THE VULNERABLE

THE VULNERABLE

"A harrowing, thought-provoking, and utterly absorbing read…
In DeJesus's high-stakes thriller, domestic terrorism collides with family wounds, and past choices turn deadly. The novel tackles urgent issues, including climate change, societal shifts caused by the pandemic, and opioid addiction, while staying firmly rooted in its thriller genre. Paced with precision and laced with brutal twists, this is a thriller that stays with you well beyond the final page."

—*Prairies Book Review*

"In *The Vulnerable,* Ed DeJesus crafts a suspense thriller that masterfully intertwines themes of domestic violence, societal scrutiny, and the acts of violence perpetrated by and against vulnerable individuals. The character development is one of DeJesus's strongest skills. The Vulnerable is compelling and incisive, deftly balancing elements of suspense with compelling social commentary. DeJesus highlights the fragility of life, the impact of violence, and the complexity of human relationships with a keen narrative! You won't be able to put down this emotionally rich narrative. A five-star review!

—The Book Commentary

THE VULNERABLE

A Suspense Thriller

Ed DeJesus

INDIES UNITED PUBLISHING HOUSE, LLC

First publication April 2025
Indies United Publishing House, LLC
Cover design by Lisa Orban

Hardcover: 978-1-64456-809-5
Paperback: 978-1-64456-810-1
Kindle: 978-1-64456-811-8
ePub: 978-1-64456-812-5

Library of Congress Control Number: 2025903976

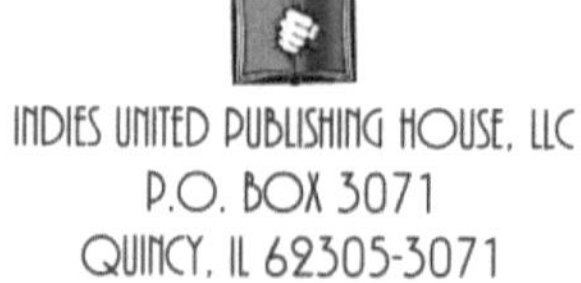

INDIES UNITED PUBLISHING HOUSE, LLC
P.O. BOX 3071
QUINCY, IL 62305-3071

DEDICATION

For all the vulnerable people—their fate often makes us sigh. And for all who have grieved—and never got to say goodbye.

*"Don't waste the time. Time is the final currency,
man. Not money, not power—it's time."*

—David Crosby

PROLOGUE

Sept 14, 2019

Dick DeCosta helped his son carry the final truckload into Dan's new home.

Dick had the auto shop install a new catalytic converter and remove his company's signage from his Tacoma pickup before he gave it to his son. He was relieved Dan didn't want to take over his solar company. It made it easier for him to shut it down, sell his Massachusetts properties, retire early with his wife in a secure high-rise condo in Fort Myers, Florida, and not worry about leaving Dan alone.

Dick looked at the text message the Boston FBI office said was sent from a burner phone.

NEXT TIME, WE'LL EXTRACT THE DRIVER!

The police said catalytic converters were being stolen more frequently. But Dick knew these idiots didn't give a damn about the environment or the value of the precious platinum, palladium, and rhodium in his converter. This text was a direct threat from the far-right extremists who had sabotaged one of his solar farm projects and shot out the panels on the roof of another. It was more blowback for his controversial best-selling book on climate change, *Greenhouse Gases and the Gaslighters*, the existential crisis of our time.

He recalled his book's tour interview with Bill Maher two years earlier. Maher had said, "Love it. You're a ballsy Desert Storm vet calling out corporations and politicians supporting fossil fuels and gaslighting clean energy. Thank you for your service."

Against his publisher's recommendation, Dick would use a pen name for his next book.

Chapter 1

Amy Johnson was glad her shift at Walgreens ended soon. She could then pick up her three-year-old son, Jayden, from daycare. Thursday, February twenty-seventh, had been crazy with customers picking up prescriptions and supplies to prepare for the third major snowstorm this month to hit Lowell, Massachusetts.

A tall, clean-shaven man wearing a gray hoodie over close-cropped hair put a Red Bull can on the counter. She didn't recognize him without his beard and mullet until he spoke.

"How ya doin', Amy?"

"Good… Thanks."

"Wicked naw eastah comin'. No school tomorrow."

"Anything else?" Amy asked, hoping to get home before the nor'easter started.

"Hard box of Mahbos."

She placed the pack of Marlboro cigarettes on the counter, and he asked, "How's Robin?"

"She don't work here anymore." Amy printed the receipt and said, "Twelve eighty-two."

He handed her a twenty, "So, ya boy won't be in daycare tomorrow. Who watches him when you work?"

She gave him his change and replied, "My mom." She knew he didn't believe her.

He grabbed a pen from the counter, wrote on the receipt, handed it to her, and said, "Tell Robin I fahgive her. And to call me at that numbah."

Amy nodded and slid the receipt into her jeans pocket. She then scurried to clock out and rushed out to her Camry. The creep was now smoking in a Nissan Sentra. Amy sped off but couldn't lose him. When she arrived at the daycare center, they were putting a jacket on her restless son. Amy sent Robin a text.

> Sean's back. He knows about Jayden 😳 You can't stay here!

After she buckled Jayden in his car seat, Sean was gone. He knew she lived in a tenement on Middlesex Street. Her phone dinged with Robin's reply.

> OMG 😱 I'm sorry. Storm's coming. Can't sleep in my car. I'll freeze to death 😭 Please, 1 more night.

Amy knew Robin had to come to her apartment to get her things. She consented.

> Just tonight. Can't have that psycho around when the storm ends.

* * *

Saturdays never seemed to go as planned for Rebecca Bouchard. Her husband, Brandon, a Manchester, New Hampshire paramedic, was tired after shoveling. By the time they finished food shopping and put the groceries away, February twenty-ninth was half gone. The 2020 winter storms were getting more extreme.

When Rebecca got pregnant with their second child, Brandon insisted she use their safer, all-wheel-drive Toyota RAV4. He drove their ancient Dodge Caravan to work, but transmission problems sank it last month. Down to one car, Rebecca was now forced to cut back her hours at Target. So, when her younger sister, Robin O'Rourke, said they could have her all-wheel-drive Subaru Outback, they were thrilled. But they had to get it today, and it often needed a jump start.

Rebecca and Robin grew up thirty miles northwest of Boston in Lowell, Massachusetts, the melting pot mill town. Robin, who'd had a run of bad luck, was couch-crashing at Amy Johnson's Lowell apartment. Robin worked at Home Depot just over the border in Nashua, New Hampshire. She'd told Rebecca she'd transfer to the Manchester store and live with them; she'd help Rebecca with the new baby, and they could use her Subaru.

Yesterday, Robin called stressed about Sean, her abusive ex. Unfortunately, the call kept breaking up. Rebecca thought Robin said she'd be taking a bus to the Cape and wouldn't need the Outback. She'd signed over its title and left it in the glove box; they could pick it up at the bus station's parking lot in Tyngsboro. Robin followed up with a text on Saturday at 8:04 a.m.

> My car won't start! It's in the guy's driveway that I've been dating. 36 Buckingham St., North Chelmsford. Keys inside. TTYL

Rebecca mapped the address on her phone—forty minutes south of Manchester. But there was no TTYL; they never got to talk later. Robin still had not replied to her text or voice message when they drove their Rav4 down Route 3 to pick up the Outback. Rebecca was worried and tried to hide it from Brandon and Brianna, her three-year-old daughter, strapped into her safety seat. They exited the highway onto Groton Road in North Chelmsford. The late afternoon sun on this leap day helped the salt melt the snow on the secondary roads.

"Turn right onto Buckingham Street," the iPhone instructed.

Her husband slowed down as the tires crunched loudly over the snow-packed, less-traveled side street. *Almost there,* Rebecca thought. She stretched her seat belt out over her seven-months-pregnant belly, then said, "Oh look, Crystal Lake's over there."

"It's Freeman Lake," her know-it-all husband said, "named after Chelmsford Selectman Bruce Freeman, who got the state to fix the broken dam that flooded."

Rebecca replied, "My dad said in the olden days, Boston's Crystal Ice Company cut up the frozen lake and hauled the ice away on sleds." *Bet you didn't know that smarty pants.*

Fresh-plowed snowbanks surrounded rural mailboxes at the end of each driveway, obscuring the house numbers on the cottages, ranches, capes, and colonials clustered around the frozen lake. Rebecca's phone flashed 4:52; with the setting sun sinking behind the tall trees, it would be dark soon. Her phone squawked, "Your destination is on the left."

They pulled into a cleared driveway with enormous snowbanks and a two-car garage attached to the mudroom of a cape-styled home. They jumped out and approached the gray Subaru. Its roof was crusted with thick snow, and its body was covered in road salt. Brandon got behind the steering wheel. No keys. They spotted Robin's phone charger on the console. But the horn didn't work.

"Battery's dead," he said. "Glad I brought my jumper cables."

They found the registration and signed title in the glove box. Brandon left the registration there and stuck the title inside the vest pocket of his EMT Jacket. Rebecca opened the Outback's rear passenger side door; taped moving boxes and bags cluttered the inside.

"Oh no! Brandon!" she exclaimed.

An open box and a white plastic bag full of linen were smeared with blood and more on the flipped-down rear seat. Rebecca reached for a blood-stained hand towel.

"Don't touch it!" Brandon shouted. "Get in our car and behind the wheel. I'll check with the homeowners."

She stepped over blood spots on the icy driveway, climbed inside the SUV, and locked the doors. Her husband rang the bell on the mudroom's entrance. She called Brandon, saw him adjust his earbud, and heard him say, "Door's open, Becca. I'm going in, don't hang up."

"Be careful," she said as she put the phone in speaker mode in the dashboard's holder.

Her husband—a trained first responder—had been in many dicey situations in tough inner-city neighborhoods. At six-feet-one and two-hundred-twenty pounds, the former high school wrestling team captain was strong and fearless. *He'd know what to do.* Her husband stepped inside the mudroom door and announced himself. "Hello. Anybody home?"

She heard him exhale deeply, then exclaimed, "Whoa, blood on the mudroom's floor… and more in the kitchen." She shivered and checked on Brianna, who was asleep in the back seat.

Oh God. She recalled last year they'd picked Robin up at Lowell General's emergency room, her head bandaged, her eye swollen shut. She told Rebecca she'd awakened the night before, half-naked and missing her cash and credit card. She believed Sean's drug supplier, Miggy Morales, slipped her a roofie and raped her. Robin then had it out with Sean. He said she probably led Miggy on and nearly killed her before the cops arrived. Rebecca and Brandon brought Robin to their home from the hospital to recuperate. Brandon said that day, "If Sean comes looking for her, I'll break him in two."

Rebecca knew Robin still had a restraining order on the abusive opioid addict. She hoped Sean had not found his way back into Robin's life. Or she hadn't fallen into another troubled relationship with the guy she'd recently met. Rebecca thought Robin finally seemed happy but withheld the man's name from her, saying instead, "Becca, I don't want to get my hopes up."

Rebecca heard Brandon shout, "Hello! Hello! We came for the Outback… anybody home.

He told Rebecca, "I hear banging; it's either upstairs or in the garage."

Breathing heavily, he said, "Party remnants… floor's a mess with blood and broken glass."

A light went on in the house, and she could hear him opening kitchen drawers. He said, "Bag of weed in here. Bingo, car keys." He paused. "I don't believe this."

"What?"

"Two sets of keys—both Toyotas. No Subaru."

She heard him walking around the house until he whispered, "Shit. The banging stopped."

She could hear his breathing grow heavier. Then suddenly, a man shouted at Brandon.

Her husband quickly whispered, "Call nine-one-one. Park in the street."

Rebecca then heard Brandon pleading. "I don't want any trouble. Put that down—"

She put Brandon's call on hold, tapped 9-1-1, frantically backed the car out of the driveway, and parked on the street. A female dispatcher answered, "Nine-one-one, what's your emergency?"

Rebecca explained the situation, provided the address, and added, "My husband, an EMT, is in the house. He saw lots of blood and drugs."

"Police are on their way. Don't hang up. Stay in your car, put the emergency flashers on."

Rebecca turned on the flashers and noticed her daughter stirring in the back seat. Reaching back, she said, "It's okay, Sweety." Patting Brianna's head, she pushed her red wavy hair aside. She sighed, realizing how much her daughter resembled Robin as a toddler.

"You still there?" the dispatcher asked.

"Yes, comforting my little girl in the back seat."

Rebecca then shuddered. *Did Robin get out of that house? Will Brandon get out?* She made the sign of the cross and began to pray.

Chapter 2

Officer Mick O'Malley cruised by the huge snowbanks outside the Chelmsford Seniors Center's plowed and sanded parking lot. It was ready for tonight's bingo game. The squawk box's dispatcher announced, "B and E in progress. Proceed to thirty-six Buckingham Street, North Chelmsford."

"Roger," he said, turning on the flashing lights of his Ford SUV squad car. He then took a right onto Groton Road and flew by a pulled-over car. Only a minute away, the squawk box announced another 9-1-1 call at the same address. A second cruiser dispatched: domestic violence and drugs.

After nine years on the force, the middle-aged Sergeant O'Malley figured the second call was the situation. He bounced along Buckingham Street and pulled up behind a vehicle with its emergency flashers. The driver's hand was out the window, frantically beckoning him. He cautiously approached the woman talking with a dispatcher on her phone's speaker.

The panicked, pregnant lady explained, "My sister's missing. Her car is in the driveway.

It has blood on the seats. My husband, an EMT, is in the house pleading with someone. He said there's blood everywhere. He's on hold," she nodded at her phone. "Should I switch to his line?"

O'Malley spotted the second cruiser approaching and said, "Not yet."

Too volatile, he thought. *Don't want to spook them 'til we see what's in play.*

The other cruiser pulled alongside him with its windows down. O'Malley said, "Kyle, hostage situation, call for backup. We'll go in now."

Officer Kyle Saxon called for backup and jumped out of his vehicle. At six feet and two hundred-ten pounds, Saxon was four inches shorter and thirty pounds lighter than O'Malley, who led the way with their weapons drawn up the icy, blood-speckled driveway. Huge snowbanks provided them cover. But the breezeway's door was ajar.

O'Malley raised his hand, "I'll go in this way. You ring the front doorbell. If no one answers, pound on the door and announce yourself."

O'Malley spotted a roll of blood-stained duct tape on the mudroom floor. He quietly approached the closed house door and listened for activity inside. He heard the front doorbell and stepped back in case anyone rushed out. There was dead silence. He then heard Saxon pounding on the front door and shout, "Police! Open up!"

Inside, a man shouted, "Let 'em in!"

O'Malley whipped open the door, his weapon aimed at a man in the kitchen, with a sharp knife in one hand and a hammer with a bloody handle in the other. The crazed bearded suspect looked toward him and glanced back at Saxon, converging from the next room.

"Drop them. Now!" O'Malley shouted.

"Woah! He's the thief!" the suspect blurted, pointing the knife in his left hand toward the open-concept living room, where the EMT stood near the oncoming Saxon.

"Ahhh, fuck!" the man screamed when Saxon's taser jolted him. He then dropped the knife and hammer, fell to his knees, and grabbed his left forearm.

O'Malley pounced on the man's back, who grunted when his chest and his face hit the floor with a hard thud and screamed after another taser strike. As Saxon kicked the knife away, the perp kicked the taser gun from his hand. O'Malley holstered his weapon, yanked the man's left arm up behind his back, grabbed his other arm, and cuffed him. The wild man groaned and squirmed on the floor. The hammer slid out from under his chest, and O'Malley kicked it aside.

A third officer charged in to help them lift the wriggling guy off the floor and slam him against the kitchen wall. Two officers then held the suspect face-first against the wall. O'Malley patted him down, found a cell phone and Subaru keys, and tossed them onto the counter.

"This is my fuckin' house!" the man shouted. "You can't do this to me."

"What's all this blood from?" O'Malley demanded.

"My hand. I had an accident." His right hand was wrapped in blood-soaked duct tape. *She put up a fight,* O'Malley thought.

"Where is she?"

"Who? … I live alone."

"Get him outta here," O'Malley said. "I'll look around."

The other officer and Saxon muscled the angry suspect out of the house. O'Malley checked the master bedroom at the rear of the house: a messy bed, no girl or blood. The walk-in closet and the main bath were clear. He darted through the living room and bolted up the stairs. He checked the bedroom, an office, closets, and the bathroom—no signs of a struggle.

He then bounded down the stairs, where he found the basement door. He switched on its light and descended the steps to check behind the furnace and storage containers. There was no blood.

O'Malley was out of breath when he found Detective Jon Evans, with plastic gloves, snapping photos of red stains on an area rug by the fireplace. Evans had already bagged the bloody hammer and the kitchen knife. He was now walking around the blood-splattered island, snapping photos of a shattered wine glass and coffee mug on the floor. The plainclothes investigator, with a two-day stubbled beard, looked at him.

O'Malley said, "The rear bedroom, upstairs, and basement are clean."

Evans nodded. "I told the EMT to wait in the street. We'll want to talk to him."

O'Malley pointed at the cell phone and Subaru keys. "We took these from the perp's pockets after we cuffed him."

The two men soon found the perp's wallet and identification in a kitchen drawer. Evans opened the cabinet door under the sink and whistled when he pulled a blood-soaked dish towel from the trash container. He then flipped a switch to a floodlight near the atrium door, illuminating the rear deck, bloodied snow gloves, and safety glasses under a ladder. Evans then aimed his phone's flashlight around the deck and snowbanks. There were no footprints or blood in the snow; he returned inside.

O'Malley shouted from the laundry room, "Jon, look at this!"

They bagged a Tom Brady Patriots jersey in the laundry basket; it had red stains on the front and back near its bottom. They then headed for the garage and bagged the blood-stained roll of duct tape. The Toyota pickup truck's cab and bed were clean, as was the Prius in the next stall. The recycle bin and trash containers looked proper next to the shovels and snow blower.

Inside the Subaru, they found a bloody hand towel and a blood-spotted Home Depot utility knife. Half of the luggage deck was cleared; a body could have been placed there. Evans took pictures and told O'Malley, "Call for a tow truck. We need to impound the Subaru."

The two men then headed for the street. Evans removed his plastic gloves and put them and the evidence bags in his car's trunk. His phone displayed 5:28 p.m. when he called the techs to dust the place for fingerprints and retrieve blood samples. Evans told O'Malley, "Before we talk to your suspect, let's speak with the EMT."

* * *

SIX HOURS EARLIER.

A bone-chilling wind blasted the powdered snow across the drifts in Dan DeCosta's backyard and smacked his face. Stinging white crystals clung to his dark, trimmed mustache and beard. He pulled his woolen Boston Bruins beanie over his ears, zipped up his North Face ski parka, and shoveled his rear sundeck. The latest of three storms subsided Friday night. It was Saturday morning, and Dan was still removing snow around his new home. Yesterday, he used his snowblower to clear the wide driveway, producing massive snowbanks. He'd posted impressive pictures to his family's WhatsApp chat. They'd escaped to warmer climates and had no sympathy. His younger sister, Samantha, posted:

    Ugh! 🧖

The edgy software engineer worked in San Francisco and had set up the group chat to keep their scattered family informed. His dad replied:

    Wow! I don't miss those winter workouts. Take it slow.

His mom posted a picture of her and his dad by a sundrenched pool at their Florida high-rise condo and captioned it:

    Want to get away? 😎

Dan lifted his snow-packed shovel over the deck's railings and dumped it onto the mounds piling up in his backyard. His lean six-foot frame was in great shape because of his consistent workouts at his employer's fitness center, but all this shoveling after partying with Robin last night tested his conditioning. He now realized how good he had it in his garden condo as they provided snow removal. But Dan had sold it for the down payment to the three-bedroom cape with a two-car garage he'd planned to share with his ex-fiancée, Shannon. Sadly, he had to put an abrupt end to their engagement and their purchase agreement.

His dad had owned numerous properties and had talked him into going through with a great deal on the undervalued bank-owned property and co-signed the loan. Six months later, Zillow priced his North Chelmsford home with a view of Freeman Lake at $90,000 more. His gas fireplace made the frigid evenings very cozy with Robin, who, like the snow, had recently dropped into his life. The shapely, fun-loving redhead routinely cuddled with him by the toasty hearth; it hastened their disrobing.

The bright sun had finally broken through the overcast skies. Dan looked up at the rear roof of his house and hummed George Harrison's "Here Comes the Sun." Snow was melting at the top of his solar hot water collectors, but the drifts below were damming up, and long glistening icicles hung from the roof's edge. His dad designed and installed the solar system. He'd want to know about this and would have suggestions.

Dan cleared the deck, brushed the snow off his boots, and entered his newly remodeled kitchen through the thermal Atrium door. He piled his hat, gloves, and parka on the kitchen's bar stool. His phone charging on the counter displayed a missed call and message on February 29, 2020, at 11:43 a.m. He hoped it was Robin getting back to him; they'd barely said goodbye when she left early this morning. No such luck. He dropped a Folgers pod in the Keurig and played the voice message from his mom on the speaker-phone.

"Hi, Dan. Hope you're keeping warm. We're at a Red Sox spring training game. It's eighty-six degrees. Let me know when you can get away— I'll book your flight on us. Love ya. Bye"

Rub it in, Mom. Her generous invite was tempting and irritating.

But Dan worried about Robin. All week, she'd sent him texts about changes coming. She called Thursday night and said, "No matter how bad the storm is, I *must* see you Friday."

The storm tapered off Friday afternoon, so he'd clear the driveway by dusk. Robin had pulled in with her tired Subaru Outback and its cargo area packed with bags, boxes, and luggage. He had her park in front of the stall where he kept his new Toyota Prius. The hybrid was low to the ground and useless in deep snow. An eight-year-old Toyota Tacoma previously used in his father's business, Sold on Solar, occupied the other stall. The dependable four-wheel-drive truck his dad gave him before he moved to Florida served Dan well this winter.

Dan had helped Robin carry farewell gifts from her coworkers at Home Depot: a pizza, a bottle of wine, and a half-eaten cake. She announced, "I'm moving in with my sistah, Becca, and her family in Manchestah, New Hampshah. No more Mass income tax."

Dan braced himself for another shattered relationship. *At least it's not over; she'll just be forty minutes away.* They made the most of what they knew would be their last night together for a while. The buzz-filled night of fun and intimacy with the ginger-haired beauty made him forget about the severe winter and unfulfilled dreams he once had for this house and his ex, Shannon.

Early that Saturday morning, he'd felt a soft nudge; Robin lifted the covers off his head, kissed his cheek, and said, "Goodbye, Dan, my sweet man…I'll miss you."

"Miss you too," he puckered his lips for an air kiss, then pulled the covers over his head.

He needed more rest before tackling the snow cleanup. He had to sleep off Robin's cheap wine and the potent pot his cousin, Eric, gave him for Christmas, which got them both stoned for the first time last night. He heard a car door close in his driveway and then dozed off.

At 10:19 a.m., Dan rolled out of bed and emptied his bladder. He washed up in the sink and found strands of Robin's red hair; he missed her already. He dressed warmly, entered his kitchen, and started his coffee.

Empty IPA bottles, red-stained wine glasses, an empty wine bottle, rolling papers, and a bag of weed littered the kitchen island's counter. Dan stashed the pot in the drawer where he kept his car keys and dumped the empty bottles in the recycle bin in his ice-cold garage. He pushed the button to shut the overhead garage door Robin had left open and noticed her Subaru, which often needed a jump start, was still parked in the driveway. *Why didn't she ask me for help? Who picked her up this morning?*

In the mudroom, near the bench where he kept his parka and boots, he found Robin's car keys and a note written on the backside of a farewell card from her Home Depot co-workers. Dan put on his jacket, dropped the Subaru's keys in his pocket, laced his boots, and read Robin's perplexing handwritten note.

> *Dan,*
> *I didn't want to wake you. Sorry, my car won't start. The stuff in the luggage area is for Becca—she'll come and get it. Sorry about Brady's shirt and my urgency to move. I'm sorry about everything. You're the best!*
> *Take care.*
>  *R*

Dan scratched his beard and wondered. *Hmm, sorry about everything. Why didn't she mention who she drove off with?*

Chapter 3

It was a bright, sunny Saturday in Fort Myers, Florida. By noon on the twenty-ninth day of February, the balmy Gulf of Mexico breezes pushed the temps into the mid-eighties. Meghan walked alongside her smiling retired father, Jim McCormack. They followed the crowd of locals and snowbirds sporting Boston Red Sox jerseys and baseball caps. They passed through the turnstiles of Jet Blue Park—the unmistakable aromas wafting from the footlong Fenway Franks and sausages simmering in grilled peppers and onions. The Sox and the Minnesota Twins were stretching and warming up on the lush green baseball diamond. Meghan captured pictures on her phone as her father pointed and barked out the replica features and dimensions of Fenway South.

"There's the Green Monstah. Three hundred and ten feet down the line from home plate; thirty-seven feet, two inches high." She photographed the Green Monster wall in left field.

Her dad stood near the screened fence, his silver hair covered by his Red Sox cap. She snapped pictures of a beaming David Ortiz, "Big Papi," the loveable, recently retired Red Sox star, towered over her dad. A petite blonde woman behind her suggested Meghan join her dad. The lovely, evenly tanned woman, sporting a shapely Red Sox tank top, used Meghan's phone.

Meghan thanked the thoughtful woman, who then said, "Dick, move up."

A fit, bronzed gentleman with dark hair and graying temples joined her. He asked Meghan, "Could you take ours?" *My pleasure, handsome.*

Meghan snapped shots of the attractive mature couple, with David Ortiz behind them.

Her dad's gravelly voice bellowed, "Dick DeCosta! How the heck are ya?"

The handsome guy grinned at her dad, "Jimmy Mack! Been quite a while, ole friend."

They shook hands, leaned into their shoulders for a manly hug, and gently slapped each other's back. Her dad, with his bulging beer gut, released their embrace and smiled at the man's pretty wife, "And this… must be your daughter, ha-ha."

DeCosta placed his arm around his shapely wife's tiny waist, "Joanna, you remember Jim McCormack, a former CEC colleague—lived in our old neighborhood in Maynard."

Computer Equipment Corporation (CEC) was headquartered in Maynard, MA, twenty-five miles west of Boston. Meghan and her older brother, Mitch, were raised there. Beaming with pride, her dad wrapped his arm around her shoulder, "This *really is* my daughter. Doctor Meghan McCormack."

Joanna extended her hand and said sweetly, "Hi, so nice to meet you, Doctor."

"You as well. Please… call me Meghan."

"Call me Jo. Welcome to Fort Myers, Meghan," she cheerfully added. "We retired here in January. Where are you from?"

"Bedford, Mass," she felt self-conscious about her pale skin. "I visit every Christmas. This is my first time at the ballpark."

Her dad lifted his cap, ran his fingers through his thinning hair, and said solemnly, "She's helping me out with my wife, Peg. She, um… the hospice nurse, is with her now. We'll probably leave by the sixth inning."

"Oh, dear, I'm so sorry," Jo said, gently touching Meghan's wrist.

Jo's husband frowned and put his muscular arm around her dad's shoulder, "Mack, buy you a beeah before the game starts?"

Her dad nodded, and the woman's husband said, "Jo, we're in this front row, seats one and two. Why don't you and Meghan wait there for us?"

"Okay," she said. "Please bring me a bottle of watah. Meghan, do you want anything?"

"Water would be great. Thanks!" Her dad and Mr. DeCosta headed off.

Meghan then sat with Jo and explained, "Everyone expected Dad to go first. Mom's a former nurse. She always took care of him and neglected herself. Pancreatic and now liver cancer. Chemo bought her a few months. All we can do is keep her comfortable."

Jo sighed, and Meghan continued, "Last month, I quit my physical therapist job at the Lahey Clinic in Burlington." Meghan completed her Doctor of Physical Therapy (DPT) and a master's in nutrition and kinesiology.

Jo smiled, rolled her right arm, and said, "Physical therapist, eh? Maybe you can fix my frozen shoulder. Ha, ha. I love tennis. Do you play?"

"No. In warm weather in Boston, I'd play golf with my boss or ride my mountain bike. Hope to do both year-round now. With Florida's aging demographics, healthcare workers are in high demand. I'll find a job later."

Jo gave her a once-over. "You bike—it shows. You look fantastic. And left Bawstin just in time. My son texted blizzard pics. I don't miss snow."

"Nor do I. And I have no one up north now. We lost my older brother, Mitchell, to opioids. It took its toll on my parents. They think I'm their last hope for grandchildren." *And that's never going to happen.*

Jo frowned, "Oh, my. I'm so sorry for your family's loss."

"Thank you," she leaned closer. "Caring for Mom got me away from my charming boss, head of orthopedic surgery. He cared more about my anatomy than my PT skills."

Jo hugged her. "I'm so sorry about your mother. And men... always needy and greedy." With her big shiny rock and gold bracelets, Jo's soft fingers gently patted Meghan's hand. Her grey-green eyes twinkled, "You're highly skilled, gorgeous, and confident. You'll do well in Fort Myers."

"Thank you! You're so kind. But I worry about Dad. He'll be lost without Mom. She cooked for him and kept him on his meds. He's seventy-four, diabetic, and loves his beer."

Jo nodded, then asked, "Where do your parents live?"

"In a fantastic high-rise condo overlooking the river, east of downtown. The twin towers have an infinity pool, tennis, pickle ball courts, gym, and gorgeous sunset views."

"Spectacular views!" Jo exclaimed. "We have many friends there. We still own a unit we bought three years ago to rent to snowbirds. We planned to retire there until we fell in love with a bigger place. More room when our kids visit."

"Oh? Where did ya end up?"

"A high-rise on the west side, a short walk downtown. It overlooks the river and a marina. Still waiting for our son in Chelmsford and daughter in San Francisco to visit."

"Sounds nice. When I can get a break from my mom's needs, perhaps we can do lunch downtown." Meghan couldn't believe this stunning woman and her hunky husband were retired.

"I'd love that," Jo said. They exchanged contact info.

Meghan's dad and Jo's husband returned armed with beers, water, and roasted peanuts. Knowing her mother was in hospice, the four hugged farewell and promised to get together at the appropriate time.

Meghan was glad her dad discovered old friends, and the attractive couple intrigued her. Maybe it's because she'd had so little contact with anyone since she arrived, or she was excited to hear Boston accents. Either way, she couldn't wait to pick her dad's brain to learn more about Jo and Dick. Both made her pulse quicken.

Chapter 4

Dan ate leftover pizza. His phone dinged. *Robin?* He sighed and opened his father's text.

Hey, how goes the battle?

Attached was a picture of his parents at Fenway South with David Ortiz. Happy for them, Dan considered texting back with a picture of Robin and recalled what led to the stunning pose last night. Robin looked through his kitchen drawers for a corkscrew and found his cousin Eric's pot and rolling papers.

"Holdin' out on me, eh?" she said.

Didn't know you toked. I haven't since Christmas when my cousin left me that weed."

"It's legal, let's pahdee."

Dan poured the wine, Robin rolled the joint, and then they partied and wore out his bed like newlyweds on the final day of their honeymoon. In the aftermath, Robin sat on the rug before his glowing fireplace, holding a glass of red wine. The Tom Brady jersey she had borrowed from Dan barely covered the top of the alluring redhead's tantalizing thighs.

He texted Robin's photo to his father with a caption:

The snow sucks… but the company's quite nice and cozy.

His dad replied:

Indeed! I see you have the luck of the Irish. And I don't mean Brady.

He laughed and wondered how Dad knew Robin was Irish. He wanted to call him and explain how serendipitously and quickly his relationship had heated up with the fiery redhead, who, like his dad, was from Lowell.

Dan entered his name, number, and email for a Home Depot drawing; the first prize was a cordless drill. The next day, he returned and claimed his free metric ratchet set. As he was climbing into his pickup truck to leave, he spotted a shivering young woman looking helpless with the hood up on her car. Dan offered to help start the Subaru and saw that her cargo area was jammed-packed. He wondered if she was moving or living out of it. The jumper cables he had in his truck did the trick, and it jump-started his first female contact in over six months.

"I don't know how to thank you!" she said through chattering teeth.

"No need," he told the intriguing wide-eyed girl. "Can I buy you a coffee?"

"Ooh, sorry. Not tonight. But I'll take a rain check." *I'll never see her again*, he thought.

When the first monster snowstorm was forecasted, he returned to Home Depot to buy a Toro snow blower. Robin, working at the Customer Service Desk, where he had to pay for it, explained, "If you qualify, you'll get a hundred dollahs off this purchase if you open a Home Depot credit card today."

Dan had excellent credit. Robin took his application and accepted his offer for a drink. She punched out in twenty minutes.

Carlos, the Latino sales associate who sold him the Toro, wheeled it out front and helped load it into his truck. Robin pulled her car up behind them. Carlos said, "She got jou the big credit card deal… Big Red, she likes jou."

Everything about Robin is big, he thought and chuckled at Carlos's moniker. She had a big red wavy head of hair, a big smile, big blue eyes, and big bones, and he sensed behind her big breasts was a big heart.

Robin had followed him to the Bahama Breeze Restaurant, minutes away on Middlesex Road in Tyngsboro. They entered, sat at the bar, ordered margaritas, clinked their glasses, and Robin toasted, "Here's ta the Aries." She knew he'd turn thirty on April 6 from his credit card application.

"Not fair! I don't even know your last name… age, or address."

The smiling fellow ram replied, "O'Rourke. I'll be twenty-seven on March twenty-seven. I'm staying at Amy's apartment in Lowell. She's a single parent. I babysit her little boy. Hope to save money; return to Middlesex Community College once I get back on my feet."

"Is your family in Lowell?"

She shook her head. "My dad died of lung cancer when I was ten and my sistah was fourteen. We then moved to the Bishop Markham Projects on Gorham Street. Mum did her best, waitressing at the Owl Diner. My sistah, Becca, married her high school sweetheart, Brandon. He's an EMT in Manchestah, where they live with their little girl and a baby on the way. Mum married a retired truck drivah. They traveled cross-country in an RV. Settled in Reno, Nevadah. Mum left me her Subaru."

"All-wheel-drive Outback, great in snow," Dan said. *Yours needs work you can't afford.*

Robin frowned, "Spent a few nights in the Outback last summah." She twirled the umbrella in her drink. "Someday, I'll get to the tropics, like my Aunt Kelly. She vacationed in Key West in search of her lost shakah of salt. She *nevah* came back. Ha-ha."

Her hearty laugh, turned-up nose, and caring blue eyes fascinated him. Her Lowellian-Boston vernacular sounded like his parents, who destroyed their Rs. The distinct dialect of Lowellians who moved to other states or the suburbs usually disappeared in their children. Dan should know—he and his sister pronounced words in standard American English, but everyone knew that a *watah bublah* was a water cooler, and if you were late for *suppah*, your dinner was in the microwave.

He ordered jerk chicken wings and more margaritas.

"These wings are wicked good," Robin said. "So, what's your story?"

Dan told her he grew up in Chelmsford, an affluent Lowell suburb, but didn't mention it was in a ten-room colonial his father custom-designed. "My parents retired to Florida. My younger sister, Samantha, graduated from UC Berkeley and lives in San Francisco. She's a smart, savvy techie." He didn't mention she was bisexual and had a female partner.

Dan continued, "I graduated from U Lowell. I'm an environmental engineer working at GreenEx Corp. I made my North Chelmsford home by Freeman Lake more energy efficient."

"Nice area, and close by," she grinned. "So, Dan DeCosta, where do you come from?"

"Came from my mother, who has French Canadian parents."

"Of course. I mean your surname's origin."

"Portuguese. My great-grandparents came to Lowell in eighteen-ninety from Lisbon. The name DeCosta means you lived by the river or the coast."

"I *love* the beach," Robin said, raising her glass, "Here's to the coast."

By this point, they were feeling the tequila.

Robin explained, "I met my ex, Sean Cassidy, on Saint Patty's Day at the Gaelic Club in Lowell. We got an apartment togethah. He use ta be fun… a nice guy." She sighed and continued, "Sean was doin' great as an electrician apprentice but liquored up every payday. His bruthah died in Afghanistan; it devastated him. He totaled his SUV and spent a month in the hospital on oxycodone. Sean became dependent on booze and pain meds, then opioids. He lost his job, hawked my engagement ring, ruined my credit, and then took it all out on me."

Dan scratched his beard, "Where's Mister Nice Guy now?"

Robin frowned. "One brutal night, I called nine-one-one. The second crewzah to arrive was his uncle, Bill Cassidy, a Lowell cop. Bill couldn't save our relationship, but he probably saved my life. Sean's drug supplier, Miggy Morales, was found beaten to death a week later. His uncle got him into a rehab centah down the Cape." *She runs in tough circles; she deserves better.*

"Good," he gently touched her wrist. "A rehab center is the best place for him."

"I still got a restraining ordah on him." Robin touched Dan's hand in return. "You're the first guy I've shared that with. Must be those trusting, deep brown eyes."

Dan raised his eyebrows, smiled, moved closer to Robin, and said softly, "I know what it's like to be let down by someone you thought you'd spend the rest of your life with."

Robin squeezed his hand. Dan felt sad. Relative to her, he'd lived a charmed, protected life. He paid the tab. She said, "Thank you! Now it's time for Home Depot to delivah ya snow blowah."

Dan exited the parking lot and made sure her Subaru followed close behind. They struggled and giggled, getting the Toro off the truck and into his garage. Robin asked to use the bathroom. Dan directed her to the one accessible from the hallway and his adjacent master bedroom. He then turned on more lights and stood beside the island in his remodeled kitchen.

Robin looked around and proclaimed, "*Very* nice!"

"Thanks, and so are you."

Dan embraced her. Their lips met, and they kissed passionately; tongues rotating, they frantically tore at each other's garments. After the lustful rush, they stopped and gazed into each other's eyes before Dan took her hand and led her to his bedroom, where they slipped under the chilly sheets and warmed one another. Dan then discretely reached into the nightstand's top drawer and grabbed a condom. The action was intense, heated, and, for both, long overdue.

After succumbing to fatigue, they gasped for air beside one another. *Wow!*

He looked at her flushed, smiling face and said, "Sorry, it's been a while."

"Me too! … and I'm *not* sorry."

They chuckled and faced each other. Her fingers stroked his chest while his hand ran over her soft hip and tender glute. Her fingers headed south, and she said softly, "Not sorry *at all*."

Her hand adeptly supplied more stimulation for him. *That didn't take long.*

They began again gently, much more tenderly. As the night wore on, they clung to each other. Her friend's apartment was ten minutes away, but he didn't need to start humming Bob Seger's "We've Got Tonight" to persuade her to stay.

Following that fateful night, she spent most nights at Dan's after her

Home Depot shifts.

Dan refocused, finished his coffee, and sent another text to Robin. He then stepped outside and took photos of his solar panels on the snow-packed roof and its massive icicles, then texted the pics to his father with a caption.

Ice dams are making me nervous.

He went back inside and put his phone on the counter. He used his bathroom and washed his hands when his phone buzzed. *Robin?* Dan dashed to the kitchen.

"Hey, Dad."

"Dan! How ya holdin' up?"

"Barely. We got another twenty inches. The solar collectors were melting at the top. But it's all jammed below that."

"Saw your pics. The snow will slide off your panels. But you need to clear the snow and ice dams below, or you could have watah damage in the mudroom's ceiling and walls."

"What do you suggest?"

"Get a snow rake with an extension. Reach up and pull the snow down. Throw ice-melt crystals on the ice dams and then break them up with the claw end of a hammah. And wear safety glasses."

"Okay, Home Depot has snow rakes." *Robin no longer works there… or sleeps here.*

"So… where'd you find that gorgeous Gaelic guest?"

"That's *Robin.* Uh, long story. Short ending. Ha-ha." His attempt at humor to mask his anxiety didn't fool his dad. "How'd you know she was Irish?"

"Red hair. And a shamrock tattoo with a heart in the centah on her wrist."

His dad spotted the shamrock when Robin held the wine glass. Robin told Dan she got the tattoo on her other wrist, a rose, and the words "*Be Kind*" to shield herself from Sean's beatings. She never explained the tattoo on her shoulder blade with the words, *"Still I Rise."*

"Dan. Mom wants to talk. I'm putting you on the speakah—"

"Thanks, Dad. Have to snag a snow rake to clear the roof. Talk later. Bye."

Dad will handle things with Mom. He treasured his parents but relied on his father's advice and always tried to please him. His dad's voice was more often in his head than his teachers, coaches, and managers. Dad always stressed, "Focus, Dan. Ask yourself—what's the most important thing to do in the next five minutes?"

Get a snow rake at Home Depot and ask which co-worker picked Robin up this morning.

Chapter 5

Meghan and her dad left the Red Sox game to relieve her mother's hospice nurse. It was too hot to drop Dad's Mustang convertible top.

"Joanna DeCosta seems nice. How well do you know her husband?"

Her dad smiled, "Dick's a retired tech exec and entrepreneur; we go back forty years. The first time we worked together, my project was behind schedule. I was told to use Dick DeCosta, the company's top CAD guy, to design my circuit board. The long-haired dude with the thick mustache completed the design six days before schedule."

A successful techie. Meghan figured. *With those guns, he looks ex-military.*

"Dad, most people call you Mack. Why did he call you 'Jimmy Mack?'"

"Ahh. 'Jimmy Mack' is a Motown song by Martha and the Vandellas. Dick was always humming tunes or talking about rock groups at work." Her dad cleared his smoker's throat and explained, "Dick declined my lunch offer and a beer. He said, 'Thanks, Jimmy Mack. But I eat lunch and help my wife at The Music Stop, our record store downtown. It's busy at noon.'"

"Wow!" said Meghan, "Mitch lived in that record store. He'd bring home bags filled with albums and sheet music. Mom said Hippies owned it. Ha-ha."

"Your brother loved playing drums and keyboards. Drove your mother nuts. Dick and Jo bought their first house in Maynard. He worked at CEC days and the store during his lunch hour and weekends and attended college nights. The DeCostas were the coolest trendsetters in town. When Jo decided to have kids, he sold the store and designed and built multiple homes in upscale suburbs."

"Aggressive guy," Meghan said.

"Very aggressive! Dick bolted up the corporate ladder. He left CEC to be the VP of engineering for a global startup. After putting their kids through college, Jo worked in HR. Dick was CEO of an internet startup—later, he owned a solar company."

Cool couple. They owned a record store and, later, so accomplished. Meghan couldn't wait to get home and cheer her mom up about meeting her parents' old friends.

* * *

The Sox were leading when Dick was replying to his son about the redhead. Jo sang "Sweet Caroline" between innings with fellow fans reaching out, touching hands, shouting, "So good! So good!"

After the Sox won, they headed to the parking lot in search of Jo's new Audi A5 hybrid. Dick preferred his Audi Q8 e-tron, which they drove down to Florida from Massachusetts. It was now eighty-eight degrees and sunny, so they would not drop the A5's ragtop.

Dick's phone dinged; he glanced at the text.

"Who's that?" Jo asked.

"Dan sent pics of snow on the solar panels. He's worried about ice dams."

Jo said, "Call him."

They climbed into the Audi. Dick called Dan and advised him on how to deal with the snow and ice buildup. Jo motioned that she wanted to talk to her son. Dick said, "Dan, I'm putting you on the speaker."

"Thanks, Dad. Gotta snag a snow rake and clear the roof. Talk later. Bye."

Jo whined, "I don't want him on a roof. He should hire someone for that."

"He has to learn to take care of a house. He'll be fine."

Dick learned home repairs from his dad and more by working with contractors on the properties he'd owned. His son wanted to learn but was alone at his snowbound home. *Dan was evasive about Robin.* Dick sensed something else was going on.

Jo's Audi crawled through the snarled traffic; she let her frustration out. "Dan's moody. I called him twice, left voice messages, and offered him airfare. He *nevah* returns my calls!"

"Kids prefer texts… But I agree. Dan could use a getaway."

Their phones chimed. Someone had posted on their family chat.

"It's Sam," Dick announced. Their tech-savvy daughter Samantha used WhatsApp to communicate with them. Jo wasn't happy about it, but everyone knew how headstrong and independent Sam was. *And she has no filter,* Dick thought.

Jo kept her eyes on the road, "What is it?"

"A selfie… Her, Khori, and Bulova, overlooking a hillside cliff."

Khori Chen, Sam's lovely partner, had named her French bulldog Bulova. Dick didn't think Bulova was a watchdog but thought it fit the loveable canine. Sam had an apartment in San Francisco near her employer; they went to Khori's mountainside cabin on weekends.

"At least one kid is happy and tells us she's alive," Jo said. "Too bad she lives even farther away and has no plans to see our new retirement home."

Dick changed the subject. "Small world running into Mack. I felt bad for him. He said Peg doesn't have much time left. And they're still grieving the loss of their son to opioids."

"So sad!" Jo said as they hit the I-75 on-ramp. "His daughter, Meghan, said she's also worried about Jim—he has diabetes and loves his booze."

"Can't blame the guy at this point. But he's thankful Meghan's here."

"Yes! And isn't she a doll?"

"*Very* attractive, and a physical therapist!"

"She'd be perfect for Dan."

"Jo, don't meddle."

"I'm not, just saying."

Meghan is quite a catch, Dick thought. She's accomplished and older than his fragile son was used to dating. Poor Dan's still reeling from his breakup with Shannon, his gorgeous fiancée. Dick wondered about the hot adventurous-looking redhead. *Was she a stray or another beauty Dan would regret he'd let get away?*

* * *

Dan drove along the Daniel Webster Highway in Nashua, NH, pulled into Home Depot, and parked his truck. His phone chimed. *Another of Sam's gloating California hillside posts.* Sam entered the workforce four years after him, and she was already earning twenty thousand dollars more. *She sure found ways to rub it in.*

Dan stopped at the store's service desk. He asked Kayla, who had a short, stylish boy's haircut and worked alongside Robin, if she'd heard from her.

"No. Sorry," said the thin brunette who'd signed Robin's farewell card. "Yesterday was her last day. She transferred to Manchester."

"Do you know if anyone here helped her move?"

She shook her head and asked Victor, the tall, lanky assistant manager standing nearby. Shrugged, then said, "Nope. Anything I can help you find?"

"Do you have snow rakes?"

"Back wall, aisle two." Victor motioned for Dan to follow him.

They grabbed the last snow rake, which had a telescoping pole. Victor's phone chirped, and he moved on to another department.

Dan carried the lengthy rake with both hands to safely navigate through the congested aisles of Saturday shoppers. He avoided the self-service checkouts and got in the familiar, friendly cashier's line. Maddie, the pretty African American woman who signed Robin's card, smiled at him as he leaned the rake against a display of batteries and other last-minute items. He grabbed a plastic jug of ice melt off a nearby pile and placed it on the conveyor belt.

She scanned the bar codes on the jug and snow rake. He asked Maddie, "Do you know if any co-workers were helping Robin move today?"

She replied, "Uhm. I don't, sir."

Dan handed her his Home Depot credit card. "Do I get a discount?"

"Sir, are you a veteran?"

"No, but my dad and grandfather served." *Grampa, RIP, fought in WWII.*

"Military gets a ten percent discount if they have an ID," she said, smiling at the customer behind him. He nodded to the old-timer with the letters DAV on his hat. *Grampa wore a DAV hat—Disabled American Veteran.*

"Thanks, I'll tell my dad." *He served in Desert Storm.*

Another man in a military cap got in line behind the old-timer. Dan felt ashamed when he realized that vets needed to show IDs. "I get ten percent off with my Depot card?"

The concerned-looking cashier shook her head, "Sorry, sir. Your card was denied. Do you have another one?"

"No way. I got it when I bought a snow blower."

"Well, sir. It's maxed out."

"Can't be! It's approved for five thousand. Please recheck it?"

"I tried twice, but it was denied. Sir, do you have another card?"

"Listen to me!" Dan shouted. "It's a mistake! Should be over four thousand left on it."

Customers began to murmur behind Dan. The old-timer DAV, his carriage full of HVAC filters, frowned at Dan. Another vet behind the old-timer threw his arms in the air.

The assistant manager, Victor, approached the register and asked Maddie, "What's up?"

As she explained, Dan interrupted, "This is *bullshit*! Recheck my credit and application."

A lingering young couple gave him dirty looks as if it appeared he was disrespecting the plus-sized, dark-skinned cashier. They aimed their phones at Dan—they'd expose him with their videos.

Great, Dan fumed. *Social media slaves in search of a not-woke moment. It's not my fault. I'm pissed at everyone who works here.*

Victor took Dan's card. "Calm down, sir. We'd be happy to do that. Please follow me to the service desk."

Dan grabbed the snow rake and stepped towards the service desk. The rake's blade hooked a display rack and yanked it over. Everyone heard the loud crash as items scattered across the tiled floor. Dan retrieved the pole but the handle end punctured through a pleated HVAC filter in the DAV's cart.

"Oh, geez! Sorry!" Dan emphatically apologized.

"You idiot!" the old-timer said disgustingly, eyeing the damaged filter.

All of the commotion caused a crowd to gather. Dan grabbed the rake and tried to drag the batteries and other scattered items into a pile. A sales associate put his hand on Dan's arm and said, "Sir, leave it! Go to the service desk."

A customer behind taunted him, "Yeah, loser, you've done enough!"

"It was an accident," Dan shouted defensively to anyone listening.

The heckler yelled, "You're an accident. Your father should have used a condom."

"Fuck you!" Dan responded and flashed the bird at his tormentor.

Dan then turned and met face-to-face with an angry man with a white-shaggy beard and an eerie smirk. The burly guy wore a U.S. Army cap and crossed his arms against his pumped-out chest. The millennial couple sneered at him and videotaped the action on their smartphones. *Friggin Instagram dolts looking for fifteen seconds of fame.* As his heart raced and his hands trembled, Dan pivoted and walked briskly towards the service desk.

The store's PA system announced, "Cleanup, main aisle."

Customers leered at Dan while he paced back and forth by the service desk. The heckling continued, "Rage shopper, main aisle, avoid service desk."

Victor, the manager, calmly explained, "Sir, you placed a 'Will Call Order' online. You specified a curbside pickup last Wednesday in the other Nashua Store." He handed Dan the order's printout.

Dan scratched his beard as he read through the list—air compressor, portable generator, portable heater, cordless drill, circuit breakers, electrical outlets, switches, Romex wiring cable, zip ties, and duct tape. *Something's fishy; Robin sold me this card.*

Dan shouted back, "I didn't order this! Someone stole my card info."

"This is your approval and notice for curbside pickup. You can dispute it online." Victor handed him email printouts and a pickup confirmation at the other Nashua store off Exit 8.

"This is crazy! Someone had to sign for this, right?"

Victor nodded. "So, call the other store and find out who!" Dan shouted. "And what's up with Robin? She sold me this credit card deal, and then she quit this week?"

"Sir, please lower your voice," Victor said firmly.

Dan dictated a text into his iPhone, "Dammit, Robin. Someone maxed out my Depot card. Call me," and hit send. *Why is she ignoring me now?*

Carlos, the associate who sold Dan the snow blower, approached him.

Dan asked, "Where is Big Red? Wait till I get my hands on her."

Carlos pointed a finger at him, "Jou, leave her alone!" He then walked away to help clean up the mess in the main aisle.

The manager asked, "Do you want the snow rake? It's the last one. If so, we'll need another credit card."

"Hell no!" Dan shouted as more people began videotaping him on their phones. "Until you reverse those charges on my card, I ain't buying a friggin' thing at Home Depot!"

He stormed out of the store, climbed into his truck, slammed the door, and tossed the printouts on the passenger seat. He was livid as he raced up the Daniel Webster Highway. At a traffic light, he banged a U-ey and narrowly missed the snowbank in the right lane, cutting off another car. A driver behind saw him make the reckless U-turn, beeped his horn, opened his window, and shouted, "Masshole!"

Dan flipped the guy off, pulled into Lowe's, and rushed into the store.

Lowe's was out of snow rakes. He bought a painter's telescopic pole, duct tape, aluminum flashing, and ice melt. *I'll make my own damn snow rake.* Dan paid with his other Visa card and was relieved when it had no unusual charges. *Robin better have some answers.*

Dan carried his garden rake and the Lowe's items into his mudroom. When he placed his wallet and truck keys in the kitchen drawer, the microwave clock displayed 3:04 p.m. Less than two hours before darkness set in, he had to de-ice the roof, assemble his snow rake, and pull the snow down.

He climbed the ladder on the deck and sprinkled ice-melt crystals across the roof's icy edge. Dan then returned to the mudroom, used duct tape to fasten the sheet metal flashing on the teeth of his garden rake, and taped the telescopic pole on the rake's handle. The pole was ten feet long and would extend another seven feet. His dad would be proud; he made his snow rake for less than half the cost. Dan grabbed his safety glasses and a hammer to chip the ice.

"Oh, shit!" He saw water stains on the mudroom's ceiling. There were even more stains on the Sheetrock and back wall. *Damn! Dad was right.*

Chapter 6

Saturdays were always tranquil for Sam, especially after a hectic week writing software. On weekdays, she and her partner, Khori Chen, a Bay area HR recruiter, stayed at Sam's one-bedroom flat in San Fran's Potrero Hill section. They'd drive to Khori's cabin in the hills on Friday nights and sleep late all weekend.

Khori headed down a mountain path with her bulldog, Bulova. The long, shiny black hair on her partner's thin figure matched the color of Bulova's short black fur. Sam pedaled in another direction, biked three hilly miles, and filled her backpack with produce from a roadside farm stand. She rode home and concocted healthy smoothies while Khori and Bulova returned.

Khori filled Bulova's water bowl on her redwood deck and fed him treats. Sam placed the smoothies on the resin table between the lounge chairs, settled in, and enjoyed the views.

"Ooh, delicious. Thanks," Khori said after tasting Sam's green smoothie.

Sam balanced her iPad on her legs and focused on the Twitter and Reddit feeds. She leaned closer. *What the hell?* She turned up the volume, and Bulova raised his ears.

"What are you watching?" Khori asked and looked over her shoulder.

"I don't freakin' believe this!" Sam exclaimed. "My idiot brother is now known on social media as 'Depot Dan.' First, he shouted at a Black cashier, then it got cartoonish. The later vids showed his anger, and the taunting he got was *so* embarrassing."

"Oh, wow! That's your brother losing it on Facebook and it's trending on Reddit and Twitter?"

Sam rattled off the tweets and headings: "'Depot Dan goes ballistic over denied credit card.' … 'Racist customer trashes Home Depot's steel display with a snow rake.' … 'Steely Dan disses vets while raking in the goods at a big box store.'"

"Sorry, but that's ugly," Khori said. "And this tweet, '#Steely Dan abuses big box.'"

Sam chuckled, "The Steely Dan band lampooned their name from a super strap-on."

"Seriously?" Khori looked doubtful.

"Google it."

"Hmm. You're right! Ha-ha!" Khori exclaimed. She then read from her search, "'Steely Dan was the name for a mechanical device described in satirical sex scenes in William S. Burroughs's banned-in-the-60s-Beat-generation novel, *Naked Lunch*. Lennon named The Beatles after the Beat Generation and included a picture of Burroughs on the iconic mural cover of *Sgt. Pepper's Lonely Hearts Club Band* album."

"Told ya. My parents owned a record store. We'd listen to their vintage vinyl Beatles, Pink Floyd, CSNY, and more. My dad said Steely Dan's *Aja* was his favorite jazz, rock, and pop combo album."

"A record store. Were your parents hippies or cool yuppies?" asked Khori.

"They won't be cool when they learn about Depot Dan."

"Yikes! Is your brother a racist with crummy credit?"

"Not racist! He's a recluse whose sustainability work on his home might've overextended his credit. We'll find out after I put these vids on our family chat. My parents will freak!"

Khori sighed. "Geez, I hope anger management issues don't run in your family."

* * *

The elevator stopped on the fifteenth floor, where Meghan and her dad entered his condo.

"Hey, Brewski," Meghan said as she patted their black labrador's head, his tail wagging. Silvia, the widowed neighbor who lived down the hall and often checked in on her mother, was leaving.

"Thanks, Silvia. Take care," Meghan said.

Meghan's mother was resting in the recliner, looking out the glass doors to the lanai. Gladys, the kind and caring hospice nurse, stood by her side.

"How's Peg doing?" Meghan's dad asked as he leaned over and kissed her mom's cheek.

"Tired today," Gladys said, patting Meghan's hand.

The nurse headed out the door and said, "Call us if you need anything."

Their dog followed Gladys to the elevator and whined. He couldn't wait to go out and find a bush to water. "Coming, Bruschi," her dad said, grabbing a leash.

Her dad, who promised to quit smoking, snuck a butt when he walked

Bruschi, named after Teddy Bruschi, the New England Patriots retired line-backer. He always had a few brewskis when he watched his teams play. He named their dogs after Boston's favorite retired athletes. Before Bruschi, their boxer was called 'Larry' for the Celtics' Larry Bird. He'd named their German Shepard, Yaz, for the Red Sox's Carl Yastrzemski.

Her dad would say, "We name the next dog Brady. Greatest quarter-back evah. The stubborn Irishman probably won't retire in my lifetime. You kids get an Irish Setter and carry on."

Dad walking Bruschi afforded Meghan the dwindling time alone with her mother. She leaned over, hugged her gently, and kissed the bandana covering her hairless head.

"Mum, can I get you a lemonade or ice?"

She shook her head no, then smiled, "Did you enjoy the ballgame?"

"Loved it," she said, showing her a photo. "Look at this picture with Big Papi Ortiz."

Her mother squinted at the iPhone and said, "That's a keepah."

"The lovely lady, Joanna, who took this picture, used to live in Maynard."

"That's nice, Meg." The frail woman looked back out at the river view.

"Her husband, Dick DeCosta, worked with Dad. They owned the Maynard record store."

She turned back towards her and frowned. "That store was bad for Mitch."

"Oh, Mum, you used to buy Mitch records there. He always played Steely Dan's song "Peg" for you… And you and Dad loved it."

Meghan's mother pointed her bony index finger at her. "Mitch started a band and fell in with the wrong crowd. And we lost him."

"I'm sorry, Mum." She placed her hand over her mother's frail, trem-bling hand. "I thought you'd be happy to know Dad has old friends living in Fort Myers."

Mum yanked her hand away. "Stay away from *them*. They're trouble!"

Woah, pain meds wearing off? She went into the kitchen and checked the nurse's log. *The last dose was twenty minutes ago, so not the meds.* She dampened a face cloth and put it on her mom's forehead. *I better tread softly with her about Dick and Jo. And warn Dad.*

* * *

Joanna and her husband had their fill of ballpark food. They'd skip their usual Saturday night out for dinner and drinks. She felt sluggish and nause-ous as they rode the elevator to the twenty-seventh floor. When they entered their expansive condo, she said, "Let's freshen up, relax on the lanai, and enjoy the sunset."

Joanna threw up her ballpark food and cleaned up. She slipped on a short, colorful kimono loosely tied around her tiny waist, which had become slimmer since her food poisoning episode. She had gotten sick after toxic runoff from Hurricane Irma contaminated the Gulf with nasty red tide and blue-green algae. They treasured their time at the Gulf's beautiful beaches but were concerned about runoff from herbicide-soaked lawns on homes, golf courses, and oil spills. Progress at a cost to the environment did not sit well with them.

Joanna then placed the booze on her quartz kitchen counter, and Dick mixed two glasses with pink lemonade and her favorite Pinnacle Whipped Vodka.

"My flight is Tuesday morning," her husband said. I'll miss the condo's board meeting but make Monday's Calusa Waterkeeper's meeting."

Joanna and her husband were raised in Lowell by hard-working, lower-middle-class families. Through hard work, prudence, and good fortune, they'd reached the upper-middle class, retired early, and lived comfortably off their assets. Her husband managed their investments and did solar consulting—not for the money—to help others in their quest to combat climate change and protect future generations. Dick captured his mission six years ago in his controversial best-selling book on global warming, *Green House Gases and the Gaslighters*. He promoted it on TV talk shows and donated most of the proceeds to 350.org and Greenpeace. He'd started his second book, but Joanna made him feel guilty about not devoting more time to enjoying their retirement. However, Dick was flying to Boston on Tuesday to chair a panel at the Clean Energy and Sustainability Conference, "The Urgency to Combat Climate Change."

Joanna thought about her busy week—Monday and Wednesday mornings were tennis with Marie Bates; Monday afternoon, a follow-up with her primary care physician as she'd ordered more blood tests; Tuesday, food shopping; Thursday, water aerobics; and Friday, hair appointment.

She tidied the kitchen counter as she replied to Dick, "I laugh when people ask if retirement is boring after working for years."

He came up behind her, slid his arms around her waist, and kissed her neck. She arched her back in response.

"Jo, you're always high maintenance, high octane, and the perfect ride."

"Oum," she purred.

"Don't change. Can't imagine retirement without my better half." He patted her butt and then headed for the elevator. "Going to get the mail. Expecting tax documents."

Joanna carried her phone and drink to their screened lanai and placed them on their russet-colored coffee table. She settled in on the loveseat, sipped her drink, and took in the panoramic view of the river, the Legacy

Harbour Marina, Centennial Park, and downtown Fort Myers. Yachts, sailboats, and speed boats passed under the three bridges spanning the broad scenic Caloosahatchee River. Her phone chimed. She opened the family chat and was confused by her daughter's caption of the video she sent.

Congrats, Depot Dan, you are the biggest 'Leap Day Loser' on SM.

I hate it when Sam picks on Dan. She clicked the link. The video showed her outraged son knocking over a store display, yelling at customers, and arguing with Home Depot employees. Joanna frantically typed a response.

Sam, I don't know what SM means, but Dan needs to explain what happened with a long overdue call to his mother!

* * *

Dick returned to the condo, reviewed his tax docs, and ignored his phone's trills. He finally read Sam's latest post in the family group chat.

Mom, SM = social media. Loser Dan will also be on MSM, Main Street Media!

He read the earlier posts and clicked on the video link. Dick's stomach churned as he watched the painful expressions on his son's angry, red face. He texted Dan.

Hey, when you get a minute, give us a jingle.

Dick grabbed his drink off the counter, took a sip, and watched Joanna pace back and forth on the lanai. *She'll remind me that I told Dan to get the snow rake and that she wanted him to hire someone to clear his roof.* He guzzled half his drink and headed to the lanai to join high-octane Jo.

Chapter 7

Ashley Brinkley put her items on the convenience store's counter and grabbed a SNICKERS bar. A second flashing cop car flew by North Chelmsford's Triangle Store on Route 40—all lights but no sirens. Ashely, a reporter for the *Lowell Sun*, figured it meant there couldn't be an accident or fire. *But what did it mean?*

"Something's going down," she told the store owner.

He shrugged, put her receipt in the bag, and said, "Thank you."

The local news banner on the store's flatscreen highlighted, "Breaking News: Chelmsford man's rage at Nashua's Home Depot fires up the Internet."

She'd seen it earlier on Instagram. It was not good, not good at all. The video of a guy shouting at store employees and Army veterans upset her, and the social media vultures she called 'The Cancel Culture Crowd' annoyed her.

Ashley turned off Route 40 onto Buckingham Street. She spotted the flashing lights in her quiet neighborhood, a few doors down from where she'd lived all her life. She parked her Honda CRV in the driveway and entered the house. Her mother was by the window.

"Lots of cops going up the street," Ashley's mom said.

"Yeah, Mom. I'm gonna walk up there. Could be a news story for me."

"Be careful!"

Ashley tucked her SNICKERS bar and phone in her coat pocket and walked cautiously along the icy road toward the flashing lights. She then took a position opposite the driveway from all the action at the cape with the two-car garage.

Oh no, this is where that cute guy who drives the Prius lives. She'd seen the new homeowner move in last fall. Like everyone in the neighborhood, he'd wave back to her and her mother when they stood near their mailbox watching him move in. Mom said, "That house is too big for one person."

Ashley recently ran into him at the Triangle Store. He always greeted her with a charming smile. He had dark, well-groomed hair, a clean-shaven face, and dark, dreamy eyes; he resembled Adam Levine. She never missed an episode of *The Voice*. When a Maroon Five song came on her car radio or social media feed, she'd think about her neighbor and how to get him to notice her more.

An ambulance arrived. Neighbors gathered along the snowbanks with their phones ready. Kenzie Carpenter, a young teen, waved to her. A dramatic news story was unfolding—far different from the usual town meetings Ashley covered in Lowell's suburbs. She opened her SNICKERS and took a bite. A concerned pregnant woman then stepped out of an SUV and moved toward an EMT who was walking up the driveway of the house that was crawling with cops.

* * *

"Thank God, you're out!" Rebecca Bouchard embraced her husband. He let out a big sigh and kissed her forehead.

She looked up at Brandon, "Did you find out about Robin?"

"Not yet... Glad the police let me out."

They watched two police officers escort a handcuffed, agitated man to the ambulance. The crazed man, blood running from his nose onto his mustache, motioned towards her husband and shouted, "He trespassed! He should be the one in cuffs! You're making a big friggin' mistake!"

"Where's the Outback keys? Why is there blood in the car?!" Her husband hollered back.

The angry man spewed profanities at Brandon.

"What have you done to my sister?" Rebecca shouted

"Wait, who?" The man then slipped on the ice and dragged a cop down with him.

"Robin ... Where is she?"

"She's gone!" the crazed man shouted as he struggled to get up from the icy road.

"Becca, let the police handle this," Brandon said.

The cops dragged the bloodied perpetrator past the ambulance to an idling cruiser, pushed his head down, and shoved him inside.

"Let's go, Brandon," Rebecca said to her husband.

"We can't. Cops told me to wait 'til they finish inside." Brandon crossed his arms and leaned against their Rav4.

Sergeant O'Malley, the huge police Rebecca had spoken with earlier, and a shorter, plainclothesman approached them and asked. "Folks, can we speak with you?"

"Of course," her husband replied, and the shorter man turned on his phone to record them.

"Thank you for rescuing him," Rebecca said to O'Malley.

"I'm Detective Evans," he said, exchanging a handshake with her husband.

"Brandon Bouchard, and my wife, Rebecca. How can we help?"

"Why were you in the house? How did you get in?"

"We came to get her sister's car in the driveway." Brandon pulled a document from his vest pocket and handed it to Evans, "She signed the title over to us."

Evans glanced at it, handed it back, and said, "Go on,"

Rebecca interrupted, "But there were no keys. And blood in the back seat."

Brandon continued, "So, I rang the mudroom's doorbell. No answer. It was open. I entered through the kitchen and shouted, 'Anybody home!' Still no answer. I looked around for the keys and saw more blood and mess on the floors."

"How do you know this guy?"

"I don't even know his name," Brandon said.

"My sister gave us the address this morning," Rebecca added.

"When you saw the blood, why didn't you leave and call nine-one-one?"

"As an EMT, I've seen worse, and we were worried about her sister," Brandon explained. "Becca and I were talking on our phones, and I had her call nine-one-one."

O'Malley nodded.

Brandon told O'Malley, "This crazed guy came charging into the kitchen with a hammer in his hand, and well… you saw what I saw."

O'Malley asked, "So what happened?"

"I told him I didn't want any trouble."

"Did he attack you?" Evans asked.

"He kicked a stool at me and grabbed a knife. I backpedaled toward the front door and said I'd come back another time for the car. That's when the police rang the doorbell."

Evans said, "We're impounding the car. A tow truck is on its way."

"Battery's dead anyway," Brandon said.

"Forget the car!" Rebecca shouted. "Where's my sister?"

"That's what we hope to find out," Evan said. "When did you last hear from her?"

"Eight this morning," she said and showed him Robin's text.

He glanced at it, "Call her."

She did, then said, "Again. It went right to voice mail."

Evans said, "We'll ping her phone. Hopefully, its GPS will indicate where she's at."

"She planned to live with us in Manchester. Yesterday, she said she was going to the Cape and wouldn't need her car," added Rebecca.

Evans pointed at the house, "That cape?"

Rebecca shrugged, "Or she meant Cape Cod, where her ex, Sean Cassidy, is in rehab."

"No way," Brandon said, shaking his head. "He beat her up pretty bad—she's got a restraining order on him."

"Oh?" Evans said and looked at O'Malley. "We'll check him out too."

"I'm hungry." Little Brianna whined from her car seat.

"Anything else, Detective?" she hinted.

"All set for now," Evans handed her his card. "Call me if you hear from your sister or think of anything else."

"Thank you, we will."

O'Malley asked Evans, "Want to talk to the perp now?"

"Not here. Let's get him down to the station."

* * *

Ashley and her young neighbor, Kenzie Carpenter, videoed on their phones the shouting match between the EMT and the angry man the cops dragged from the house. Ashley had a sick feeling. *Something terrible happened to a woman.* The attractive man who lived there had grown a dark beard and had a dark side that frightened her. Idling engines drowned out the ensuing hushed discussions between the police, the EMT, and his pregnant wife. Then, the cruiser drove away with the handcuffed man peering out the window.

Kenzie called to Ashley, "That's Depot Dan! I'm posting this Leap Day Loser video on Instagram!"

"Wow, Kenzie." *It is him.* Ashley ran across the road to the EMT in his SUV.

"Sir. Oh, sir. I'm a *Lowell Sun* reporter. Do you know why they arrested that man?"

The EMT said, "Not sure. My wife's sister is missing. That's her car in the driveway."

"What's her name?"

"Robin O'Rourke. We haven't heard from her since early this morning."

"That's the crazy guy at Home Depot," Kenzie bellowed behind her at the startled EMT.

"What? … Robin works at Home Depot. Not me," the EMT said defensively.

"Not you," Ashley explained. "She meant the guy they arrested. He had trouble at Home Depot today. It's trending all over social media."

"Sorry, we have to go," the EMT said before closing his car window and driving away.

Wow! Wicked interesting! Ashley got it all on video, plus the SUV's New Hampshire plate. She'd submit a story for the *Lowell Sun's* Sunday edition. She'd miss the morning print edition, but the online version would hit the internet as soon as her editor approved it. She'd check with the Chelmsford Police about an arrest at 36 Buckingham Street and for missing person updates on Robin O'Rourke.

Ashley then thought about her cousin Kayla, who worked at the nearby Home Depot. She might know the missing girl. She hoped Kayla worked Sundays. If she did, she'd have a follow-up story for Monday!

Chapter 8

With Dan's hands cuffed behind his back, it was impossible to brace himself in the cruiser. Every bump and turn made him recoil when his throbbing shoulder hit the car door. A stabbing pain shot across his ribs where he was bruised when the big cop jumped on his back, and Dan fell on the hammer. Every thump on the frozen roads and breath he took was excruciating until they mercifully stopped in front of the Chelmsford Police Station on Olde North Road.

A fierce headache, sore shoulder, and tender ribs overshadowed the pain in his sliced hand and his bloody, broken nose. Dan thought the cops tore his rotator cuff and cracked his ribs. They'd slammed his head into the wall; he might have a concussion. Ever since Dan discovered his Home Depot card was breached, everything spun out of control along with his anger, leaving him with deep regrets and fear. Unfortunately, Dan had no phone to call anyone for help. He had to figure a way out of this nightmare.

The police officers escorted Dan into the station and removed his handcuffs. A tall, fit woman in uniform, Officer Hall, took his fingerprints and gave him a tissue. Dan winced in pain as he blew his bloody nose. The officers then ushered him through a steel door into a pale green room with fluorescent lights in a suspended ceiling. *Better than a jail cell*. The chilly room's steel table and four metal chairs were icy cold. Dan rolled his sore shoulder and felt a large bump on his aching forehead. He had blurred vision, struggled to breathe, and needed to pee.

The door opened; a plainclothesman with weekend stubble and short brown hair entered. He was accompanied by a cop much bigger than the one who cuffed Dan at his house. The man sat across from Dan; his gray fleece pullover had a maroon Town of Chelmsford logo on the breast. The hulking uniformed cop sneered at Dan, placed an iPad on the table and turned on the video recorder.

"Mister DeCosta, I'm Detective Jon Evans; this is Sergeant James Morehouse. We have questions about today. You have a right to remain silent. Anything you say can and will be used against you in a court of law. You have the right to an attorney. If you cannot afford an attorney, one will be provided for you."

Questions about today? Dan had a sinking feeling and wondered if he should have an attorney present. He felt like crap and ached everywhere. The iPad displayed 6:57 p.m. He nodded, deciding to move the interrogation along.

"Would you like a coffee or water before we start?"

"Both," Dan winced and held his chest. "Black coffee and water to wash down Advil."

Evans grinned. Morehouse grumbled, "This ain't Dunkin, and we're not a pharmacy."

"My ribs hurt when I breathe."

"Hold your breath then—you'll do us all a favor," Morehouse said.

I wouldn't need Advil if you pricks hadn't roughed me up.

"We'll see what we can do," Evans said. Morehouse shook his head with disgust. The mammoth officer lumbered out and left Dan alone with Evans.

Evans will play the good guy. He guessed Morehouse—big enough to be an NFL nose tackle—would relish the bad cop role. *I better be careful.*

Dan said, "I have a lot to talk about. I'd appreciate it if you let me use the restroom first."

Evans smiled, "Like what?"

"People robbing my house. Stealing my credit card identity."

"Everything about you—nothing about Robin O'Rourke."

"Sure, she uh… must know about my credit card mess."

Dan did his best to empty his bladder as a tall cop stood behind him. He then washed his hands and threw water on his face. The mirror reflected a shiner below his left eye and a purple egg-sized lump on his forehead. Dan dabbed the caked blood off his mustache and beard. He unzipped his jacket, lifted his sweatshirt, and touched the tender bruises. The hammer's head left its mark and cracked his ribs.

When Dan returned, Evans and Morehouse sat across the table from him, along with three Styrofoam cups—one with coffee, one with water, and the third with a blue pill inside.

"Thanks," he said, washing the Aleve down with water. He sipped the bitter, lukewarm coffee and struggled to breathe.

Evans switched the video recorder on and began, "After the fight, where did you take Robin O'Rourke?"

"We didn't fight. I was clearing snow off my roof when I saw a guy rifling through my kitchen. I figured he took Robin and came back to rob me, so I called nine-one-one. Your guys came into *my house* and trounced on *me*. Why the hell am I even here?"

Evans leaned forward, "*You* were threatening the EMT whose wife called nine-one-one because her sister is missing."

Morehouse added, "And *you* had a bloody hammer and a knife, resisted arrest, and kicked a police officer. It's on their body cams and on here." He pointed at the iPad.

Evans said, "So, stop the BS. Answer the questions. After she put up a fight, where did you take her in her Subaru?"

"We… she left early this morning. Her car wouldn't start. She left me a note. Someone else must have taken her." Dan sat back in his chair and grabbed his chest.

"Where's the note?"

"In the kitchen drawer by the fridge. It's on the back of a farewell card from her coworkers."

Evans grabbed his phone. "I have techs there now." He spoke into his phone, "Wilson? Check the kitchen draw next to the fridge. If you find a greeting card, take pictures of all sides and text them to me."

Evans continued, "So, she spent the night with you. How long had you known her?"

"We met last month at Home Depot, where she works. She drops by after her shift."

"Home Depot," Morehouse snickered. "Of course. You're Depot Dan."

"What's that supposed to mean?" Dan looked at Evans for an explanation.

"Don't play games with us." Morehouse jumped up, and Dan sat back.

"The infamous *Depot Dan*," Evans said, "trashing displays, shouting at employees and vets—it's all over the internet. Don't tell me you haven't seen it?"

"I haven't. People were taping stuff that was none of their business. My Depot credit card had thousands charged for stuff I didn't purchase—someone stole my identity!"

"I'd show you the videos," Evans touched the iPad, "but I don't want to upset him." He motioned at Morehouse. His mean face turned red, veins bulging out of his thick neck.

"Don't ever disrespect vets!" Morehouse bellowed. "My nephew is in Afghanistan. And my cousin didn't make it back from Iraq."

"My dad and grandfather served. I wasn't disrespecting vets. It was an accident. I told you about the credit card—Christ, I'm the victim."

"Spare us your sympathy crap. There's blood all over the house, in her car, and we have the weapon you used. Where'd you move her body to?"

"I didn't take her anywhere. I cut my hand on a broken glass."

Dan held out his duct-taped hand. Morehouse grabbed it with his huge mitt and shouted, "You cut your hand on the knife when she fought you off. Admit it!" The brute then pressed his thumb into the nasty wound, making it bleed again.

"Ow, Jesus!" Dan yanked his hand free. "I didn't! I'd … never hurt her."

He shook his throbbing hand and kept an eye on Morehouse. *Find a fly to torture, you big prick.* Dan then tried to control his painful breathing.

Someone knocked on the door. Morehouse opened it a crack, and an officer stated, "Lieutenant wants you both in his office. It's about DeCosta."

Morehouse tapped Evans's shoulder, "Let's go." He looked at Dan, "Not *you*. Depot Dan ain't going anywhere tonight."

Dan sipped the cold coffee; acid churned in his stomach. He felt nauseous; his head was pounding, his ears still ringing from a possible concussion. He wanted to lie down. Dan leaned over the table as his ribs burned in pain. He ran his hands through his hair and tried to focus on what to do next.

Ask Evans for my phone. Get a lawyer before they crucify me.

Chapter 9

Dick joined his upset, red-faced wife on the lanai, and she asked, "Have you seen Sam's posts?"

"Yes," he replied, "I texted Dan. Told him to call us."

"I'm calling him now!" Jo paced and left an angry message for Dan. Dick embraced her to stop her from trembling. She'd been shaking a lot lately, which is another reason for follow-up tests with her doctor on Monday.

A bell ring signaled another family group chat. This time, Sam included an Instagram link with her comment.

OMG! Chelmsford cops arrested him.

A video titled—Leap Day Loser Depot Dan arrested at his home—showed their son handcuffed and struggling with a bloody nose being dragged toward a police cruiser.

Dick pulled out his phone.

Jo said, "Maybe he'll take your call."

"Not him. Cops probably have his phone. I'm calling Harlan King."

He didn't answer; Dick left a message, "Harlan, sorry to bother you and Christina on a Saturday night. Our son, Daniel, was arrested by the Chelmsford Police. Find out what the charges are and get him released. Call me with an update."

Harlan King, a tall African American criminal defense lawyer, handled pro bono cases for minorities. Joanna's widowed sister, Paula Rondeau, raised three teens in Lowell. She always had trouble with her only son, Eric. A Lowell vocational grad and a good carpenter, Eric got caught stealing tools from a union shop. Harlan got Eric off with community service, probation, and fines paid by Dick.

King gained notoriety when he successfully defended the innocent Black boyfriend of a single White parent whose babysitter was stabbed to death in her apartment. The deceased babysitter's family sued his client and Harlan but later dropped the charges when the real murderer was brought to justice after he confessed to his drug counselor. Attorney King is now well respected and busy.

* * *

Fishbones, the popular seafood restaurant in Chelmsford, was always packed on Saturday nights. Harlan King sat alone at the bar, nursing a Stella Artois while he waited for his entrée. Snowstorms canceled his wife's return flight from a nonprofit convention in Washington, DC.

The bartender placed another Stella before him, "Compliments of the gentleman in the corner table."

Stephen Coben raised his martini glass to King. Harlan raised his bottle and nodded to the successful real estate developer sitting with his wife and another couple. Coben built a home for Harlan and Christina in his exclusive subdivision in Westford.

Harlan's phone rang. He adjusted his earbud and greeted his loving wife, "Hi, gorgeous."

Christina said, "I'm booked on JetBlue. Arriving at Logan on Sunday at three-fifteen."

"Great! I'll pick you up. I'm looking forward to Italian food in Boston's North End."

"Is that *all* you're craving, Harley?"

"I waited a week, Sugar. I can hold out for dessert back in Westford."

"How do you know I can wait?" she taunted in a throaty tone that had captivated him since he first heard her speak.

Christina Turner-King was executive director of Second Chance—a non-profit for needy families in the Greater Lowell area—where he'd met her at their scholarship awards night. He sat in the audience and admired the poised, attractive woman. Her cultured face, like Diana Ross, with breasts like Beyoncé, and legs like Tina the Queen of Rock, Christina Turner, walked up to the podium and mastered the ceremony like Maya Angelou.

Deontae Collins's long dreads and tats stood out when he accepted his Second Chance scholarship. His heartfelt words of thanks to his single mother, three seats away from Harlan, set off quite an applause. Next, Deontae thanked Harlan King for defending him pro bono and turning his life in the streets around. Then Christina's eyes met his, and she led another round of applause.

After the ceremony, Harlan invited her to dinner. Eventually, after two years of steady contributions to Second Chance and dating, Harlan proposed to Christina. She jumped into his arms and said, "Thought you'd never ask."

Harlan's meal arrived. He ended his call with Christina and noted a voice message from Dick DeCosta. He devoured his lobster risotto and thought about how much he and Christina appreciated Dick and Jo. They'd spent a getaway weekend at the DeCosta's luxurious high-rise condo and were happy the dynamic, industrious couple got to retire early.

The DeCostas were regular contributors to Second Chance. Dick facilitated a grant to install solar panels at the community center and helped with fundraisers. Harlan told Christina, "Dick is a gifted speaker. He energizes an audience with his enthusiasm."

Christina chuckled, "He'd talk Popeye into donating his last can of spinach."

Dick's company, Sold on Solar, also held job fairs and training seminars at the center. His Sneakers and Boots on the Roof program hired minorities and veterans as solar trainees.

Harlan adjusted his earbud and listened to Dick's urgent message about his son when a *Lowell Sun* headline popped up on Harlan's phone's notifications.

Chelmsford man arrested, search on for a missing Lowell woman.

He settled the check and crossed the frozen parking lot behind Fishbones. Harlan then called Chelmsford Police and told the desk sergeant to let Chief Patterson know he was coming to see his client. He started his Lexus SUV, turned on the heated bucket seat, and read the *Lowell Sun* story in full. Harlan wondered why the story referenced Dick's son with the 'Depot Dan' moniker. He googled it, then clicked an Instagram link captioned:

Leap Day Loser and Home Depot racist-shopper disses vets.

Harlan reviewed DeCosta's actions and demeanor in the videos. The racist accusations and the veteran incident appeared to be overblown. He knew how Dick and Jo raised their kids. In fact, Harlan and Christina enjoyed chatting with Dan at his parents' holiday gatherings. Harlan thought Dan was bright, polite, and respectful to everyone. But he had to admit that Dan's frustrated reactions to his credit card denial and toward other shoppers that day were more than unflattering. Harlan was more concerned about the domestic violence charge and the missing Lowell woman. He forwarded the Lowell Sun story link in a text to Dick DeCosta.

I'm headed to Chelmsford Police Station. I'll call you later.

* * *

Dick read Harlan's text, showed it to his wife, and opened the story in the *Lowell Sun*.

North Chelmsford Man Arrested, Search for Missing Lowell Woman Continues
By Ashley Brinkley |abrinkley@lowellsun.com|
PUBLISHED: February 29, 2020, at 6:50 p.m.
Early this evening, Chelmsford Police apprehended Daniel DeCosta, 29, at his North Chelmsford home for domestic violence and resisting arrest. DeCosta—AKA 'Depot Dan' for his angry outburst at Home Depot in Nashua, NH—blew up social media today, sparking backlash from veterans and civil liberties groups. DeCosta was captured on video tonight being hauled away by police from his Buckingham Street home. His blood-streaked face and hands indicated a struggle took place on the property. Police are actively looking for a missing Lowell woman. Robin O'Rourke, 26—employed by Home Depot in Nashua—has not been heard from since Saturday at 8:00 a.m. Police impounded O'Rourke's blood-stained Subaru Outback from DeCosta's driveway. Chelmsford and Lowell authorities are urging the public to contact them immediately if anyone has any information on the whereabouts of Robin O'Rourke.

Joanna's hands shook while she read the story with Dick. He held her and said, "I'm changing my Tuesday flight to Boston. I'll grab the first one out tomorrow."

"I'm coming too."

"Jo, you have a doctor's appointment on Monday. Harlan and I will handle this."

She sobbed, leaned into his chest, then said, "Pack the bigger suitcase. You'll need more clothes than four days. Don't forget Dan's house keys."

"Thanks, babe. I have warmer clothes in Dan's guest room." *Hope I'm back in a week.*

Dick put Dan's key in his laptop's carry-on bag. He was glad he'd already completed his Clean Energy conference presentation.

Jo dictated a text message on her phone, "Marie, sorry. I can't make tennis on Monday. You were right—I need to rest before my doctor's visit."

* * *

Evans and Morehouse sat in Lieutenant Sinclair's office. Chief of Police Paul Patterson was on the speaker phone listing his concerns about the suspect.

"DeCosta's rap sheet is clean?" Peterson asked.

"No priors, speeding tickets, not even a parking ticket," the lieutenant replied.

"His attorney, Harlan King, is on his way in. Did DeCosta admit to anything?"

"Not yet," said Evans. "He's good at deflecting, but he had the woman's car keys on him when we collared him."

"All that blood! Depot Dan's lying and hiding something!" Morehouse shouted.

The chief asked, "Any progress on Cassidy, the woman's ex?"

"He lives in Lowell with his mother and borrowed her car," Sinclair said. "The LPD still has a restraining order on him. They're trying to locate him."

"Any GPS hits on the woman's phone?"

Sinclair said, "None. The last location was DeCosta's house this morning. We're pushing the judge for warrants. Should have a list of all her calls tomorrow and DeCosta's."

"Did you look at DeCosta's phone?"

"No," Evans said. "He claims he's the victim. We'll ask his attorney for the password."

"Put DeCosta in a cell before King arrives. We can hold him on the arresting charges 'til he sees the judge Monday morning. Focus on finding the woman!" The chief ordered, then cautioned, "Be good to King. The press loves him, and we don't need a media circus. Bad enough, Depot Dan has already flooded the internet. Don't tip off the newspapers or TV stations that his attorney is Harlan King."

* * *

Morehead and another cop escorted Dan from the room and past an array of jail cells, three of which were occupied by town drunks and homeless men who were happy to be warm with free meals. They put Dan in the last cell on the left and locked the steel gate. His cell consisted of three dingy-gray concrete walls and a dreadful hopper in the rear corner.

Dan laid down on the steel bench and used a woolen blanket as a pillow for his throbbing, spinning head. He slid his hand under his sweatshirt and gently stroked his tender ribs. He was pissed at the cops, mad at Robin for selling him the credit card, and disgusted with himself for his foolish rage. Dan struggled to control his breathing and take his mind off the pain and this nightmare.

He decided to close his eyes and recall the good times with Robin. She'd stopped in after her Home Depot shift when the first blizzard began to accumulate. They had sat on the bar stools at the kitchen island, washed down Chinese takeout with beers, and laughed over the silly fortune cookies. Snowbound for the night, he had turned on the flatscreen TV and asked her, "Netflix?"

"Maybe latah," she said, then selected a Music Choice channel, and Taylor Swift started things off.

They had cuddled on the area rug by the gas fireplace to Dan + Shay's

"Speechless." Then Bruno Mars belted his hit, "Locked out of Heaven." Robin jumped up and started dancing to the beat. Dan joined her and slipped on the hardwood floor, but she held him up. She then took his hand and led him to his bedroom, where she made him feel like he was locked out of heaven.

Dan sighed and tried to breathe—his ribs hurt like hell. He was locked in the cold, dingy jail with a stuffy broken nose and gasping for air. Dan massaged his temples and tried to ease his throbbing headache. His long, exhausting day had gone from shoveling snow off his deck to raking snow off his roof to an avalanche of troubles. He foolishly thought the cops would blame the guy who tried to rob him, but instead, they trampled on him and buried him deeper into the blood-spotted snow.

Chapter 10

Harlan arrived at the Chelmsford police station. His courtesy call to the chief paid off; the police were cooperative and focused on finding the missing woman. Lowell police were now trying to locate the woman's ex as they'd had a violent relationship. Detective Evans suggested he take Dan's phone to get the timelines for the calls with the woman. *All Good.*

The atmosphere changed when instead of a conference room, Sergeant Morehouse walked Harlan to a cell where he spotted Dick's son lying in a fetal position facing the wall. Rather than opening the locked gate, Morehouse stepped into the adjacent empty cell.

King tapped the metal gate with his client's iPhone, "Dan, hey … sit up."

The young man looked over his shoulder, grabbed his chest, and rubbed his eyes. "Mr. King!" He winced, got up, and stumbled towards the gate. Dan had bruises on his forehead, a shiner under his right eye, and dried blood in his nostrils. He stuck his wounded right hand out between the bars and shook Harlan's. "Thank you so much for coming."

Thank your parents. Harlan nodded, pulled his phone out, and hit the record button.

"What happened to your hand?"

"Sliced it on a broken glass in my kitchen." Dan gripped the cell bars with both hands, leaned forward to rest his head against them, and closed his eyes.

"You, okay?" Harlan asked. A toilet flushed in the next jail cell.

"Head's killing me. I think I have a torn rotator cuff and cracked ribs." Dan lowered his left hand to his chest and winced. "And my Home Depot Credit card was breached."

He might have a concussion. Looks like the woman had put up a fight, or maybe he had duked it out with her ex-boyfriend.

"So, you and the woman were fighting over your Home Depot card?"

"She sold me on the credit card. But we never fought."

"Well, where is she?" Harlan shouted as the noisy toilet was flushed a second time.

"Don't know. She left early this morning when I was sleeping. Never returned my texts."

"Wait. Start from the beginning."

"I got up a few hours later to shovel. Saw her car in the driveway. Dead battery. She left me a note apologizing."

"She was living with you and left with another guy?" The toilet flushed again.

"No. She stays the nights she works at Home Depot. Said she was moving to her sister's in Manchester today." Dan grabbed his chest. "I went to Home Depot to buy a snow rake; they denied my credit card. I got stuff at Lowe's and was clearing my roof when I saw an intruder in my house. Thought he was robbing me. I called nine-one-one, and—"

"Stop!" Harlan raised his hand. "You called nine-one-one?"

"Yeah."

He handed Dan his phone, "Show me the call."

He pulled it up for Harlan, "I called the cops on the guy, but they grabbed me instead." The toilet flushed again. *Asshole in the next cell.*

"You fought with the guy in your house, and the cops arrested you for that?"

"No. He tried talking his way out of my house when the cops rushed in, tasered me, and drove me into the kitchen floor. Then they threw me against the wall, cuffed me, and dragged me here."

Christ, what a mess. "Sit down. I'll be back in a few minutes."

Harlan showed his disgust for Morehouse standing by the toilet in the next cell. He stormed into Lieutenant Sinclair's office, where he was speaking with Evans.

"Your guy flushing the toilet is not helping! If you want to find the woman, I need to talk to my client in a conference room."

"That's to protect his privacy from the other jailbirds," Sinclair said. "The woman's top priority; we'll accommodate your request." He motioned at Evans to handle it.

"Thanks. Can I have the arrest report?"

Sinclair lifted it off his desk and handed it to Harlan.

Evans said, "You can read it in the conference room—follow me."

"Hold on," Harlan said, scanning the report. "The log shows two nine-one-one calls, six minutes apart."

Sinclair nodded.

"My client made the first call," Harlan said, then asked. "Where are the arresting officers who wrote this report?"

"Back out on patrol—both work second shift."

Harland followed Evans to the conference room.

"We'll bring him out," Evans said. "Ask him about the blood on the floors, on a towel in the trash, and in the woman's car. And why did he have her keys on him when we collared him?"

Evans closed the door. Harlan took photos of each page, then read the report:

The bodycams were on during the takedown of the suspect at 36 Buckingham Street, where a possible hostage situation was unfolding. O'Malley and Saxon spotted an angry man armed with a hammer and knife, threatening Brandon Bouchard, an EMT, and the brother-in-law of Robin O'Rourke; the woman believed to be held hostage and still missing. The suspect …

Harlan flipped the report over on the table when Morehouse and Evans escorted Dan into the room. Dan sat, folded his arms, and leaned over the table's edge with his head down. The cops sat down, too. Harlan met their eyes: *Not what I had in mind, fellers.* He'd wanted to speak with his client alone but knew the priority was finding the woman first. He decided to change the tactics to Dan's advantage.

Harlan set his phone to record, and the cops did the same with theirs. He then handed his client's phone to him and said, "Dan, pull up the texts you made to Robin O'Rourke today."

Dan found his text stream and handed the phone back to Harlan.

"Dan, you texted Robin at ten fifty-two a.m."

> How's it going? U should've woken me. I'd have jumped your car or given u a ride.

"You texted her again at twelve-fourteen p.m."

> Who picked u up? Where r u now?

"Again, no reply," he looked at both cops. You sent the final text at two-eighteen p.m."

> Dammit, Robin. Someone maxed out my Depot card. Call me.

"No call back from her," Harlan looked at Dan. "I'm guessing you were at Home Depot when you sent the last text. Is that correct?"

Dan nodded, "Yes."

Morehouse pounced, "Then she shows up at your place."

Evans added, "You fight—it goes too far. You take her body somewhere in the Subaru."

"No! No! No!" Dan roared and pounded the table. He then seized his chest as he gasped for air. Exhausted, he bent over and laid his head down on the table.

"Dan, look at me," Harlan instructed. He snapped photos of his client's badly bruised face and asked, "Your head and chest hurt… shoulder's torn?"

"I can't breathe." Dan stood up and raised his sweatshirt. "I think my ribs are cracked."

Harlan took a picture of the bruise on Dan's left side, then gingerly touched Dan's shoulder and eased him back in his seat.

Harlan looked back at Evans and Morehead—they were fuming. Then everyone turned towards the thud they all heard. Dan had keeled over and hit the floor. Harlan rushed to kneel next to him. Lying on his side, blood seeped out of his nose and mouth as Dan's face turned blue. Evans grabbed Dan's wrist and checked for a pulse. Harlan put two fingers on Dan's neck.

"He needs medical attention now!" Harlan shouted. "Get an ambulance!"

Chapter 11

Amy Johnson's little boy, Jayden, was asleep in his room. She heard heavy footsteps on the front porch and peeked through the Venetian blinds at the cruiser parked out front. The loud knock on the front door of her first-floor apartment made her switch the porch light on and peer out the peephole. She recognized the Lowell cop Robin had called Uncle Bill, who'd saved her from her violent ex-boyfriend. Amy unlatched the deadbolt, opened the door as far as the safety chain would allow, and felt the cold evening air.

"What's this about?" she asked Officer William Cassidy.

"Sorry to bother you," the broad-shouldered cop asked. "Is Robin inside?"

"No. She moved out."

"Where to?" Vapor rose from his mouth.

"Manchester, to live with her sister, Rebecca."

"You sure?"

"Yeah. I heard her tell her mother, who lives in Reno."

"Robin was reported missing by her sister."

"Oh, God!" She removed the chain and opened the door. "Come in."

"Thank you," the middle-aged cop said. "When was the last time you heard from her?

"Friday morning. When we hugged goodbye." Amy sighed.

"My nephew, Sean. Has he been by looking for her?"

"Not here. Thursday, he stopped into Walgreens and asked about her."

"Hmm… What did he say?"

"That he forgave her. Left his number on a receipt for her to call him."

"He just got out of rehab and doesn't have a cell yet. Do you have that number?"

"I saw Robin put it in her phone and block the number. Wait here. I'll check if she tossed it in a box with other stuff she left behind."

"Found it." Amy handed him a Walgreens receipt. He held it near the light.

"It's his mother's landline." He stuck it in his pants pocket and reached for the door.

"God help her!" Amy said as he stepped out onto the porch.

He handed her his card, "Thanks. Call me if you hear from either of them."

* * *

Saturday had been a busy one for Sean Cassidy. He took the Plain Street exit off the Lowell Connector and waited at the light across from the Lowell Car Wash, where he and his older brother Chris had worked. It was near the Veterans of Foreign Wars (VFW) club. His dad and brother were members after tours in Vietnam and Iraq until those conflicts ultimately took their lives.

The light changed. Sean headed home and parked his mother's Sentra in her driveway. It was covered in highway road salt from miles to the job site he'd worked at in Merrimack, NH, and a side trip he made to Manchester, looking for a grey Subaru Outback. He hung his hat and coat on hooks in the hallway, now filled with the aroma of his mother's cooking. She was in the kitchen talking to her sister, Fran, twisting the landline's phone cord around her finger. She pointed at the pot of beef stew on the stove. *Thanks, Ma.* The kitchen clock showed 6:13 p.m.

Sean devoured a bowl of stew, sopping it up with sourdough bread and washing it down with a glass of milk. He belched; his mother frowned. "Scuze me," he said.

He headed upstairs, showered, dressed, and returned downstairs. Ma was still on the phone.

"Hold on, Fran," Ma said, covering the mouthpiece. "Where ya goin'?"

"Downtown, catch the Bruins game," he replied.

"You can watch it here."

"Haven't seen my friends in six months. Trust me, Ma. I'll be good."

She opened her purse, "Get me my Megabucks tickets." She gave him five bucks and her prefilled Mass lottery numbers.

"Okay, Ma." He kissed her forehead.

Sean heard her say, "Fran, I got Uncle Bill on the other line. I'll call you back."

Time to go! He grabbed his wool Bruins beanie cap and his brother's camouflage field jacket, rushed outside, and jumped in the Sentra. He drove up Chelmsford Street and passed through Lincoln Square; the Gaelic Club was still boarded up. *Shame, it's where we first met.*

Sean then headed toward downtown Lowell, hoping to bump into his Irish buds at their favorite watering holes. He drove down Appleton Street, took a left on Elliott Street, and passed by Elliot's Famous Hot Dogs eatery.

He'd had lunch there with his Uncle Bill Thursday before the storm started. His uncle stressed, "You must stay clean and away from Robin." He had no intentions of falling off the wagon but made no promises about her.

He took a right on Middlesex Street and stopped at Garcia Brogan's restaurant. The half-Irish, half-Mexican venue had trivia tonight in place of an Irish band. *She won't be here.* He drove down Gorham Street, parked in the lot next to a four-story red brick building, and entered Towers News Stand. *Ma won't let me in the house without her Megabucks tickets.*

Towers's narrow aisles were filled with snacks and newspapers. A couple stood at the register to buy the soda and chips they had picked out. Sean stepped into the store's much larger seedy section where guilty-looking men sorted through the smut mags, porn DVDs, and sex toys. He chuckled. *Towers's adult biz is always on the upswing.* He returned to the center aisle.

"Hard box a Mahbos," he said, handing the clerk his mother's prefilled lottery picks.

Sean stuffed the lottery tickets in the car's glove box. He drove down Central Street, turned left onto Middle Street, rolled along the cobblestone, and found a parking spot. He locked the car, turned the collar up on his camo jacket, and headed into The Old Court Irish Pub.

* * *

The Pub's boisterous Saturday night crowd was getting louder. Due to the snowstorms, Tim, the head bartender, hadn't seen it this busy in over a month. *People are tired of being cooped up.* The hockey game blared on both TVs—the Boston Bruins and Pittsburg Penguins were tied. Patrons stood two rows deep behind the bar stools as every table was filled with diners devouring fish and chips, bangers 'n mash, and shepherd's pie.

"This is crazy!" shouted Casey Cregg, Tim's excited new barmaid.

Tim was busy serving Boomers on his end of the bar. Casey, the hot blonde, tended to the Millennials at the other end, who were filling up her tip jar. Tim Sullivan topped off two more pints of Guinness for his regular customers.

"Thanks, Sully," said the gray-bearded guy running the tab.

Sully kept an eye on the corner table where Beau Jaynes and Mickey Ward, two of Lowell's most recognized Irish boxers and Golden Gloves champions, sat with their wives. Ward's battle with Arturo Gatti, in the bloodiest match ever, won *Ring Magazine's* Fight of the Year Award. Mickey's boxing career was depicted in *The Fighter,* filmed in Lowell. Mark Wahlberg, who produced it, portrayed Mickey Ward. Mickey's step-brother Dickie Eklund—an excellent boxer in his own right and known as the "Pride of Lowell" for going ten rounds with Sugar Ray Robinson—was portrayed by Christian Bale, who won the Oscar for Best Supporting Actor.

"GOAL!" the crowd screamed when Brad Marchand scored for the Bruins. Everyone was high-fiving and watching the replay, except for Casey's upset customer.

"Problem?" Tim asked Casey as he rinsed beer mugs in the sink beside her.

"I made him a Captain Morgan and Coke. He don't want it."

Tim made eye contact with the guy in the Bruins beanie and a camo jacket. The man leaned between two customers sitting on stools and said, "Sully, I axed fa a Coke."

"Hey, Sean! Didn't recognize you without your beard." *And your mullet.*

"I just got oudah detox. No rum!"

"No *problem*," Tim said, then added, "Your uncle, Bill, was in earlier looking for ya."

"That so?"

Tim nodded while he filled a glass with ice and Coke. When he looked up, he saw Sean Cassidy heading out the door.

"On the house," Tim said as he dumped the Coke down the drain.

Chapter 12

Harlan watched the paramedics load Dan into the ambulance. The oxygen helped his skin color improve; he was conscious but not moving. He followed the blaring ambulance led by a police cruiser through Chelmsford, into Lowell, across the Merrimack River, down Route 113, onto Varnum Avenue, and up the hill to Lowell General Hospital.

Harlan considered calling Dick but wasn't sure he understood everything that happened at Dan's house. The cop's scenario that the woman returned and a struggle took place was possible. He needed more information about the blood in the house, the car, and the missing woman. Harlan was now deeply concerned about Dan's condition. *I better wait 'til I learn more before I call Dick.*

* * *

Sean stopped abruptly at the Princeton Boulevard and Wood Street light. The sirens blared when the Chelmsford cruiser led an ambulance through the intersection. He was relieved it wasn't Lowell cops. *I gotta get over this paranoia.*

He crossed Wood Street, continued down Princeton Blvd, and passed the town line into Chelmsford, where it became Princeton Street. He'd check out an Irish hangout in another town, where no Lowell cops, especially his uncle Bill, would be looking for him.

The Glenview Pub and Grill in Chelmsford was built in the mid-fifties. "Their corned beef and cabbage boiled dinner is as good as Ma's," Chris said to Sean the first time his brother took him there on St Paddy's Day. On Saturday nights, they usually had a big karaoke crowd.

Robin loved karaoke. After a few drinks, she'd get up with her girlfriends, and they'd sing Irish rocker hits, like the Cranberries' "Zombie." She'd sing Sinead O'Connor's "Nothing Compares 2 U" and point at him. She'd belt out U2's big hit "One" and make him join her. Together, they'd sing their hearts out. Then he'd lift her, show everyone what it meant to carry each other. He sighed. *I wish I could turn back time.*

Sean pulled into Glenview's plowed, empty parking lot. He parked near the brick building's entrance, flashed his high beams, and read the sign on the green double doors.

Under New Management Spirits Coming Soon

He hadn't been here in a year. He was depressed; he'd run out of places to look for her. Soon after, a black and white pulled behind him, blocking him from backing out. Sean lowered the window. A tall Chelmsford cop approached him, "What are you doing here?"

"Nothin', sir. Just wondering why it's closed."

The cop shined a flashlight inside the Sentra. "Shut the car off. License and registration."

"Yes, sir." He handed Officer Saxon his license and his mother's registration and waited inside his car. He looked in his rearview mirror; the cop was talking to someone. A few minutes passed; another Chelmsford cruiser pulled in. Saxon approached Sean's door. He handed him back his license and the registration, and Sean put it back in the glove box.

"Step out of the car."

Sean cooperated. Then a much bigger cop, Sergeant O'Malley, asked, "Where're the car keys?"

"My jacket. What's the problem, offasah?" he asked politely.

"Open the trunk."

Sean walked to the rear and opened the trunk. The larger cop aimed his flashlight at the box of Romex cable, electrical switches, electrical tape, and his tool belt. The cop used his flashlight to nudge a shovel, a roll of duct tape, trash bags, tie wraps, and rope. O'Malley aimed his body camera at the trunk's contents, shut the box, and nodded at the other cop.

"Hands on the trunk. Spread your legs," Saxon instructed.

They patted Sean down, took his car keys, cuffed him, and then led him into the back seat of Saxon's cruiser.

"I've done nothin' wrong. Why am I being arrested?"

The cop ignored him and drove off, followed by the other cruiser.

* * *

The Lowell General's ER staff took Dan for X-rays and a CT scan. Harlan sat in a chair across from the nurses' station. The female cop, Officer Hall, who drove the Chelmsford cruiser ahead of the ambulance and helped admit Dan to the hospital, sat two chairs away from him.

Harlan read the police report he'd copied earlier on his phone. *The police are responsible for Dan's wounds and will have to answer for it,* he thought, especially when his father finds out. Due to the possible hostage situation, the cops will justify their actions, especially if the woman turns up harmed and Dan is implicated. He had concerns about all the blood and Dan having the Subaru's key when they arrested him. He didn't know when he'd be able to get Dan's explanations to question him further about the woman.

An ER nurse in blue scrubs approached Officer Hall and him and said, "We stitched up his hand. He has a broken nose. The doctor will be out shortly."

Dr. Lee extended a hand to Harlan and said, "It's not as bad as we first thought. No cerebral bleeding or obvious brain damage. But he's not out of danger yet. We'll know more after the next rapid CAT scan."

"Uh-huh. What's your diagnosis?" Harlan asked, and Hall listened closely.

"Concussion, deviated septum, torn rotator cuff, two fractured ribs, may have resulted in hemopneumothorax."

"Meaning what?" Harlan asked the Chinese physician that he towered over.

"A punctured lung. The cracked ribs are high. If lower, he might have ruptured his spleen, requiring immediate surgery. Long recovery, weakened immune system for life."

"Can we see him now?"

"We gave him locals and analgesics for the pain. He's drowsy." Dr. Lee motioned to the nurse. "They can have a few minutes with him now."

Harlan and Officer Hall entered Dan's room. His eyes were shut, oxygen tubes ran up his nostrils, IV tubes clung inside his left arm, his wrists were taped to the side rails, and he had a bandaged right hand. Hall looked at Harlan and shook her head. *Won't learn anything else from Dan tonight.*

He leaned close and said, "Dan. Hey Dan."

His glossy eyes opened.

"Doing any better?"

He gave a slight nod.

"Do you remember what happened to Robin?"

He uttered, "She's gone."

Officer Hall leaned over, "Gone where?"

He rolled his eyes up as he searched for an answer and said, "Home Depot?"

Then Dan closed his eyes and drifted away. Harlan's phone chirred—a text from Dick.

Harlan, any updates? Call, I'll be up.

* * *

"Good work, guys," Evans said to officers O'Malley and Saxon; they were all in Lieutenant Sinclair's office. He was wrapping up a call with the Low-ell Police, informing them they had picked up Sean Cassidy for questioning. Sinclair ended the call and explained, "Sean Cassidy's uncle is Sergeant Bill Cassidy, LPD. He's on his way here."

Evans and O'Malley headed for the conference room. O'Malley said, "I know Bill Cassidy and all the Irish cops in Lowell. He's one of their best—and a good man."

They sat across from Sean, who was detained for questioning; they skipped the Miranda.

"Mister Cassidy, I'm Detective Jon Evans, and you've met Sergeant Mick O'Malley. We have a few questions about today. Officers Saxon and O'Malley said you have cooperated with them. Should you continue to do so, this should go quickly."

O'Malley asked, "Why do you have duct tape, tie wraps, and a shovel in the trunk?"

Cassidy shifted in his seat, grinned, then replied, "Uhm a 'lectrician. Tools o' da trade."

Chapter 13

Dick kissed Jo good night, stepped onto the lanai, and texted Harlan, asking for an update. The night was still warm; a breeze splashed the river's water on the docks of the brightly lit marina below. He answered his phone, "Harlan, thanks for getting back to me. What happened at the station?"

"Sorry, I couldn't call earlier. We had complications. We're uh… at Lowell General."

"Why? Is Dan, okay?"

"Is Jo listening in?"

"She's sleeping. Fill me in."

"According to the police report, captured on their bodycams, Dan was threatening an EMT in his house with a hammer and a knife. They tasered him and took him down hard. We were in the station's conference room, trying to find out what happened to the woman when he passed out. We had an ambulance bring him here. He's—"

"Passed out… from what? What's his condition?" Dick paced back and forth.

"Conscious, but not stable. He has fractured ribs, a broken nose, and a torn rotator cuff. May have a collapsed lung, too."

"Ouch!" *Who did this?*

"He's heavily medicated and dozing. They're doing another CT scan." Harlan took a deep breath, "Doctor said it could've been worse!"

"Oh?"

"No brain damage. No damage to his spleen, or they'd have operated immediately."

"It's bad enough. What are the charges? What happened to the girl?"

"Resisting arrest, assaulting an officer, domestic violence. We don't know anything about her yet. But they're looking for her ex-boyfriend who had a violent history with her."

"What'd Dan say about her?"

"He hadn't heard from her since early this morning when she left his house. He has text messages trying to reach her all day. She never replied."

"What the hell happened at Home Depot?"

"He said she sold him the credit card and that someone maxed it out. We didn't explore it further as finding the woman is paramount."

"That mess has been all over social media!"

"Yeah, but Dan's no racist. It's all viral cancel-crowd hype."

"I know. But he lost his cool. Something put him over the edge."

"Social media crap should fizzle out soon. Unless the woman—"

"What?"

"Hold on, here comes the nurse." Voices could be heard in the background. Then Harlan said, "No collapsed lung, no bleeding in the brain."

"Good. So, what about the woman?"

"Dan said her car wouldn't start and that she left him a note. He thought she got a ride to her sister's house. But her sister and husband arrived at Dan's house to get the girl's car. They found blood in the car, more inside the house… then they called nine-one-one."

"Christ. This is far more serious than I—"

"Yes! But here's the thing. Dan said he was clearing snow off his roof when he saw the guy in his kitchen. He called nine-one-one first. I checked the arrest report."

"Hmm. So, what's next?"

"We wait 'til he's stable enough to speak. May not be until tomorrow morning, though."

"Harlan, uh. Thanks for being there with him. Christina must be worried about you."

"She's stuck in DC. I'm picking her up at Logan tomorrow afternoon."

"I got an early flight out, landing in Logan at ten-thirty."

"I'll pick you up."

"You got enough to deal with. I'll Uber to Dan's house, get his truck. Should make it to the hospital by twelve-thirty."

"Don't touch anything at the house. It's uhm… a crime scene. Call when you land."

"Text me with any updates on Dan. And thanks again."

"Will do, good night."

* * *

After Harlan ended his call with Dick, he overheard Officer Hall speaking on her phone, explaining Dan's condition. "Okay. Roger that. I'll inform his attorney."

Hall reported, "They picked up Cassidy for questioning. He's no longer a person of interest. No other leads on the woman. They want Evans or me present when you speak with DeCosta."

With the spotlight back on Dan, Harlan had a decision to make: Go home, get some sleep, and be here early tomorrow, or stay all night and wait for Dan to come around so he won't be interrogated without his attorney present.

* * *

Sergeant Bill Cassidy slid behind the cruiser's wheel as his nephew, Sean, jumped in the passenger's side without a word. He pulled out of the Chelmsford Police Station and headed towards the Glenview Pub to get Sean's mother's car.

"What am I going to do with you?" Bill continued. "You're lucky your mother and the owner of Small Electric vouched for you—and no one saw you near Robin."

"Luck o' tha Irish," Sean said.

"Look. You can charm your mother and your rehab counselor—"

"I proved to her and Ma I could do this."

"That's nice, but—"

"But nevah enough fa you. Huh Uncle, Bill? Nevah fa you."

"We've had this conversation, Sean."

"I'm clean. Nevah touchin' anythin' again."

"Not the booze and drugs. You violated a restraining order! Just didn't get caught."

"If you say so."

"Where did you get the electrical gear and supplies?"

"A friend owed me a favah."

"Yeah… What'd you do for him?"

"I needed work. I called Hectah Hernandez, who works for Small Electric. They needed an ordah picked up at Home Depot and delivered to a job site in Merrimack, New Hamsha. We rough-wired a business condo. Two day's pay undah da table."

He pulled into the Glenview and parked next to the Sentra. "That's all good. But you must stop looking for Robin."

"Just want to letah know, I forgive her. Chelmsford cops didn't say why they were lookin' fa Robin. She in trouble?"

"*You* need to *thank her* for calling the cops—you almost killed her. You could've had your head smashed in like Miggy Morales. Lucky you ended up in rehab instead of prison."

Sean's mother was his alibi the night Morales, a bisexual with a rap sheet for petty theft and drug peddling, was found in the woods behind Chelmsford's Route 3 rest stop. It's where undercover cops busted drug dealers and men who have sex with men for indecent exposure. They reported the homicide as a hate crime or drug deal gone bad but never found the tire iron used to beat him to death or the wire cutters that snipped his dick off and shoved it in his mouth.

Bill's nephew turned away and looked out the window. He put his hand on his surrogate son's shoulder and patted the Camo jacket. "I'm happy for you. Proud of you for trying to get things together. But I'm sorry, Sean. I think Robin skipped town when she heard you were looking for her."

Sean furled his lips, grabbed the door handle, and jumped out, "Been a long day. I gotta bring Ma her winning Megabucks ticket."

Bill followed him from a distance, ensuring Sean pulled into his mother's driveway.

Chapter 14

Dick barely slept last night. He left Jo a note on the kitchen counter before he left for his early Sunday morning flight to Boston. He parked his Q8 e-tron SUV in the airport's long-term lot and checked his large suitcase. Once aboard, Dick settled in the aisle seat, opened his laptop, and sipped his coffee. Although the police report justified their brutal takedown, the ugly defense photos Harlan took of his battered son angered him. Dick also worried about the missing woman and couldn't imagine Dan harming her or anyone.

Dick checked his @soldonsolar Twitter feed. A #extremeweatherdeaths story depicted why and how many lives had perished worldwide due to climate change. He retweeted the story and revised his PowerPoint presentation for the Clean Energy Conference session he was chairing. Dick hoped it didn't attract any of the militants who had sabotaged his solar projects last year. The pilot announced it was sunny and forty-one degrees when they landed in Boston at 10:21 a.m.

* * *

Detective Jon Evans was back in the Chelmsford Police Station on Sunday morning. He scrubbed social media for the missing Robin O'Rourke and found no Twitter, Instagram, or LinkedIn accounts for her. But she did have a Facebook page. It listed that she works at Home Depot, attended Middlesex Community College, lives in Lowell, and is not in a relationship. Evans noticed that she had deleted all her posts, but others' tagged posts remained.

Her sister, Rebecca, tagged Robin with her niece, Brianna, sitting on her lap. Ed Mulligan tagged her in a photo with other Home Depot employees. Bonnie Boyle tagged her with Sean Cassidy in October 2018 at a Glenview karaoke night and on St. Patrick's Day in 2017 at the Gaelic Club. *She had an online social life, but now it's private.*

Evans then read the lab results. *DeCosta's hiding something.* The blood on the Subaru's seats, towel, and the utility knife inside the car matched Robin's blood type obtained from an ER report on her domestic violence injuries reported last year. Blood and red wine stains on the rug by the fireplace and a Brady jersey mixed with blood spots also matched.

The blood in the mud room, kitchen, carving knife, hammer, and towel under the sink matched DeCosta's blood type on his recent hospital record. The labs—along with the mess in the kitchen and the wound on DeCosta's hand—led Evans to believe Robin put up a fight. *So where is she now?*

Evans printed Robin's phone usage log—texts and calls, local and out-of-state. He cross-referenced the numbers to phone directories to identify the owners of the calls and texts. He noticed Thursday evening calls to the woman's mother in Reno, Nevada—a three-hour time difference—and her sister Rebecca in Manchester, New Hampshire. He called the sister.

"Hello, Rebecca? This is Detective Evans."

"Hi… Have you found Robin?"

"Sorry, still trying to locate her. Have you spoken with your mother? It's six-thirty in Reno; I didn't want to wake her."

"I spoke with Mum last night. Robin told her on Thursday that she'd live with us in Manchester. How about her ex, Sean?"

"We questioned him last night. He hasn't seen her and has an alibi for Saturday. Robin's phone records show texts on Saturday morning with San-jay Patel. Do you know anything about him?"

"Patel? Don't think so. Sanjay, wait! Maybe it's Jay. He gave her a ride to work one day when her car wouldn't start. She knew him from Middlesex Community College."

"Got it. Thanks, stay in touch."

"Yes!" He shouted to himself. Sanjay Patel had also texted with Robin three weeks earlier. Evans asked Lieutenant Sinclair to get Judge Clark to approve a broader emergency search warrant to allow them to trace the phones on the missing woman's call log, specifically Patel.

* * *

Dick texted Jo that he'd landed in Boston and would call after he spoke with Dan and Harlan. He then grabbed his suitcase from the luggage carousel. Dick noticed that many Asian travelers were wearing facemasks to protect themselves from the coronavirus raging in China and Italy. He hoisted his laptop bag on his shoulder and dragged his suitcase along the pedestrian bridge to where his Uber ride awaited. Along the way, the raw, cold Boston breeze smacked his face. Dick zipped up his black leather bomber jacket, adjusted his wireless earbuds, and called King.

"Hi, Dick," Harlan answered "The nurse said Dan's doing better. I'm at home now and heading into the hospital shortly."

"I should make it to Chelmsford in an hour, the hospital by noon. Any word on the woman?"

"Still missing. Cops picked up her ex last night—"

"Oh, good."

"Not really. He had an alibi and is no longer a suspect."

"So, it's back to Dan?"

"Afraid so. Hopefully, we'll learn more when we speak to Dan."

"Yeah. Text me Dan's room number. See ya there."

The olive-skinned Uber driver placed Dick's luggage in the rear of his white Ford SUV. Dick settled into the warm back seat. The driver's rear pouch was stuffed with paperback books and a first aid kit. College textbooks filled the passenger's seat.

"Sir, you're going to North Chelmsford, is that correct?"

"Yes. Buckingham Street, alongside Crystal Lake."

"Never heard of that. Is it near Freeman?"

"It is Freeman Lake. Sorry. Showing my age. You know the area?"

"Yes, sir, I live in North Chelmsford."

They made it through the Ted Williams Tunnel and headed north on Route 93. They drove up I-95 as the quiet Uber driver eyed Dick from time to time in his rearview mirror. Dick checked the paperbacks behind the driver's seat: Jodi Picoult, David Baldacci, James Patterson, Lee Child. A closer look revealed a blood-spotted first aid kit.

"Take a book," the driver said. "Riders finish them and leave them behind." *Good English, no accent, born and raised here,* Dick figured.

"Thanks, but I've read them. Must be boomer's books. Everyone else reads Kindles and tablets."

The driver smiled as they exited I-95 onto Route 3 and headed north. *Twenty minutes from Chelmsford now.*

"How long have you been driving for Uber?" Dick asked.

"Two years. This is my last trip from Logan. Gotta study for exams. I go to U Lowell."

"My son graduated U Lowell in twenty-thirteen. Environmental engineer now. What's your major? When do you graduate?"

"Computer Science. Class of twenty-twenty-one."

"Good for you! I spent forty years in the computer industry. Do you have any experience with blockchain technology?"

"My data structure classes covered it. It's in the forefront."

"My daughter, who's a software engineer, is into it. She was recruited by West Coast crypto firms."

"Did she go to U Lowell?"

"No, UC Berkeley. She keeps pushing me to buy Bitcoin."

"Have you?"

"All crypto is volatile. I bought a little Bitcoin and more Ethereum. I have always been an early adopter of technology and have invested in many different areas. Did you buy any?"

"My classmates have. You're the first boomer I know that bought," he said with a smile.

They exited the highway, turned off the main road, and slowed when they hit the snow-packed side street.

Dick instructed, "Pull in here." He'd prepaid the fare and tip through the Uber app.

The driver turned into the driveway, which was surrounded by massive snowbanks. He then put Dick's bags on the ground and mumbled, "Déjà vu," as he shut the tailgate.

"Thank you, sir!"

Dick surprised him with an additional cash tip. "Thank you, and good luck with school."

Dick spotted the yellow police tape stretched from the stair railings to the garage. He shook his head, *Crime scene.*

* * *

Evans sat in Officer Nate Thornton's cruiser and set up the tracking software on his iPad to triangulate Sanjay Patel's location and movements. He knew Patel lived in North Chelmsford with his parents but didn't know if he was there now or with the missing woman. They waited in a store parking lot two blocks from his parent's condo. Evans then used his iPad to ping Patel's phone. The tracker showed him traveling north on Route 3, moving past Lowell, and entering Chelmsford. Patel then turned off the highway onto Route 40.

Evans said, "He's headed toward his parent's house."

Evans eyed the tracker as Patel turned off Route 40.

"Drive toward Freeman Lake!" Evans shouted.

They then sped off with their flashers on, no siren.

"Shit. He stopped," said Evans as he zeroed in on the address.

"Where?" Thornton asked.

"The house where the woman disappeared. I'll call for backup."

Evans and Thornton arrived at 36 Buckingham Street and cut off a white SUV backing out of the driveway. They jumped out, and each took a door with their weapons pointed at the dark-skinned Middle Eastern driver. "Step out of the car!" Thornton ordered.

The driver killed the engine, opened his door, raised his hands over his head, and stepped out. A taller, dark-skinned man lingered near the garage. Evans pointed his weapon at him, "Halt! Don't move!" The man froze and turned both palms up.

"Identification," Thornton said.

The suspect handed him his license. Thornton returned it, nodded at

Evans, and said, "Turn around. Hands up on your car."

Thornton searched and cuffed the driver before they walked him to their cruiser. Evans opened the car door and kept an eye on the other man in the driveway standing perfectly still.

Patel said meekly, "I'm an Uber driver. Why am I being arrested?"

Another cruiser pulled in.

Evans confronted the well-built man in a black leather jacket near the garage. "Identification," he said.

The sun-tanned older man handed him a Florida driver's license with a veterans designation.

"The Uber brought me in from Logan." He showed Evans the Uber receipt on his phone.

Evans glanced at it and handed his ID back. "You related to DeCosta, who lives here?"

"He's my son. I came to get his truck. I'm going to the hospital to see him and our attorney, Harlan King."

Our attorney. "Don't touch anything in the house. It's been dusted."

"No problem. What do you want with my Uber driver?"

"He was the last one to text the missing woman."

"Oh? Can I talk with him?"

"No. We'll handle it."

"Right. Could you please move his car and your cruisers so I can leave?"

Evans nodded. DeCosta said, "Thank you." He then used his phone. "Harlan, I'm at the house, and so are Chelmsford's finest."

This guy's worse than his lawyer, Evans thought. The Florida man continued his phone conversation, ducked under the yellow caution tape, and headed into the house.

* * *

Dick explained to Harlan that the cops were driving off with his Uber driver, the last person that texted the missing woman.

"Really?" Harlan said. "Maybe they'll back off from Dan now."

"Hope so. We need to hear his side of the story. I'll be at the hospital in thirty minutes."

Dick opened the door to the mudroom, stepped over the puddle of blood, and placed his laptop bag and suitcase on the sitting bench. He then carefully entered the kitchen and maneuvered across the blood-splattered floor littered with broken glass and a shattered mug.

Dick grabbed paper towels to open the kitchen drawer without leaving his fingerprints and seized the truck's keys. He then opened the atrium door and stepped outside. A ladder he gave his son leaned against the roof as melting icicles dripped onto the deck. He examined an improvised snow rake—an extendable handle duct-taped to a garden rake. Dick guessed Dan made it. *Clever. Well done.*

Dan's rake and effort did the trick—the solar collectors were clear. However, the roof's overhang had no soffit vents. Whoever built the garage and mudroom addition missed that essential roof ventilation requirement. Dick made his way back into the mudroom, which had water stains on the back wall. The Sheetrock would have to be replaced, and mold would have to be removed. *Poor Dan… when it rains, it pours.*

Dick grabbed his laptop bag from the bench, entered the garage, and jumped in the Toyota pickup. Home Depot printouts on the passenger's seat matched Dan's credit card dispute; he stuck them in his laptop bag. Dick reversed out, hit the clicker for the garage door to close behind him, and squeezed by the Uber car in the driveway and a second cruiser. Neighbors had gathered on the street by now, and a teenage girl was recording the commotion on her phone. Dick was glad to be on his way.

Chapter 15

Ashley Brinkley's *Lowell Sun* editor and colleagues praised her for scooping Depot Dan's arrest. She knew a little about Home Depot herself. Ashley asked the sales associate at Home Depot's customer service desk where her cousin Kayla was.

"She's in the break room. I can page her?"

"Don't bother, I know where it is. I worked here eight years ago."

She texted Kayla, stood outside the break room, and scanned the familiar bulletin board. Robin O'Rourke was February's first-place winner for credit card promotions; Kayla took second, and Maddie third. Kayla stuck her head out and waved Ashley into the break room.

"How ya doing, Kayla?"

They hugged, giggled, then sat together on a couch.

"Tired. Don't usually work Sundays. We're shorthanded at the service desk."

"You work hard; they're lucky to have you."

"Thanks. I read your story online. Is Robin still missing?"

"Far as I know. Bet it's been wild here since the Depot Dan shitshow?"

"Crazy! Nashua and Chelmsford cops came in. Management told them they had not heard from Robin. The cops are not pressing charges on anyone yet. We're all worried about Robin."

"What about the customers and employees?"

"Nutso…. Generous customers are now paying for veterans' items at the register. It's uncomfortable for Maddie. She tells everyone the guy didn't offend her. The store's tape showed him reacting to unknown charges on his Depot card; the snow rake was an accident. Everything was way overblown."

"Social media hype to get followers. So, what department did Robin work in?"

"Service desk with me. Friday was her last day. We had a party for her in the breakroom. I thought she'd return to pick up her apron on the table;

friends are still signing it."

Ashley recalled writing farewell notes on the Depot's orange aprons for popular departing coworkers. *I never had a party or a signed apron.*

"Did she say where she was going and why?"

"Moving in with her sister and transferring to the Manchester store. Distancing from an abusive ex."

"Did he come here looking for her?"

"Not sure. She has a restraining order on him. Although Friday, she sounded anxious on the service desk phone. I heard her say, 'Perfect! Thank you, lord.'"

"Did you ask her about that?"

"I got busy with a customer, and she went to the break room, where her old iPhone was always charging."

"Did you know Depot Dan?"

"I'd seen him shop here. Didn't know he'd dated Robin until he came in looking for her Saturday when the credit card incident happened."

"Does he have bad credit?"

"He had excellent credit. Rumor is someone loaded up his card with online purchases." She looked around and lowered her voice. "Management told us to say no comment on any media inquiries. Don't put that in writing."

"Sure, understandable. By the way, congrats… saw you came in second for getting leads and opening credit cards. I sucked at that when I was a cashier."

"Thanks. Robin was good. She usually came in second behind Ed, who beat everyone else. But he got canned last weekend. So, we all moved up by default."

"Ed, who?"

"Ed Mulligan, lead generator for service and installations—windows, siding, roofing—"

"Why'd they fire him?"

"Rumor has it he sold leads to unauthorized contractors. But management said they fired him for stealing gift cards. Charlie in electrical thinks it was both."

"Interesting."

"Hey, Layla," said Carlos, a cheerful coworker entering the break room.

"It's Kayla," Ashley corrected the husky Latino worker.

"No worries," Kayla said. "Carlos has a nickname for everyone."

Carlos told Ashley, "Fast Ed and Big Red, both gone. Jou gonna win the contests now."

"Ha, no way." Kayla shook her head.

"Fast Ed… meaning Mulligan? Who's Big Red?" Ashley asked.

"Robin. She has red hair."

"Oh? And both are gone in the same week." *Wicked interesting.*

Kayla shrugged. "I gotta get back to the service desk."

They walked toward the store's front. Ashley told Kayla, "Text me if anyone in the store hears from Robin."

* * *

Harlan sent a text to Dick:

> Dan's in ICU, room 260. They took him down for a CT scan. I'll be in the cafeteria.

He grabbed a coffee and sat at a cafeteria table. Someone left the sports section of the *Lowell Sun;* other Sunday edition sections were scattered at nearby tables. Harland read the sports section's top headline.

> Free Agent Tom Brady—moving on from the Patriots?

Two female nurses and a male nurse in blue scrubs were eating on the table beside him. One mentioned the online story about Depot Dan. Harlan listened in.

"We have him in CCU," a young nurse bragged. "Cops brought him in last night—concussion, cracked ribs."

The nurse's voice raised the attention of two women and a little girl sitting at the next table. Harlan shook his head. *So much for patient privacy and HIPAA laws.* He read a text from his wife.

> Boarding in forty minutes, on time to land in Boston at 3:15.

He'd spoken to Christina earlier, giving her the abridged version of Dan's ordeal. She said, "Poor Jo must be worried sick."

The female nurses said goodbye to the male nurses, leaving Harlan with a clear view of a little girl with her mother and an attractive blond he thought he recognized. He sipped his coffee and buried his nose back in the sports section.

"Mister King." Harlan looked up at the lovely young woman he and Christina knew. "How are you?" she asked.

"Doing well, Shannon. How are things with you?"

The well-developed woman who filled out a light blue cashmere sweater and tight blue jeans said, "I'm good. This is my sister, Cheryl, and her daughter, Taylor."

"Pleased to meet you both," he said, rising from his seat. Tiny Taylor, with dirty blond bangs, said, "We're visiting Grammie."

"Oh?" Harlan looked at Shannon for an explanation.

"My mother slipped on the ice Thursday. Broke her hip."

"Ouch." Harlan frowned.

"She's doing better today," added Cheryl; the pretty woman was unmistakably Shannon Nickerson's older sister. She grabbed Taylor's hand and headed off.

Harlan then spotted Dick DeCosta walking toward him. He turned to Shannon, "Well, I hope your mother has a speedy recovery."

"Thank you." The young woman's eyes widened. "Hello, Mister DeCosta."

"Hi there, Shannon. How've you been?" Dick said.

"Good, thanks… Great tan! You've been to Aruba again?"

"Ha, no. I'm retired in Florida."

"Nice! Well, tell Dan I was asking for him," said Shannon, flipping her hair over her ear.

Dick nodded at her. The shoulder-length blond with snug blue jeans and leather boots walked away and looked equally perfect from behind.

Harlan shook Dick's hand, and they sat at his table. *Dick's pissed, no time for small talk.*

"How do you know Shannon Nickerson?" Dick asked.

"She works for Stephen Coben. He built our house in Westford."

Dick replied, "Isn't she a paralegal?"

"Yes. She handles the contracts for Coben's attorney and then coordinates sales upgrades with homeowners. Christina loved working with her. She's gorgeous and thorough."

"Yup, and Dan let her get away. They were engaged and buying the lake house together."

"Wow! Small world."

"Shame he couldn't trust her. It crushed him. He tore up the agreement and hadn't seen any other girl in months until he ran into this redhead."

"Wait. What redhead, the missing woman?"

"Yeah, Dan sent me her picture." Dick pulled out his phone.

Harlan enlarged the photo—a mesmerizing redhead sitting in front of a fireplace with very little covering her long legs and shapely body.

"Stunning. He sure finds the beauties." Harland smiled as he continued to gaze at it.

"Yeah, and he seems to find the trouble too."

"May need this photo for evidence."

"Not funny, Harlan." Dick grabbed the phone back from him.

"She's holding a wine glass and wearing a Brady shirt they found with blood," Harlan retorted.

"Sorry, you're right. I'm not on my game. I'll forward it to you."

"The cops arrested *your* Uber driver, the last one who had contact with the woman?" inquired Harlan.

"Yeah, small world," Dick replied. *Touché.* Harlan nodded.

"Now we know how she left Dan's house. But we don't know if she returned later like the cops believe," said Harlan.

"What did Dan say about that?" asked Dick.

Harlan saw the beleaguered look in his bloodshot eyes. "He was groggy. Unfortunately, they took him for his X-rays before I could ask him."

"Poor guy. By the way, do you know anything about credit card fraud?"

"No, but I'll learn once we clear Dan of these other charges," Harland reassured. He then tossed his coffee cup in the trash receptacle and hurried behind Dick, who was already leaving the cafeteria.

* * *

Dick and his attorney entered Room 206. Dan had an IV drip in his left arm, his right hand was bandaged, an ice pack laid on his chest, oxygen tubes ran up his bruised nose, and he had a black eye and a purple lump on his forehead. *The friggin cops did this to him?* Dick tried to remain calm, reached for Dan's left hand, and gently squeezed it, "Hey, Dan,"

"Hey…. Sorry about all this," his son frowned.

"Yeah, well. We'll get you healed and then out of this mess," Dick said.

Harlan nodded in agreement.

A doctor in light blue scrubs and graying hair made notations on the computer setup next to Dan's bed, then spoke. "You're breathing a little better. The scan and X-rays look good. Does your shoulder still hurt?"

Dan winced. "My ribs hurt more, especially when I breathe."

"The nurse will show you how to use a spirometer, improve your breathing, and measure your progress," said the doctor. "In the meantime, take shallow breaths every few hours to prevent your lungs from collapsing. Ice your chest and keep a pillow on it. And tomorrow, we'll move you to a regular room."

"How long will he be in the hospital? Dick asked.

"Five to seven days," the doctor replied. "And no heavy lifting or driving a car for at least two weeks. The cracked ribs may take a month or longer to heal." The doctor exited quickly.

"I'm done shoveling this winter," Dan replied.

Dick looked at his bandaged hand. "What happened here?"

"I cut it on a broken wine glass."

Dick glanced at Harlan, who then set his phone down to record.

"I saw the mess when I got the truck," Dick continued. "Cops think you and the missing woman fought when she came back later. Can you fill in the rest for us?"

"No! Ouch!" Dan cried in pain. "Dad, Robin never came back. I don't even know who she left with."

Harlan interjected, "Chelmsford police picked up an Uber driver. He was the last person to make phone contact with her."

"Huh… They say where the Uber took her?"

"Don't know yet. They are questioning him now."

"Hope those pricks treat him better than they did me." Dan held his chest and grimaced.

Dick winked at Harlan and asked, "What's that porcupine story your uncle told you?"

Harlan smiled, his pearly white teeth shining on his dark-skinned face. "My Uncle Sammy from Roxbury did a lot of jail time. He told me, 'Before you go to law school, you best know the difference 'tween a porcupine and a police car.'" Harlan leaned closer. "Uncle Sammy said, 'The porcupine has the pricks on the outside.'"

"Ah, ha, beautiful. Ow." Dan grimaced. "Don't make me laugh. It hurts."

Color finally returned to his son's face. "We'll deal with the porcupines later, including Home Depot. Let's focus on Robin. Why so much blood in the house, and why were you threatening the EMT with a hammer and knife?"

Dan raised a finger. "I need water first." He sipped from a glass with a straw in it.

Dick checked his phone. A text from Jo and a similar question from his daughter, who posted in the family chat.

What's the story with Dan? Is the woman still missing?

Dick responded to the chat.

We're with him now. He's OK. No updates on the woman yet.

No need to spread panic, Dick thought.

Then they all heard a ding. It was Dan's phone. Harlan retrieved it from his coat pocket and handed it to Dan. "Check your messages, see if you heard from Robin."

Dan placed his fingertip on the iPhone and returned it to Dick. "Dad. You check before the battery dies."

Dick pulled a charge cord from his laptop bag, plugged it in, and checked his son's text and phone messages. Several were from him and Jo, but none from Robin. He opened the family chat, which had nineteen unread posts.

His son was never in the loop with viral videos, or he chose to ignore them. Dick believed Dan had no clue as his anger seemed to be all directed toward the cops. Dick scratched his head. *So, what happened in that time space? Did Robin come back to the house?*

Chapter 16

Dan swallowed the water. He asked his dad, "Anything from Robin?"

"No. And you never read the family chats. Do you have any idea how many stories and social media videos are out there on you?"

Dan shook his head. "Cops told me I dissed vets. I told them it was an accident and that someone had stolen my identity. They didn't give a shit."

"It's shameful. What were you doing all that time after the Home Depot fiasco?"

Dan adjusted his oxygen tubes. "I went to Lowe's, but they had no snow rakes. So, I bought stuff to make my own. You'd be proud of me."

"I am. Good job improvising and clearing the snow and ice."

"Thanks, Dad—"

"Go on," Mr. King said, placing his phone on the bed to record everything.

"When I returned from Lowe's, I got the ladder, threw ice melt on the roof, and made the snow rake in the mudroom. I attached flashing to the garden rake with duct tape and the painter's pole on the handle. I nicked my thumb on the flashing and used duct tape to stop the bleeding. I had less than two hours before dark."

His dad and lawyer pulled chairs up on each side of his bed.

"I rushed into the house with the rake, and the long handle knocked a wine glass off the kitchen island to the floor. My coffee mug was rolling. I dropped the rake and lunged to snag the cup but missed it. I braced my fall with my right hand and landed on broken glass. It embedded deep into my palm."

Dan raised his bandaged hand. "The blood squirted everywhere. I ran my hand under the water to flush out the shards. I dried my bloody hands with a dish towel, used paper towels to make a bandage, and dropped the bloody towel in the barrel under the sink. I went to the mudroom and wrapped duct tape around the paper towel bandage. The blood and mess on the floors could wait. I was fighting daylight and had a shitload of roof work to do."

His dad nodded and said, "Right—the most important thing to do in the next five minutes."

"What happened next?" Mr. King asked.

"I dragged the snow down with my rake. I used the hammer to chip through the ice. The gash on my hand bled on my gloves. The hammer slipped from my grip and fell on the deck. It was getting dark; I'd had enough. The kitchen lights were now on. I removed my safety glasses and peered through the atrium door. I saw the kitchen drawers were pulled open, and a bag of weed was now on the counter. I thought maybe Robin had returned for some pot."

"But it wasn't Robin. Right?" his dad asked.

"No. This big guy walked by," replied Dan. "I thought I was being robbed, so I ducked down."

"Then you called nine-one-one," Mr. King blurted.

"Yeah. I told the dispatcher I had burglars in my house. She said, 'Police are on their way. Get outside and wait in the street.' I told her I was stuck on my back deck with five-foot drifts around it. I couldn't get to the front of the house."

Mr. King said, "According to the police report, you didn't wait outside."

"No. I saw the guy go into my living room. I told the dispatcher, 'I got this; I'm going inside.' I put my phone in my pocket and snuck in. I then raised my hammer and shouted, 'What the hell are you doing in my house?'"

"You never hung up from nine-one-one?" asked Mr. King.

"No. The startled intruder spun around. He had a wireless earbud and was talking to someone. He was my height, probably thirty pounds heavier. I asked, 'Who are *you*? What do you want?' He raised his hands and said, 'I don't want any trouble. Put that down—then I'll explain.'"

"He told you to put the hammer down?" Mr. King asked.

"I wasn't about to let my guard down, especially when he was talking with someone else who could be near. I shook my head no and said, 'I'm all ears.'"

"That's when the cops showed up?" Dad asked.

"No. He stepped forward, crunched the broken glass on the floor, and froze. That's when I kicked a bar stool in his direction, which made him back up. I then grabbed a sharp knife off the counter, pointed it at him, and raised my hammer. He started backpedaling into the living room, angling toward the front door. I knew it was bolted, and the cops were coming."

"Did you advance toward him?" Mr. King questioned.

"Never. I stayed beside the kitchen island. Then the guy said, 'We came for the Subaru.' Then the front doorbell rang. The cops announced, 'Police open up!' I said back, 'Let 'em in.' As the intruder let the cop in. Another cop threw open the mudroom door with his gun pointed at me."

Dan took a shallow breath, winced, then continued. "The big cop yelled, 'Drop 'em!' I shouted, 'He's the thief!' and pointed at the intruder in the living room. Out of nowhere, the other cop tasered my left arm. It stung like hell. I screamed and dropped the knife and hammer. The cop tasered me again as I was falling to the floor; the huge cop pounced on my back. I landed chest-first on the hammer, and my face hit the floor. I told the cops they were making a mistake and couldn't do this to me in my own fuckin' house. But they cuffed me anyway, threw me against the wall, emptied my pockets, dragged me outside, and took me to the station."

"They took your phone and her car keys. Why were her keys in your jacket?" Mr. King inquired.

"Uhm… she left her keys with a note on the mudroom floor, next to my jacket. Guess I slipped them in my coat pocket and forgot I had them."

His dad's phone dinged again. He glanced at it, put his hand on Dan's wrist to pause his recollection, and looked at Mr. King. "Don't you have to get Christina at the airport?"

"Yes. She said it's on time. I got a few minutes yet," said Mr. King

"Yeah, but—head out now. Check with the cops about the Uber driver and get the nine-one-one tapes. Ask if they are doing anything about the credit card crap."

"Okay," the lawyer said, took his phone, and moved around the bed near his dad's side.

Dad patted King on the shoulder and said, "Harlan, thanks… for everything."

"No problem, I'll call you later. Dan, take care. We'll get you through this."

"Thanks! Mister King."

Dad said, "Relax, drink more water. I'm going to use your private bathroom."

* * *

Joanna took Advil for her headache, read the Sunday newspaper, and tried to keep her mind off Dan. Then, her phone reverberated. It was a text from Christina King. She hadn't heard from her since she and Harlan spent a weekend getaway at their new condo.

> Jo, so sorry to hear about Dan! Thank God no brain or lung injuries. I'm in DC, waiting to board my flight back. Wanted to let you know I'm here for you. Luv, C.

What the hell? Her hand shook uncontrollably. She swore at her husband. *Why am I the last to find out? I'll sound like a fool if I ask Christina.* Joanna composed herself and replied.

Thanks, Christina. You're so thoughtful. Luv Jo

Too angry to call, Joanna texted Dick.

Where's Dan? Where are you? For God's sake, Christina knows more than I do!

She gathered the newspapers and cried. Her husband's reply did little to calm or clarify.

At Lowell General with Dan. Harlan and I are getting statements from him. Jo, I'm sorry. I'm still not caught up on everything. I promise I'll call when I can to explain. Love you.

* * *

Detective Evans had Sanjay Patel, the Uber driver, in the cruiser's back seat. They were headed to the station. He turned the iPad's recorder on, "I'm detective, Evans. Officer Thornton's driving. Mister Patel—how long have you known Mister DeCosta?"

"Sir, I met him an hour ago. Picked him up at Logan."

"Did he seem nervous, make phone calls? What did you observe?"

"Weary like most after an early flight. No calls. Talkative, intelligent gentlemen and generous tipper."

"What did he talk about?"

"Colleges, his children, technology."

"What did he say about his son, Dan DeCosta?"

"His son went to the same college as me."

"You know he's been all over social media and the local news?"

"Yes. He never brought it up."

They pulled into the Chelmsford Police Station. Evans and Thornton escorted Patel to the conference room, uncuffed him, and they all sat down.

"What do you know about the missing woman? Did you know she was last seen at the house you drove to?"

"You mean Robin?"

"Yes, we mean Robin O'Rourke. Is she one of your Uber riders?"

"No, sir."

"Do you drive full-time for Uber?"

"Part-time. I'm a full-time student at U Lowell."

"Sanjay—or is it—Jay? Robin has never been in your car before?"

"She has, sir. But not as a customer."

"On a date?"

"As a friend. I knew her from school."

"Robin went to U Lowell?"

"No, sir. Middlesex Community College. I met her there. I transferred to U Lowell after I got my associate degree."

"And you kept in touch?"

"No. I ran into her at Dunkin's a few months ago. She said she worked at Home Depot and had dumped her ex. We exchanged numbers. She called a few weeks later, stuck in Lowell—her car wouldn't start. So I gave her a ride to work."

"When did you last see her?"

"Yesterday she texted. She needed a favor. At eight-forty, I picked her up at the house on Buckingham. Then I drove her to the Tyngsboro bus station at the Park and Ride."

"Where was she going?"

"She mentioned taking the nine-fifteen Boston Express bus to South Station."

"And you haven't heard from her since then?"

"No. She asked me to charge her phone. Her old model didn't fit my charge cord."

"Was she upset, acting strange?"

"She was stressed and rushing. She had sliced her fingers on a utility knife she kept in her car. I dressed her wound with a first aid kit in my car. I then unloaded her luggage at the bus stop. Robin then entered the office to buy her ticket, and I stayed by her suitcases until she came out. She thanked me—hugged me tight—felt like goodbye forever."

"Did you see her board the bus?"

"No. I had to pick up a rider in Lowell."

* * *

Dick was disappointed with Harlan for telling Christina about his son. He used his son's hospital room's lavatory and replied to Jo's text, hoping to appease her and buy time. Dick hoped the cops would get a lead from the Uber driver on the missing woman soon.

He returned from the bathroom and helped a nurse get Dan up. They walked him and his IV stand to the bathroom. Dick pulled out the Home Depot printouts from his laptop bag and examined the credit card purchases—electrical supplies and expensive equipment for a construction site—nothing Dan would need.

Dick then read the email confirmations for the will call pickup order. *That can't be right.* His son's email address was dan.decosta@gmail. But the order confirmation listed a dan_decosta@gmail. The variation made it look like Dan's, and it would never get to his inbox.

Dick used his laptop to research Home Depot's will call process. It was easy to game, including sending someone else to pick up the order. All you needed was a credit card number, phone, and two email addresses for notifications. He started an online order for items to repair the water damage at the house he and his son owned.

Dan returned from the bathroom. Dick asked, "So, how'd ya meet the red Robin?"

His son smiled. He could now talk freely without being recorded. "In Home Depot's parking lot. Her battery was dead. I jump-started her car."

"And you lived happily ever after by your fireplace."

"Ha, no, don't make me laugh. It hurts." Dan held a pillow to his chest. "But you'd be proud of me. I was careful. At least until yesterday."

"Mom and I will always be proud of you *and* Sam. We just want you to be happy."

"I know. I didn't want to disappoint you again. You both adored Shannon, but Robin is nothing like her… or anyone." *Oh boy, he's screwed.*

"How'd you charm the ginger-haired goddess into your winter wonderland by the lake?"

Dan smiled, then filled his father in on the courting details. He explained that she was independent and more resilient than any woman he'd ever known. "She was raised in Lowell with her sister by a single mom. She had a tough life—especially after her asshole ex ruined her credit. After that, she quit college and lived out of her car. But she's always smiling, never complains and is fun to be with. The cops are wrong. No fuckin' way we fought. Something happened to her."

Dick said, "Think she had anything to do with the credit card breach?"

"Hope not, but someone stole my info and faked the emails and online purchases."

"Definitely," Dick said. He read Harlan's text aloud, but only what his son needed to know.

"Cops have a bus lead on Robin's departure. Not investigating stolen identity. Dan should file a dispute with Citibank online."

"I told you Robin never came back."

"Good. You need to call the eight hundred number or freeze your card online."

"The card is in my wallet. Back at the house unless the cops took it."

Convinced they had to act themselves, Dick called an old friend in Boston. He told him he was in Lowell and filled him in on Dan's problem. His friend said, "Send me an email with the specifics. I'll get someone on it."

"Thanks, Lee. You at the bureau now?"

Lee Grisham lived in Newton, MA, but was currently vacationing at his condo in an exclusive golf community in Fort Myers.

"Small world," Dick said. "I recently retired and bought a high-rise condo downtown.”

“You’re only twenty minutes away. We should get together for a round of golf,” Lee replied.

Dick ended the call. His son now had an astonished look on his face. “What?”

“The *bureau*? Mom said the family had protection because of your book.”

“Fish and Wildlife Bureau,” he smiled.

“Come on, Dad. How do you know anyone at the FBI?”

“Long story, short ending, Dan. Ha, ha.” *Your line, my secret.*

“Fair enough, Dad.”

Dick headed for the door. “You want anything at the cafeteria?”

“Ribeye, medium rare, fries, and a beer.” His son grinned. *That’s good.*

“Got it. Fruit cup, large lemonade with Metamucil.”

“Daaadd.”

Dick was relieved the woman might be safe; it would take the heat off Dan. But he worried about how the social media mess could affect his son’s future. He had kept the unresolved legal matters with the police and Monday morning’s arraignment that Harlan mentioned in the text from Dan.

He felt confident Lee Grisham, the special agent in charge of the FBI’s Boston office, would resolve the credit card scam. But pissed at himself for slipping up and calling in front of Dan. He prided himself on being two steps ahead. But he was tired and stressed, and his anger toward the cops made him react too quickly. Dick hoped this screwup and the dark, delicate past wouldn’t come back to bite him and his family someday. If need be, he’d say he first encountered Grisham when the FBI protected his family from far-right extremists over his controversial book. And it may reoccur after his podcast coverage at the Green Conference.

Dick filled his cafeteria tray and gathered his thoughts. *Focus on the next five minutes.* After he ate, he’d email Lee Grisham, then call Jo.

Chapter 17

Evans had Thornton give Patel a ride back to his car. Tyngsboro's Boston Express ticket office—where O'Rourke paid cash—confirmed the description Patel gave them. Robin had no active credit cards. Her Home Depot checks were automatically deposited to a bank account. But on Friday at 4:33 p.m., she withdrew all but five dollars from an ATM minutes from where she worked.

Evans checked bus schedules leaving Boston's South Station—Greyhound had a 10:45 a.m. to Hyannis in Cape Cod. He requested a review of South Station's cameras to confirm the woman's arrival on the Boston Express bus and any Greyhound connections. The redhead, dressed in a black parka, black jeans, and black boots, had bandaged fingers on her left hand.

Evans got a call from a *Lowell Sun* reporter, Ashley Brinkley, whose cousin worked with Robin at Home Depot. She said, "Robin O'Rourke and Ed Mulligan were tagged in a Facebook photo. Mulligan and O'Rourke ended their Home Depot jobs the same week. I wondered about their Irish connection."

Mulligan resided in Nashua, NH, and had other Facebook posts of him in Provincetown, MA. Evans would follow up later with the Nashua and Provincetown Police. Ashley pressed him on his prime suspect. He said DeCosta would be arraigned Monday morning in Lowell's district court but didn't tell her he was in Lowell General Hospital and his attorney was Harlan King.

* * *

Joanna's husband called and sugarcoated her son's injuries, justifying the cop's actions. She didn't understand why Dan was arrested or had credit problems, but Dick assured her he'd clear that up in a week or so.

"Jo, you're right. The cops overreacted. But they confirmed the woman skipped town on a bus. So, things are settling down."

"Monday I have a doctor's appointment. Tuesday, I can catch a flight."

"Not a good idea. It's cold and icy—snow everywhere, and we're getting another storm midweek. Call me after your doctor's appointment."

"But I want to see him… help care for him."

"He'll be in the hospital for five to six days."

"Okay… bring him a change of clothes and a robe."

"I will. I'm bringing him fruit from the cafeteria. He's got an appetite and is doing better already."

"Thank God."

"Love ya."

"Love you too. Give Dan a hug for me." Joanna wiped a tear away.

* * *

Dick heard the family chat bell and read the post from Sam with her comment:

Dad filmed making a getaway.

An Instagram video headline: More action at Depot Dan's home, Uber driver arrested.

Damn, she has no filter. Sam, this is not helping! He dictated a text to Jo.

"Please tell Sam to knock it off. Update her on Dan's condition, the woman, and mistakes the cops and Home Depot made. Luv ya."

He entered Dan's hospital room and cringed when he heard another family chat ding. His son was gazing at his phone and looked pissed. He'd caught up on Sam's posts, the ugly reaction from the Home Depot videos, and his arrest.

"I'll take the lemonade; you eat the damn fruit." Dan winced and turned away.

Dick put the drink and fruit on the tray, sat in a side chair, and opened the family chat. Dan had posted a selfie video of him with oxygen tubes, a bruised face, and a bandaged hand. He indignantly stated, "Robin and I *never* argued. I'm not racist. My credit card was breached. I called nine-one-one about an intruder. But the asshole cops beat me up instead… So, screw you, Sam, and your lame-ass social media cancel crowd."

Tell us how you really feel, Dan.

Dick worried about Jo. She'd be heartbroken by her children attacking each other and upset with how bad Dan looked. *And bullshit at me for not filling her in on everything.* His phone dinged—a text from Jo.

I'm not calling Sam for you. You kept secrets from me. Because it's your solar panels, and you told Dan to get the snow rake!

He shook his head. *Yep, I'm a bad parent and a worse husband.* On the bright side, he no longer had to shelter his wife, tell Sam to knock it off or update her on her brother's situation. *Thanks, Dan. You got this.*

* * *

Evans called the Nashua Police. Home Depot fired Ed Mulligan, and a search warrant was issued for his automobile and apartment for stolen goods. The landlord had let the police into his abandoned apartment, and they determined he'd skipped town abruptly.

The Nashua Police were working with the Provincetown authorities in Cape Cod, where Mulligan and two other men had a summer rental. Evans called South Station at 3:48 p.m. They transferred him to the technician, who reviewed the video footage.

"Yes, sir. The red-haired woman in the black jacket arrived at the South Station bus terminal. No, I did not see her board the ten forty-five for Hyannis."

Evans replied, "Please check other Greyhound departures for Cape Cod destinations."

"Sir, I leave in ten minutes. No OT is authorized. I'll note your request for the second shift supervisor. It might not be reviewed until Monday morning, though."

"I see. Have the supervisor call me. Thanks." *Damn! Well, at least she's alive.*

* * *

Kori observed Sam pacing back and forth during a rare call she made to her mother.

"All right, Mom, I love you too. Good luck at the doctor's tomorrow."

Sam ran her fingers through her short blond hair and shouted, "You idiot!"

Khori touched Sam's shoulder. "What's wrong? Is your mother okay?"

"She's been having stomach problems and the shakes. She's having more tests tomorrow. My brother's problems aren't helping, and neither am I."

"What's the latest with him?"

Sam handed her iPhone to Kori. "Look at this."

Kori played Dan's distraught video. "Oh my. What's he in the hospital for?"

"My mom said cracked ribs, a concussion, and a broken nose."

"Poor guy. Cops whooped him—that's *crazy.*"

"Dan was arrested for domestic violence, resisting arrest, and assaulting a police officer."

"That ain't right!"

"It's bullshit! His credit is ruined. The social media cancel crowd is over the top. And I made it worse by ragging on him. I feel terrible!"

"Call and apologize."

"Dan's pissed, he wouldn't take my call. Besides, he's in the critical care unit and needs rest. My dad's with him. And I promised my mom I wouldn't bother him on the family chat."

"Then message him on Facebook."

"He's not on Facebook or Instagram. He hates social media."

"For God's sake, stop making excuses. Text him!"

"You're right. I needed an attitude adjustment first. Thanks, I love you."

Sam hugged her tightly. Khori saw what she had sent to Dan.

So sorry about all you're dealing with. 😭 Feel better, big brother

Chapter 18

Dick laced up his LL Bean boots, which he'd kept in Dan's guest bedroom closet. They were better for icy, snow-packed parking lots than his Florida shoes. He took pictures of the water damage in the mudroom for insurance purposes. He was meeting Harlan for Dan's Monday morning arraignment at Lowell's new district court.

Dick drove the Toyota pickup down Route 40 in North Chelmsford and passed through Vinal Square. He cruised along Middlesex Street and entered the city of Lowell, where he grew up. Many of the storefronts were now owned by Cambodian families who'd immigrated to Lowell after the Vietnam War. As multiple generations of European immigrants had done before them, second-generation Asian Americans now held elected school board and council seats representing their burgeoning neighborhoods.

The last time he and Jo visited downtown Lowell, they enjoyed the three-day summer folk festival. It featured live rock, jazz, folk, and blues bands, crafts, and food vendors serving African, Asian, Brazilian, Burmese, Greek, Latin, Portuguese, Polish, and other cuisines.

He drove across the Lord Overpass; Lowell's new seven-story justice center and district court was visible on the corner of Jackson Street. The state-of-the-art sustainability building is exceptionally energy efficient and has a LEED platinum rating. It features a chilled beam HVAC system, photovoltaic panels, and sophisticated system controls.

Dick continued on Middlesex Street and took a left on Canal Street to Jackson Street, where its renovated red brick textile mills were now housing modern apartments, artist lofts, business units, and private schools.

The historic first in the nation's industrial city of Lowell was named after Francis Cabot Lowell, who brought power loom technology from England; later, his partners built textile mills along the mighty Merrimack River, which fed a system of canals that powered its cotton mills. The arduous task of the French Canadian, Greek, and Irish immigrants who dug the six miles of canals in the 1800s will never be forgotten. Tales of the mill girls who lived in the boarding houses with as many as six in a room and the generations of immigrants who worked on the spindles and cotton looms on the production lines would always be part of the lore and pride of the city's inhabitants.

Dick's grandparents and parents all toiled in the red brick factories, made sacrifices to yield a better life for each succeeding generation, and ingrained in him a strong work ethic to ensure a better life for his children.

Lowell is the birthplace of many well-known TV and movie stars. They include Michael Ansara and Michael Chiklis; Academy Award winners Betty Davis and Olympia Dukakis; Scott Grimes; Ed McMahon; and tough-guy actor Robert Tessier, who epitomized the rugged city. Lowell built monuments and parks dedicated to their beloved Beat Generation author, Jack Kerouac, whose novel *On the Road* influenced Bob Dylan, The Doors, Willie Nelson, Patti Smith, and Bruce Springsteen. In 1975, Dylan and poet Allen Ginsberg, the Ambassador for Peace and Equality, visited Kerouac's gravesite in Lowell's Edson Cemetery and recorded it in the movie *Renaldo & Clara*.

Lowell author Elinor Lipman has a dozen bestseller books, including the novel *Then She Found Me*, which was made into a movie starring Helen Hunt, Bette Midler, Colin Firth, and Matthew Broderick. Andre Dubus III, a UMass Lowell professor and best-selling author, his novel, *House of Sand and Fog,* made the big screen starring Jennifer Connelly and Ben Kingsley. These celebs left their mark in Lowell and never forgot where they came from. *Nor will I,* thought Dick.

He parked, entered the new justice center, and followed the lengthy line through courthouse security. The massive two-story atrium lobby was adorned with murals, dates, and pictures honoring Lowell's historic textile mill girls.

His tall African American attorney—sporting a dark blue, three-piece suit, colorful tie, and matching pocket square—waved at him. Harlan King shook his hand and explained, "This is *the first day* this court is operating. The politicians and media are here to tour the seventeen separate court-rooms."

Dick recognized the mayor and other city officials. "Beautiful facility. It's the first LEED platinum-designated courthouse in Massachusetts. I'm impressed. I wish it were under different circumstances."

Harlan nodded, then said, "I checked the docket—Dan is fourth or fifth."

They sat up front in the crowded courtroom. Harlan said, "If Dan had stayed in the Chelmsford jail, the police would have driven him here today, and he'd be in one of the forty-seven new holding cells."

Thankfully, his son was spared the embarrassment of standing in handcuffs and speaking to the judge in front of the overflowing public audience, all mumbling behind them.

The bailiff shouted, "All rise!"

The judge began, "Welcome. This district court is officially in its inaugural session." Everyone applauded as the judge softly gaveled them into silence.

The bailiff introduced Dan's case. The judge reviewed the previously signed complaint by the arresting officers, O'Malley and Saxon. They included domestic violence, resisting arrest, and assaulting an officer with the defendant's foot. The judge asked where the defendant was.

King rose, "My client was forcibly arrested and wrongly accused. He was protecting himself in his own home from the intruder *he* had called nine-one-one on. The officers tasered him, knocked him to the floor, and caused severe injuries. My client cooperated during the interrogation at the police station until he blacked out and was rushed to Lowell General Hospital, where he remains in the critical care unit."

The crowd murmured, and the judge gaveled and stared them down to silence. Harlan asked to approach the bench. The judge nodded. Harlan handed him 911's printed transcript, pulled out his phone, and showed a picture of his client lying in the hospital bed. The judge reviewed everything, shook his head, and asked about the missing woman.

"Your Honor, the missing woman—my client was falsely accused of attacking—left unharmed with an Uber driver and took a bus out of town. Everything my client said during his arrest and questioning has all been proven to be true. We motion for a dismissal of all the charges."

The judge looked at the police officers and responded, "At this time, I'll grant a continuation, and the defendant will be released under his own recognizance."

The red-faced police officers were disgusted. But Harlan told Dick, "At the time, they thought they had a hostage situation. They probably have no regrets and got paid overtime today to come in and fulfill their duty."

When they left the courtroom, Dick asked Harlan what the continuation meant.

"It means the judge didn't want to create a media frenzy or embarrass the police, so he shut this down quickly, which is good."

"But a continuation will bring it all out later."

"A future hearing date will be set unless the cops drop the charges. They will once they locate the woman unless she or the EMT press charges."

"Can we sue for the injuries?"

"Sure, but I believe this will never go to court unless you or Dan want to file for damages, medical expenses, and lost wages later."

"Let's get the charges dropped first."

Chapter 19

Ashley moved among the media and politicians swarming in the impressive atrium of Lowell's new justice center. She waved back to Paul Marion, the former community relations director for UMass Lowell and her alma mater, who also worked for Lowell's Historic Preservation Commission. Paul stood by Lowell historian Richard Howe Jr., whose Middlesex County Register of Deeds would relocate to this building.

She sat at the end of a middle row in the district courtroom and was surprised that Harlan King, a respected defense attorney, represented DeCosta. A handsome, well-tanned older gentleman with a black leather jacket sat beside King. He resembled her neighbor.

She heard the murmurs when Attorney King explained his client was hospitalized. *Hmm,* she thought, *Detective Evans never mentioned that.* Ashley didn't hang around for the other sessions. She rushed to the parking lot, called Lowell General, and asked about Mr. DeCosta. He'd been moved from critical care into Room 420 and can take visitors now. She headed toward the hospital and thought about an excuse for dropping in on her neighbor. She schemed she was visiting a friend who used to be in Room 420.

* * *

Dick jumped in his truck. The second call he made while following Harlan was to Jo. He told her he'd called the hospital as Dan had been moved to a private room. He explained the continuation by the judge and the fantastic job Harlan did.

"And the woman is no longer missing. That's good news," Jo said. "What's next?"

"I'm grabbing a bite at The Owl with Harlan, then to the hospital."

"Sam called me…. Said she texted an apology to Dan. And she'd make it up to him."

I can't get into this now. "Great. Call me after your doctor's visit. Love you, babe."

"I will. Love you too."

Dick and Harlan sat in a booth, sipping coffee, devouring the Owl Diner's famous omelets—named after streets in Lowell. They quietly discussed everything from lawsuits to identity fraud and the FBI—none of which was to be mentioned to Christina.

He paid the waitress, and as they exited the diner, he exchanged friendly greetings with David Daniel and Stephen O'Connor, distinguished Lowell-area authors whom he had autographed books of theirs in his library. They knew his controversial book, *Green House Gases and the Gaslighters*, sparked good and bad local press coverage. He figured they'd also read the ugly stories about Dan in the Lowell Sun or on social media. Dick hoped that died down before he returned to Lowell and Boston to promote his latest book, *Climate Change is Chilling*.

On his way to the hospital, he called his insurance company. He had multiple home, auto, boat, and business policies with them. They said he'd hear from an adjuster soon.

* * *

Ashley bought chocolates in the hospital's gift shop. She pushed the ground floor call button, and the elevator doors opened. Inside, a nurse held an IV stand by DeCosta, who was sitting in a wheelchair. He had oxygen tubes up his nose, a black eye, and ugly bruises on his forehead.

"Excuse me," she said as she squeezed in. The fourth-floor button was already lit, so she pushed the top-floor button for the birthing center. *I need a new excuse now.*

The nurse asked, "Visiting a newborn?"

"Yes, a colleague… had a boy," she said and caught Dan's eyes.

"Hello there," he said.

"Oh, hi." Ashley looked at the nurse. "We're neighbors." She tilted her head toward him, "Gee, what happened?"

"Long story."

When the elevator's doors opened, the nurse wheeled him out.

Ashley called out, "Sorry! Feel better!"

"Thanks," he waved goodbye with his bandaged hand. *Yikes, the cops went too far.*

Ashley got off at the top floor to rehearse a new approach. She looked at the sleeping newborns inside the nursery's viewing window and sighed. She'd be thirty-four in June—her childbearing clock was headed for a landfill, like landlines replaced by cell phones—men always want the latest models.

She used the reflection in the glass to fluff her shoulder-length brown hair and adjust her designer eyeglasses. She rode the elevator down, whistling Maroon Five's "This Love." Her stomach churned in anticipation of meeting her dreamy Adam Levine doppelgänger neighbor.

* * *

"Good job," the nurse said, putting an ice pack on Dan's chest when he finished his spirometer breathing exercise.

His friendly neighbor entered his room with a box of chocolates. The warm smile on her thin face and long nose framed with purple eyeglasses presented an air of intelligence and shyness. The full-figured woman he'd seen in his neighborhood was covered in a long parka over jeans.

"Hi there," she said. "They released my friend this morning. The mother's doing fine. Her premature baby is still in the nursery."

"Ah. I'm Dan." He tried to sit up and extend his right hand.

"Ashley." She gently shook his bandaged hand.

"Nice to officially meet you," he said, eyeing the chocolates.

"Rather than flowers, I got these figuring she'd share with me."

"Wise choice," he said.

"I thought so, but selfish. Want one?"

"Sure."

She opened the box. "Solid or cream-filled?"

"Solid, thanks." He popped it in his mouth and savored the dark chocolate.

"Delish," she said as she bit into a pink cream-filled. Dan sipped water through a straw.

"So… what's the baby's name?" he asked.

"Oh. Uhm… Adam."

"Like Apple," he pointed at his iPhone.

"Like Levine," she said. "And sugar," pointing at the chocolates.

He knew Adam Levine, the lead singer for Maroon Five, had a song titled "Sugar." He thought of another Levine song, adjusted his oxygen tubes, and said, "Like 'Harder to Breathe.'"

"Exactly. But I'm sorry. What happened to your chest?"

"Cracked ribs. Luckily, my lung didn't get punctured. No shoveling. Doctor's orders."

"I guess not. So, what happened?"

"Cops, uhm… I was in the right place at the wrong time."

"I saw the cops at your house. It's a shame. And social media is so unfair!"

"Yeah, I hate it. I deleted my Facebook and Twitter accounts last year." *To ghost my ex.*

"Maybe I can help. If you don't mind a picture." She aimed her phone and snapped one before he could even respond.

"I *do* mind."

"My bad."

What's she up to? "Ashley… Uhm, what's your last name?"

"Brinkley."

"Like, Christie. The model Billy Joel married," he said proudly.

"Ding, ding!" She gave him another chocolate.

His dad walked in with his carry-on bag, which, he hoped, had his charger and earbuds.

"Hey, Dad," he said.

Ashley's eyes widened when she saw his father. "Hi, I'm Ashley, his neighbor. And I was *just* leaving."

"Hi," his dad said.

"I'll leave these with you," Ashley said, putting the cover back on the chocolates.

"Thank you, but no. *Please*, share them with your mom."

"Aww," she smiled and nodded. "'Bye, take care."

Chapter 20

Dick wondered, *who's the brunette with the chocolates*? She introduced herself and left quickly. He filled Dan in on what transpired at the courthouse and explained the judge's decision to continue.

"You guys never told me I was due in court."

"Harlan did great—the cops weren't happy. He showed the judge the nine-one-one transcript, the hospital's report, and photos of your injuries."

"Good. Let's sue the fuckin' porcupines."

"Let's get the charges dropped first." Dick changed the subject. "The new courthouse is LEED platinum-certified. Incredible building."

"I know. Greenex bid on it. We lost out to a firm more connected at the state house. So, now we have a new CEO with fed contracts. I have a new manager, and they announced a small reduction in the workforce, which is planned for Q2."

"You're a senior engineer; you should be safe from a layoff."

"I'm good. And I can't wait 'til I get to work on the state's coastal and marine project."

"Sounds good. Did you let GreenEx know you can't attend the Bawstin conference?"

"I emailed my manager. Said I cracked my ribs. Didn't mention how it happened. He said take as much time as I need."

"Good. You handled your neighbah well."

"Thanks! She lives a few houses away with her mom."

"Oh? Has she seen your fireplace?"

His son grinned. "Ha, no," he chuckled and winced. "Met her today."

"What's her name? Ambah?"

"Ashley. Ashley Brinkley, like Christie."

"Hmm… sounds familiar."

Dick looked through his phone messages and found the link to the story Harlan sent him.

"Your model neighbah is also a reportah for the *Lowell Sun*."

"You're shitting me."

"Nope."

He clicked on the link and showed it to Dan.

Chelmsford Man Arrested...
By Ashley Brinkley |abrinkley@lowellsun.com|
PUBLISHED: February 29, 2020, at 6:50 p.m.

Dan was furious. Dick surmised, "She witnessed the arrest and got a story out quickly. That's why Harlan knew details early and rushed to the police station." *Saved your butt.*

"I'm screwed. She took my picture... I'm such a fool."

"Don't be so hard on yourself." *Geez, he's so vulnerable.*

"I can't trust anyone."

"When the time is right, we might be able to use Ashley, like Ambah, to put out our own alert." He thought, *I have her email and know where she lives.*

"Amber—not Ambah. You sound like Robin from Lowell." His angry son looked away.

"Don't mock her or anyone from Lowell—the people are gritty."

"You missed the point, Dad," his son frowned.

No, Dan. You miss Robin.

* * *

Ashley wrote her brief follow-up story and checked in with Detective Evans before submitting it. She fought the urge to mention how the cops screwed up. She didn't want to lose her sources there. Ashley asked about O'Rourke, Mulligan, and the Cape instead.

Evans said, "The woman was spotted at South Station, but not the Cape. Nor Mulligan—Nashua Police have a search warrant out on him." *That's wicked interesting.*

She told her editor she covered the arraignment in the new courthouse, verified with police that the missing woman left town on a bus, and confirmed that DeCosta remained in the hospital. She didn't mention that she visited the patient and had a photo. Ashley was working on a more extensive follow-up, including the Home Depot incident.

Her boss said, "Stay on it. Today's follow-up will be online in thirty minutes."

Ashley checked her Instagram and Reddit alerts. *Oh, crap. Too late!*

> Depot Dan is in critical condition after a weekend bout with the police. Missing woman Greyhound bound, safe and sound, but still not found.

Sourced at 9:00 a.m. DeCosta's case did not come up until forty minutes later. Ashley had no idea where this came from. Her boss and the police could not pin this on her or others at the arraignment. *Someone else is controlling the narrative now.*

* * *

Chief of Police Paul Patterson wasn't surprised by DeCosta's continuance. But pissed that King had let the heavily-media attended arraignment know about the 911 transcript and the hospital. Patterson called Evans and Morehouse into his office.

"Evans, find the woman. Get her domestic violence complaint. We know she had wounds. DeCosta must have lied. The lab reports support that."

"I'm on it, Chief."

"Morehouse, call Bouchard, the EMT. Get him to file a complaint about the hostage situation. His wife's nine-one-one call supports that."

"Exactly, Chief," Morehouse said, cracking his knuckles.

"The EMT *was* trespassing," Evans said. "DeCosta's nine-one-one call supports that."

The chief said, "Yeah, but it's worth a shot, along with his wife's collaboration."

Morehouse ended his call with the EMT and updated Evans: "Bouchard said he and his wife felt bad for everyone. They're more interested in getting the Subaru back than filing complaints, especially with DeCosta in the hospital."

Evans called Rebecca Bouchard. He understood how remorseful the pregnant, stressed-out woman felt about everyone impacted by her missing person complaint. He began in a sympathetic tone. "Hi, Rebecca… How are you doing today?"

"Doing okay. But uh… I have good news and bad news. Not sure where to begin."

We all need good news. Start there, take your time."

"I just spoke with Robin! She's fine. Her phone died Saturday morning. Anyway, she said nothing happened to her at Dan's house."

"Fantastic! Where is she?"

"That's the bad news. She had to get away from Sean Cassidy. She doesn't want anyone to know where she is—not even Dan. She's ashamed about everything that happened to him."

"Please have her call me. We need a statement from her."

"She doesn't trust the police. Sean's uncle is a Lowell cop, and she knows they're looking for her."

"Understandable, but you know… *she can trust me.* We need an explanation about her blood in the car and house.”

“She cut her finger on a utility knife opening a moving box in the cah. She kept the knife in her glove box to protect herself when she left Sean’s place.”

“Plausible…” *Matches Patel’s statement.* “But there’s also matching blood in the house and clothing. Give me her number. Tell her she’ll hear from me.” *We already have a warrant—we can get her number off your call list.*

“I can’t. But I’ll pass it on. Doubt she’ll take your call.”

“My email address is on the card I gave you. Have her mail her explanation.”

“I’ll let her know.”

“Thanks. And uh. Do you have Triple A?”

“We do. Why?”

“Call them. Have them tow your Subaru. They’ll even put the new battery in for you at your house. I’ll inform the guys at the impound lot.”

“Thank you, Detective. Much appreciated.”

Chapter 21

Joanna sat in the chilly, air-conditioned examining room and tried to steady her hand. The tremors were getting worse. Her primary care physician, Dr. Sarandakos, asked, "Are you still nauseous and getting headaches?"

"Yes, and the shakes. It all started when my tennis team went to the beach. I'm the only one who went swimming. Friggin' red tide and blue-green algae."

Sarandakos nodded. "Lots of neurotoxins are in that water. Other patients have had eye-ear infections and respiratory illnesses. You lost weight and are dehydrated. That might explain the headaches. You also have a history of hypertension. Your blood pressure is higher than usual."

"I play tennis, and I always drink watah. Maybe I'm not used to the heat."

"Maybe. I'm more concerned about your white blood cells and high blood pressure."

"I checked my symptoms online. Uhm, they list leukemia—"

"Your spleen and liver are fine. The tremors and headaches are another concern. I've ordered more tests. I don't want to scare you. It could be Graves' or Parkinson's. I'm referring you to Doctor Silas, a hematologist. You may also need to see a neurologist. Okay?"

"Uh-huh. Do I need to fast?" *Cancer, Parkinson's, not okay. What the heck is Graves'?*

"No fasting. I'll send prescriptions for your nausea and blood pressure to the pharmacy. Stay hydrated. Double your water intake and avoid alcohol."

"Thank you, Doctor." *Avoid alcohol, easy for you to say.*

Joanna texted Dick she'd call him later. She got the meds at the pharmacy and took them when she got home. She then used her computer in their den to research her symptoms. Her older sister, Paula, called. She lived in Lowell, saw the news about Dan, and knew about Joanna's health issues.

Paula had previously dealt with breast cancer and cared for their parents before they died from cancer and heart failure.

"Hi, Paula." She put her on speaker and focused on her computer monitor.

"Jo, how'd it go with your doctor?"

She filled her in and discussed her symptoms for Graves' and Parkinson's disease. Paula had told her about 23andME, an ancestor-based website—where she and her children submitted their DNA—and received genetic health risk and carrier reports. Paula had gifted a 23andME kit to Joanna; she'd already submitted her saliva in the DNA test vile two weeks ago.

"Be good if you had your DNA health risk profile now."

"Yes. Be another week or two before I get my report."

"I'll get an email notice of a family match. I don't recall seeing anything about Graves' or Parkinson's in my reports, but Aunt Theresa had thyroid cancer."

"Ugh," Joanna said, ending the call and continuing her online research.

* * *

His son was doing breathing exercises on the spirometer while Dick priced Sheetrock and roofing at big box stores. His phone rang. The insurance adjuster scheduled 9:00 a.m. for tomorrow morning. *Perfect.* He'll be going to Boston tomorrow night for the conference.

"That was fast." Dan gave a thumbs-up about the insurance claim.

A female police officer walked in. "How are *you*?" Officer Hall asked, handing Dan an envelope containing his personal belongings.

"Thanks. I needed my wallet. The hospital needs my insurance card."

Hall nodded and looked at Dick, who extended his hand to her. "I'm his father. Does this mean he's free to go, and the charges are dropped?"

"He's on his own recognizance. I don't know about the charges. The woman's sister called and told us she is safe."

"Yay!" Dan exclaimed, perking up. "Where is she now?"

"Her sister said she's hiding from her ex and doesn't want anyone to know where she's staying. I'm sorry, that's all I know. You take care." Officer Hall left quietly.

Dan called Robin. "Figures, her number is no longer in service."

A nurse took Dan's insurance info, and twenty minutes later, an orthopedic surgeon entered the room. He said the X-rays confirmed a torn rotator cuff. He explained Dan could have arthroscopic surgery tomorrow morning. He'd then be in a sling for a week or more, and it would be several additional weeks before he could drive a car. He'd also need physical therapy.

"What do you think, Dad? You've had the same surgery."

It's painful, son. "You can't drive or lift weights for a month with cracked ribs. And post-surgery, you'll be recovering here instead of at home. Might as well get it over with now."

"Yeah. I agree." He signed the paperwork to authorize shoulder surgery.

* * *

Evans requested Rebecca's call list to obtain Robin O'Rourke's new phone number. He still needed her signed explanation. The database would not be updated with today's calls until overnight. Chief Patterson called a meeting for everyone.

The chief informed them that the FBI and local police arrested Edward Mulligan in Nashua, along with Juan Sanchez, who worked for Seth Small, an electrical contractor. Sanchez signed for DeCosta's will call order at the contractor's desk at Home Depot's Nashua store. There were also warrants on Hector Hernandez of Chelmsford and Sean Cassidy of Lowell; both were identified on the store's security camera picking up the items for Small Electric.

"Wow, small world," Evans said. *DeCosta really was a victim.*

Evans returned to his desk, opened the email from South Station, and read the video summary. The red-haired woman, carrying two suitcases and a backpack, boarded an Amtrack sleeper train. It departed Boston on Saturday at 10:53 a.m. and arrived in Orlando, Florida, on Sunday at 12:44 p.m. It dispelled Evans's theory of the woman returning to the house.

* * *

At 4:40 p.m., Dan's food tray arrived. Dick headed to the cafeteria. He hadn't heard from Jo and didn't want Dan to overhear their conversation. He preferred FaceTime, but it wasn't conducive while walking down hospital corridors.

"Jo. How'd it go?"

"Been busy. Booked blood tests online. Scheduled an appointment my PCP referred me to and researched everything the doctors will test me for."

"What doctors?"

"Hematologist. And later a neurologist."

"What did your PCP say?"

"Said they'd check my thyroid—it could be leukemia, Parkinson's, or Graves'. I'm a freakin' mess."

"Take a deep breath. The specialist will pinpoint it early and get you the proper treatment. You'll get through this."

"Yeah, but I'll be a wreck until I know what's wrong with me. I can't sleep and am losing my appetite."

I'll be a wreck, too, Jo. "Look at the bright side, Jo. You'll qualify for medical marijuana. Ha! That'll take care of your appetite and sleeping."

"Sure. It's not the eighties, Dick."

I know, Babe. I'm trying. "Try to get some rest. I'll call you tomorrow. Love ya."

"Love you too."

Dick finished a turkey sandwich, sipped coffee, and called his nephew, Eric. He had roofing experience and had done handyman work for Dick on his income properties. Eric was five years older than Dan, a hard worker, but wasn't always reliable. The good-looking guy could charm his mom and his aunt Joanna into anything. Many of his handyman jobs were referrals from women—many were single moms.

Dick explained the repairs the house by the lake needed. Eric said, "Heard Danny took a beating from the cops. How's he doing?"

"Better. But it's still hurting. Cracked ribs, rotator cuff surgery tomorrow. I want to get this done before he gets home. He'd appreciate—"

"Don't know about that. He never replies to my texts. But anything for you, Uncle Dick."

Eric agreed to put vents in the roof's overhang, replace the edge shingles, and install ice shields. But he wouldn't do the Sheetrock; he hated it.

"Crazy winter, I got a lot of calls for leaky roofs," Eric said. "I'll be by Wednesday to give you an estimate. I'll get the materials on Saturday."

Not good enough. Snow is forecast for Wednesday night. "I'm only in town this week. I don't need an estimate. I'll have the materials there tomorrow. I'll pay you cash to get this done before the next storm hits. Okay?"

"Okay, Uncle Dick. You've owned several homes; you know what it takes."

He returned to Dan's room. A young nurse's aide finished shaving his shoulder area to prep him for tomorrow's surgery. They turned to the TV when a news anchor announced, "The deadly novel coronavirus that spread from China to Italy—where thousands have succumbed and flooded their hospitals—has moved rapidly across the globe. Multiple US cases confirmed in Washington, California, New York, and now Boston, Massachusetts."

"Dad, this is scary. Cable news showed the caskets of people dying in Italy. And now breakouts in the States."

"I haven't been following it. But I will." *Been busy lately.*

He used his laptop to complete a Home Depot order for shingles, ice shield, flashing, soffit vents, Sheetrock, and paint. He made a will call order for pickup on Tuesday, March 3.

"Got my roofing order for tomorrow. I'll see you before I go to

Bawstin," said Dick.

"What's the rush? We don't know what the insurance company will pay," replied Dan.

I'm trying, son. Before his conference, he hoped to do everything he could—work on Dan's issues and then get back to Jo. He rattled off his plan.

"Thousand-dollar deductible. Don't matter. I need the roof fixed before Wednesday night's storm. I lined Eric up. I'll deal with the Sheetrock and mold, too."

"Screw Eric! I don't want him near my house."

Technically, it's mine too. "Come on. You know, he went to trade school because he couldn't afford college. Cut him some slack; he works hard."

"Right. He's always got a hard-on for my girls! Good thing he never saw Robin."

"He's like a big brothah to you. When he was dating that single mom, Cheryl, he set you up with her gorgeous sister, Shannon, at that concert."

"Don't go there, Dad." Dan's eyes turned to tonight's episode of *Jeopardy*.

"I know you dumped Shannon ovah trust issues. But guys were bound to hit on her. Stop holding grudges, especially with family. Whatevah Eric did... let it go."

"Never! Can't trust her or Eric. He shagged her!"

"Seriously? Hope you didn't let ya jealous streak run its imagination."

"Dumbass, Eric told me! We were having beers at his apartment, watching the Bruins. He kept pushing his bong at me, saying it was superior pot."

Dan adjusted his oxygen tube and continued, "The stoner mentioned Shannon stopped by to cop weed for a friend's bachelorette party. Then he bragged, 'When Shannon gets high—she's even wilder in the sack than Cheryl.'"

"Woah...What'd you say to him?"

"I headed for his door and said, 'Wish you hadn't done that—I *was* going to marry her.'"

"He was stoned—probably goofing with you. Did Shannon deny it?"

Dan shook his head. "I couldn't eat or sleep. It killed me, but I had to ghost her! A week later, she showed up at my condo in tears. I came right out with it. 'Eric said he gave you some weed, and you gave him everything else in exchange.' She cried, said she was sorry, that she loved me. Claimed Eric got her really high, one thing led to another—and it happened before we were engaged. Another lie."

The expression on his son's face revealed that he regretted venting this to his dad.

"Wow! Tough one." Dick touched his son's arm. *I remember you lost weight.*

"Shannon was bawling and begged me to sit down and talk it out. It tore me up—but I knew I'd never forgive her—never trust her. I ripped up our house sales contract. She screamed hysterically. I opened the door and told her to leave. I shouted over her balling, 'I never want to see you again—and if you don't leave me alone—I'll tell your sister, Cheryl!'"

"Whew!" Dick watched a *Jeopardy* contestant choose 'Women and Science for $500.'

"Come on, Dad. She fucked *my* cousin—*her sister's* boyfriend! Would you trust her after that? … And marry her?"

"Probably not." *But love's blind. I've dealt with worse and hope you never find out why.*

Chapter 22

Early Tuesday morning, Dick put his coffee on Dan's kitchen counter and listened to Lee Grisham's updates on the arrests of the credit card scammers. Grisham added, "The O'Rourke woman was unharmed. She took an overnight Amtrack to Orlando, Florida."

This will please Dan and Jo. But they can't know I got Grisham involved. Yesterday, he told Harlan never to mention anything about the FBI to Christina and Jo. He called King and relayed the arrest lists, including Sean Cassidy.

Harlan said, "Cops now know Robin never returned to Dan's house. They're in a weak position. I'll update my letter to Chief Patterson. He never returns my calls. I'll try Evans. He's been cooperative throughout this investigation."

Dick added, "Mention the cops also tore Dan's rotator cuff. He's in surgery as we speak."

Dick swept up the broken glass and debris, then washed the blood off the floors and counters. Last night, he gathered the yellow police tape outside. The adjuster arrived on time, took photos, and assessed the damage in the mudroom and roof. He'd file his claim report and email it to Dick shortly. It would come with a bill of materials he'd use as a checklist against his Home Depot order. Dick lined Eric up to help him unload his truck at the house later today.

He called the hospital. The doctor said his son's surgery went well. He'd be in his room before lunch but groggy from anesthesia and pain meds for several hours. He called Jo, updated her on Dan, and asked about her progress.

"My hematologist appointment is in the Cape Coral Cancer Center next Monday."

I hate cancer! "Okay, I'm working on house repairs. I'll see Dan later and then go to Bawstin."

Jo was pleased when he said Eric would fix the roof work. He didn't mention Dan's problem with Eric and Shannon—hoped it never came up—it would break her heart. He told her the cops arrested the credit card scammers—and that it was part of a larger ring in the Northeast.

"Thank God they did something good for Dan. Give him a hug for me."

"I sure will, babe. Love ya. Bye."

* * *

Evans reviewed Rebecca Bouchard's cell phone records. Yesterday, she called her mother in Reno after a ten-minute incoming call from Roger Gibbs near a cell tower in Orlando. He guessed the girl used Gibbs's phone to call her sister.

Evans used his cell phone instead of his desk phone, which would appear on caller ID as Chelmsford Police. A man answered.

"RG Tile. Gibbs here."

"Hi, yes, I'm trying to reach Robin—"

"Sorry, bud. No Robin or Bee Gees here." He hung up.

Evans called back, "This is Detective Evans. I'm trying to get a message to Robin…."

"I'm Roger Gibbs. Robin Gibbs is dead. And so are you if you prank me again."

Roger that. Evans knew Gibbs had blocked his phone. He called from his desk and left a voice message requesting that Robin O'Rourke call or send an email stating what transpired on February 29 at DeCosta's home. *Just following orders, Mister Gibbs.*

* * *

Kayla took the outside call at Home Depot's service desk. She confirmed that Mr. DeCosta's will-call order was ready. He told her he was on his way there, so she called her cousin, Ashley.

"Guess who's coming in to pick up an order for the house two doors down from you?"

"Not Dan, he's in the hospital."

"Nope. Dick DeCosta. Sounds a lot older. Do you know him?"

"Dan's father—met him at the hospital."

"Cool. I'll let Ryan, the store manager, know. Everyone feels bad about what happened to Dan. The Nashua cops arrested Ed Mulligan—he'd taken Dan's info when he signed up for a drawing—before he applied for the credit card. Robin had nothing to do with the breach."

"Great," Ashley said, "Chelmsford Police said Robin took a train to Orlando, Florida."

"So glad she's safe."

* * *

Dick grabbed his camo fatigue jacket from the guest closet. He didn't want to mess up his black leather jacket handling Sheetrock at Home Depot. His company's name, Sold on Solar, and logo were embroidered on the camo's breast pocket. He'd ordered field jackets and polo shirts with company logos for the veterans he recruited and trained.

He showed his ID to Kayla, who worked behind Home Depot's service desk, for his 10 percent military discount. The store manager and the assistant manager apologized for what had happened to his son. They already credited Dan's card. Kayla snapped pictures of the managers presenting Dick with a $100 gift card for Dan and applied it to his order.

Ryan, the store manager—a military veteran—was delighted when he discovered Dick's solar company had hired the vets for the Boots on the Roof training. The managers helped him load the materials into his pickup and asked when he'd complete the work.

Dick explained, "Can't get to it until Saturday. I'll be in Bawstin for a Green Conference."

They wished Dick's son a speedy recovery.

Dick texted Eric to meet him at his house. He figured the Depot discounts and labor costs he'd save with Eric would cover the insurance deductible and then some. He drove up Buckingham Street. Ashley, the *Lowell Sun* reporter, was standing by her mailbox. She gave him a big wave and smiled. He returned the gesture.

* * *

Eric Rondeau drove his banged-up Ford F150 down Buckingham Street and followed his uncle's loaded Toyota pickup. An interesting-looking brunette standing near the road waved to his uncle, caught Eric's eye, and smiled at him. He wondered if she was married. He pulled into the driveway behind Dick. His tall favorite uncle greeted him with a manly hug.

"How ya doing, dude?... And how are your mother and your sisters doing?"

"Good, good. We're all good," Eric replied.

They hauled everything off Dick's truck and stored it inside the mudroom.

"Let's look at the roof." His uncle led him out onto the deck, where they discussed the addition's poor quality.

"I agree, Uncle Dick. They should have installed soffit vents and ice shield."

The doorbell rang. Uncle Dick opened the mudroom's outside door.

"Hi, thought you might like these." He heard a high-pitched voice.

"Oh… Thank you! Come in." Dick stepped aside to let in the woman Eric spotted a few doors down. Attractive face, long nose, and glasses. *Hello there!*

"Hi, I'm Ashley," she told Eric. "My mom made brownies." She handed the Tupperware container to Uncle Dick. They both grabbed one. *Yum.*

"Thanks," Eric said. "I love me some freshly baked brownies. Mighty sweet of you."

"This is my nephew, Eric."

He looked her over. *Sweet and very nice… Ash.*

"Nice to meet you, Eric." They shook hands—he felt like she hung on longer.

"Nice to meet you, Ash—lee," Eric said as she flipped her brown hair behind one ear.

"Are you a contractor?" she asked. Her curious eyes peered through her fancy glasses.

"Yep. I'll be fixing the roof tomorrow," he said, looking at his uncle. "You're staying in Boston tonight, right? I'll need a key to get in."

Dick nodded and handed him the key.

"But I'm not touching this inside damage," he said, scanning the water-stained walls, torn Sheetrock, and insulation drying out with a fan.

"I'll deal with it Friday when I return from the conference."

"What conference is that?" she asked in a high-pitched nasal voice.

"Clean Energy and Sustainability," his uncle replied.

"Ah. You're in the solar business?" She pointed at the logo on his jacket.

"Was. I retired to Florida. Only consulting and helping others now."

"I see. So, how is Dan doing?"

"He had shoulder surgery this morning. Going to see him after I clean up and change."

The sympathetic girl nodded, "Tell him I wish him a speedy recovery."

"I will, and I'll bring him the brownies. Thanks for being so thoughtful."

Ashley smiled at Eric. "You're *welcome*. Bye, guys."

Eric held the door open for her. He watched her stride down the walkway in her brown high boots as her blue-jeaned hips swayed. *Bye, Ash.*

His uncle handed him cash. "Here's half. I'll give you the rest Friday."

"Thanks!" His uncle overpaid. And always offered incentives for a perfect job. He'd never let Dick or his aunt Joanna down.

Eric drove down the street, hoping to catch up with Ashley. He spotted her looking at her phone by her driveway. He beeped, and they waved at each other.

* * *

Ashley read her cousin Kayla's text, which included a picture of Mr. De-Costa with the store's managers attached. Kayla said they gave him a veteran's discount plus a gift certificate for his son. Ashley called Kayla, explained she'd been to DeCosta's house, and told her to run a suggestion by her store manager.

A horn beeped, and Ashley waved at the handsome, rugged-looking guy with the mullet and gray hoodie. Eric had strong, rough hands—like her deceased father had—from working in construction all his life. She totally respected that. Aside from asking her mother if she needed any roofing work, she wondered how she might get to know this man better.

Her cousin thought her suggestion was great and would get back to her. *I might have two follow-up stories now, and maybe I'll also see Eric the Great.*

Chapter 23

Dan felt the excruciating, unbearable pain penetrating across his left shoulder and chest. The tight bandages and sling made lifting himself with his right bandaged hand impossible. He pushed a button on the bed's right-side rail for pain meds. But it was impossible to reach the call button on the other side. The morphine kicked in and eased the pain but not the agony.

He grumbled to an empty room. "Geezus, Dad. Why'd you talk me into surgery." *Not everyone has your freakin' high pain tolerance.*

He remembered Mom telling him, "Dad broke three bones in his foot a week before his scheduled shoulder surgery. He hobbled around in a foot cast and shoulder sling for weeks while working at the office and their record store." His workaholic father, who bulldogged through every obstacle, set the bar high. Too high!

His dad told him, "Dan, someday you'll find a passionate soulmate like I did with Mom. Life will get easier. You'll have a partner to take on the world and enjoy the fruits of your labor. And your best work will be your children."

Dan sighed. *I'll never bring kids into this world.* He felt like many millennials—they weren't sure they wanted to raise kids in today's crazy expensive world—and kill themselves trying. *Call me selfish.*

He loved his dad, but the older he got, the more he learned about his father's determination and successes. After seven years in the workforce, Dan realized how difficult life and relationships can be. He resented living in the shadow of his dad's accomplished life—the thought of measuring up was sometimes overwhelming.

The nurse said, "You've been out quite a while. How do you feel?"

"Horrible. Can you get me up more?"

She adjusted the bed, "There, try to reach the call button now."

He did. She switched the call light off and asked, "Feel like eating?"

"Feel like vomiting." She held a stainless-steel container near his mouth. He spit up.

He asked for his phone and earbuds. Sadly, there were no texts from family, coworkers, *or Robin*. He thought something terrible had happened to her and was relieved when he learned she was safe. *Why hasn't she gotten back to me?* He was confused, angry, and depressed.

But he listened to a voice message from his mom.

"Hi, Dan. Good luck with your surgery and recovery. Dad said the police arrested the guys who used your credit card. Call me when you feel up to it. Miss you, love you."

Thanks, Mom. Not up to talking with anyone.

He scanned his email. His inbox was full of GreenEx updates about the conference.

What the hell is this? An email from TMorrison. Tamara Morrison was the admin for Toni Thompson—the VP of human resources—copied along with his manager, Neil Crosby.

Subject: Notice of Termination

An attached letter, written with legalese, identified company violations in the employee handbook, complete with references.

Terminated for Unacceptable Public Conduct. Unbecoming and frowned upon with inappropriate, racist innuendos, disrespect for citizens and veterans, and lying to a superior regarding absence from work.

Un-fucking-believable! When will this freaking nightmare end? He reached for the spittle container, vomited, and howled from the painful dry heaves. *My life's become a giant shit sandwich, and every day, I take another stinking bite.*

Dan pushed the meds and call buttons.

* * *

Samantha signed off from the Zoom call with her Coinbase coworkers. She grabbed a banana off her kitchen counter and listened to her mother's voice message. It was an update on Dan's surgery and credit card scammer arrests.

She was concerned after researching her mom's symptoms for leukemia, Parkinson's, and Graves'. She'd call her after tweeting another update on Dan's latest setback and mock the cops for arresting the real culprits. Someone beat her to it. *Woah, a picture of Dad trending on social media?*

Depot Dad, a Gifted Vet.
By Ashley Brinkley |abrinkley@lowellsun.com|
PUBLISHED: March 3, 2020, at 3:05 p.m.
Army veteran Ryan Hannigan, Home Depot's Nashua, NH store manager, presented a $100 gift card to fellow veteran Richard DeCosta. He

accepted the gift on behalf of his son, Daniel DeCosta—currently recuperating at Lowell General Hospital from injuries sustained after a dubious arrest at his North Chelmsford home. The gift was reparation for DeCosta's breached Home Depot credit. FBI agents, along with police in Nashua, NH, Lowell, and Chelmsford, MA, have arrested perpetrators involved with scamming big box stores and victimizing DeCosta and others.

Sam posted the link on her family's chat with the caption.

Way to go, Dad! 👏🙌

Sam FaceTimed her mother. "Hi, Sam! How are you, and Khori?"

"Good, and Khori's great… Did you see the family chat?"

"Yes! The *Lowell Sun* reporter did an excellent job." Her mom looked pleased.

"Yeah, and Dad always shakes things up."

"Don't remind me." Her mother's eyes looked away.

"So, how are you feeling?"

"The same. Shaky, especially after I play tennis."

"You should stop playing until you know what you're dealing with."

"With all the unknowns and Dan and Dad up north. I need to keep my mind off things."

"Yeah, I guess. When do you get your blood test results?"

"Hopefully tomorrow. You on a lunch break?"

"Doesn't matter. I told you I changed jobs. I work from home now."

"Good, the coronavirus is breaking out in California. Be careful."

"I will. What's the latest on the missing woman?"

"She took a bus to Orlando."

"Cool. You'll probably run into her someday."

"Orlando is inland, three hours north of Fort Myers. People go to Disney to vacation or find jobs there. We live on the Gulf Coast in Southwest Florida. Someday, you'll visit and see that it's our paradise, not Splash Mountain."

"It's a small world, Mom," she countered, remembering her parents took her and Dan to Disney when she was five. "We'll get to Fort Myers. I promise."

"Hope so, Sam. I really hope so." Her mom looked worried.

Sam saw Dan's reply to the family chat pop up.

"Gotta go. Keep me posted, Mom. Love ya."

"Love you too. Bye."

Sam reread her brother's disturbing reply to her previous post.

Of course. Dad's my friggin hero.

Chapter 24

Dick put his luggage and Ashley's Tupperware container in the truck. He knew from firsthand experience Dan would be wracked with pain the day of shoulder surgery and complicated further with cracked ribs. He hoped to cheer him up with brownies and the Home Depot news.

He parked in Lowell General's visitor's lot and read Ashley's *Lowell Sun* story. He recalled telling Dan they might use Ashley to put pressure on the cops. *I can't take any credit for that.* He wondered how she got the photo and details from Home Depot. He'd underestimated her. She was a good neighbor and a good reporter.

He waited for the hospital elevator and read another chat post. He was stung by Dan's terse reply to Sam. *Shit… you stepped in it again.*

Dick exchanged a nervous smile with the nurse applying an ice pack to Dan's shoulder and chest. He saw the familiar blue sling and white bandages securing his son's shoulder. Their eyes met. Dan frowned and turned away.

Dick placed the brownies on a side chair and asked, "How do you feel?"

"Like dying… like fuckin' dying."

"When was the last time you had a pain dose?"

"Don't know," Dan answered tersely as he repeatedly thumbed the meds button.

"Did they explain it's programmed to control the doses per hour?"

"How do you know?" he snapped at him.

"If it weren't, you'd OD. Back when I had shoulder surgery—I had to summon the nurse for the morphine needle." *And you get irritable when it wears off.*

"Right. You've seen it all… Desert Storm hero."

He touched his bandaged hand. "Dan, look at me. What else is going on?"

Dan turned. His eyes were welled up. "I got fired!"

"Why? How?"

"HR sent me a termination email for the Home Depot fiasco. Friggin' cancel crowd!"

"Oh, Christ!"

"I violated handbook rules and lied to my manager about my absence from work."

"That's ridiculous!" Dick shook his head. "I'm sorry, Dan. Send me that email."

"Why? So, you can stick your nose in this too!"

"Sawree. But you, uh—might have a wrongful termination case."

"My fuckin' corporate hero. You think you can fix everything—fuckin' sick of it." *Ouch!*

"You'll have hospital bills and no health insurance!"

"Won't matter. They can take my house and my car. Sue the cops. Won't fuckin'—."

"Your mother and I can help. Remember, she was in HR."

"You think so, huh? Get me my damn phone."

Dick held it for him. He found the email and forwarded it. *He can always get another job.*

"We both have experience with these incidents. You can always fight it."

"If you say so." Dan turned away again.

I know you're hurting, Dan. I'm trying. "Want a brownie?" He opened the Tupperware. Dan looked at them. "I need a drink first."

Dick held a water cup with a straw up to Dan's mouth. He sipped, then devoured a brownie. "This is good. Did you get these from Mrs. King?"

"Ashley brought them to the house. She's thoughtful and resourceful. We under—"

"I don't care about her. Stop meddling in my life!" Dan turned away again.

"I didn't. I'm not—"

"You always do. *You* talked me into buying the big house that *you* found."

"You sold your condo. You needed to live somewhere."

"I could've rented or bought another condo. And *you* put solar on the roof. I wouldn't be in this friggin' bed—this mess if—"

"You got a great buy—and have twice as much equity now. And you're one of the most eligible bachelors in town."

"Right, but you don't meddle. You just gaslight me." A tear rolled down Dan's face. "And expect me to do what you want for me—not what I want for me."

Bam! Another uppercut to my solar plexus. "Not true, I—"

"It's so hard," he sobbed, his nose running. "You don't know how hard it is being your son!"

An ice pick through my heart. "Only when I screw up. I'm sorry… Truly sorry," Dick said. He handed his son a tissue. "I never want to do anything except." *What I think is best for you.* "Except help you." *That's what dads do.*

But his son had already looked away and tuned him out. Dick sat back in the chair, exhausted, frustrated, and disappointed. His heart ached for Dan; he'd let him down again.

With the TV off and the room deathly silent, he opened his phone and read Dan's termination email. *Hmmm. Toni Thompson, HR? Sounds familiar.*

He googled GreenEx. He located the CEO and the staff's pictures and bios. The CEO was a retired Air Force major. VP, Toni Thompson, an African American woman. No wonder they terminated Dan after all the negative social media hype about race and veterans. *Damn shame.*

His phone rang. He answered, "Harlan, what's up?"

"I haven't heard from the chief. I spoke with Evans. He agreed the charges were probably a mistake, but it's out of his hands."

"Send the letter to the chief anyway."

"I will tonight. How's Dan?"

"He's in a lot of discomfort—struggling with morphine." *Life in general, and me.*

"Poor guy. He must be happy about Home Depot clearing his credit. I saw the *Sun* story. You did an excellent job getting the reporter to flip the narrative on Dan."

"Honestly—I had nothing to do with the *Sun*."

Dan turned to face him.

"Or Home Depot. They surprised me with the gift card," admitted Dick.

"Either way, great photo op with your Army fatigue jacket."

"I wore my field jacket to avoid ruining my leather one. I think the reporter, Ashley, Dan's neighbor, planned all this. Even stopped in here to visit him yesterday."

"Wow! Dan has a way of attracting women."

"Yup, he's a chick magnet. Unfortunately, he doesn't trust them." *Or me.*

"Tell him I got fired!" His son blurted. Dick held up a finger to hold Dan off.

"Hey Harlan, does the name, Toni Thompson, ring a bell?"

"Christina knows her well. She's a regular donor to Second Chance. Why?"

"I'll explain later. I'm heading to Bawstin shortly. I'll be at the Marriott Long Wharf for the next two nights and at the Clean Energy Conference during the day. Keep me posted."

"Why didn't you tell him I got fired?" Dan asked.

"I didn't think you'd want anyone to know, and you wanted me to stay out of things."

"Don't we need a lawyer to fight GreenEx?"

"Sure. A corporate lawyer. Harlan's a criminal lawyer."

"Screw GreenEx. I don't want to work for them anymore."

"Don't blame you—but there are medical bills."

Dick zipped his leather jacket. "No matter how bad things are—nevah, give up." *Besides, no one gets away with screwing my family. No one!*

Dick grabbed the brownies.

"Leave those. They're delicious." his son said.

He put them back on the nightstand. "But no more sugar now. You need to rest."

Dan nodded. Dick touched his son's wrist. "You'll feel much better to-morrow." *Trust me.* He pressed Dan's pain meds button.

"And even better every day after that," *I promise.* Dick said, "Good night."

Dan closed his eyes and drifted off. While he slept, Dick snapped Dan's picture and texted it to Harlan with a message:

For your letter to the Chief.

Later, he'd send the picture to someone he needed to thank. Now, he had to drive to Boston and deal with black ice and white-knuckle rush-hour traffic. He had to devise a plan to deal with Dan's latest problem. Then, he had to call Jo about her blood tests and Dan's termination without upsetting her more. *God help us.*

* * *

Joanna had the TV softly playing on the music channel. She filled her stain-less-steel shaker with vodka and other spirits, shook it like a pro, and poured it into her chilled martini glass. She took a big sip off the top and carried it to the living room. She raised the TV's volume and sang along with Lee Ann Womack's chorus, "I Hope You Dance."

She'd told Dick that as long as she could stand, she'd want to dance. She hoped her children did the same and embraced life to the fullest. She even said she wanted Womack's song played at her funeral. Dick said, "I'd rather play it while you're alive." He often danced with her while he sang David Bowie's disco hit "Let's Dance."

Dick had left for Boston three days ago, but it felt like a week, as so much had happened to Dan. She hated waiting for Dick's updates and re-sented him for leaving her behind. Getting a FaceTime call from Sam in-stead of her WhatsApp posts was nice, as the posts often led to tension in the family. Dan's harsh response directed at his father worried her. She knew him better than anyone and wondered what else had happened to her reclusive son, who had been prone to anxiety attacks since he broke up with his fiancée.

Joanna knew Dan would be hurting from the surgery. She was painfully familiar with the agony of post-surgery. Having had an emergency appendectomy and children delivered by cesarean sections—she had the bikini cut and abdominal scars to remind her. Dick would stroke her tummy and say, "Jo, you needn't worry about these life marks; they depict your motherhood and courage." *I do worry. I can't wear a bikini.* Dick, on the other hand, wore his scars like a badge of honor. The Desert Storm vet proudly told the stories behind his shoulder, ankle, hernia, and knee injuries sustained from active duty tours.

She flipped to the tennis channel, which mentioned possibly canceling tournaments due to the coronavirus. The virus cases were increasing in California, where her daughter lived, and in Massachusetts, where her son and husband were. Dick had promised to call hours ago. Finally, her phone rang. She took Dick's FaceTime call and shut the TV off.

"Hi, what took so long?"

Her husband's weary face came into focus. "Sorry, babe. Just got to my room. Brutal commute, with black ice and congestion. Glad we left the rat race early."

Me too. "How's Dan?"

He frowned and shook his head. "Hurting. He was angry and delirious from the morphine. You know how bad the first day of surgery is."

Sure do, but. "What else is going on?"

"He got terminated. Overreaction to the cancel crowd on social media."

"Oh, faw Gawd sakes!" *That's why he's pissed at you.* "They can't do that."

"You worked in HR. Check out the senior staff at GreenEx, and you'll understand why."

"I will later. Give me the details and tell me we will fight this."

"We'll fight it to at least cover his medical bills."

"Exactly!"

"What about you? Any test results back?"

"Not yet."

Dick informed her about Dan's employee violations and the GreenEx senior staff. He also explained his three-pronged strategy to fight it. She agreed it was worth a shot and would do her part to follow up with Christina and Sam. Dick encouraged her to console Dan on the phone tomorrow—to help him build his self-esteem.

"Don't FaceTime him. Text him first, so he'll call you back when he can sit up."

Thanks, Dick, you finally let me help. "Okay, Love ya 'bye," she said.

He blew her a kiss before the call ended.

Happy to get involved, especially while stuck in Florida, Joanna finished her drink and put the glass in the sink. She hoped Dick was right on all accounts and hoped to get the test results Sam and Dick had asked her about. She could sense they were as nervous about her health as she was, which increased her anxiety even more. Joanna shut the lights off in her big, empty condo and went to bed.

Chapter 25

Wednesday, March 4, Dick had breakfast in his Long Wharf Hotel room. He sent an email to attorney Jack Reiner—employed by a prominent Boston firm specializing in corporate law—whom he'd worked closely with when he was VP of engineering for a global service provider. He hoped Reiner would handle the case with the quick resolution Dick had outlined. GreenEx execs and their attorneys would soon realize they made a hasty, ill-advised decision to terminate Dan.

Last night, he emailed Ashley to thank her for her positive story and attached Dan's hospital photo. This morning, she replied and asked if he'd approve her follow-up plan for another story.

Ashley, I approve. But credit everyone else and don't mention my name.
You got it, Mr. DeCosta. Say hi to Dan.

Dick attached his Clean Energy Conference badge to his beige long-sleeved Oxford shirt with the embroidered Sold on Solar logo. He stopped by the vendors' booths. Most exhibitors were optimistic for an upswing in business this year. With a presidential election, there is hope for a new administration supporting clean energy, plus electric vehicles, charging stations, and new battery applications were on the rise.

Dick entered the conference room and greeted the session moderator and panel members. The cover slide illuminated a large projection screen.

2020 Panel Session
The Urgency to Combat Climate Change
Chair: Dick DeCosta
President of Sold on Solar, Renewable Energy Consultant
Author of *Greenhouse Gases and the Gaslighters*
Email: Dick@soldonsolar.com
Twitter: @soldonsolar

The moderator, Dr. Merrill Jablonski, thanked the Clean Tech Media Group, whose global podcasts captured the sessions on YouTube, then she introduced Dick. He thanked her and introduced his esteemed international panel to the packed room. Many familiar faces applauded, along with a sizable increase in millennial participants. The younger generations had much more at stake and a greater urgency to address climate change.

Dick began, "Raise your hand if you attended this conference in two thousand-ten?" About a third of the hands went up.

"At that time, 2010 was the warmest year ever recorded. We emphasized future projections of land and water temperatures, rising carbon, and increased sea levels. Well, please accept our apology—they were *wrong!*"

A hush came over the perplexed audience. A millennial shouted, "Okay, boomer!"

Many younger attendees and a few older ones chuckled. Neither Dick nor the panel smiled. He turned on his screen and read the first bullet on his opening slide.

—"Global warming changes dominated by greenhouse gases have rapidly accelerated since the UN's Intergovernmental Panel on Climate Change reported those findings ten years ago."

He continued:

—"The past decade was the *hottest ever* recorded globally—with five of the past six years eclipsing the records. Every decade since nineteen-eighty was warmer than the preceding one since temperature records began in the nineteenth century."

He showed the next screen and solemnly announced.

—"In the past twenty years, there were roughly 11,000 extreme weather disasters worldwide which caused nearly 475,000 deaths and $3 trillion in economic losses."
These unrelenting perils—extreme flooding, wildfires, tornadoes, hurricanes, heat waves, rising sea levels—can no longer be accepted *as merely natural disasters*."

"Dam straight!" a Gen-X man shouted. "They're man-made tragedies."
Dick nodded and surveyed the audience before he read his last bullet:

—"In 2018 alone, 8.7 million people died prematurely from illnesses related to air pollution from fossil fuels. One in five deaths worldwide!"

Dick's final slide listed issues, solutions, goals, and actions, including monitoring environmental, social, and governance (ESG) for large and small companies. The panel took turns addressing them, and the enthusiastic audience interactively participated. A reporter from a right-wing rag— that routinely mocked global warming—shouted out:

"If the Earth is warming, why have we had multiple nor'easters and cyclone bomb blizzards this winter?"

Dick replied, "Warmer air can hold more moisture than cold air."

He turned to Professor Roberta Sizemore—an atmospheric scientist on his panel, "Doctor Sizemore, would you care to elaborate on your findings?"

"Think of the atmosphere as a sponge," Sizemore said. "Air holds 4 percent more water for each additional degree of increasing temperature." She put up a slide.

—"Seven of the top ten largest snowstorms in Boston and New York happened since 1995. Twenty-two degrees Fahrenheit was the average Northeast winter temperature in the early 1900s. It's averaged twenty-six degrees in the last three decades, and recent winters have averaged thirty."

Sizemore added, "The oceans capture more than 90 percent of the heat from greenhouse gases. They're getting warmer and carrying more moisture across the country. Torrential downpours hit the tropical regions and southern states, with their high humidity producing record flooding. It flows to the north and east, which generates intensive snowstorms."

"It's all a hoax," retorted the gray bushy-haired reporter.

A woman shouted at him, "I pray your grandchildren hold an intervention for you!" Everyone roared, and the red-faced reporter used both hands to flip them off.

A millennial shouted, "See a therapist before you harm yourself or a loved one!"

The angry reporter stormed out of the room, and the crowd cheered.

Dick wrapped up the session with his closing remarks:

"We must prevail over politicizing climate change—it's too dangerous not to. We have 9 million species and 7.7 billion humans, but there is only one Earth and one life to live."

The audience applauded.

"So, please join us for a pledge." Dick placed his right hand over his heart. Many stood.

"We pledge to devote our lives and exhaust our efforts… to protect *all the vulnerable inhabitants* on our precious planet."

It culminated with a thunderous ovation. Handshakes and accolades were shared among the panel and attendees who lingered for follow-up questions. But Dick politely excused himself and grabbed his laptop—he had other pressing matters.

Attorney Jack Reiner replied to his email. He'd draft the letter and meet Dick at the Marriott for a cocktail at five, where he'd sign Jack's retainer. Dick texted Jo.

Full steam ahead with the legal fight.

* * *

Joanna and Marie Bates finished their practice match and said goodbye. Joanna sat on the tennis bench, drank water, and toweled off her perspiration. Her phone dinged. She felt faint when she tried to open it. Her focus was marred by blurriness. She finally deciphered Dick's text; the legal fight was on. Her hands trembled as she dictated her response.

"Great. I'll let Christina know. We already discussed GreenEx. Dan texted me. He'll call me after his lunch."

Joanna went home, took a pill for nausea, and showered. She then called her primary care physician and asked about her test results. The nurse said, "Doctor Sarandakos left you a message yesterday on your e-health chart. It also has the blood test results, which were negative."

Oh, I never checked it. "Meaning what?" Joanna asked.

"You do not have Graves' disease."

"Great!" *I think.* "Well, what else?"

"The doctor wants you to follow up with the hematologist and the neurologist as soon as possible."

"Thank you." *Guess I better book the neurologist, too.*

She canceled next Monday's tennis match for the hematologist appointment but wouldn't give up Wednesday's tennis. She scheduled the neurologist for the following Thursday. There was no Graves' disease, two appointments next week, and a lawyer for Dan. She felt better.

I'm having a good day. Don't ruin it, Dan. Call me.

Chapter 26

Dan felt better after having juice, toast, and warm coffee. The nurse's aide gave him his earbuds and iPhone, which displayed, Wednesday, March 4, 9:18 a.m. He read a text.

Dan, I'm playing tennis, please call me later. ♥ Mom

He dictated a reply, "Mom. I'll call after lunch." He hit send with his thumb. The *swoosh* in his earbud verified it was sent. He could communicate with everyone again. *Except Robin.*

Dan checked his email. He was still getting messages from GreenEx about the conference. *The fools fired me yesterday but never notified the team or shut off my email account.* He accessed the Sustainability Conference via the virtual attendance portal and located his father's session. It started thirty minutes earlier; he'd catch up through the recorded podcast. Dan paused the podcast when the doctor and the nurse entered his room.

"How are you feeling today?" the surgeon asked as the nurse put an icepack on Dan.

"Better than yesterday. But can't do much with this sling and cracked ribs."

"It will delay your post-surgery progress, so you'll be here a few more days. A physical therapist will show you routines to work on at home. For starters, squeeze this rubber ball."

Dan squeezed the ball the nurse attached to the end of his sling.

"Good," the doctor said. "You must ice the shoulder several times a day for the first week. Do you have someone to care for you at home and drive you to the PT appointments?"

No, I'm all alone in that house. "I'll check with my father."

"Your insurance covers the PT sessions."

"Great." *I don't have insurance at the moment.*

"Tomorrow, I'll check how the incisions are healing. Try to ease off the pain meds."

When the doctor left, Dan pushed the pain meds button. *Thanks for *reminding me.* Then he went back to the podcast. His dad's opening remarks and slides were sobering. But he thought the goals and ideas the panel discussed were exciting. The pledge to protect the environment, which Dan had already devoted his career to, gave him hope. *I'll find another job.*

Six years ago, his father gained notoriety for his controversial book, *Greenhouse Gases and the Gaslighters*, after he promoted it on Oprah and Bill Maher's HBO talk show. His dad also got trashed on Twitter by conservative journalists and received severe threats from right-wing extremists. *The threats are much worse now that the country is more divided.* However, Dan was proud of his dad's message and happy the audience embraced it. He recalled his dad's advice before his first technical job interview.

"Dan, presentation is everything." He meant your image and how one carried themselves with confidence. "It doesn't matter if you walk into a classy restaurant or a bar in a rough neighborhood, sit with engineers and intellects, or in a corporate board room—act like you belong. And remember, the smartest person in the room is the room in total."

"How so, Dad?"

"Don't be intimidated, Dan. Make direct eye contact with the interviewer. Do your homework. Know the company's strengths and needs. Show your curiosity and listening skills by acknowledging them. Ask people what they need and how you can help them first."

"You never know unless you ask," Dan said, repeating one of his father's adages.

Dad replied, "Exactly. People love to tell you what they know. It makes them feel good about themselves, and you for listening and complimenting them. From there, you can control the conversation. And never… bullshit. Stick to the facts."

"Dad, I never BS people. I don't know how to lie and sell."

"Dan, every day, you're selling you. How you look and conduct yourself is critical to making people believe in you."

"Easy for you, Dad. You're the ultimate salesperson."

"I…*you* can sell anything you're passionate about and well-versed in. Use and practice what you're advocating."

His dad's passion for the environment was on full display today. He felt he'd let him down after he gave him his pickup truck and said, "Dan, along with the truck Sold on Solar, is yours if you want it."

"No thanks, Dad. I don't want to learn more about it or run a business like you."

He felt terrible about pouring his heart out to Dad yesterday. In that weak moment, he'd said many spiteful things he now regretted. But he meant it. *I'll never command a room like him. And I don't want to.* "I want to be me, Dad. Not you!"

* * *

Dick finished eating lunch with his session panel. He checked Twitter; many tweets were positive—and as always—many were attacks on his presentation. He blocked a few bad guys and ignored the rest. Eric sent a text with pics of his progress on the roof. Harlan copied him on his letter to the chief of police to drop the charges. It included graphic photos and Dan's medical procedures. Harlan's follow-up text said he hadn't heard anything from the chief. Jo sent a text saying she does not have Graves' disease, and she scheduled a neurologist appointment. Dan hadn't called yet.

* * *

Joanna read a disturbing article in the daily *News-Press* about the Calusa Waterkeepers. The story mentioned how runoff from rainstorms produces higher bacteria readings on the beaches, which made her stomach churn and head pound. Her phone rang.

"Dan! I'm so glad you called… How ya feeling?"

"Hi, Mom. Not good. Lots of pain, but not as bad as yesterday."

My poor baby. "I can imagine. What did you eat for lunch?"

"Tomato soup, grilled cheese. Tough with one arm in a sling, the other hand bandaged."

"When did the doctor say you could go home?"

"In a few more days. I have to ice the shoulder and start physical therapy after my ribs heal.… I'll need help."

"You'll need health insurance for PT and hospital bills. And you have to deal with STD."

"I have cracked ribs, not herpes?"

Men… Their minds are always in the gutter. "STD … stands for short-term disability. Text me the link and login info for your employer's insurance. I'll submit the claim for you retroactively on Monday. That's another way to get a jump on GreenEx."

"Dad told you I got fired… don't tell Sam."

Oops. "I already spoke with Christina King. She knows the VP of HR."

"Thanks, Mom. Dad said we need a corporate lawyer, not a criminal one."

"Dad already has a corporate attorney from Bawstin dealing with it."

"That was fast. I thought the Clean Energy Conference consumed him."

"Nevah, underestimate your farthah." *Can't believe I said that.*

"Right... Dad's my hero."

He's writing checks for two law firms. Give him a break. "The cops arrested the credit card thieves…At least that's cleared up."

"Screw them. The bastards should pay for my medical bills. Let's sue—"

"Dan, we're paying for all your legal bills. Let us decide the priorities."

"Sorry. You're right. I'm friggin' angry. I didn't deserve *any* of this!"

"I know. When did you take your pain meds?"

"I pressed the button twice since we've been talking."

Geez, I'm not helping. "You have to take it easy with that stuff."

"Easy for you to say."

"Dan, we're just trying to help."

"Sorry, Mom. Uhm. How are *you* feeling? Dad said you had stomach problems and were getting blood tests."

"About the same. I got good news today, though, as one came back negative."

"Good… Well, uh… I better let you go."

"I ain't going anywhere." *Neither are you.* "So, tell me about Robin."

"Well. She's from Lowell, beautiful, and fun to be with. Down to earth, grounded. Not a phony like Shannon."

"Yeah, well. Shannon was gorgeous, and she knew it."

"I thought you adored her, Mom."

"I did. We were happy for you. But I thought her eyes were bigger than her heart."

"Did Dad say something about her?"

"No."

"Then what do you mean about big eyes?"

"She'd only ask me about our trips to Aruba or talk with Dad about the boat and our place at Lake Winnipesaukee. She was disappointed when Dad said we sold them."

"Hmm. She kept talking about booking Aruba for a destination wedding, but her parents couldn't afford it. I had payments due on the engagement ring, and she wanted to buy furniture for the house before we owned it."

"Exactly. Christina told me Shannon's now dating a lawyer from Westford who is going through a divorce."

"Oh, wow!"

Yep. You ditched the right one—too bad she kept the diamond. "So, when do I get to meet Robin? I can fly up there and help care for you."

"I don't. Uhm… Haven't heard from her since Saturday."

"I heard she went to Disney. She'll probably be back after her vacation."

"Maybe. But doubt it. Cops said she left to get away from her abusive ex."

"Sorry to hear that. Why don't you stay with us? Rehab down here."

"No way. And I gotta see a physical therapist. So, forget about it."

"I know one personally. Lovely girl. Just moved here from Bawstin. She'd be perfect—"

"Mom. Please! … Don't meddle."

I'm not, just saying. "I'll work on the GreenEx insurance. You take care. Love ya, bye."

Chapter 27

Rebecca pushed aside her little girl's red wavy hair, gazed at Brianna's beautiful freckled face and blue eyes, and kissed her forehead goodnight. She reminded her of Robin when she was three. She wondered when she'd see her sister again; she'd miss the arrival of her second child. Rebecca rubbed her aching lower back, sat in her recliner, and struggled to find a comfortable position to watch *Jeopardy*. Her phone rang, an unknown number; she ignored it. A text popped up with a message.

Becca, this is my new cell. Call me back. R.

Rebecca added it to her contacts and called, "Hey, when did you get the new phone?"

"This afternoon… so different from my old one, lots to learn."

"I know, right?"

"I saw Dan's videos. What a freakin' mess. He got arrested. Plus, social media attacks and his credit cahd… I sold him that. He must hate me!"

"A real shame, but we can't change the past. You settled in now?" asked Rebecca.

"Not yet. It's beautiful but hot and different. Did you call Ma—tell her I'm safe?"

"Yes. She's pissed. Auntie K and her haven't spoken to each other since Dad's funeral."

"I know. It's hard on all of us. But I had to look out for myself. And others—"

"Sean's sick. Brandon would've killed him if he came near you, me, and the baby."

"Exactly. Sean probably would've gone after Dan, too. Poor guy didn't need that."

"Right. We got the Outback towed here and a new battery installed."

"Great. Sorry again for all the confusion. If my phone hadn't died—"

"It's not your fault. And Brandon and I feel bad about the nine-one-one call we made."

"You were worried about me. Are the cops still bugging you?"

"Detective Evans wants you to call or email him. Needs a statement about what happened Saturday and the blood in the house. I told him don't—"

"No way. They'll track me down. I don't owe them shit."

"I know. They were just trying to protect Brandon. Now they want to cover their butts for botching the arrest. The poor guy is still in the hospital. Brandon and I are sick about it."

"So am I. Oo no…," her sister sobbed. "I read the story about Dan in the hospital. It's good the store fixed his credit and arrested the thieves, but—"

"Yes. We met the *Sun* reporter when they arrested Dan. She's nice. She called and asked how I was doing—and if you were safe in Orlando. I told her you applied for work at Disney."

"Good… but I feel terrible about what Dan's going through. He'll never forgive me for misleading him."

"Probably not. But when the time is right. You should call and apologize."

"I don't have his numbah. I lost all my contacts and photos on my dead phone," explained Robin.

"Didn't they retrieve it off the old SIM card when you got the new phone?"

"I lost my phone, probably on the train when I fell asleep."

"Wait… aren't all your contacts still on the cloud?"

"Didn't have cloud backup. Couldn't afford that plan."

"Shame." *Gotta cheer her up.* "So… how was Disney?" asked Rebecca.

"Amazing. Different from when you and I went with Ma and Dad. We had a one-day pass. Space Mountain was wicked cool!"

"Glad you had fun; it's freezing up here."

"Sorry… Send me Brianna's pictures to show Auntie K. She says hi."

"How's Aunt Kelly doing?"

"Great in her new salon. She bought me tops, shorts, and a new bikini."

"Nice! Stay out of trouble and wear sunscreen. Redheads burn easily," Rebecca teased.

"O-K. Big Sistah. Love ya. Bye."

* * *

Robin ended her call with Becca and put her phone on the dresser in the bedroom, which her aunt said was hers for as long as she needed a place to stay. *Paradise,* she thought, after sleeping in her car and Amy's couch to escape Sean. He'd ruined her physically, financially, and emotionally. *Lucky to be alive. I'm blessed my godmother took me in.*

The mirror in her private bathroom reflected her sunburnt face, neck, and pale white back. She touched the scripted tattoo, *"Still, I Rise,"* on her shoulder blade. Last summer's reminder of how low things had gotten after Miggy Morales, Sean's drug supplier, slipped a roofie in her beer. She awoke the next day half naked—knew she'd been raped—and her money was gone. Robin confronted Sean about it and flushed his drugs down the toilet. That's when he nearly killed her. However, Miggy was found beaten to death a week later, which gave her some solace, but she always wondered if Sean did it. *All in my rearview mirror now.*

Robin washed her hands and removed the Band-Aids on her fingers; the cuts had healed. If Amy hadn't taped all her moving boxes the night before, she wouldn't have sliced her fingers opening the one with her toiletries and sunglasses. No freakin' way she'd tell the cops about blood in her car, especially after they beat on Dan. And it is way too personal to explain her blood in the house. Her period had ended on Thursday, but she was spotting after their wild love-making on Friday. She'd conveniently masked the blood on the Brady shirt and the scatter rug in front of the fireplace by dabbing red wine on the spots.

Robin and Dan had partied from the moment she'd arrived with the wine from her coworkers, and they smoked pot together for the first time. All of it made it easier for her to enjoy her final evening with him and avoid explaining that Sean was stalking her and how going to Becca's house wasn't safe. She knew Dan wouldn't accept that, and he'd never understand how violent Sean could be.

She'd planned to call Dan on the train to Orlando, but her phone died. When Jay arrived, they drove off before she realized she'd left her charger in her car. Unfortunately, neither Jay nor anyone on the bus or train had a charger that fit her outdated thirty-pin phone port. Robin wished she could have a redo or go back, hug Dan, and nurse him back to health. But there was no going back. She figured she had a better chance of getting hit by lightning in Florida than ever hearing from Dan again.

Robin removed the price tags on the shorts and tops she found on sale; she needed tropical weather clothes. Her Aunt Kelly said, "Rachel, honey, you spent enough on your new phone. Consider this an early birthday gift."

"Thank you so much, Auntie K. You and Uncle Rawjah have been spoilin' me since you picked me up at the train station."

"I'm sorry, Rachel. But Roger and I were tired of watching you jump into our pool with those ragged cutoff jeans and faded T-shirts."

"I know, huh? I love this bikini. And I'm not sorry. Ha-ha. Not sorry at all."

After twenty-six years of everyone calling her Robin, she still hadn't gotten used to being called by her birth name. Born in the spring, red-breasted robins nested outside the bedroom she shared with her sister. Becca was only four when her father started calling her little sister Red Robin, which stuck.

Her father's sister, Aunt Kelly, never had children. Her godmother, Kelly, spoiled her ever since she was baptized—Rachel Robin O'Rourke—at St. Patrick's Church in Lowell. Every Christmas and on her birthdays, her aunt faithfully sent gifts or generous money cards addressed to Rachel. She'd call to thank her godmother personally. And Auntie K would always tell her, "Rachel, come visit us. We have plenty of room; stay as long as you like."

When Amy said Sean was back stalking her, she had no alternative but to get away for her safety and Rebecca's, and sadly Dan's, a wonderful guy she hoped she could have a future with. Robin had called her aunt from Home Depot's service desk as soon as she got word.

Auntie K explained, "It's cheaper to take a train to Orlando than fly. We'll pick you up at the station and drive you to our house in Cape Coral."

Kelly and Roger then surprised Robin with a detour to Disney World on Sunday. They left Orlando on Monday, and Uncle Roger let her use his phone to call Becca.

Robin slipped into her new black bikini. *Love it*. She then joined Auntie K and Roger by their screened-enclosed pool.

* * *

Sean Cassidy was released on his own recognizance and escorted out by his uncle, Sergeant Bill Cassidy. His uncle's attorney said, "Sean did not sign for the stolen goods or resell them—he was merely a laborer hired to load a van at Home Depot."

Sean sat in his mother's kitchen and read the *Lowell Sun* story about the missing woman and the suspect arrested at his North Chelmsford home. He also read the follow-up story on DeCosta recuperating in Lowell General Hospital. He figured Robin had been sleeping with him. *Gotta pay Depot Dan a visit; he'll know where Robin is*.

* * *

Joanna was happy Dick FaceTimed her from his hotel room. She talked about the doctors, Dan, Samantha, and Christina, while he gave her the abridged version of his meeting with Attorney Reiner, his Green Conference, and her nephew Eric's work at Dan's house.

Her husband continued, "Harlan said Chelmsford cops didn't return his calls or acknowledge his letter requesting they drop the charges."

Ridiculous. "How the hell can they get away with that crap?" she shouted.

"Why do dogs lick their balls?"

Because they can, she'd heard that one before. "This isn't funny, Dick… Dan wants to sue the cops for his medical bills."

"I know. He's also got a mortgage, car payments, and no job."

"What'd you tell him?" She saw the determination on Dick's face.

"I said one thing at a time. We need the charges dropped and expunged from his record. That's what we're paying Harlan to do."

Joanna had muted the TV but saw the banner across the bottom of the screen.

"Oh, my God!" she shouted. Joanna's hands were shaking.

"What? What's wrong?" Dick asked.

"California Emergency. Turn on cable TV."

California's governor declared a state of emergency after a medical screener contracted the coronavirus. Four more cases were identified in New York. The Health and Human Services director has ordered 500 million N95 respirators to respond to the novel virus. The CDC has lifted federal restrictions on coronavirus testing for every American.

"Gotta go, Dick. I'm gonna call Sam. Love ya, bye."

Chapter 28

Thursday morning, the nurse removed Dan's IV, gave him his pain meds orally, and put ice on his chest and shoulder. He did his spirometer breathing routine and squeezed the rubber ball attached to his sling with his left hand. A physical therapist reviewed an exercise list with diagrams required to rehab his shoulder at home. Dan hoped to be discharged tomorrow.

Cable news covered the California emergency and the New York governor's daily press conference. The deadly virus is now called COVID-19 because it originated in China in 2019. Dan worried about his sister, Sam, who lived in San Francisco with Khori, her Chinese partner.

Dan appreciated the emails from his GreenEx colleagues. Most said, "Hang in there. I wish you a speedy recovery." The IT manager, Dominic Silveira, a close friend he worked out with at the GreenEx gym, said, "We got your back, Dan." He wondered why HR hadn't instructed Silveira to terminate his email account. *Or had they?*

His auto insurance company sent a renewal invoice for his Prius. He checked his online banking account—thankfully, his car and mortgage payments went through. Dan worried about making future payments with no wages. Once his dad returned to Florida, he'd sell the truck to make mortgage and car payments until he found a job.

Dan ate the last brownie and sent a thank you email to Ashley for the sweets and the positive story she wrote about Dad and him. He figured everyone knew he was in the hospital now. *Why haven't I heard from Robin?* She'd essentially ghosted him, like he did to Shannon. Dan figured his odds of hearing from Robin were worse than winning the battles with GreenEx and the porcupines.

* * *

Thursday morning, Ashley submitted her coverage of last night's selectmen's meeting for the neighboring town of Tyngsboro. She reminded her editor she'd return to DeCosta's house for a follow-up story. Ashley had fun yesterday with Eric. Dan's rugged and handsome cousin wasn't as tall as him; she could look right into his blue eyes, which followed her around DeCosta's house. Ashely felt they were both looking forward to pushing their flirting to another level.

She pulled her hair into a ponytail, squeezed into a tight pair of jeans, and pulled on a gray, well-worn Hampton Beach sweatshirt; she didn't care if it got dirty. She imagined Eric's strong hands soiling it before his workday ended.

Ashley checked her social media news feeds. *Whoa, I didn't see this coming!* She scanned the surprise story with a familiar disturbing photo of bandaged Dan asleep in his hospital bed.

Depot Dan Down for the Count and Canceled.
Think you had a bad day? Dan DeCosta—victimized by a credit card scam and unjust social media attacks for a February 29th misconstrued incident at Home Depot—was only trying to buy a snow rake to clear his leaking snow-packed roof. But it snowballed into an avalanche of troubles all day for DeCosta. The environmental engineer is currently recovering from surgery and wounds inflicted by the police after he called 911 on an intruder in his home. To add insult to injury, DeCosta is now burdened with mounting medical and legal expenses after being terminated by his employer, GreenEx Corp, who reacted prematurely to the overzealous, misinformed social media vultures.

Ashley was concerned. *Dan's hospital picture points to me.* She emailed Mr. DeCosta, apologizing for the story and saying she never leaked this. She promised her planned follow-up story would be entirely different.

* * *

Khori carried the grocery bags into her partner's apartment and shouted, "Sam, more in my car!"

Sam followed Khori back to her Range Rover. She grabbed the paper products she felt lucky to have as the market's shelves were getting bare, and Sam took the jumbo-sized dog food bag. They carried them inside and made sure Bulova did not scoot out the door. Sam returned to her laptop, smiling and whistling Daniel Powter's pop song "You Had a Bad Day."

She's in a good mood, Khori thought, considering how upset she was last night after talking with her mother about COVID-19 and her brother's problems. Khori put the groceries away. She had thirty minutes before her interview with a candidate—previously scheduled at her office—but was now a Zoom call due to California's COVID lockdown.

Like many Coinbase engineers, Sam routinely worked at home on her laptop. She was usually focused, serious, and quiet. *So why is she smiling and humming tunes?*

Khori sidled up to Sam, "You hit the lottery and will leave me after the pandemic ends?"

"Ha. Never," she pecked Khori on the lips. "I'm just happy about my choices."

"Meaning you love me and French bulldogs."

"Uh-huh. And glad I chose software. I could have been in marketing— like my mom wanted. I minored in journalism."

"Why so happy today?" Khori asked.

"Cuz I can work at home in my sweats. If I were in marketing, I'd be all dressed up with nowhere to go and have to kiss up to the power-hungry, gutter-minded men who think they could get me in the sack."

"You're too moody to deal with men. You're better off in software. But you did an excellent job marketing yourself and doing interviews," Khori said, and then she kissed Sam's cheek.

"Thanks. My parents also think I'm a good writer. Read this," Sam said and clicked on the story. Khori saw Dan's photo. She read Sam's informative story about him getting canceled.

"That's terrible! He lost his job… how can you gloat over that?" Khori asked aghast.

"I'm not. This is why," Sam said, pulling up a text from her father.

Well done, Sam. Perfect to put pressure on GreenEx and the cops!

Sam grinned and showed her a text from her mother.

Love it, Sam. Stay safe. Hugs to you and Khori.

"Your parents put you up to this?" Khori nervously scratched her head.

"My dad has lawyers challenging my brother's company and the cops. He said, 'If social media can wrongfully condemn an innocent victim—it can also be used to turn the sentiment around for the underdog.'"

"I hope he's right," Khori said with uncertainty.

"We all do. My brother's going through hell—physically, financially, and mentally. He has bills and hasn't heard from the missing woman."

"Why would he want to?"

"My mom says he's holding out hope for her. They're both victims. She ran away from her abusive and stalking ex."

"Oh, Sam," Khori sighed. She hugged her tightly. They'd also been victimized. She by a narcissistic, perverted husband—she'd recently divorced—and Samantha from blatant sexual harassment by a superior at her previous job.

Khori, nine years older, felt like Sam's big sister at times. She'd recruited and mentored her for her first two jobs. Sam had to escape from a male project manager in a company where she excelled and enjoyed the work. Sam's instincts told her it wasn't worth reporting the harassment and risk tarnishing her reputation. She decided to take what she'd learned to another firm.

Sam had poured her heart out to Khori over lunch, "Get me something quick in the same field—cryptocurrency, blockchain technology."

Khori found Sam a better-paying job where she rarely worked in an office. Celebrating over dinner, they shared their own sordid stories and realized their vulnerability. Cautious at first, they discovered their empathy for each other had soon blossomed into a caring and then passionate relationship.

Chapter 29

The Green Conference was great for investing and recruiting talent. Dick attended the session—New Product Announcements and Emerging Technologies. A few startups piqued his interest. They improved lithium battery storage, utilized hydrogen cells, and developed white reflective paint to eliminate the need for air conditioning and dramatically reduce buildings' carbon footprint.

Dick accepted a lunch invite from Clayton Marshal, a former employee. Clay had come a long way. The Generation X African American dominated sales in his region and climbed to director. After seeing Clay's CEO pitch his company, he wanted to learn more about the startup.

"Hey, Dick. Great to see you."

They shook hands and got their sandwiches. Clay paid, and they headed for a private table.

"VP of business development for a burgeoning startup. Proud of you, Clay."

"Thanks, Dick. Coming from you, much appreciated."

"I'm not surprised," Dick said as they sat down. "You were a sponge and always stayed focused on the next five minutes."

"Always. But anyone who hangs around you gets brainwashed into thinking they can do anything."

I should have offered him my company, Dick thought. "Thanks. I caught your CEO Bakari Bashir's pitch today. Good stuff. Exciting product."

"Doctor Bashir is passionate about the product he's been working on since leaving MIT. He's headed this way. Do you want to meet him?"

"Sure."

Clay waved to the olive-skinned CEO wearing an open-collar button-down under a blue suit. Dr. Bashir excused himself from the MIT professor who'd attended Dick's session yesterday.

"Bakari, this is Dick DeCosta."

They shook hands and pulled up a chair. Clay slid a water bottle toward his boss, who said, "Thank you, Clayton."

"I liked what I heard today," Dick said. "So, how's the conference going so far?"

"Thank you—going well," Bakari said. "We're getting traction. Now, we need to secure the next rounds of capital."

"How are you doing with VC?" Dick knew minority-led startups often get aid grants, then first-round venture capital funding. Securing subsequent rounds was difficult.

"Getting there," Bakari said. "But not as fast as our initial investors would like." He looked at Dick, then back to Clay.

"I heard you stepped away from Sold on Solar," Clay said. "What's next for you?"

Dick smiled at Clay. *Set up by the sponge.* "Retirement. A little consulting these days."

"Clay tells me retirement is out of character for you," Bakari smiled. "Would you be interested in coming on board with us?"

"Oh? In what capacity?" Dick asked out of courtesy and curiosity.

"I need a COO to drive the operation and supply chain. And a CFO to join us in the VC rounds."

Dick knew VC investors had a bench of C-level managers. It gave them board seats, control, and insights into their investments. "I'm honored, Bakari. But I must pass. I promised my wife I'm committed to retirement and sunshine." *And writing books.*

"Sorry to hear—but I understand," Bakari replied. "Could you kindly recommend us to any VC who might want to kick the tires?"

"Yes. And invest. But I'd have more clout and reassurance if I were on your board of advisers." *Insight and control from afar with a minor time commitment.*

"Done," Bakari said, extending a hand to seal the deal. "Clayton, please follow up and arrange access for Dick. And send him our sales projections."

"Be happy to."

Bakari stepped away to give an interview with a young woman with press credentials.

Clay said, "Always impressed with how decisive you are, Dick."

Dick never made a move without research and at least two good reasons. He believed the product could help the environment, and he'd invest in a potential winner. Dick bid farewell to Clayton. He then looked at the pictures attached to Eric's latest text and called him.

"Eric. The place looks good. I'm impressed. And relieved. Thanks!"

"Yep. Thank Ash for that. It's moving along fast."

"You mean Ashley?" *He moves fast—he calls her Ash.*

"Yeah, Ash, ain't afraid to get dirty. She pitched in and wore gloves and a mask. Later, she brought sandwiches from the corner deli."

"Has it started snowing yet?"

"Lightly. Heavy wet stuff is on its way. Could be ten inches or more," reported Eric.

It's too messy for Dan's snow blower. It jams up every few feet. "I'll pay you the balance tomorrow. Can you plow the driveway? I'll pay for that, too."

"Can't. After the last three blizzards, my tranny broke. I can't put it in four-wheel drive."

"Will your plow fit on Dan's truck?"

"Sold it to the garage that towed my truck and patched it up. Hope the Ford makes it till spring… gotta get a new truck."

"Okay. Is Ash… is Ashley still there?"

"She's taking pictures. Want to talk to her?"

"No. I'll—"

"Ash, my uncle wants to talk to you."

"Hello, Mister DeCosta."

"Hi. Eric says it's moving quickly. Is he being a gentleman?" *Or moving fast on you?*

"Yes. And… yes. I think you'll be pleased. I am," Ashley replied.

"Great. Well, thank everyone for me, and remember to keep my name out of this."

"You got it. I heard Eric talking about the snow. Is Dan coming home tomorrow?"

"Hope so. I'll be going to the hospital tomorrow."

"Great. I hope to see you both tomorrow."

Dick waited for the conference shuttle bus to his Marriott Hotel and spotted the guy in the suit who was hovering near his meeting with Clay. The suit nodded at a man wearing sloppy fatigues and faux boots—he looked more militia than a veteran. The bearded, fatigue guy followed Dick onto the bus. Dick got off at a different hotel to be safe. Sloppy G.I. Joe did, too. Dick then entered the lobby, went through the hotel's restaurant, exited a side street door, and walked two blocks to the Mariott.

Dick then had the front desk move him to a different floor, and he ordered room service. Tired of the gloomy COVID-19 news, he turned the TV onto the music channel to calm his nerves. One of his favorites by Bob Seeger played "Against the Wind." The song made him think about how much older he was now, and yet he was still running from the anti-green lunatics. *Wish I didn't know now what I didn't know then.*

* * *

Ashley's phone rang. She took the call from Detective Evans and walked into the kitchen to be out of earshot of Eric and the others.

"Hey, Ashley," said Evans. "You leak the story about DeCosta getting fired?"

"No! Poor guy's been through hell. I didn't know he got fired 'til I read it. But we, uh… I'm working on a wicked good follow-up story."

"Oh? What's so good about it?"

Ashley explained the angle and then mentioned another idea for Evans to consider.

"I'll run it by them. But the chief's fuming over that story and plans to call your editor."

"Call my editor. He'll verify I'm not the source and what we are working on for tomorrow's wrap-up."

Ashley hung up with Evans, turned around, and met Eric face-to-face. "Ooh. You startled me." He snuck up behind her.

"They're packing up now," Eric grinned. "Better say goodbye."

"Yes! Let's go say goodbye." *I've been waiting all day to be alone with you.*

Chapter 30

Rachel joined Aunt Kelly and Roger Gibbs who were enjoying a drink by their screened-enclosed pool. After vacationing in Florida, Roger, a tile installer, realized it was in high demand due to the tropical humidity. He and Kelly moved from Dracut, MA, three months before Rachel's dad passed away; both started new ventures. Consequently, Kelly missed her brother's funeral, and Rachel's mother never forgave her aunt.

Kelly has half a dozen hair stylists working for her. Roger had worked for a builder in Cape Coral, where they settled. He built up his own business with crews working for several home developers. Four years ago, they sold their modest home on the Cape and made a killing. They built a new sprawling four-bedroom, three-bath ranch with a three-car garage, an enclosed pool, and an outdoor kitchen. Each holiday season, they host a pool party for their employees. They never had children and love having Rachel living with them.

"Rachel," Kelly said, "You look great in your new bathing suit."

She'd gotten used to jumping in the refreshing pool; it helped her sleep better. After surviving a brutal New England winter, she still hadn't adjusted to the heat and humidity in Southwest Florida. *Thank God I work in air conditioning all day.*

It had been a long, interesting day. She rode with Aunt Kelly to her Cape Cuts hair salon and worked as a receptionist until one. She then had four hours of orientation and training at Lowe's, conveniently located in an adjacent shopping plaza. Rachel started her employment file with her baptized name instead of Robin. She didn't want anyone from her former company or Sean to know where she now lived.

Blessed, she thought. She has a new life in paradise with a clean slate and plans to finish her degree. She'd start next semester at Florida Southwestern State College (FSW). What more could she ask for? How about finding someone at Lowe's as nice as Sean used to be? Better yet, finding someone as kind, caring, and trustworthy on the college campus as Dan.

* * *

Thursday evening, Joanna enjoyed her cocktail on her lanai. Spectacular pink and purple cloud formations hovered on the horizon just after sunset. Her head was throbbing. She planned to ask the doctor about her neck pain and cloudy vision. *Probably stress.* She worried about Dan and her daughter in California with the COVID-19 breakouts. She missed her children and her husband.

After sunset, she turned on the TV, watched *The Voice*, and cheered when a contestant chose Kelly Clarkson as a coach over Blake Shelton. She thought about her hair appointment the next day with Kelly Gibbs. They shared many stories about cold winters and their hatred for driving on snowy roads back in Massachusetts. Kelly always did a fantastic job coloring and cutting her hair; she made her look and feel better.

Joanna scanned Facebook and complimented her new friend Meghan on her gorgeous sunset post she'd captured on the other side of town. She inquired about her mother's condition. Meghan replied via Messenger. Joanna felt closer to this younger woman from Boston who was caring for her mother in hospice. Unlike the frosty reception her mother always had for Joanna, she hoped things would be better with Meghan.

* * *

When Meghan's mother dozed off, Meghan turned off the bedside lamp and opened the master bedroom's sliding door to the lanai of her parents' high-rise condo. She loved to snap pictures of the striking sunset skies. Her Facebook post garnered numerous likes and envious comments from her friends in Boston. Her old boss, Dr. Allan Hansen, commented, "Breathtaking." *He always lets me know he's watching me.* She considered blocking him but enjoyed taunting him from afar.

Her friend across town, Joanna DeCosta, commented:
Beautiful pics. How is your mother doing?

She sent Jo an IM: Mom's still battling. Thank you so much for asking.

Meghan then perused Jo's posts of sunsets and beach scenes. The lovely woman and her husband were fit and even more attractive in their bathing suits.

Beautiful family

She commented on Jo's 2018 Christmas post. Jo's perfect family of four made her sad. Before her older brother, Mitch, had overdosed, she had an ideal family, but soon, it would only be her and her dad.

Meghan zoomed in on Jo's son, Dan DeCosta. The young, good-looking, dark-haired man had the same European features as his handsome father. She then clicked on the profile of his attractive sister, Sam DeCosta, and scanned her posts. The young, attractive woman with short, stylish blond hair had much of Joanna's beauty but no resemblance to her father. She looked great pedaling a mountain bike, with long legs and a well-toned body.

She left the lanai and found her dad in the den, sitting in his recliner, sipping a beer, watching his favorite cable news station. Her diabetic half-deaf father, who refused to get hearing aids, always had the volume up on the station she couldn't stand. Meghan sat at the desk by the window, logged into her father's computer, and searched for physical therapist positions in Fort Myers. She had to update her LinkedIn profile with keywords to match job openings. A commercial came on, and the TV's decibels doubled.

"Dad. I'm trying to find work. Put on sports. You've heard the same stuff repeatedly." *Presidential campaigns, COVID-19, conspiracy theories.*

Her dad coughed, changed the station to ESPN, and patted Bruschi's head. The dog's eyes followed the banner rolling across the screen—Tom Brady testing the free agency market.

"Thanks, now lower it—don't want to wake Mom."

"Her meds put her out," he replied. "I'm gonna need meds if Brady leaves the Patriots."

ESPN covered the spring training games. She thought about the De-Costas she'd met at Jet Blue Park. She searched LinkedIn and found Joanna DeCosta—her father was already connected to Dick DeCosta. Joanna had a lovely profile photo and professional summary—a retired HR benefits specialist. She then read Jo's children's profiles. Dan—environmental engineer, oceanology. Samantha—software engineer, blockchain technology, cryptocurrency evangelist. *What a well-rounded family. Jo must be so proud. I hope we can get together soon.*

Meghan then read Jo's husband's profile. Dick DeCosta: venture capitalist, renewable energy consultant, former solar company president, internet CEO, engineering VP for a multi-national service provider, software developer, published in Artificial Intelligence, and published author of *Greenhouse Gases and the Gaslighters*. She thought the title sounded controversial; she searched for Dick's book on Amazon. She read the *NY Times* bestseller blurb: "DeCosta's hard-hitting exposé shines sunlight on the top fifty corporations producing global greenhouse gas emissions."

Fifty hot buttons for green activists, she thought. *I prefer Fifty Shades of Grey. Tee-hee.*

Meghan finished updating her LinkedIn profile and submitted job applications for companies in Fort Myers, Naples, and Cape Coral. She kissed her father good night, checked on her mother, and turned in.

Chapter 31

Friday morning, March 6, Toni Thompson, VP of HR for GreenEx, watched the plow push the wet, slushy snow around the Burlington, MA, office park. *What a mess,* she thought, when she turned back to her computer and filed Christina's email with the others that had flooded her inbox, triggered by the social media backlash.

The outside council instructed the senior staff not to discuss the potential litigation with anyone. Unfortunately, the evening before the letter arrived from DeCosta's attorney, she'd unwittingly discussed it with her friend, Christina Turner-King, who convinced her that GreenEx had misjudged the circumstances and the false accusations of the upstanding young man she'd vouched for.

The expediency of DeCosta's attorney and their grievances caught them off guard, as did their mediation offer, which was rejected by her CEO, ratcheting up the tension. Dan's termination and hospitalization—now sensationalized on social media—inundated Toni with angry employees volunteering to speak on his behalf. She was overwhelmed with requests to resolve this.

DeCosta's dilemma put GreenEx in an unflattering position. For starters, it set off fireworks with their top clients. Their CEO, Major Tom Eldon, and their public relations department and attorneys were scrambling to figure out how to save face without backing down. Yesterday, Toni declined to answer questions from the *Boston Globe* and the *Lowell Sun*. This morning, her office phone had inquiries from Boston TV stations and cable news outlets. Toni instructed Tamara Morrison—her assistant—to hold her calls except those from the CEO or outside counsel.

She perused DeCosta's personnel file. He had flawless attendance, sterling performance reviews, and a strong work ethic. The recently promoted senior engineer had accumulated paid time off days and three weeks of vacation. She read the *Lowell Sun* story Christina sent her about DeCosta's father—a veteran posing with Home Depot's store managers who cleared up his credit card breach. She added Christina's info to her talking points on the slide presentation she'd prepared for her CEO's conference call this morning with PR and outside counsel.

* * *

Dick took Route 93 North on the Central Artery and crossed the Zakim-Bunker Hill Memorial Bridge—under a magnificent, cabled tower—built as part of Boston's Big Dig project. The highway's surface was cleared from night's heavy sleet and snow. He took a call from Lee Grisham.

"Hey Dick… Heads up. Since your podcast coverage at the Green Conference—violent activity threats are picking up from extremists on social media and the dark web."

No surprises here, Dick thought, and eyed a black pickup in his rearview mirror, passing several cars, then abruptly swerving into his slower middle lane.

"Lee. My daughter's in Frisco, my son's in the hospital, Jo's in Florida. We left Chelmsford six months ago. So, we're all safe."

"Hope so, Dick. These are far-right militants and neo-fascists; they've become more empowered in the last four years. Be careful!"

Dick knew the militants, incited by far-right hate groups, targeted oil pipeline protests and sabotaged solar farms and wind turbines. They cared more about the filthy fossil fuel jobs than about climate change and a clean environment. *Shame,* since *clean energy jobs had a brighter future and were not hazardous to their health.*

"Will do. Thanks, Lee. Maybe we'll hook up in Florida in a few weeks for golf."

He turned off 93 North onto Route 95, as did the black pickup. He thought about the Twitter attacks—which he routinely ignored after he presented somewhere—another reason he's better off retired and out of Massachusetts. Dick was also glad his son didn't want the reins to his solar company.

Dan was being released from the hospital. Lately, his relationship with his son had been strained. Poor Dan struggled with physical and emotional trauma, which had unleashed unexpected resentment toward Dick. His son's words hurt but sunk in.

"You expect me to do what you want for me. Not what I want for me." And the crusher, *"You don't know how hard it is being your son."*

It ripped Dick's heart open as well as opened his eyes. Just as he'd never know the pain his wife or any woman went through bearing a child, he'd never know how hard it is to walk in Dan's shoes or live in his mind. He now realized he was oblivious to how his words and actions could sometimes adversely impact the people he loved the most.

Dick was decisive and results-driven, programmed to routinely plow ahead with what he assumed was best—for employers and his career, his companies and employees, and for his family. He was convinced he saw the bigger picture and knew what everyone needed. He did, but only through his eyes, not what others saw or wanted for themselves. His son and his family tolerated him—not because they appreciated and respected him for being a relentless provider—but because they loved him and were stuck with him. *I'm retired; there's no excuse now. I have to slow down and be better.*

Dick swerved into the exit lane for Route 3 North. The car he cut off blasted his horn.

"Sorry!" he shouted into his rearview mirror. *I'm trying to lose the black pickup.* He knew they'd follow him on Route 3 to Chelmsford, where he used to live, but he was going to Lowell. He took the Chelmsford exit and waited at the Drum Hill light; one car separated them. He could go right to Lowell but instead took a left, crossed over the highway, took North Road, and pulled into the Chelmsford Police Station. The pickup with out-of-state plates slowed when they drove by. Now out of sight, he turned back toward Lowell, and minutes later, he arrived at the hospital.

* * *

Dan swallowed his meds. The doctor removed the sutures from his right hand and said the incisions on his shoulder healed well. Dan then squeezed the rubber ball with his left hand—he passed the test. The nurse gave him a bundle of bandages and his prescriptions for oxycodone and muscle relaxers to take home. "Book physical therapy sessions at the rehab center," she said. He wondered if she knew he'd lost his health insurance.

The cheery nurse's aide buttoned his plaid woolen shirt, put the sling on, and zipped his North Face jacket halfway up. His father grabbed his gym bag, scripts, and bandages. Everyone they passed bid him farewell while the aide pushed Dan in his wheelchair down the corridor into the elevator. His dad took him from there and pushed him outside into the bright sunlight. His red pickup, covered in white road salt, was impossible to climb into with a sling. Dad helped him, secured the seatbelt around him, and stuck dark sunglasses in Dan's right hand.

"Thanks," he said. The sun's glare off the snow was blinding but revitalizing after being stuck in a hospital all week.

They drove away from Lowell General Hospital, coasted down Varnum Avenue, and turned onto Route 113 Boulevard. Dad drove cautiously. The seat belt rubbed Dan's throbbing shoulder and tender ribs whenever they hit a pothole or braked for traffic.

Dan wanted to change the oldies radio station that his dad loved, but he didn't want to upset him, so he tolerated it. At least the volume was *low*.

His dad still hadn't said a word. *I wonder if he's mad or afraid to say anything*. Dan felt terrible about the way their last conversation went. Maybe he wants me to feel bad; perhaps he's just thinking about the next five minutes. They stopped at a traffic light; their heads turned toward the Merrimack River Bridge.

"The Rourke Bridge built thirty years ago was supposed to be temporary," his dad finally said. "I bought an investment condo up the road. I sold it after a year and made a quick forty K—then bought our Lake Winnipesaukee vacation home. Those were great times."

"Yeah, fun times. And I loved the boats," Dan said. They both smiled.

Dad always told stories about why he bought this place and sold that one. *I guess he's not mad. Talking about business is the only way he communicates with me.*

"I'll never be a landlord, Dad." *Don't have the stomach. Can barely afford one house.*

"Don't blame you… And you'll never have to. I made more money in real estate than as an engineer and needed tax shelters and extra income for your college funds."

Exactly. I'm not bringing kids into this crazy, costly world. Probably never marry.

More silence. The radio played a Simon and Garfunkel hit, "Bridge Over Troubled Water." Dad raised the volume. The light changed. They crossed the Rourke Bridge. Dan felt every bump across his upper body. He squeezed the rubber ball attached to his sling. He worried the thirty-year-old temporary span might collapse before they crossed the river. *Note to self: Don't use this bridge…and stay out of Lowell General Hospital.*

* * *

Dick drove cautiously to avoid the potholes that, after every winter in Massachusetts, were as unavoidable as sesame seeds on a bun—you learned to roll with them. He went through a rough patch with Dan the last time they spoke. Dick felt he had no way to break the ice or avoid the rabbit holes. There wasn't any good news on the cops or GreenEx. He didn't want to mention Eric fixed the roof because it would remind Dan of Shannon. He wasn't going to ask if he heard from Robin. It was an uncomfortable ride for him—and worse for his fragile, downtrodden son.

They'd stopped at the Rourke Bridge traffic light earlier, and he recalled selling a nearby condo to buy their waterfront condo. He mentioned the fun times in their vacation home, hoping to break the ice. *I'm trying, son.*

It got a warm response—Dan mentioned the boats were fun. He sensed the resentment again when Dan said, "I'll never be a landlord." Dick could relate; he hated worrying about tenants and repairs. But getting ahead and saving for his kids' college education was necessary.

Dick did it the hard way by working full-time and taking computer science courses in the evenings. He'd sold all his investment properties and reinvested them in the kids' college trust funds he managed with stock securities.

Dick dreaded the thought of having to shovel the wet snow on Dan's double-wide driveway. More silence. He turned up the volume to Cat Steven's ballad, "Father and Son." Every time the truck hit another pothole, his son winced.

"Dad, lower that. Better yet, change the station."

But it's a great song, son. "Sorry," he said and changed the station.

"Blinding Lights," by The Weeknd, was playing. They both liked the upbeat tune. *Peace and harmony*, Dick hoped.

* * *

Dad finally changed the station to a song Dan liked by The Weeknd. *What the hell am I going to do after this weekend?* He squeezed the rubber ball attached to his sling when he realized how handicapped he'd be once his dad left for Florida. *How will I change my dressings? Drive to physical therapy, get groceries, and cook?*

They turned onto Buckingham Street. Many neighbors were still shoveling last night's snow, made heavier by the melting sun. He spotted sweet Ashley at the end of her driveway. *Maybe she can come by and help me out.*

Dad pulled up alongside her and zipped Dan's window down. Ashley was giggling at someone behind her. He saw Eric standing by his beat-up F150, parked behind Ashley's car in her cleared driveway. They both approached the open window and shouted, "Welcome home!"

"Thanks," he said.

His dad asked Eric, "What's up?"

"Ash had me check the storage shed's roof. Her mom wants it repaired."

He calls her Ash... Eric's a horn dog! He squeezed the rubber ball and focused on the melting snowbanks.

"Everything good at the house?" his dad asked.

"Everything is wicked good," Ashley said.

Eric said, "We'll follow you up there."

They jumped in Eric's old pickup. Dad drove on past the bend in the road.

"Christ. What now?" his dad mumbled.

They spotted the police cruiser parked in front of his house and an unmarked vehicle parked by the driveway's entrance.

"The friggin' *porcupines* are back!" Dan shouted. His heart raced, and his shoulder throbbed.

His dad's phone rang. He stopped the truck beside the cruiser and answered, "Harlan, what's going on? Cops are at Dan's house.... Great, but I'm confused. I'll call you back."

They turned into the driveway. Detective Evans was shoveling wet snow near the mailbox. *They're digging… for more useless evidence?* Dan fumed.

Evans waved Dad into the partially shoveled driveway. O'Malley, the huge cop who'd cuffed him and tore his shoulder, was digging by the garage, and Saxon—who tasered him—was digging by the steps to the mudroom. Eric pulled his truck in behind his dad's. Ashley aimed her phone and videotaped the cops. Dan looked at his father. *When will these pricks leave me alone?*

His dad shut the truck off and replied, "Harlan said he had no clue why the cops were here since the charges were just dropped." His dad jumped out, approached Dan's side, and helped him out of the truck.

Evans and the two cops converged on them. They all shouted, "Welcome home!"

Dan swallowed hard, "Thank you." He was tottering, and his eyes were welling up behind his sunglasses. He had wild, mixed emotions. *Get the hell off my property.* But he managed to compose himself.

His dad asked Ashley, "Did you do this too?"

She nodded and said, "Help Dan get in the middle of these fine police officers. I need a group photo."

Dan squeezed the rubber ball, kept his anger in check, and forced a smile. Everyone shook hands. His dad refused to be in the photo. He handed him off to Eric, who stood next to Detective Evans. The two huge cops stood by with shovels, and Ashley snapped away.

Then Eric helped Dan up the steps. The cops stayed outside shoveling. *Their way of apologizing,* Dan thought: *They could come back and mow my lawn for a year, but I'll still sue the pricks for my medical bills and lost wages.*

They stepped into the mud room. All the walls had been repaired and painted, and the floor was sparkling clean. Ashley took more photos and then showed Dan her phone with other pictures: several Home Depot employees, including the store manager and Victor, the assistant manager, had volunteered their time and skills the previous two days. Eric waved to his father to follow him outside on the deck.

"Eric cleared the snow off the deck this morning," Ashley said. "He knew your dad would want to check the roof." The sunbaked roof was shedding water onto the deck.

Ashley opened the cover of a box of Dunkin Donuts on the kitchen counter. He couldn't resist the chocolate-glazed and bit into one.

"Eric brought them. He said cops love donuts," she said in her high-pitched voice. "Shall we call them in to join us?"

"Let them finish shoveling first," Dan said.

She giggled.

He moved closer, "Thank you for being such a great neighbor… Ash."

She stepped back, "It's Ashley, like Brinkley. Only Eric can call me Ash—and get away with it. Ah-ha-ha."

Dan squeezed the rubber ball. She smiled at Eric outside on the deck as Dan's heart sank.

* * *

Toni Thompson sat in the GreenEx conference room with her CEO, Major Tom Eldon, the PR director, and the VP of sales, who had reviewed their clients' reactions. Most agreed with the PR director, except for the defense contractors brought in by the major—the company should reinstate De-Costa or minimally cover his medical bills.

"No," said the outside council, "The terminated employee can get Cobra to pay for it."

"Exactly," said the major, the ornery CEO's face was red.

"But It will cost him a lot more," Toni countered. "He'll be ineligible for unemployment benefits because we fired him for willful misconduct. How will he cover insurance payments and a mortgage? It will ruin his credit."

"He'll get another job!" the major shouted. "But not with any defense contractors."

She thought the Air Force major had his head in the clouds. *Ground control to Major Tom.*

"He'll be unemployed during a pandemic; no one is hiring now. Did you look at the slides I sent over?" Toni asked the attorney on the speakerphone.

"Yes. I get it. His father's a Desert Storm vet. But you already terminated him."

"He hasn't signed the letter yet. Why not negotiate the terms they offered?"

"Because he's facing felony charges for assaulting a cop, we don't have to."

"Damn straight," the cantankerous major added. "Next agenda item."

Toni agonized over deciding whether she should play her last card. The IT manager, Domenic Silveira, told her two employees were building a

Crowdfunding site to pay DeCosta's legal and medical bills, and he'd help them. He warned her it would blow up social media and further embarrass the company. She urged them to hold off until she'd work out a compromise. Toni knew the major would fire three or more employees, possibly her, for not bringing it to his attention sooner.

Her phone dinged: a text from Christina Turner-King. Toni Thompson announced to the room, "The police have dropped all the charges. The court will expunge it from his record."

Chapter 32

Joanna spent Friday morning filling out her family's medical history online before Monday's hematologist appointment. Her father had high blood pressure and died of a heart attack, like her older brother. Her mother had early dementia and succumbed to ovarian cancer. Her older sister Paula had a lumpectomy and radiation; she's been cancer-free for eight years. *Detection and treatments were more successful today*, she thought. Still, it made her anxious while she waited to hear about Dan.

She thankfully got good news. Christina texted the Chelmsford Police, dropped the charges, and cleared Dan's driveway as a peace offering. Dick called and explained that GreenEx agreed to most of their attorney's demands and changed the reason for termination to a voluntary reduction in the workforce, effective April 6. The extra month meant his health insurance would cover Dan's hospital bills. He'd also go on short-term disability and receive 60 percent of his salary after using his accumulated sick days.

Before Dick sent his demands letter, he told Jo he'd ask for a month's severance for each year of service—Dan had five. She said, "He's a terminated engineer, not an exec—he'd be lucky to get five days."

"You nevah know unless you ask," Dick said. "It's a starting point."

She was pleased when Dick said, "Dan's getting five weeks severance. He has a clean personnel file and wages for the next month with health insurance. And between severance and accrued vacation, he'll get a lump sum check for eight weeks and can collect unemployment 'til he finds a new job."

"Good job! Is Dan happy with it?" *I am.*

"I just found out from Reiner—took the call out on the deck. Dan's inside eating donuts with Eric and the cops. I hope he'll be happy."

"He better be," Joanna said. "It's what's best for him,"

"I know, but… I never asked him what he wanted. I got busy with the conference, the lawyers, and the house. He was—"

"In the hospital," she finished his sentence. "Don't worry about it."

"Call him. Say, your HR experience knew this was the best way to go."

Hmm, you want me to take credit? That's a switch. "I'm late for my haircut appointment. Maybe tonight. Love ya. Bye."

* * *

Joanna waited at the long Cape Coral traffic light behind an idling motorcycle. She laughed at the driver's T-shirt: IF YOU CAN READ THIS, THE WIFE FELL OFF.

She pulled into the shopping plaza, parked the Audi, entered Cape Cuts Salon, and sat in the waiting area. Kelly—her stylist and the owner—was with another client. Two other stylists were clipping away, chatting up their aging male customers. A new young woman sat at the reception desk talking on the phone. The lovely redhead hung up and looked at Joanna.

"Hi. Do you have an appointment?"

"One-thirty. With Kelly."

"She's finishin' up with anothah customah."

Her Boston accent made Joanna smile.

Kelly and her client watched her new receptionist ring up the charge, print the receipt, and tell the silver-haired woman, "Your hair looks perfect. Enjoy your dinnah."

"Thank you. Have a nice day," the woman said, then left.

"Jo!" Kelly waved Joanna over. "Want you to meet my godchild, Rachel."

"Hello, Rachel. You must be from Bawstin," Joanna said to the freckled-faced beauty with a slight sunburn.

"Use ta be. Not anymore, ha-ha."

The pretty woman's ocean-blue eyes looked at Kelly, "I better get goin'." Then,

the full-figured redhead in tight, faded jeans grabbed her handbag and rushed out.

Joanna settled into Kelly's stylist chair. "When did Rachel start working here?"

"This week," Kelly said, draping a protective gown around her shoulders. "And she started at Lowe's in the next plaza. She walks there and back."

"Energetic."

"She's saving for Florida SouthWestern State College in Fort Myers. Living with us now."

"What a lovely young woman."

"Isn't she, though?" Kelly said in her proud, raspy voice. "Reminds me of Amy Adams."

"I can see that—but she's taller."

"She's big-boned like her father—my brother, Tommy. May he rest in peace."

"Sorry for your loss. Where's her mother?" Joanna hoped she wasn't prying.

"Reno. Hasn't spoken to me since Tommy died of lung cancer."

Rachel from Reno... used to be Bawstin. Dan would like her.

"How'd your root canal go?" Joanna asked. Kelly had to reschedule around it.

"Great. I paid extra for nitrous oxide—it keeps me relaxed." Kelly chuckled.

"Me too. My Bawstin dentist used nitrous—even my ob-gyn. He'd crank up the laughing gas. It was the only way to have a pelvic exam. I didn't care what he did down there."

Kelly laughed, then changed to a serious tone. "Last time in, you had an eye infection and stomach problems... feeling better?"

Joanna filled her in on her medical issues. Then, she said her daughter in California was stuck in COVID lockdown. She avoided discussing Dan's problems because she didn't know where to begin, and it didn't portray him well.

Hair stylists are great listeners because they know everything that's going on in your life. Many are better than psychotherapists—they don't pry or analyze you—you open up more naturally. When they're done, you feel more beautiful outside and inside, and then they say, "See you next time. Hope you feel better then."

"Thanks! Take care, Kelly."

* * *

The HR woman at the Fort Myers Rehab Center called Meghan. She said, "Doctor McCormack, I'm impressed with your PT credentials and rehab experience with orthopedics, brain trauma, and dementia care. I'd like you to meet with our medical director on Monday. He may want you to start the following Monday."

"I'll be there on Monday," replied Meghan. "But I can't commit to any start dates now."

"That was quick," her dad said once she got off the phone. "Yeah. I applied on LinkedIn."

Her dad said, "After I got laid off, Dick DeCosta helped me on LinkedIn. He gave me good referrals and helped me land jobs at Intel and Cisco. He has an enormous network."

"Yes," Meghan added, "You never told me he was published in *Artificial Intelligence* and wrote a book on climate change."

"Dick's a greenie. He also launched several companies. He's well-known."

"Wow! I guess. And he helped you get jobs during tough times. I remember how worried Mom was about Mitch and me. We were in college then."

"Always worrying. She wanted Mitch to go to med school—hated that he went to Berklee College of Music. Good thing you ended up a doctor."

Bruschi barked. It was time for his walk. Her dad grabbed the leash.

Meghan brought her mother the meds. "Who was worried about Mitch?" she asked. *Mom's antenna was always tuned to talk of Mitch.*

"Nothin' on Mitch. Dad said after he got laid off, Dick DeCosta got him into companies."

Her mom snapped, "He's meddled enough in our lives. I told you... *stay away.*"

"Meddled? I might not have made it to med school. Life would be different—"

"Yes! Mitch would be alive. I'd have three doctors caring for me."

"Mom, what are you talking about?" *God, she's shaking!*

"Forget it. Promise me you'll never talk about this with Mack."

"Okay, Mom. I promise." *Since when did you call him Mack instead of Dad?*

Chapter 33

Dick settled up with Eric and grabbed a donut before the cops finished the rest. After they bid farewell to Chelmsford's finest, Dick thanked Ashley again before she and Eric left the house together. Detective Evans returned with a bag and put Tom Brady's jersey on the counter. "Hang on to this," Evans said to Dan. "It will be worth a bundle someday."

Dan nodded, lowered his sad eyes, and slumped over his stool.

He's probably remembering memories of Robin wearing it, Dick thought. He asked him, "How're you feeling?"

"Drained. Do you know where my meds are?"

"Left your stuff in the truck. Be right back."

We have to wean him off the oxy.

He went to Dan's mailbox and returned with a stack of mail and Dan's stuff. After his son took an oxy, he rifled through the mail and set aside the bills. Dick opened an envelope addressed to him and endorsed the insurance check.

"Wow. That was quick," Dan said.

"Yep. All the work is done and paid for. Sign below me."

Dick used Dan's phone, scanned the check, and completed the online deposit.

"Thanks, Dad!"

"You're welcome. You can use the cushion."

"Sure do, since I don't have a freakin' job."

"My lawyer called. We got you STD wages and health benefits for a month and a lump sum severance package with vacation pay—nearly two more months' salary. Mom had a lot to do with that. She got Christina to put the bug in Thompson's ear.

"Are you sure about that?"

"Think so. Mom can fill you in. She's the HR expert. Right now, I gotta deal with my taxes and your prescriptions." Dick headed for the door. "I'll pick up dinner too."

The pharmacist handed Dick the prescriptions. He signed for the muscle relaxers to help Dan sleep comfortably and the oxycodone, which he didn't condone. He also grabbed a box of facemasks for his flight back. He then stopped at his tax accountant's office in Chelmsford, less than a mile from the home he and Jo left last fall to retire in Florida.

He was getting a modest fed refund. On his way to pick up dinner, Dick called Jo.

* * *

Joanna started on a grocery list for things she'd need before Dick came home tomorrow. *Or would he*? She never asked. Her phone rang.

"Hi, babe. How ya feelin'?"

"Tired, taking a nap soon. Marie and Ted invited me to dinner and downtown's art walk. Might as well; I got my hair done. I'll be home early."

"Good. Say hi to them for me. Are the nausea meds helping?"

"Yeah, now just my neck aches and my ears ring. Guess you've been talking about me."

"Oh, did you call Dan?"

What's wrong now? "Not yet." She heard ominous sirens blasting on Dick's end. "What's that racket? Where are you?"

"Outside the accountant's office. Fire trucks and first responders are roaring by. Two more stops, then I'll pick up dinner."

"How's Dan look?"

"Weak. He can't care for himself. Can't drive. I'm worried about him getting dependent on oxy."

Don't tell me you canceled your flight! "So, what are you going to do?"

"Call him. Get him to come back with me tomorrow," replied Dick.

"Last time I asked, he said no way." *NFW, to be precise.*

"Yeah. But—"

"He was in the hospital and holding out for Robin. Maybe now—"

"You nevah know—"

"Unless you ask," Joanna finished his sentence.

"Right. And he needs reassurance from you about the GreenEx compromise."

"What did he say when you told him?"

"Not sure he bought it or understands. Fill him in. It's a good icebreaker for Florida."

"I'll do my best," she replied.

"I know you will, Jo. Gotta go. Love you. Miss you."

"Miss you too…"

Joanna worried about them. Dick wasn't his usual take-charge self. He was pulling back on things—she hadn't seen that in him since Samantha was born.

* * *

Dan checked his online balances. The US Treasury had deposited his tax return, adding to his cushion. He thought about how much his parents had come through for him. *Too bad I'm stuck here all alone in a damn sling.* He tossed the Brady shirt—with the dirty load from the hospital—into the washing machine. He grabbed the detergent but couldn't unscrew the cover. *Screw this, I give up.*

Dan peed instead and did his best to wash his hands. He thought about putting a trash bag over his shoulder so he could shower.

His phone started buzzing. *Robin?* He rushed back to the kitchen.

"Hi, Mom."

"Dan! How do you feel?"

"I'm exhausted and aggravated."

"Why, what's wrong?"

"I can't do shit with one hand! Can't even shower."

"When your dad had his right shoulder surgery. He had a sling and a boot cast on his left foot. He had to sponge bathe and couldn't shower for weeks. I had to drive him to his office, or he wouldn't get paid."

"Yeah, well, I ain't, Dad. And at least he had a job."

"You don't have to worry about work until you've healed. We got GreenEx to keep you on a month with benefits, plus a lump severance pay worth another two months."

"Thanks, Mom. Dad told me what you and Christina King did to make it happen."

"Everyone helped. But what will you do about rehab and driving? Come back with Dad. I'll book the flight."

"I don't know. Let me think about it." *Robin might be back from Orlando next week.*

"Don't wait too long. Dad's flight out is at three thirty."

He's retired. Maybe he'll stay 'til I get rid of the sling.

* * *

Dick put the pharmacy bag, the pizza, and the beers on the island's counter and the Home Depot bag on a bar stool. On the couch watching TV, his son shouted, "Dad, Dad! Look at this!"

The local news reporters were on the scene. Firetrucks, police cruisers, and first responders were scrambling in front of their former home in Chelmsford as black smoke filled the air. Charred ruins were scattered about the unplowed driveway. A time-delayed bomb had been detonated in the mailbox, setting the garage ablaze. Solar panels on the roof were riddled with bullet holes—authorities believed—shot with a sound-suppressed weapon.

A neighbor told the TV reporter, "Thank God no one was home. The family's attending a wedding in the Bahamas."

Fearing something like this, Dick had sold their home seven months ago and moved to Florida. His children grew up in the huge colonial he'd customed designed for his young family. It pained him to see this horrific, needless act. Visibly shaken, his son's eyes welled up as well.

"Was that intended for you? They'll come after me next," said Dan.

Dick patted Dan's knee and replied, "Don't know. The security cameras I had installed will help find the lunatics." Dick changed the subject. "Let's eat," he said, helping Dan get up from the couch.

"Dad. I started my laundry but couldn't get the detergent open. Can you?"

"I'm on it," Dick replied. He added his clothes and returned to the kitchen, where Dan nibbled pizza.

He opened bottles of IPA and handed one to Dan, "Here's to warmer weather."

They both took a slug of beer. Dan asked, "What's in the Depot bag?"

"Suction safety grips for your shower." Dick bought them at Home Depot, where he thanked the manager and employees for replacing the Sheetrock and painting the mudroom.

Dick offered, "I'll change the bandages after, don't worry about getting them wet."

"Thanks! I'm gonna need help. Can you stick around a few weeks?"

Dick looked into his son's eyes, "Is that what you want… and is best for you?"

"Yes! Maybe 'til I get rid of the sling and can drive?"

"What do you think is best for your mother, who has health issues?"

Dan hesitated. Dick chewed on his pizza. They heard a knock on the kitchen door.

"Uncle Dick," Eric said, sticking his head inside from the mudroom.

"What's up?"

"Brought you back your house keys." He slid them on the counter and eyed the pizza.

"Grab a slice," Dick said.

"Beer?" Dan offered.

"Thanks. Don't want to ruin my appetite," he said, raising both palms. "Taking Ash out to dinnah tonight."

Dick looked at Dan. They both burst out laughing.

"What's so funny?"

"Nevah, seen you pass up free drinks and food," Dick smiled.

His son added, "Never seen you waste a heartbeat to make moves on a woman either."

"Hey! I really like Ash. I knew her deceased dad. Worked with him framing houses years ago—I was just learning the trade."

"Small world," Dick said.

"Yep. And Ash is down to earth. Not like all the entitled—"

"Gold diggers and frauds," Dan said.

"Exactly, dude," Eric said, running his fingers through his thick mullet.

His son opened the kitchen drawer and pulled out a plastic bag. "Here. Take this. I'm struggling to breathe. I won't be doing any of this again."

"Primo weed," Eric said. "Now, that won't ruin my appetite. Ha-ha."

Everyone laughed. Eric bid them farewell.

* * *

Joanna's neighbor and close friend, Marie Bates, said, "Your hair looks great."

"Thank You," she said, locking arms with her as they headed toward downtown Fort Myers for Friday night's Artwalk.

"What are you ladies craving tonight?" asked Ted, Marie's husband, catching up to them.

"Salad and Capone's veggie pizza works for me," Marie, the vegan, replied.

"Alfresco with martinis first," Joanna added.

Joanna and Dick always enjoyed the Bates, who'd retired in 2015 from their government jobs in Virginia. They'd met the vegan couple on vacation in 2018 at The Lodge, a sports bar in downtown Fort Myers. Later they invited Joanna and Dick to their spacious condo overlooking the marina. Dick told Jo, "When we retire, this is where we should live. It's awesome, close to everything, and has security guards."

They loved the Bates, who were active in politics and passionately cared about the environment and protecting animals. The handsome older couple were in great shape and seemed to defy the aging process. Marie— Joanna's petite and curvy tennis partner—got her to join the league. Marie liked to indulge; she preferred her martini or margarita glasses half full— with another round ordered.

The crowded downtown streets were routinely blocked off from traffic—for Artwalk, the first Friday of the month, and—Music Walk, the third Friday of the month. Jo and the Bates walked over the multicolored stone pavers in the middle of First Street and lingered near the artist tents displaying paintings and photography. Other vendors hawked clothing and jewelry. They then went to Capone's, known for their homemade pasta, coal-fired pizza, and Chicago-style gangster theme. The ladies drank Cosmos while

Ted had a cold Stella. They enjoyed their sidewalk table, people-watching, and the balmy evening breeze. Although it was snowbird season, the crowds were noticeably thinner because of COVID-19. Several older people wore facemasks.

The trio strolled the streets, passed by more art vendors, and enjoyed the live bands and performers, drawing crowds that filled their tip jars. Marie began dancing in the street. Joanna joined her until she felt faint, stopped, and leaned against a lamppost. Ted came to Joanna's side.

"Let's go to the Hideaway before it gets too crowded," said Joanna.

They walked to Dean Street and entered the jam-packed Hideaway bar. Their favorite local band, The Kapo Kings, had the place hooting and hopping to their Eagles's cover of "Already Gone." The boomer-heavy crowd erupted in cheers when the band's talented frontman, Kenny, launched into an upbeat song he'd written, "Cigarettes and Gasoline." They sang along and danced in the packed aisles. Marie had a salty margarita, Ted had another beer, and Joanna drank water and washed down a pill for her nausea.

While Marie and Ted bopped to the Kings' rendition of David Bowie's "Fame," Joanna missed Dick, who loved to dance. She hoped to hang in for more of the band's Bob Seger and Prince covers. Joanna then leaned on Ted.

"How ya doing, Jo?" Marie asked.

"Worn out, one more song," Joanna replied.

Ted dropped a five in the Kings' tip jar and shouted at Kenny, "Yo—Petty time!" He put his finger and thumb to his lips like he was toting on a joint. Kenny nodded. The band played Tom Petty's "Mary Jane's Last Dance."

Joanna loved the song, but her ears were ringing. She popped another Advil in her mouth. *One more time to kill the pain.*

Chapter 34

Saturday morning, Meghan called the hospice office. Her mother had a rough night and was laboring. They agreed to send a nurse to show Meghan and her father how to administer morphine with a dropper. In the meantime, Meghan had to bathe her. The red scar on her stomach where they operated on her liver still looked raw. Further down was a decade's older semicircle scar—a reminder that she'd been delivered by C-section.

Unfortunately, her mother refused to eat. Meghan feared yesterday's conversation with her mom about Dick and her father worsened matters. She'd promised her mother never to speak to her dad about the DeCostas again. And she'd never mention her mother's outrage about them to her father.

* * *

Joanna parked at the liquor store. She needed to restock before Dick arrived. She spotted Jim McCormack lifting the trunk to his silver Mustang convertible two spots over.

"Hello there," Joanna said.

Jim put a case of Bud in his trunk next to a bag of dog food. The silver-haired gentleman with bushy eyebrows turned, "Oh, hi, Jo."

"How's Margaret doing?" She eyed Jack's bag of Maker's Mark bourbon and Jameson.

He coughed, "Hospice changed her over to morphine drops."

Joanna hugged him. "So sorry to hear that."

"Thanks! I gotta get back and help Meg."

"Say hi to her. Take care."

Joanna got her booze, then drove to the crowded Publix grocery store and put on her facemask. Employees and other customers were now wearing masks. The shelves were now sparse, and the cashier lines were longer than usual, filled with shopping carts overloaded with toilet paper.

Joanna put the groceries away when she got home and changed into her pink shorts and Pride tank top. She walked with Marie to Centennial Park for the start of the LGBTQ gathering. The two women shared a special bond. Marie had a transgender daughter in Virginia. Joanna always supported the gay community but became more so once Sam became involved with Khori.

Before the Pride walk ended, she felt weak and begged off. Marie suggested they grab an iced coffee at Starbucks. The caffeine helped. Joanna posted pictures of the event for Sam and Khori on the family chat. Sam responded.

Thanks, Mom 🤍 🌈

After a shower, she turned on the local news. They announced the first COVID-19 death in Lee County—which encompasses Fort Myers, Cape Coral, and other towns—then showed footage of the walk for equality. Joanna made a vodka tonic and switched to the tennis channel. She couldn't wait until Dick and Dan arrived from Boston tonight.

* * *

Dick got up early and made breakfast. He didn't know if it was because his son gave up on Robin and consented to his parent's wishes or because of the militants who bombed the home he grew up in, but he was relieved when Dan decided last night to go to Florida with him.

"Guess everybody would be better off if I go to Florida," Dan had said. "I need a change of scenery, and I'm looking forward to seeing Mom and your new place."

"Mom will be thrilled. Don't ruin it by talking about the house fire. She'll worry herself to death. And don't mention it to Sam. Okay?"

"Okay, Dad. I get it."

Dick packed Dan's large suitcase and gym bag with the essentials and summer clothing he'd need in Florida. He put Dan's bags in the mudroom and was headed upstairs to the guest bedroom when Harlan called him.

"We saw the horrible news about your firebombed home. You, okay?"

"Yes. Thanks. Please don't bring it up with Dan. Make sure Christina *never* mentions it to Jo. It's local news. No one except the FBI knows I was the target—hope it stays that way."

"Will do. See you soon."

Then Lee Grisham called. The FBI had retrieved camera footage from the cloud off Dick's security system, which is on the same server as the solar panels he'd installed at his Chelmsford home. They had additional leads on an out-of-state truck spotted in the area on Thursday and Friday. "We'll get them, Dick."

"No doubt. Thanks, Lee."

When Dick finished packing, he looked out the window at Freeman

Lake. The majestic North Chelmsford water tower on the frozen lake's other side reminded him of the night he and Jo went parking at the dead-end street and fogged up the cars' windows. He married the girl of his dreams when she was young, and she became more beautiful every year.

Jo made him happy and proud. He always looked better with her by his side, which gave him confidence and kept him focused. He'd never have been as successful without Jo. She was a great business partner, a loving wife, a super mom, and a reliable homemaker—she did everything exceptionally well. He missed her and was worried about her health.

"Dad, they're here!" Dan shouted up the stairwell.

Dick had planned to take an Uber into Logan Airport, but Harlan insisted on driving, as he and Christina planned to do a little shopping in Boston and dining in its Italian North End.

Dick hauled their bags downstairs, where Harlan and Christina were speaking with his son and looking out on the deck and Freeman Lake.

"Nice place you got here," Christina said, examining the kitchen island's granite and the shiny hardwood floors.

"Thanks," his son beamed proudly.

"How many bedrooms?" Harlan asked.

"Three and two full baths." Dick pointed to the living room, "And a gas fireplace."

"Great location and lake views," Christina added. "I have an assistant looking around Chelmsford and Westford for a new home. I'll have to tell her about this area."

They locked up the house. Harlan helped Dick load the luggage into his Lexus SUV. He helped his son climb into the back seat. Christina strapped her seatbelt and put on her sunglasses.

"Nice hybrid," Dan said, looking at the interior.

Christina replied, "It's much better than the gas-guzzling Lincoln Navigator he replaced."

"Yep. A wise man told me," Harlan said, eyeing Dick in his rearview mirror, "I better get with the environmental program, or he'd find another lawyer."

Dick chuckled, "All I said was hybrids qualify for a tax credit."

"Wait till you get my invoice and expense voucher," Harlan said.

"I knew an Uber would be cheaper," Dick said. Everyone laughed.

"Mister King, thank you again for all you did for me with the police and getting me to the hospital. And Mrs. King, thank you for helping with GreenEx."

"Thank your parents," they both said in unison.

Harlan dropped them off at JetBlue departures. Most people were wearing facemasks inside the terminal. Dick put on his mask and helped Dan with his before they passed through security.

Jo used her frequent flier points to upgrade Dan to business class; the flight attendant helped him with his seatbelt. Dick took his seat in coach, buckled up, and closed his eyes for the three and half hour flight.

It had been a grueling, gut-wrenching week. He felt like he'd worked a month of Mondays at minimum wage. After dealing with the Green Conference, cops and lawyers, social media and the FBI, hospitals, and home repairs, his checkbook was a little lighter and his heart much heavier. He'd gotten his battered, heartbroken son out of trouble and safely away from Massachusetts, where COVID cases were rising and militants were roaming.

They landed at RSW airport in Fort Myers. When they got to Dick's Audi SUV, it was dark, seventy-nine degrees, with a warm, balmy breeze. He texted Jo.

In the car—we'll be there shortly!

He couldn't wait to take his son to their new condo. It would make Jo happy. She wasn't feeling herself lately, but he knew how good she'd feel when he hugged her tightly and felt her heart beating for him as strongly as it did the day they wed.

* * *

Sean finished eating and put his dirty plates in the sink. He listened closely while his mother gossiped on her kitchen phone with her sister, Fran; she'd spoken with Robin's mother, who lives in Reno. Since they both waitressed at the Owl Diner, Aunt Fran had known Robin's mom long before Sean dated the feisty redhead. Mrs. O'Rourke told Fran that her daughter now lived with her aunt in Cape Coral, Florida. Sean remembered Robin raving about her favorite Auntie K, who owned a beauty salon there.

Gotta get to Floridah, Sean thought, *but I ain't got the money… yet.*

Chapter 35

Dan enjoyed the smooth, quiet ride in Dad's Audi Q8 e-tron SUV. He eyed the tall palm trees lining the sidewalks of MLK Boulevard as they approached downtown Fort Myers. His parents bought a high-rise condo three years earlier with fantastic river views. His dad said it was a turnkey deal, fully furnished, perfect for renting to snowbirds.

The first time Dan visited Fort Myers was in 2018. He had taken in a Red Sox spring training game with his parents, and every night, they dined al fresco in several of the downtown restaurants. He craved a thick, juicy burger at Ford's Garage—named after Henry Ford, who'd followed Thomas Edison to Fort Myers in the early 1900s.

His dad pulled into their impressive high-rise complex with two majestic buildings and drove under a steel security gate through an underground garage to a reserved parking spot. He'd never seen so many high-end luxury vehicles, sports cars, and convertibles under one roof. The place was a fortress loaded with security cameras, *much safer than living in Chelmsford*, Dan thought, and now understood why his father retired here.

His dad waved at a security guard, loaded their bags on a luggage cart, wheeled them over the marble lobby floors, and entered a private elevator for his parents' tower. Dad punched in his security code, then hit twenty-seven. There were buttons for thirty-three floors. They stepped off the elevator to a private lobby and entered the dual fire-safety doors.

"Oh, wow!" Dan exclaimed as he stepped inside the foyer and saw how large and luxurious the open kitchen and great room were relative to their rental. *Breathtaking*, he thought, looking at the magnificent views through the ten-foot, floor-to-ceiling glass sliders and the lanai. Mom rushed inside and greeted him with open arms.

"Dan! You made it!" His petite mother hugged him and wouldn't let go. He gritted through the pain in his shoulder and ribs. *Can't complain— nothing like a hug that enables you to feel the heartbeat of another.*

"Mom, this place is awesome!"

"Thanks, we love it. I'll give you the tour later."

His dad hugged her and gave her a quick kiss on the lips, then hugged her again. He was happy for them. Then, Dad grabbed Dan's bags and walked down the hall.

"Follow, Dad," Mom said. "Your room is at the other end."

He entered the bedroom with a side door to an adjacent bathroom. A king-size bed and a private balcony awaited him. Dad pointed at the two bridges spanning the river, "They connect Fort Myers to Cape Coral."

"Fantastic views here." *Perfect for recuperating,* he thought, *and safer than Chelmsford.*

His mom unpacked his luggage while he checked out his dad's study. A desk beside a large picture window offered panoramic views of the city and river. A bookcase with family photos and a shelf devoted to his dad's favorite *Lowell authors*—David Daniel, Andre Dubus III, Jack Kerouac, Elinor Lipman, Jacqueline McDonald, and Stephen O'Connor. The next shelf had Dad's book on climate change and his published journals. There was also a bronze sculpture of Rodin's *The Thinker.* Dan nodded, *Dad's the thinker in the family.*

Mom showed him the view from their master bedroom: a marina below with countless cruisers, speed boats, and sailboats. Beyond were three bridges spanning the river, and views of downtown lit up the cityscape.

"What's under construction with the big crane?" he asked Mom.

"The Luminary will be a twelve-story Marriott Hotel with three restaurants and a rooftop lounge overlooking the river. Should be opening this fall."

"Cool. Can we go to Ford's Garage for dinner?"

"Long wait in snowbird season. But I made reservations at Kings Kitchen; it's only a two-minute walk."

They sat outside and shared loaded tostones, beef empanadas, and lobster tacos. Surprisingly, Dan did all right with one arm and washed it down with a beer. His parents enjoyed margaritas while a salsa band revved up the crowd. Dan took it all in under the starry skies and warm tropical evening air. The only thing missing, he thought, *was clicking margarita glasses with Robin.*

* * *

Across town at the McCormack's condo, Meghan, her dad, and a hospice nurse were gathered around her mother Margaret's bed. Meghan held her hand. Her dad leaned over and kissed Mom's forehead, "Love you, Peg," the nickname he called his wife of forty-four years. Their dog, Bruschi, was panting on the master bedroom floor. They left the room when a Catholic priest arrived to administer Margaret's last rites.

Her dad was the first to spend time alone with her mom. Meghan then exchanged places with him and now had the candlelit bedroom alone with her mother.

"Mum, I'm here." Meghan kissed her cheek and patted her thin bony hand. Her mom's glazed eyes locked into the shadows on the wall.

She mumbled weakly, "M-Mitch…." Her parched lips parted and then closed.

"It's okay, Mum. You'll be with Mitch soon."

Meghan swallowed hard and let out a deep breath. The candles flickered, drawing her mom's eyes to her brother Mitch's flowered urn on the dresser. Meghan held back a tear. Mum's thin, sunken face turned to her; her glazed blue eyes sent a chill up Meghan's spine. Meghan kissed her forehead and said, "Love you."

She then gathered everyone and Bruschi. The hospice nurse directed her dad to hold Mum's right hand and Meghan the other. The nurse then made a sign of the cross and administered morphine on the frail woman's tongue. A moment later, Margaret McCormack took her last breath. Meghan hugged her weeping father tightly. She then wiped her tears away on her trembling father's shirt.

Thirty minutes later, the Cremation With Care drivers wheeled Margaret out the front door on a gurney. A draft rushed into the bedroom and blew out a candle on the dresser.

Her dad grabbed a Maker's Mark bourbon bottle and two shot glasses. Meghan joined him on their lanai, and they toasted to Peg.

* * *

Sean entered the Owl Diner. He figured a fellow contractor would be having breakfast. He snagged the counter seat beside the dude scrolling on his phone. The server poured Sean black coffee as he ordered a Fletcher Street omelet with extra toast. The roofing contractor he had met on a few job sites finally looked up from his phone.

"How ya doin', man? Long time no see," said Eric Rondeau.

"Good, Brutha," Sean fist-bumped him. "I got outah rehab. Pickin' up odd jobs."

"Good for you," Eric said, then sipped his coffee.

"Saw ya pichah in the *Lowell Sun*. Cops with shovels, helping a guy in a sling."

"Yeah, my cousin, Danny DeCosta. I repaired his leaking roof."

"Ah. What happened to your cuz?"

"Cops beat him up, cracked his ribs. Botched arrest at his house. They dropped the charges and shoveled him out to make amends."

"He need any 'lectrical work?" *I'll payem a visit, crack more ribs.*

"No. He's recuperating in Fort Myers, Florida, with his folks."

"Wish I could get to Floridah—find some work." *Robin's there, maybe with Depot Dan.*

"Greg Gaudette and I went there three years ago—helped out after Hurricane Irma. Nice to live there. But too freakin' hot to be up on roofs."

Sean's omelet arrived. He dug into it as Eric continued.

"Greg stayed. He lives in North Fort Myers, doing appliance repairs and HVAC. Says they're always hiring. Course he knows electrical like you."

"Greg's a smaht dude. We did 'lectrical together. That anywhere neah Cape Canal?"

"Cape Coral. It borders North Fort Myers. Greg did AC work there. I did roofs."

Don't have a car. Bus might get me there. "You still got Greg's numbah?"

"I do." Eric scrolled the contacts on his phone.

"Thanks!" Sean added Greg's info on the new phone his Uncle got him.

Sean called Greg Gaudette and left a message. Greg called him back on his lunch hour. He gave him the company's website and tips on how to apply for positions at Home Tech Squad (HTS). Greg would get a finder's fee for workers who last at least six months.

"You have to pass a drug test," Greg said.

"No problem, dude. I spent six months in rehab. I'm a changed man."

"Okay, Sean. Give it a shot. And good luck."

Sean checked the company's website, located in Fort Myers. *I'll give it a shot.*

Chapter 36

The digital clock on Joanna's nightstand displayed 9:23 a.m. Daylight savings had sprung the clocks ahead an hour. The gorgeous sunsets would appear later now. She raised the shade to expose the wide river and marina below. Two neighbors were fishing off the condo's seawall; others were walking their dogs. A group of ladies were in the pool doing water aerobics.

Waffle aromas filled the condo as Dick poured batter on the hot iron.

"Morning, babe. Yours is cooking, this one is Dan's. He's on the lanai."

Her son looked comfortable in his gym shorts, tank top, and sling. He sipped coffee at the glass-top table. She put Dan's plate before him. "Want me to cut this up for you?"

"Morning, Mom. Yes, please."

He added syrup, stabbed a piece, took a bite, and said, "Ooh, so good. Haven't had Dad's waffles in ages."

She checked her phone and read a text from Christina and a link to a story about her son.

"Great story in the *Lowell Sun* about Dan," she said to Dick plating waffles. "You never told me about the store's Volunteer for Vets program."

"Too busy with the other stuff," Dick said, carrying their plates outside.

It's always good when someone else cooks for you, thought Joanna.

"Dan, nice follow-up by the *Sun* reporter. She even had Eric in the pictures with the store manager. Want to see it?" She pulled her phone out.

Dan said, "We know, we were there. Ashley lives a few doors down. She visited me at the hospital and sent brownies. She put the Home Depot people up to it—shamed the cops into shoveling my driveway."

"Resourceful woman. Is she married?"

Both her husband and son laughed. "What?" she asked.

"She's already dating Eric," her son said.

"Well, Eric's always been a charmer. Hasn't he?"

She scanned Facebook. "Oh my God! Peg passed away."

They stopped eating.

She said, "Meghan posted, 'My beloved mother took her last breath last night and is now in heaven with my brother Mitch.'"

Dick said, "Poor Jack, he loses his wife, son, and brother in two years."

"No arrangements yet," Joanna said. "I'll have a fruit basket delivered."

"How did they die?" her son asked.

"Mother died from pancreatic cancer," Joanna said.

"Mack said opioids killed Mitch," Dick added. "His brother died of a heart attack after Hurricane Michael destroyed his mobile home on Panama City Beach. Which reminds me, I have to get quotes on hurricane shutters."

"Oh wow. Wait, who is Mack?" Dan seemed confused.

"Jim McCormack, a former colleague of mine. We go back forty years."

"They live in the same high-rise as our rental," she said. "We met his daughter, Doctor Meghan McCormack, at the Sox game. She moved here to care for her parents."

She found Meghan's post with David Ortiz. "I took this photo of Meghan and her dad at the ballpark." She showed Dan.

"Woah!" Her son said. "She's a doctor?"

"Yeah. Physical therapist. I told you about her and—"

"Mom, stop meddling."

"I'm sorry." She lowered her head and picked at her waffle.

Dan touched her wrist and grinned, "Don't be. I'm kidding."

Her husband smiled and poured more maple syrup on his waffle.

He's as volatile as his father. But they're both being extra sweet right now.

* * *

Rachel took in the sights from the back seat of her aunt's Kia Sorrento SUV. They were stalled in Sunday morning traffic, waiting to cross the Matanzas Pass Bridge to Fort Myers Beach on Estero Island. Her uncle Roger griped, "It's always backed up during snowbird season."

Becca sent her a text and link to a *Lowell Sun* story. It included photos of Dan in his sling with the cops and a photo of her former Home Depot coworkers painting the walls in Dan's mudroom, where she'd left him a note and her car keys. She'd left Dan's house believing she did the right thing for everyone but was sad about the outcome. *I gotta move on.*

The traffic started moving, and when they reached the arc on the top of the bridge, she marveled at the beautiful turquoise water in the Gulf of Mexico. They then hauled a cooler, chairs, blanket, and umbrella to the packed public beach. It was a gorgeous cloudless day with a warm offshore breeze, eighty-four degrees. Rachel pulled off her T-shirt, put her ponytail through the rear slot on her cap, and kicked off her flops. Her feet sunk into the soft, soothing sand. Relative to the brown, coarse sand on New England beaches that scorched your feet, Fort Myers's sugar-white, cool sand felt like talcum powder.

Rachel felt naked as the hot sun singed her pale shoulders. She applied sunscreen everywhere she could reach; Aunt Kelly put more on her back. She stretched out on the blanket and set her phone's timer to turn over in twenty minutes. After Rachel adjusted her earbuds, she cranked the volume to Harry Styles's "Watermelon Sugar." As she zoned out, she vividly recalled the time she'd smoked weed with Dan. They had munched on pizza and cake, sipped wine, got naked, and giggled under the sheets. He kissed her forehead and said, "I'm going to kiss every inch of you." He kept his word and drove her crazy.

After sun worshipping for an hour, Rachel walked to the shoreline. Warm, gentle waves felt terrific as she swam out and joined Kelly and Roger treading in the Gulf's bath-like water. When they got out of the water, she felt the eyes of men gawking at her dripping wet black bikini. The other women on the beach were either well-tanned blonds or dark-skinned brunettes. Her pale, freckled skin and red hair stuck out like a tourist in a foreign country. *Eventually, I'll fit in if I don't burn to death first.*

They dried off, and Aunt Kelly said, "Let's grab lunch."

They walked over the colored pavers in Times Square to the PierSide Grill and Famous Blowfish Bar. The hostess seated them waterside at an umbrella-shaded table overlooking the beach. A continuous parade of beachgoers walked along the shore and under the wooden fishing pier that extended out over 560 feet. Fisherman's Wharf was lined with people casting their lines into the water while others posed for pictures as boaters motored by.

Kelly and Rachel ordered Margaritas. Roger ordered a beer and Gator Bites. Roger insisted Rachel try a beer-battered gator bite. She was pleasantly surprised; the fried alligator meat, firm like pork, tasted like chicken. A guy with shoulder-length hair strummed his acoustic guitar as they enjoyed their meals. Everyone applauded his cover of Howie Day's "Collide."

Perfect weather, good food and entertainment, fabulous waterside views. *Paradise*, she thought, sipping her salt-rimmed margarita. *The only thing missing is sweet Dan DeCosta.*

* * *

Dick helped Jo clear the dishes and asked, "What time is your appointment?"

"Ten.", she said and frowned.

"I'll hit the gym early and take you."

"You don't have to. Dan might need you here."

"He'll be fine," he said as he hugged her.

Dick brought the Sunday *News-Press* out to the lanai and handed the sports section to Dan. Dick appreciated their editorials and investigative stories covering climate change, rising sea levels, red tide, and the blue-green algae water issues that were threatening the vital estuaries.

The paper was not kind to the politicians owned by big sugar, real estate developers, and fossil fuel corporations. They all contributed to the toxic nitrogen runoff from chemical fertilizers, failing septic systems, and municipal waste flowing into the rivers and the Gulf and leaching into the aquifers, the sacred source of Florida's drinking water.

Dick said, "Dan, read this article on how Hurricane Irma's heavy rains produced toxic ground runoffs that contaminated the Gulf and increased red tide that closed the beaches for two seasons. Your mom got sick from it."

Dan said, "A student and a Gulf Coast University professor co-wrote this."

"Yes, FGCU," Dick added, "Many campus buildings are LEED certified. They care passionately about our watah and climate change."

"Good to know," his son said, then spoke into his phone. "Hey, Siri. Website for FGCU."

Dick was proud his children had STEM degrees. He sometimes regretted being too busy with his career and businesses to complete his engineering degree. He took solace that neither did mega tech entrepreneurs Michael Dell, Bill Gates, Steve Jobs, and Mark Zuckerberg. He and Jo were far from wealthy, but they did their jobs, paid for their kids' educations, and retired comfortably.

We live well now, Dick thought, *but significant health issues could shatter our early retirement dreams.*

* * *

On Sunday, Sean looked at the HTS job openings and applied online for two. He listed Greg Gaudette as the job referral and Eric Rondeau and Uncle Bill as references. On Monday, he got a favorable call from the HTS office. They set up a phone interview for Wednesday but stressed they preferred a face-to-face meeting.

Whatevah, he thought. *I'm one step closah to getting to Floridah.*

Chapter 37

Joanna and her husband sat in the Cancer Center's waiting room with spaced-out chairs and floor markings noting the recent COVID-19 social distancing policies. Courageous face-masked patients—with young and old weary eyes—were called upon and entered the doors to the chemo and radiation treatment areas. A young phlebotomist took her to the lab, where Joanna gave more blood.

Twenty-five anxious minutes later, Dr. Silas, the hematologist, examined the lymph nodes around her neck and under her arms. He pressed gently on her thyroid gland and said, "Joanna, you do not have thyroid cancer."

"What about—"

"Leukemia?" the doctor finished for her. "Negative. I checked your blood under the microscope myself. It's rare when I get to tell a patient you don't have cancer—go home and don't return."

Relieved but confused, she asked her husband on the way to the car, "What about my neck pain, tremors, and ringing ears?"

"We'll discuss those with the neurologist on Wednesday," Dick said.

On their ride home, she mentioned the possibility of Parkinson's disease.

Dick replied, "My parents used to call this Medicare Hell-care. They'd both gone through hell worrying as they were sent from one specialist to another."

She sighed, "I'm not old enough for Medicare and not in a hurry to get there."

"We should be okay with my TRICARE veteran's insurance," he told her.

* * *

Meghan had driven her BMW X5 to Florida from Massachusetts in February—her Guru mountain bike was mounted on a tailgate rack. The SUV and roof carrier fit most of her belongings, luggage, PT equipment, and a golf bag. She had several shoe boxes and clothing shipped down. Her dad parked his Mustang in one of his two underground spaces and sold Peg's car; Meghan parked her BMW in her mother's spot.

She parked in the Fort Myers Rehab Center's lot. By midday Monday, March 9, she'd accepted their job offer. They agreed to a March 23 start date. In the parking lot, she checked her phone. There were more condolences on Facebook, this time from Lahey Clinic coworkers. There was also a text from Allan, her former boss. She didn't respond. But on the drive home later, he called. She put him on the car's speakerphone.

"Hello, Meghan. So sorry about your mother. It's good that you were with her for the remaining time. She's in a better place now."

"Thanks, Allan. It's been tough on my dad, too."

"I bet. I know it's too soon to think about it, but your position will still be here when you're ready to return."

"Thanks, but I accepted a job in Fort Myers as I need to keep an eye on my dad."

"Oh. Congratulations. Good luck, take care, and please keep in touch."

"Thank you. Bye, Allan." *The only thing you want to keep in touch with is my body.*

All caught up in her messages, Meghan entered the condo.

"Sorry for your loss," Jessica, the receptionist, said, hugging Meghan in the lobby.

Jessica handed her several sympathy cards and a fruit basket from the DeCostas. Meghan and her father were overwhelmed by the empathy from their condo neighbors. Many inquired about services for her mother. Jim McCormack had previously served on the association's board of directors. The current board offered her dad the condo's gathering room for a celebratory memorial. She scheduled it for 5:30 p.m. next Friday, March 13.

* * *

Jim McCormack had already made the cremation arrangements. His wife requested a portion of her remains to be kept with her son Mitchell's urn; the rest scattered off Marco Island. He said, "Meg, I want some ashes left in your mother's urn, where I can join her after my cremation."

"Absolutely, Dad. Absolutely," Meghan sighed, knowing when that inevitable time came, all she'd have left would be memories, ashes, and urns.

Jim was the youngest and last survivor of five his parents raised in Melrose, Massachusetts. His brother, Tim, a retired bachelor, lived in a mobile home park near Panama City Beach, which was destroyed in 2018 by the Category Five Hurricane Michael. A month later, a heart attack took Tim's life. Jim wouldn't admit it, but he knew climate change had increased the intensity and the damage to Florida's communities and coastlines.

Jim contacted Peg's sister, Elizabeth, and her husband, Walter Baxter.

The Baxters lived near their children and grandchildren in Hartford, Connecticut, and wintered in The Villages, a vast development in Central Florida. Elizabeth lobbied her sister, Peg, to buy in The Villages, but Jim insisted on staying in Fort Myers near the Red Sox spring training park.

He never cared for Walter—the crusty eighty-year-old, retired insurance executive was more condescending than his wife, who always found fault with Peg's appearance and life choices. The Baxters loved Meghan but often criticized his son Mitchell. And when he succumbed to opioids in Massachusetts, they didn't attend his funeral. Elizabeth said she and Walter would attend her sister's celebration of life gathering.

* * *

Joanna and Dick returned from the Cancer Center and found Dan on the lanai, checking the condo pool below.

"Is the pool heated?" Dan asked.

"Yes," Joanna said.

"Can't wait 'til I get this sling off so I can swim laps."

"Swimming is good. But stretch out your shoulder with PT first," her husband stressed.

Joanna's phone dinged. She read Meghan's thank-you text for the fruit basket and her invitation to a celebration of life on Friday in honor of Peg.

They all moved to the living room, and her husband controlled the TV's remote. The Dow, S&P 500, and NASDAQ hit new yearly lows. Airline stocks led the losers, and Bitcoin, Ethereum, and Coinbase were all plunging. Her husband changed from the business channel to cable news.

"No wonder," Dick said, "Italy announced a countrywide lockdown."

They viewed the horrific footage of nurses and doctors wearing hazmat suits and trailer trucks loaded with dead bodies. Joanna gagged, used the bathroom, and swallowed a pill for her nausea. When she returned to the living room, the news had worsened.

Dick reported, "A cruise ship is stuck outside Fort Lauderdale because people tested positive for COVID. The governor declared a state of emergency for Florida."

Dan added, "Wow, Dublin and Boston have canceled their Saint Paddy's Day parades."

She'd had enough. Joanna went to the den and logged into her computer to research Parkinson's disease. She had a few PD symptoms—tremors and minor losses of automatic movement that affected her tennis game. The Parkinson's Foundation noted that reliable tests like MRIs or CT scans were often used to detect other health issues and rule out PD.

She learned that Linda Ronstadt's incredible singing career was cut short by Parkinson's, and beloved actor Alan Alda had announced he had it. The PD Foundation's biggest poster boys were Muhammad Ali and Michael J. Fox. Encouraged by the progress and support for treatments and research, she made a modest online donation to the PD Foundation.

* * *

Tuesday, Dick decided they'd take Dan to the Thomas Edison Museum on McGregor Boulevard. Jo loved the enchanting botanical gardens on the Edison and Ford estate grounds, highlighted by orchids, over 1,000 tropical plant species, and one of the largest Banyon trees in the world that Edison planted in the late 1920s.

Edison's second wife, Minor, and 'Tootie' McGregor—wife of Ambrose McGregor, President of Standard Oil—began a beautification project in the city. They trucked in Royal Palms and planted them along Riverside Drive, now called McGregor Boulevard. Fort Myers is home to many varieties of palms, and thus, it's named "The City of Palms."

Edison's close friend, Henry Ford, built a vacation home beside his. Dick loved the architecture of the renovated Edison and Ford summer homes. He and Dan admired Ford's Classic Model A automobiles and were amazed at the inventions displayed in Edison's 15,000-square-foot museum. With nearly 1,100 patents, some of the household items improved or invented by Edison include the light bulb, cinema, the phonograph, microphone, toaster, electric coffee pot, fan, waffle, curling irons, hot plate, Christmas lights, spark plugs, and electric meters.

Dick said to them, "I wish they'd rename 'Lee County' to 'Edison County.'"

"Great idea," Joanna said. The city removed the controversial Confederate statue of General Robert E. Lee and had been grappling with renaming the county.

"Wishful thinking," Dick added. "There is too much paperwork and county records to change, and there is not enough political will here to make it happen."

* * *

Dan stood on the back balcony Wednesday morning, resting his sling on the railing. He felt the heat from the easterly sun while he took pictures of the city and river views 270 feet below. Last night, he captured the setting sun from the westerly lanai. He posted them all on the family chat for his sister with the caption.

Sam, the pics don't do it justice. U need to C for yourself.

He squeezed the rubber ball attached to his sling and watched his father's Audi leave the condo complex to take his mother to her doctor's appointment. He stepped back inside, went to his parents' master bathroom, and surveyed their medicine cabinet.

He opened a vial with four Percocet tabs prescribed by his father's dentist. *He don't need these.* he pocketed three. Dan then found his mother's Vicodin; there had to be twenty. He swallowed one, put two in his pocket, and left the rest. *Mom's hurting.* He grabbed the Advil caps and put a handful in his other pocket.

Dan returned to his bathroom and stuffed the other pills in his container of Advil. He put it on the counter next to his muscle relaxers and his depleted vial of oxycodone. *I have to wait until I get back to Lowell.* If the doctor wouldn't approve a refill, he'd call Eric, who has friends that could hook him up.

The mirror reflected that he needed a haircut. And the beard, which is good to have up north during the winter, now had to go. He needed the sun's vitamin D to heal faster and wanted some color. Shaving with one hand took a while as his ribs and shoulder still ached. He popped more Advil and iced his shoulder afterward.

* * *

The nurse checked Joanna's blood pressure. It was higher than usual; her husband furled his lip. The neurologist then introduced himself.

Joanna described her symptoms to Dr. Royce and added, "I'm also stressed about the coronavirus."

Royce examined her right eye, "When did you first notice the droop?"

"After I went swimming during the red tide. I got conjunctivitis."

"And the sharp pains behind your ear?" he inquired as he examined her right ear canal.

"And she's a little forgetful these days," her husband added.

She shook her head.

The doctor entered a notation on his laptop. "I've ordered an MRA and CT scan for tomorrow. And I want to see you on Monday to discuss the results."

"What's that?" she asked. "A test for Parkinson's?"

"It stands for a magnetic resonance angiogram. We'll check for any cranial fluid buildup, which might rule out Parkinson's."

Dick said, "Brain scans, and—"

"Might explain the memory loss, indicative of MCI, mild cognitive impairment."

The doctor viewed his laptop again. "You have a history of hypertension, and your mother had dementia. The nurse will give you the lab orders and the prep instructions."

"Thank you, Doctor Royce." *I'm not looking forward to more tests or waiting.*

When they returned to the condo, they found their son sitting shirtless and sweating in the hot sun on the back balcony. Joanna looked at his cleanly shaven face.

"Dan, you need to put on sunscreen. You're already burning!"

"Okay, Mom."

She gave Dan sunscreen and then made salads for lunch.

"Mom, GreenEx emailed my termination agreement. I printed it out. Will you review it before I sign and scan it back?"

"Of course."

"Where can I get a haircut?" Dan asked her.

"I get mine at Cape Cuts. They style men's hair, too," Joanna added. "They have a new attractive receptionist with red hair. You'd love her."

"Really? What's her name?"

"Rachel… from Reno, Nevada, she used to live in Bawstin."

"We don't need to drive to the Cape," her husband said. "There are barbers in downtown Fort Myers. After we finish lunch, I'll take you to Blakes."

"Thanks, Dad."

Blakes Barbershop had no appointments available. Dick and his son had to wait at Dapper Cuts on Second Street for one of their five barbers' chairs to free up. They watched TV there and checked their phones; Wednesday, March 11, 2020, was peppered with bad news. The World Health Organization declared COVID-19 a worldwide pandemic. The president announced a travel ban on China and other Asian countries for everyone except US citizens abroad. And the NBA suspended basketball games for thirty days.

* * *

In preparation for her CT scan and MRA Thursday, Joanna was injected with a contrast dye via an IV tube. She felt claustrophobic and freaked out by the clicking and whirring sounds of the donut machine that enclosed her head. Her husband sat in the waiting room, then took her to lunch at Panera Bread.

They went to the Edison shopping mall, where she bought birthday gifts for Dan. She knew he needed clothes for Florida and something more appropriate for Mrs. McCormack's celebration of life. She knew Dan needed to get out. *And he needs to meet this beautiful woman.*

When they got home, her son was watching TV. Cable news covered the governor of New York's daily COVID press conference. The stock markets were tanking due to pandemic fears. Her husband switched on ESPN to find Major League Baseball had canceled its spring training games, and the NHL suspended its hockey season.

* * *

Even though they chuckled at his Boston accent, Sean felt good about his phone interviews. They said the senior manager would still want to meet him in person. Sean suggested a FaceTime call. Both men laughed and said their boss would probably prefer it over Zoom.

Sean said, "Tell'em I'm available tomawrah."

After the interview, Sean called his friend Greg and compared notes. Greg said, "Both managers already spoke to me. They like your experience. I own a premanufactured house in a mobile home park. My girlfriend, Lacy, lives with me. You can sleep in the back room, on the daybed until you get settled in and help with expenses."

"Can't thank ya 'nuff," Sean said.

"Get the job first. Then you'll buy me a rib eye and a case of beer. Ha-ha."

Sean checked Greyhound bus tickets from Boston to Florida. The train from Boston to Orlando was faster and cheaper. And a bus from Orlando to Fort Myers would work.

Chapter 38

Meghan hired Emily, a young neighborhood girl who walks dogs, to watch Bruschi during her mother's celebration of life. Her mom's sister, Elizabeth Baxter, and husband, Walter, arrived last night and stayed at the Indigo Hotel in downtown Fort Myers. They arrived at her parents' condo hours early and tested her patience.

"Nice view," her uncle Walter said, "but it's too confining in a high-rise for me."

Elizabeth said, "We prefer ground level and riding our golf cart at The Villages."

They were snowbirds in Central Florida's sprawling Villages retirement community for six months and lived in Hartford for the other six months to be near their grandchildren. A Yankees fan, Walter enjoyed goading her father about his beloved Red Sox.

Walter boasted, "Mack, the Yankees have Aaron Judge and Stanton. They'll hit a hundred home runs and win the pennant."

"Probably right," her father coughed, then said, "If they even play baseball. COVID has suspended the games."

"Ha, the Chinese Flu," Walter countered. "Everyone knows it's a hoax."

Meghan hated that her father agreed with her overbearing uncle. She changed subjects, "Aunt Elizabeth, have you heard of the DNA website Twenty-three and Me?"

"No, dear. What's that about?"

"They match your DNA with siblings and ancestors. It produces a health history report and shows genetically inherited diseases such as heart failure, cancer, diabetes, etc. I submitted Mom's saliva and my DNA kit."

"Interesting. Did you learn anything?"

"Results take a while. I submitted the kits two weeks ago. Will you excuse me? I must get ready for the celebration."

Her light blue sundress, conservative enough for the sad occasion, fit her fine figure nicely. She opened her mother's jewelry box and chose white pearls to honor her. She'd have to sort out all the jewelry later.

"Lovely sundress," her aunt Elizabeth said. "And that's her favorite pearl necklace."

"Thank you, yes. You can go through her jewelry and take what you like."

"Thank you, dear. But your mother and I always had different tastes. You keep what you need and give the rest to a thrift shop."

"Good idea," she said. *I'll give it to someone who might appreciate it, like Silvia.* "Time to go to the gathering room."

* * *

Dan was bored from being stuck in his parents' condo, watching TV all week. *It's Friday the thirteenth. What could go wrong?*

ESPN announced, "The Boston Marathon is canceled." All major sports were now suspended due to the pandemic. His dad switched to the local news to get the weather forecast.

Breaking news. The mayor of Miami tested positive for COVID-19.

Despite his cabin fever, Dan was reluctant to go with his parents to a celebration of life for a family he'd never met. His father wore beige pants and a sharp-looking casual shirt, and his mom wore a pretty sundress. "You guys look great… but I have nothing to wear," Dan said.

"Early birthday gifts," his mom said, handing him the shopping bags.

He thanked her for the shirts, shorts, bathing suit, and casual shoes.

"Wear the teal shirt with your beige slacks," Mom said, cutting the tag off the shirt.

"Alright. Can I take this sling off?" he asked his father.

"No. You don't want anyone to bump into you there. Maybe after the weekend."

* * *

They arrived early. Dan scanned the large circular ballroom with impressive views of the river and the Edison Bridge behind it. A table was adorned with bouquets and sympathy cards, and another displayed family photos. He told his mother, "I'll check out the pictures."

A green vessel centered the table between a vintage wedding picture of Mr. and Mrs. McCormack and a framed photo of Margaret in her nurse's uniform. There was a family portrait of the four of them with their dog. Perfect smiles on the parents and the son with brown hair; an alluring smile on the taller blue-eyed blond. There was a separate photo of the son with dark shoulder-length hair and a guitar strapped to his back. Dan looked closer at the dude wearing a Bob Seger T-shirt. *This guy looks like old-time rock and roll.*

"My older brother, Mitch," he heard a woman say behind him. He turned. The blond, blue-eyed beauty smiled at him, "He played keyboards in his band."

"Bob Seger fan. I bet he had all the 'Night Moves.'" Dan thought he'd be cute.

"'Against the Wind,'" she said sadly. "He passed away last year."

Oops! "Sorry for your loss," he offered his hand and said, "I'm Dan. Our parents know each other." Her soft hand accepted his condolences. *In those heels, she's a bit taller than Robin.*

"Thank you. I'm Meghan. And thank you for coming."

Wow, she looks like Margot Robbie. He scrambled to hold her attention. "Uhm… what was the name of your brother's band?"

"Mitch and the Mags."

"Like magnets to attract the groupies?" he chuckled.

"MAG Wheels. A takeoff from Mitch Ryder and The Detroit Wheels," she explained. Dan shrugged. *I never heard of them.*

"'Devil with the Blue Dress,'" he heard his father say behind him.

Meghan's eyes strayed from him to his dad. He sized up the shapely woman in her light blue dress. Her white pearls accentuated her conspicuous cleavage. *She's built like Scarlett Johansson.*

"Yes! The Mags covered that song," she said. "Mitch played harmonica and keyboards. They covered J. Geils, too."

"Ah!" his father responded. "'Freeze-Frame' and 'Centerfold.'"

"You know your music," she said to his dad like an angel. Dan imagined her as a centerfold, recalling the J. Geils video on MTV.

"As do you," his dad said. He touched her wrist and said, "So sorry about your mother… How's your father holding up?"

"Thank you! Dad's doing better now," she looked across the room. "He's talking with the condo's board members. He used to be on the board."

"It must have been before we bought here," his dad said and headed toward her father.

His mom stepped up and hugged the blond. "Oh, Meghan! So sorry."

"Thanks for coming, Jo. And the thoughtful fruit basket."

"You're welcome. I love your sundress," his mother said.

The blond turned to him, "So, what happened to your shoulder?"

Dan said, "Rotator cuff surgery."

"And cracked ribs," Mom added.

"Ouch. Did you fall down a flight of stairs?"

"He wasn't drinking," Mom said defensively.

"It was an accident," he said. "Right place, wrong time."

"How long ago?" Meghan asked him.

"Two weeks. Hope to lose this sling by Sunday."

"Should be okay. It's safer to wear it in crowds," replied Meghan.

"Meghan's a physical therapist. She'd know," Mom said.

"Really?" he feigned an expression. "Can't wait to go swimming. When do you think it will be safe to stretch it out?"

"Start on your shoulder soon. Cracked ribs should avoid swimming for another week," Meghan advised.

"Can you help him out?" *Good ole mom came through again.*

"I'm starting a new job a week from Monday. I might be able to drop by your place next week, said Meghan. "Oh, gotta go. I'm getting signaled by Silvia to get the celebration started."

"Thank you," Dan added. "That'd be much appreciated." *Much appreciated!*

The bombshell therapist strode across the room to her father and a petite silver-haired woman he assumed was Silvia.

* * *

Meghan asked her father, "Do you want to say a few words first?"

He kissed her cheek and said, "Take it away, Meg."

"Thank you all for coming. My father and I appreciate the association letting us use this beautiful ballroom."

Her father added, "And a special thanks to Silvia for organizing the refreshments." Meghan hugged the smaller lady. Everyone clapped.

Silvia announced, "To honor memories of Peg, I'll start. Anyone who played mah-jongg with Peg knew what a champion she was. She tutored the newcomers, gave them her quarters to play, and then won them all back. I asked her what she did with all those quarters. She said, 'Jim feeds them to slots machines faster than I can win them.'" Everyone chuckled.

Meghan saw the joy on the faces of others who shared their stories. Sitting in the front row, Dan DeCosta said something to his mother when his dark eyes met Meghan's. *He's a nice-looking young man, but his father is a Hollywood dreamboat.*

She had a thing for older, accomplished men. Allan, her charming former boss, was married with children, but she couldn't resist his playful passes. She preferred the courting, foreplay, and tenderness from mature men over the impatient younger lovers and one-night stands. She'd lost track of her brief relationships with men and women. She smiled at Joanna's husband. Dick smiled back. The tall, broad-shouldered man resembled Jon Hamm but reminded her of Ben Affleck when she heard his Boston accent.

The buffet line diminished, and the alcohol flowed. Meghan and her father made the rounds, thanking everyone. She saved DeCosta's table for last. Her eyes focused on the handsome older gentleman smiling at her, who rose when she approached him.

She said, "Thanks again for coming."

"My pleasure," he said and gave her a gentle hug. She felt flushed.

His son adjusted his sling and said, "Can't wait to get rid of this."

"You will soon enough," she said.

Joanna pulled Meghan aside. "Beautiful tribute to your mother."

"Thank you, Jo," she said, embracing the petite woman.

"Do you think you can help Dan with PT? He's going crazy."

"Your condo's across town, right? I can get there on Monday and maybe Wednesday. Text me the address and copy your son."

"You're an angel," Jo said.

Or a devil in a blue dress, Meghan thought, catching her charming husband smiling at her again.

* * *

Like most Fridays, Khori Chen finished loading her Range Rover and prepared to leave the city for the weekend with Sam. But this time, a car slowed down, and the passengers shouted obscenities and slurs about her Chinese heritage. She flipped them the bird and returned to the apartment.

Sam said, "I need a half hour to finish this release. Then we'll leave for the mountains."

"All loaded up," Khori said. "I'm taking Bulova to do his duty."

She'd become leery about walking in the streets. Her paranoia heightened after the president announced a travel ban on China. Asian Americans were now unfairly targeted for the origin and spreading of the coronavirus.

Traffic was light in their hilly San Francisco neighborhood. Khori adjusted her face mask and hurried behind her dog. Bulova sniffed a lamppost, raised his leg, looked back, and froze.

She heard a voice bellow behind her, "Fuck'n gook, go home!"

An angry man with a shaved head descended on them. Her heart raced. Bulova growled at the deranged-looking guy with faded jeans and scruffy boots. Khori tightened her grip on Bulova's leash.

"Fuck outa here!" yelled the tall wild man. Then he grabbed Khori, threw her down on the concrete sidewalk, and roared, "We don't need the fuck'n Chinko Flu!" He then spat on her and removed his leather belt, "We'll destroy the Kung Flu!"

Khori shielded her head with her hands. Bulova darted at the brute, but he kicked him in the head. Bulova whined as he hit the curb. Khori rolled away, scooped up Bulova, then jumped to her feet. The man swung his belt wildly around his head and laughed as she took off.

"Go back to your country!" he shouted, chasing her.

Khori had a good lead but was slowed because she carried Bulova. She turned the corner onto her street; he was still coming after her. She made it into their building, entered the apartment, put Bulova down, and locked the deadbolt. She peeked out a nearby window at the madman standing by her car.

Poor, battered, and frightened Bulova had peed all over her T-shirt, shorts, and sneakers. Khori ripped off her face mask and didn't respond when Sam asked, "What's wrong?"

She entered the bathroom, undressed, stood under the shower, and cried.

Sam wrapped a towel around Khori and cringed when she saw the bruises on her knees and the raspberry on her forearm.

"What the hell happened?"

"A racist lunatic came after me. Screamed at me to go back to China. He would have beat me and Bulova with his belt if I hadn't run away. But now he knows where we live!"

* * *

Sam called 911 and took photos of Khori's bruises. She then tended to the cut over Bulova's left ear. When the police arrived, Khori explained what happened and described her attacker. Sam thanked the two officers and walked outside with them, where she stood in disbelief.

Sam shouted, "The bastard keyed her car!"

The cops took photos of the Range Rover and added it to their hate crime report. Scratched across the driver's door was *G O H O M E.*

Khori was shaken. Sam drove the Range Rover up to the hillside cabin and played Khori's favorite CD by Melissa Etheridge, but it didn't help. It took the two-hour ride to calm Khori, who begged her to consider vacating her apartment.

"Hate to give it up. It took me two years to get that primo location and rate."

"Your company lets you work from home… things have changed with COVID," Khori pleaded. "We have a reliable internet connection in my cabin. You can do this."

"My lease ends in April; the landlord needs to know by March fifteen if I'll renew."

"That's Monday," Khori said.

"Maybe I'll sublet and net a few bucks. Then, when COVID ends, I'll move back."

"Well, don't expect me to move back with you."

After they settled into their cabin, Sam took a photo of the setting sun from their back deck, which she captioned and posted on the family chat.

All safe here.

She didn't want Khori with her bruises in the photo or Mom asking if they were safe in California. She'd never mention the racist assault. Her mother couldn't handle it after all the tests she'd been through.

Chapter 39

Saturday morning, Joanna splashed her face with water but couldn't clear the blurriness in her drooping right eye. She wrinkled her nose at the lingering scent of bacon and eggs Dick and Dan had eaten. She ate fiber cereal with blueberries and then took her tea to the lanai. Dick's head was buried in the *News-Press*. While sipping coffee, Dan asked, "Mom, what time are our dinner reservations for tonight?"

"Uhm... seven-thirty at Firestones," she replied.

"You changed them?" he asked, then turned to his father, who looked puzzled.

Dick said, "Jo, you booked Izzy's for seven. We discussed this."

"Yeah, Mom. We said seafood and outside seating because of COVID."

She launched her OpenTable app; there was nothing for Firestones but confirmed Izzy's Fish and Oyster House. "Yes. I did book Izzy's at seven. Sorry, I'm in a fog this morning."

Dick got up behind her. "You okay?" he asked, gently massaging her neck and shoulders.

"Better now that I had my tea and fresh air."

Joanna checked Facebook. Silvia had tagged Meghan in a photo standing between Dick and Dan at the celebration of life. Joanna commented on it, "Wonderful tribute last night."

Meghan put a heart on Joanna's comment and replied, "Thanks, Jo. Text me your address and copy him. I'll let you know what time Monday."

* * *

Dick's phone buzzed. He headed to his bathroom for privacy.

"Hey, Lee. What's up?"

"We got the wackos who bombed your old house. Two idiots from Maine will be indicted for domestic terrorism. They won't get any news coverage, so they can't brag about it."

The FBI's special agent in charge of Boston was currently in Fort Myers and invited him to play golf at Legends Country Club.

Dick said, "Sounds good, thanks. Last night, we went to a service for Jim McCormack's wife, Peg."

"The same Margaret McCormack who worked at Emerson?"

"Yes, you have a great memory," Dick said.

"Hey, bring Jack. Always good to see folks from the Boston area."

"He'll appreciate that. We'll see you Tuesday."

Dick returned to the lanai and said to Dan, "I'm going to the gym. Want to join me?"

"Let's do it!"

Dick and his son surveyed the condo's gym. *Quiet and safe for Dan.* A slender woman was running hard on one of the treadmills. His much shorter neighbor, Ted Bates, was pumping iron. Ted, built like a running back, had a full head of hair; no one would ever guess his age. He introduced him to Dan. Ted shook his son's hand and asked, "How's Jo feeling?"

"She's tired. Hasn't been right since the red tide messed up her eye."

"Yeah, Marie said she got worse after the tennis ball hit her in the head."

"Did that happen when I was in Bawstin?"

"No, last month."

Dick wondered why she never mentioned it.

Ted headed for the door. "Dan, go easy on your dad. He can't keep up with young guys."

Dan removed his sling and asked, "How old is Ted?"

"Seventy! The gym rat is a vegan and passionate about our watah and the environment."

"Wow! Ted's in great shape. And so are you, Dad. You're rock solid."

Thanks, Dan. "Considering what you went through, you look good."

"Thanks, Dad. But I'm gonna need your help."

"I'll show you safe arm lifts on the mat. Work on your breathing. No sit-ups. Do leg raisers and scissors for your lower abs. First few weeks, you have to be careful."

"Just light stuff. I can't wait 'til Meghan McCormack starts me on PT."

"Oh? When did she agree to do this?"

"Mom asked her last night for me. Said she'd fit me in a few days next week."

"Lucky guy!" Dick said.

"I know, huh? She's a knockout."

"My Army PT instructor, after shoulder surgery, pushed it back hard. Hurt like hell. I doubt Meghan will be as rough."

Dick's phone had two texts from his wife. The most recent one said:

> Going for a walk. Picking up a few things at Publix. Do you need anything?

He replied.

Sunscreen and Advil

Jo's first was the condo's address in a group text. He didn't recognize the other number.

Must be one of Jo's tennis partners. I wish she'd slow down.

When they returned from the gym, Dick reminded Dan to ice his shoulder and put heat on his ribs. Then Joanna came in, sweaty and red-faced from her walk, carrying a bag with sunscreen and Advil. Puzzled, Dick asked, "Where's the rest?"

She looked at him strangely, "That's all you asked for?"

"Jo, you said you were picking things up for yourself."

She found the list in her pocket. "Oops."

He took the lists. "I'll get them. You drink more water and take a shower. Then rest up for tonight's dinner at Izzy's."

* * *

Saturdays at Lowe's were always busy. When she wasn't working at the cash registers, they trained Rachel in the paint department. The employees wore face masks, but they were optional for customers. A few elderly shoppers wore masks, but most contractors did not. She enjoyed chatting with the rugged-looking contractor who came in regularly.

"Don't you evah get a day off?" she asked the handsome and always polite guy.

He smiled, "Going fishing with my son, Skylar. I get him every other weekend." He showed her a picture of the little guy on his phone.

"Cute kid. Looks like his Dad." *Every other weekend. He must be divorced,* she hoped.

"Thanks, see ya next time," he said.

Rachel left Lowe's, walked to her aunt's salon, and returned a call to her sister. Rebecca said, "Give Ma a call. She wants your new address so she can send a birthday card."

She replied, "You gave her my new number, but she hasn't called. She only wants to send cards because I live with Auntie K."

"No, she's using it as an excuse for you to call her," said Rebecca. "She's heartbroken."

"Okay. You're right." *Somebody has to break the ice,* she thought.

Rachel called her mother and walked along the parking lot. No one answered, so she leaned against a tree for shade and left a voicemail.

"Hi, Ma. It's Rach… uhm, Robin. Becca told you I couldn't stay at her house with Sean stalkin' me. Auntie K offered free room and board." She paused, "I work two jobs. It's what you do when you start a new life. The same thing happened to Auntie K. She and Rawjah started new jobs. They couldn't afford airfare or time off to drive back for Dad's funeral. I hope you can find it in ya heart to fahgive Auntie K. Cuz I'm stuck in the middle here tryin' ta start ovah. Hope to hear from ya soon. Love ya, bye."

Rachel hoped her message about her aunt starting a new life with a new husband would hit home. It's what her mom did when she left for Reno and left Robin to fend for herself.

"Hey, sweety," her aunt said when she entered Cape Cuts. "Roger and I are taking you to Izzy's downtown tonight. You'll love their New England seafood."

Later that evening, Rachel felt good about how she looked in her new beige shorts and low-cut sleeveless red and beige blouse. Roger said, "Parking downtown is impossible during spring break. I'll park in the library. Not many people know about it."

"There's a band playing at Patio de Leon tonight," her aunt said as they enjoyed the warm, balmy air while walking to Izzy's restaurant.

The receptionist said, "Outside table, an hour wait. Inside, thirty minutes."

Roger shook his head, "It's six-fifty now. I'm starving."

"Let's go to 10 Twenty Five," Kelly said. "They have a second-level outside bar."

They strolled the crowded sidewalk and passed restaurants buzzing with diners enjoying food and spirits. Two handsome, well-conditioned guys in tank tops showing off their pecs and guns entered the Lodge Sports bar. Three girls in scanty dresses were reading the menu outside the Blue Sushi restaurant. Everyone looked tanned, fit, and dressed sexy. *It's the weather*, she thought. Attractive couples, young and old, eating al fresco; they looked healthy, happy, and relaxed. She felt it differed from up north, where people seemed rushed for vacation time.

They climbed the stairs to the restaurant's upper level. Kelly snagged a high-top table. It had a clear view of the patio and the band on the stage below. She ate and bopped to the beat of rock and Motown covers by the local band Deb and the Dynamics. Deb, the lead singer, could channel Janice Joplin and Bruce Springsteen while she played guitar.

The talented band with drums, guitars, keyboards, and a brass section featuring multiple saxophone players was dynamic. *Great dancing songs*, she thought, as her aunt and uncle waved back and forth with the beat. The packed patio below had people dancing and whooping it up when Deb launched into Martha and the Vandellas' "Dancing in the Street."

Rachel scoured the crowd, looking for Dan's parents. She'd seen them on Facebook posts and knew they lived in the downtown river district.

Everyone was joyful, digging the music, the warm evening, and loving the moment. But none of those happy faces gave her any hope of finding a way to get in touch with Dan DeCosta.

* * *

Dan protected his sling on the crowded downtown sidewalks. He walked beside his mother; his father trailed them as they passed by Ford's Garage. A boomer couple ate burgers while their poodle sat under their table, drinking from a water bowl. They walked by Capone's Restaurant, where families ate pizza. Two attractive women in skimpy shorts and provocative tops checked Dan out. Another snapped a photo of her gorgeous blond friend with a bulging red tube top.

Gotta love downtown, Dan thought.

Dan looked across the street. A tall redhead flanked on both sides by an older couple was heading in the opposite direction. *Big Red?* He looked again, lifted his tinted sunglasses, and wondered if the oxy he took played tricks on his eyes.

They enjoyed another beautiful evening with perfect weather, dining outside at Izzy's. Mom had a Cosmo and scallops; he and Dad had Stella drafts with their fish 'n chips. Their waitress took their picture, and Mom posted it on the family chat for Sam.

After dinner, they stopped at Scoops Ice Cream. They sat at an outside table across from the colorfully painted historic Arcade Theatre, home of the Florida Repertory Theatre. He kept an eye out for redheads, devoured his ice cream, and enjoyed people-watching. A gray-haired couple walked by. The man's T-shirt said, DON'T ASK HER; his wife's, I SPEAK FLUENT SARCASM.

He relished the endless eye-opening parade of alluring women dressed in steamy warm-weather outfits, highlighting their impressive figures, driving any man crazy who wasn't visually impaired or gay. Fort Myers is so different from up north, where people are covered up nine months out of the year and look pale and out of shape. Here, it's a sexual showcase and fitness contest year-round. Dan savored the last spoonful of chocolate ice cream. *I'm in heaven.*

They walked by Cabo's Cantina, heard music, and stopped at the crowded alleyway that led to Patio de Leon, where a band had drawn crowds. The band rocked, and a woman belted out, "Dancing in the Street."

Dan protected his sling from the crowds strolling to and from the narrow walkway. The band then launched into a perfect rendition of Paul McCartney's "Silly Love Songs." His mother rocked back and forth to the beat. As the brass blared, she yelled, "That's Deb and the Dynamics! Great local band, we love 'em!"

Dad was bopping and singing all the words to the catchy song when Mom lost her balance. Dad grabbed her arm and steadied her. She looked pale and beat. Dad told Dan, "I'd love to listen to them up close, but it's mobbed in there, and everyone will bump into you."

Dad led Mom toward the condo and said, "We'll catch them another time."

"I'm not retired like you. Might not get another time," Dan mumbled. He couldn't help but wonder if Robin had walked by earlier in the direction of the music.

Dan moped behind his parents, who were still singing. He began whistling along with them. *Now, I'll never get this silly song out of my head tonight.*

Chapter 40

Sunday morning, March 14th, Meghan pulled her beige mesh cover-up over her red stringed bikini. She packed a cooler, and Dad put the beach chairs and an umbrella in his Mustang convertible. *Miss you, Mom.* She hugged the biodegradable urn with her mother's precious remains that she'd requested be spread over the water on Marco Island, an hour south of Fort Myers. Silvia accepted lots of her mother's jewelry and agreed to watch Bruschi.

They exited the parking garage and waved to Neil, the bald gentleman at her mom's celebration, who flirted with her and offered to take her to Fort Myers Beach. She hoped to meet a fit older man like him, but not a condo renter who drove a pickup truck. Fort Myers had many millionaires, but she still hadn't met a potential sugar daddy that her Boston friends said was the ticket to paradise in Florida. *Maybe I need to scope out Naples for billionaires.*

They cruised down I-75 in the Mustang with the top down. Dad wore his navy blue Red Sox cap, and her hair was pulled back in a ponytail. She said, "Dad, the EPA says you need thirty days' notice and to be three miles offshore to have a burial at sea for caskets, even ashes."

"The EPA can kiss my ass."

They exited onto Collier Boulevard in Naples. Dad said, "The casino is not far from here. Come with me one day this week."

"I start work the following week. Sorry, and with COVID spreading, I have no desire to gamble with my health in a crowded casino." *Nor should you.*

They crossed the bridge to Marco Island. Her dad parked in a garage under the Marco Walk Plaza. "Later, we can eat at Peg's favorite Italian restaurant, DaVinci's, or the Marco Prime steak house," he said.

They dropped their beach gear on the white sand; her mother's urn was tucked in her beach bag. Dad set up the umbrella. Rows of colored umbrellas were staked in front of high-rise condos and resorts along the Gulf's gorgeous turquoise water. The three-mile-long crescent-shaped beach was fully developed with exclusive properties and enviable sunset views.

Meghan pulled off her cover-up and felt the eyes of the handsome older man sitting beside an attractive blond half his age. She sank her feet into the powdery, sugar-white sand and applied sunscreen. Meghan then walked to the water's edge, snapped photos, handed Dad her phone, and posed for pictures in her shiny red bikini. Her father returned to the umbrella.

With teary eyes hidden behind her sunglasses, she stood ankle-deep in the soothing water and gazed beyond the swimmers and the boats to the Gulf's horizon. Gentle rippling waves encircled her ankles as her feet sank deeper into the soft, wet sand while coral fragments and shiny grains receded into the sea. She felt her mother's spirit when she picked up a keepsake, a pretty multicolored seashell. *It's beautiful, Mom. I see why you loved Marco Island.*

Meghan then joined Dad under the umbrella, who had a cold beer in his hand.

"Dad, we could rent a parasail to spread her ashes over the Gulf," she said, snapping a photo of a couple floating high above the water on a parasail towed by a speed boat.

"Meg, you won't get me up there. And your mother won't care."

She posted several pictures on Facebook and captioned them: Marco memories for Mom.

"When was the last time you and Mom came here?"

"Four years ago—we spent a weekend at the Marriott Hotel for our anniversary. It's too expensive now; it's been renovated into a fancy JW Marriott."

"Is that why Mom wants her ashes spread here?"

"No," he chuckled. "She wanted to buy our retirement home here. We rented a place for a week and looked at several condos. They were too expensive and too small. We wouldn't have had any room for you and Mitch to visit."

She sighed. *I miss Mitch.*

"But you compromised, Dad. You bought in Fort Myers, an hour away."

"Where the Red Sox spring training games are, ha, ha," he cleared his throat. "She wanted Marco since the eighties when she came here on hospital boondoggle."

"When shall we honor her wish?"

He removed his Red Sox cap and held her hand, "It's low tide. Let's walk out now."

They waded out in the warm water and bumped against each wave until it splashed against her bosom. Meghan handed the urn to her dad and said, "Say a few words for Mom."

They faced the setting sun and warm southerly breeze when he raised the container and cleared his throat, "Ashes to ashes, dust to dust, as you always said, Peg, it's Marco or bust."

And with that, Dad scattered her ashes, and she did too with teary eyes.

"Rest in Peace, Mom," said Meghan. She then hugged her dad. His heart beat rapidly as he leaned heavily on her shoulder.

They returned to the soft sandy beach and sat down to dry off.

"Meg, I hope you find your mate and paradise sooner than we did."

"Thanks, Dad. So do I."

They loaded the Mustang, changed their clothes in the public restroom, and climbed the mall's steps to the Marco Walk Plaza. Several families and older couples wore facemasks. They passed by a Roman-style water fountain, surrounded by five restaurants. They dined outside at DaVinci's, where a handsome young server with a charming Italian accent took their orders.

"Here's to Mom," she said. They toasted with red wine and topped off their delightful entrées with Tiramisu.

"Peg's favorite," her dad said.

Delish, Mom.

She drove, her dad slumped in the passenger's seat; a sense of sadness and closure surrounded them on the solemn ride home.

* * *

Aunt Kelly said to Rachel, "We're going to Miceli's. Sunday's happy hour is from eleven to seven. They have outside dining and a live band."

"Might be our last chance to get out for a while," Roger started.

Kelly replied, "COVID canceled Tuesday's Saint Paddy's Day downtown celebration."

"A shame," Rachel said from the back seat. *I was looking forward to partying with my Irish aunt Kelly and Rogah.*

She forgot about COVID when she saw Miceli's outdoor tables with a view of the intercoastal waterway behind the thatched-covered stage where the band Stringtown was playing. *Wicked cool place.*

Roger ordered a bucket of Coors to enjoy with their dishes and the band as they performed Pink Floyd's "Wish You Were Here." She wished Dan were here with her.

The frontman, Kenny, tipped his cowboy hat and softly sang Eddy Arnold's "You Don't Know Me." Roger took Kelly's hand and led her to the small, crowded dance floor. Rachel watched them slow-dance gracefully. She was happy for them but sad she didn't have a man to hold her close on the dance floor.

* * *

Sean accepted the HTS offer, which required a drug test when he got to Florida. He planned to take a train from Boston to Orlando, then a Greyhound to Fort Myers. His uncle Bill said, "Jet Blue has a one-way ticket to Fort Myers cheaper if you fly on Tuesdays." It was cheaper; he'd arrive in four hours instead of two days.

He called HTS, and they scheduled his drug test for Wednesday, March 18, in North Fort Myers. He'd start work the following Monday for his HVAC training. Greg said he'd pick him up at the airport Tuesday at 6:30 p.m. They'd celebrate Saint Paddy's Day with his half-Irish girlfriend, Lacy.

It would be the fourth anniversary of the day he met Robin at the Gaelic club on Saint Patrick's Day. *Must be an omen*, he thought. He couldn't wait to see her.

Chapter 41

Monday morning, Dick watched Joanna apply her makeup. He hoped they wouldn't be late for her appointment. His phone dinged, a text from an unknown number.

I'll be there in thirty minutes. Does that work for you?

Dick replied:

Depends. Who is this?

Meghan, for your PT.

He replied that she had the wrong guy. He'd pass the info to Dan. He added Meghan to his contact list and gave Dan her number.

* * *

Meghan had the number Jo gave her. But her husband replied, not Dan.

This is Dick. You want Dan. I'll let him know.

No, I want Dick. Meghan chuckled. *It's been a while since I've had one.*

She edited the contact's name from Dan D to Dick DeCosta. *Got you now, and I know where you live.* She replied: Sorry, Dick. Thank you!

Moments later, she received a text from his son.

Hi Meghan. Dan here. C U in 30 in our lobby. What r u driving?

OK, Dan. Blue BMW X5

Meghan filled her tote bag with two water bottles, a clipboard, stretch bands, a thirty-inch PVC pipe capped on both ends, and her yoga mat. *This is a home visit.*

* * *

Dan put on his gym shorts, tank top, and sling. His dad said his initial PT would hurt, and he didn't want to look like a wimp for Meghan. He swallowed an oxy and put the vial on the vanity next to his muscle relaxers. *She's a doctor; maybe she'll prescribe more.*

He saw Meghan's BMW pull in from the lobby. The ponytailed blond, carrying a tote bag, wore black leggings and a matching top zippered halfway down, revealing her formidable cleavage.

"Thank *you* for your time and professional guidance," he said, leading her to the elevator.

"Happy to help, especially new friends from Boston," she said with a smile.

Dan felt warm. "Do you want to use my folks' place or the gym where they have mats?"

"Their place is fine for now. Gyms can be too crowded and distracting."

* * *

Meghan's quiet patient entered an elevator code and selected twenty-seven.

Can't wait to see Jo's place and her husband. She stood next to Dan as he looked down at his feet. The mirror on the elevator's wall reflected how tall and handsome the guy was. She thought he looked pretty buff in his tank and shorts, considering he'd been in a sling for two weeks. The elevator stopped and opened to a nicely decorated private lobby.

"Oh, wow!" she said, following him inside. Ten-foot-high glass sliders to a lanai and panorama vistas drew her deeper into the expansive great room.

"*Gorgeous* place."

"Thanks! My parents love it, and I'm getting spoiled here."

"I bet. Are they around?" *This place is enormous.*

"Dad took my mom to the doctor. She's had blood tests and MRIs scheduled."

"Oh. Is everything OK?" *She never said anything.*

"Not sure… I overheard them say it's not Parkinson's. But they've kept things to themselves." He frowned.

"Sorry to hear that. Tell her I was asking for her."

Meghan looked around their sweeping, tastefully decorated great room. A beautiful bronze sculpture of a nude couple caught her eye. She ran her fingers across the smooth quartz kitchen counter and looked at the wood-plank tiled floor.

"Where should we roll out my mat?"

He shrugged, "Uhm, maybe my Dad's study." He headed down a long-tiled hallway.

"We'll need pillows," she said, walking behind him.

"Okay," he turned into a back bedroom.

"Or we can use the floor in here," she said. "The scatter rug over the tile should be comfortable." *The bed's too soft. And I don't want him to get the wrong idea.*

Meghan placed her bag down, spread her mat, and caught him looking at her in the dresser's mirror. She gathered throw pillows from the king-size bed and put them on her mat before she instructed him to lie down.

"Thank you," he said when she helped him roll onto his side and back. She reached across him to grab a pillow and inadvertently brushed her right breast against his sling.

"Thank *you*," he said when her breast nearly touched his face as she lifted his head and slid a pillow under it.

Meghan removed his sling when he said thank you again. *He's as sweet as his lovely mother and as handsome as his hunky father.*

She pointed to her clipboard, "This has passive phase one exercises, active phase two exercises, plus phase three resistance routines. I'll demonstrate a few reps for you."

Meghan showed him how to lean over and circle his arm clockwise and counterclockwise. "Hold on to a chair to keep your balance," she said.

She showed him how to use his dominant hand to move his injured arm, first with the elbow bent and then straight, so he could feel the difference in the weight at each progressive angle. Dan picked it up quickly.

"Doing good…You take direction well," she said.

"Thank you, you're way too kind."

"Oh?" Meghan pulled out her PVC pipe and tapped it in her other hand like a cop with his baton. He raised his eyebrows and smiled.

"Hold this with both hands. Use your good arm to raise the other one." She went through all the motions as his eyes followed attentively.

The room was getting warm. Meghan took off her jacket and turned on the overhead fan. She demonstrated the pipe routines she typically did in a rehab center. She enjoyed performing for him in his bedroom.

Meghan then knelt next to him and helped him do three reps each. "Work your way up to twelve reps three times a day."

"I thought you'd push me much harder," he said, lowering the pipe to his waist, which drew her attention to the bulge in his gym shorts.

You're getting hard! "I'll show you phase two, which is much harder. Did your doctor give you muscle relaxers?" *I should have asked earlier. Poor guys all worked up. So am I now.*

"Yes. They're on the bathroom vanity." He pointed the pipe at the door.

She entered the bathroom and read the vial's script. *Metaxalone will kill any erection.* Then read the other prescription, *oxycodone, hate this shit.*

She returned and helped him, "Let's sit you up."

He winced in pain.

"Ribs still hurt?"

He nodded.

She opened a water bottle and handed it to him with the muscle relaxer.

"Thanks! You're a doctor, right?"

She nodded.

"Can you write refills for my meds?"

"I start at the rehab center next week. I can prescribe muscle relaxers. It makes patients more flexible in their routines." *Don't even think about oxy, or I'll shove this pipe up your butt.*

"I got enough for a week. Can you reorder both scripts for the pain in my ribs?"

She shoved the PVC pipe in her bag and put on her jacket. "We're done."

"I'm… Uh." He grunted as he struggled to get to his feet.

She placed the pillows neatly on his bed. *Stay cool for the sake of his parents.*

Meghan then rolled up her mat, avoided eye contact, and gave him the checklist, "You can use this for routines. I'll send you videos as well."

"Uhm… should I go to the rehab center next week and—"

Not a good idea. "I'll check with the center and get back to—"

"I'm sorry," he said. "We got off to a bad start. I uh—"

"You need more than PT help," she said, leaving the room. "You have to get off the oxy. Opioids are trouble. They killed my brother!"

"Oh, no. I'm *so* sorry," he said, following her down the hall and to the elevator lobby.

Dan pushed the call button for her. "I'm sorry about everything," he said, looking down at his feet. The elevator door opened. "Please don't mention this to my parents."

Meghan replied, "They have enough to worry about. *Deal with it.*"

As the elevator doors closed, she heard him shout, "I will! *Count on it!*"

She was livid. The fool thought she'd feed his oxy habit—and she was angry with herself for not handling it better. She'd let Joanna down. Meghan walked to her car and thought about Mitch. *I did the right thing.* Hopefully, it's not too late for Dan.

She drove home with mixed emotions. She felt used by the DeCostas and guilty about volunteering her services to pry into Jo's family. *It's all moot now.* Any chance of satisfying her curiosity and growing desires for Dick DeCosta had floated down the Caloosahatchee River and into the Gulf of Mexico.

Chapter 42

Joanna and her husband were seated in Dr. Royce's office. He turned on the monitor behind him and explained, "The slide on the left is your angiogram."

He pointed, "This bulge. It's an unruptured artery... a cerebral aneurysm."

"A brain aneurysm," her husband said.

The doctor nodded, "It's six millimeters. Fortunately, we found this now. It has probably been there for several years and is growing faster now."

"What triggered that?" Joanna asked.

"Usually head trauma, perhaps the infection in your eye. Alcohol, high blood pressure, and stress can all accelerate growth."

"What happens if it ruptures?"

"You'll have blinding headache pain, nausea, vomiting, loss of vision and consciousness. It requires surgery within twenty-four hours to stop the hemorrhaging. Or you—"

"We get it," her husband said.

Joanna felt nauseous and frightened. "How do we treat it?" she asked, squeezing Dick's hand.

"We monitor your blood pressure, symptoms, and its growth. Hopefully, it stabilizes. Otherwise, surgery is required to protect against hemorrhaging. I recommend you sign authorizations to activate in an emergency."

"Invasive or noninvasive surgery?" Dick asked.

"Preferably noninvasive as it lowers the risk of brain damage. An endovascular coiling procedure via a catheter through the groin area is 80 to 85 percent effective. The coil will prevent rebleeding."

"Can I get nitrous oxide before they put the catheter in?" Joanna asked. It relaxed her with pelvic exams.

"We can do that along with the general anesthesia."

"What's the percentage of rebleeding with invasive?" Joanna hoped for better options.

"Surgical clipping, close to 98 percent. We put in a titanium clip to stop it from growing. But craniotomy has a four to six-month recovery. A much higher risk of brain damage. How much varies for each person's age and the size and location of the aneurysm."

"How long is the recovery period for the coiling procedure?" Dick asked.

"Two to three days in the hospital. A week or more of healing… unless there are complications."

Joanna said, "We have time to consider these options and complications."

"Yes, unless your pain and symptoms worsen," said Dr. Royce. "I'm changing your blood pressure medication. The pharmacy will have it ready and a kit for you to monitor your pressure and heart rate. Keep a journal."

"Any special diets?" her husband asked. He handed her a brochure.

"Avoid caffeine and alcohol. It's also pollen season. Take antihistamines to avoid sneezing. People can rupture by blowing their nose too hard."

"Pollen's up. It's hot and dry," Dick said. "Wildfires everywhere across the country."

She frowned at him, always worried more about climate change than his family.

"Can I play tennis and do watah aerobics?"

"Strenuous activities are risky. Be careful and keep an eye on your blood pressure."

* * *

Dick picked up Jo's meds and a blood pressure monitor at the pharmacy and then drove her home in silence to keep her blood pressure from rising. She'd have to avoid alcohol and tennis. *She'll decide when to discuss her options and lifestyle changes.* His heart ached for her.

She took her meds and went to his study to research brain aneurysms. He knew she'd print the info and stick it in a folder like bills or travel plans. He hated her old killing trees habits. *Bite my tongue about the printer.*

Dick got a call from his snowbird tenants, who always stayed through March. They were worried about COVID travel restrictions, packed up, and were headed back to Illinois today. He told them to leave the keys on the kitchen counter and tell the front desk they'd checked out.

Good. He'd planned to go through it, make repairs, then put it on the market.

He found Dan on the lanai, "How'd it go with Meghan?"

"Great," Dan showed him the exercise list. "Do you have any PVC pipes? I need one for my PT routines."

"I'll find something in the storage cage." He used a broomstick after his shoulder surgery.

"So, did she push you hard?"

"Not really. I laid on her yoga mat in your study with pillows, and she demonstrated the exercises. She'll send me video routines. I'll need your help. She starts a new job next week."

"Happy to help. Don't play the TV loud. Mom has to watch her blood pressure."

* * *

Meghan ate a salad for lunch and hoped Jo wasn't dealing with a severe illness. She wanted to contact her but didn't want to pry or bring up her son's PT. She sent Dan a text with three video links.

Vids I mentioned. Get help with them. Good luck. MM

He replied: Thanks again! I'm sorry. I promise I won't let you down. DD
Hope so, for your sake and your parents.

With her mother gone, she'd use the gym and pool more. She put on her red Victoria's Secret bikini, applied sunscreen, and pulled on a sheer cover-up. She sat on the lounge chair and opened a Nora Roberts novel, *An Irish Wish.* Several older people gathered at the back end of the pool. A mother sat at the edge, watching her two little girls play a game she and her brother Mitch did as kids.

"Marco!" The taller girl teased.

"Polo!" The little one screamed.

Meghan's mind drifted to Marco Island. She wondered about her mother's boondoggle there with others from Emerson Hospital. That's when she'd found it convenient to slip away with her boss, Dr. Allan Hansen.

"How are you today?" asked the short elderly gentleman in a straw hat, who had attended her mother's celebration.

"Fine, thanks. Gorgeous day."

"Perfect," he grinned.

She felt his eyes scan her body. "I saw Mack this morning. He wasn't happy they canceled the St. Patrick's Day celebration. Said he's going where the Irish go to change their luck. A-ha."

Meghan called her father. "Dad, where are you?"

"Hi, Meg. Seminole Casino. Is everything okay?

"No. I mean… Yes. But why didn't you tell me you were going there?"

"You said you had PT with Dick's boy. How'd it go?"

"Fine. He's all set. I heard St. Paddy's Day is canceled. I wanted to party tomorrow," Megan said with disappointment.

"Me too. Good thing Dick invited me to play golf with his old Army buddy."

"When? where?" Meghan was intrigued.

"Tomorrow. A Boston cop. He has a condo at Legends Country Club in Fort Myers."

"Wish I could get in a round of golf before I start working," replied Meghan.

"Want me to ask Dick if you can join us?"

"That would be great, Dad!" *Really great.*

The mother toweled off her little Marco Polo girls before they left the pool area. *Ahh, peace.* She picked up the book and found her place: *An Irish Wish.*

Chapter 43

Dick found Jo on her computer in his study. He gently massaged her neck and said, "Our snowbird tenants left today. They're worried about COVID. I'm going to check on repairs and shut the watah off. You gonna be alright?"

"I'm fine. Go."

He kissed her forehead. "Want me to bring dinner home?"

"I'm not hungry. Get something for you and Dan."

I'll call her later.

He took the elevator up eighteen floors to his rental unit. The tenants' keys were on the granite counter. He shut the water main off in the utility room. Furnished with all new amenities, it wouldn't take much to get this condo ready for sale. With Jo running up medical bills, he wanted to eliminate this mortgage and net out more emergency cash.

He started his repair list. The living room needed minor paint touch-up. The TV worked and was left on the weather channel, showing frightening footage of wildfires in California and thousands evacuating from their homes. There were tornado warnings, torrential rains, and flash flood warnings across the country. The weather *always seemed extreme now.*

The master bedroom's toilet needed a new flapper and fill valve. The condo's second master bedroom and bath were in better shape, and the TV worked. Cable news had COVID-19 spreading, and New York City hospitals were filling up. He shut it off. What a scary time.

He looked out the window at the community pool between the two high-rise towers. From 180 feet above, it was hard to recognize people, but he did make out a shapely woman in a red bikini reading a book. As he took in the beautiful scene, his phone startled him.

"Hey, Mack."

The red bikini dipped into the swimming pool.

"Dick, are we still on for golf at The Legends tomorrow?"

"Yep. Eight tee time."

The swimmer stepped out of the water onto the pool deck.

"Think he'll mind if we add another golfer?" Mack asked.

"A private club booked solid in snowbird season…" The woman in the bikini squeezed water from her hair. "Don't know if they'll squeeze in another thirty minutes for a fourth player."

"Meg wants to play golf before she starts work next week," explained Mack.

Really! "I'll check with Lee and get back to you," replied Dick.

He called Grisham, who answered on the third ring, "Mister D. How are you?"

"Great, Lee. What are you up to?" Dick paced through the other rooms in his condo.

"Sipping a cold one by the pool with my wife. You ready for eighteen holes tomorrow?"

"Can't wait. I know it's short notice, but Mack wants to bring his daughter along."

"Hmm. Be faster if we play a foursome. Us against them."

"Sounds good. Thanks, G Man!"

Dick called Mack, "All set. I'll pick you up outside your lobby at seven."

He then grabbed the keys on the counter and realized the tenants hadn't left the parking garage clicker. Dick took the elevator to the lobby to check with Jessica, the receptionist.

"Yes, they dropped off the clicker," Jessica said, turning to fetch it from a cabinet.

Dick then held the lobby door open for an elderly lady carrying shopping bags. A youthful, high-pitched voice followed her, "Hold, please."

Dick continued to do so.

"Thank you!" the woman exclaimed. Then she slipped by him with damp blond hair wrapped in a sheer, accentuating a shapely red bikini.

Their eyes met. *Yikes! It's Meghan.*

"Oh, Dick! Thanks."

"You're welcome," he said, returning to the lobby desk.

Meghan lingered, "Guess I'll see you tomorrow." She smiled with a raised eyebrow.

"I'll pick you up at seven," he said.

Jessica lowered her eyes to hide her eavesdropping.

"We tee off at eight, right?" Meghan asked.

"Yes. A foursome. You and your Dad against Lee Grisham and me."

"Looking forward to it," Meghan said as she walked off.

The receptionist grinned as she handed Dick the garage clicker. He hoped her smirk wouldn't spread unfounded rumors.

Dick stopped at a deli and ordered meatball subs for himself and Dan and a small tuna for Jo. *She's got to eat something.*

Then his phone dinged. A text from Sam.

Dad, I emailed you my lease. Need to know if I can sublet.
Been Busy, Sam. I'll look it over and call you later.
Thanks. I need to let the landlord know today.

Thanks for the short notice, Sam. He hadn't downloaded his emails since he took Jo to the doctor this morning. Sam sent the lease and needed advice as it also affected Khori. Dick then read an email from Clay and Bakari Bashir, CEO of the startup he promised to invest in. He also had to review and digest the financials and sales projections to prepare for a conference call tomorrow with a venture capital firm. They'll need his cash commitment, or the VC will pass. *Damn, I shouldn't have wasted the afternoon at the rental condo.*

* * *

Dan noticed his mom was resting in her bedroom. Earlier, she'd been working on her computer and printing many things. He entered the study and spotted a manila folder by his dad's closed laptop with a sticky note from Mom.

Dick, info on options and side effects. Discuss later.

He opened the folder and scanned the info inside. Mom had underlined paragraphs on different surgical procedures for brain aneurysms. *Christ, no wonder she has to watch her blood pressure. She could end up a vegetable.*

Dan got a headache reading about the danger of ruptured aneurysms and surgery side effects. He rubbed his sore shoulder, went to his bathroom, grabbed the oxy, and thought about his promise to Meghan. Dan took three Advil instead.

* * *

Dick sat on the lanai with Dan and Jo as they ate their subs and drank pink lemonade. It was 3:10 p.m. on the West Coast. He'd promised Sam he'd get back to her about the lease. But he also had to review the financials Clay Marshall sent to prepare for tomorrow afternoon's call with the VC firm. *Gonna be a long night.*

"I left the options info on your desk," Jo said.

"Insurance options?" he deflected so Jo would get the hint.

"Yeah," she nodded.

"Okay. I'll get to it later."

"Dad, have you seen the three PT videos I forwarded you?"

Not yet. He shook his head.

"I'd like to start on phase one PT tomorrow morning," his son implored.

"Uhm, I promised Mack I'd play golf with him. I'll be back by midday. But then I have a conference call for a green startup, so it'll have to be a short PT session. Sorry, Dan."

His son frowned and looked out at the river. His wife wrinkled her nose, got up, and entered the condo.

What's the most important thing to do in the next five minutes? Dick read Sam's lease and told Jo he needed to get his clubs in the storage cage. He found an adjustable curtain rod beside his golf gear, perfect for Dan's PT. He called Sam and paced inside the parking garage. He told her she could sublet the one-bedroom apartment with the owner's written permission, but she couldn't make any money due to rent control.

"Renew the lease unless or save for a future purchase," he advised.

Sam said, "If I renew, it will offend Khori and ruin our relationship. She won't go near the neighborhood. Asians are being bullied COVID crap."

"I see, tough call," he told her. "But I like to keep my options open."

"Whatever," she sighed.

He'd renew it and keep it a secret. He hoped she wouldn't regret giving up her place if things didn't work out with Khori.

Dick changed the subject, "How close are you guys to the wildfires?"

"Close enough to see and smell smoke; we wear facemasks outside now." Then Sam pivoted, "How's mom doing? She told me she had MRIs."

"She's struggling to control her stress, and it's impacting her high blood pressure."

"What's causing it?"

"It started with red tide and eye infections. Then worries about her tests, Dan's nightmare, and COVID. It's all taken its toll. She has to cut back on tennis and alcohol."

"Geezus… Don't mention Khori's problems or the wildfires to her."

"I won't. But, uh… It'd be good if you could come visit soon."

"Yeah. But Khori will say I abandoned her."

"Compromise. Move in with her. Then come visit. Maybe she will, too."

"Can't make any promises." *I know you can't, but family comes first.*

Dick gave Dan the curtain rod for his PT. He then spent a few hours absorbing the financials to prepare for the VC call. Jo was sleeping when he got to look at the file she'd left him. Both options concerned him. He went to bed and prayed Jo would remain stable and Sam would be safe. He also hoped she'd come to Florida soon because time wasn't on Jo's side.

Chapter 44

After five hours of sleep, Dick showered, shaved, and dressed in his St. Patrick's Day golf attire: tan shorts, a green polo shirt, and a tan cap that said 'Go Green' in emerald green letters. With coffee to go, he drove across town. Upon his arrival, Mack and his attractive daughter were waiting outside the twin high-rise buildings with their golf bags.

"Top o' the morning," Mack greeted Dick.

He loaded their gear in his SUV. Meghan took the other back seat, and her dad rode shotgun.

"Have you played at Legends?" Meghan caught Dick's eye in his rearview mirror.

"It'll be my first time. I recently hooked up with Lee, an old military buddy."

Mack asked, "How does a Boston cop afford a second home and country club fees?"

"Lee's wife inherited the house at Legends from her father, Bob Adams—an attorney from Newton."

"Luck of the Irish," Mack said, adjusting his green Boston Celtics cap.

They met and shook hands with Lee Grisham, the strong six-four heavy hitter in great shape. Dick rode with Lee in his golf cart, and Meghan drove her father in the other cart.

Meghan approached the tee in her snug white shorts and emerald green top, with her blond ponytail sticking out the rear of her white cap. She hit her opening drive down the middle of the fairway. Dick and Lee were surprised at how far it traveled.

"Outstanding form," Lee said to Dick.

Perfect, he thought.

"Great drive, Meg," said her dad.

She said, "The ball carries further in warm Florida air." She then smiled at Dick to step up to the tee.

Dick said to Lee, "You go first."

Lee put all of his 240 pounds behind his drive, which Dick figured went another seventy yards further than Meghan's.

Meghan was amazingly competitive and remarkably poised all morning. Dick matched Mack on their drives and puts. When Lee wasn't taking calls from his office, he coached them throughout the match. Everyone congratulated one another for shooting respectable high nineties except Lee, who scored eighty-seven on the par-four, eighteen-hole course. Lee invited them to the clubhouse for an Irish lunch and a St. Paddy's Day drink.

They headed to the clubhouse in separate carts. On the way, Lee told Dick, "She's not just a pretty face, she's pretty good."

"Well, she's a doctor. She's had a lot of practice. Ha-ha."

"And her mother's a nurse, not as attractive but equally tough," Lee said. "We couldn't get anything out of her. She kept claiming HIPPA laws."

"I didn't know you questioned Margaret during your investigation."

"We wouldn't be playing golf today if you hadn't tipped us off," Lee smiled at him.

"How's that?" Dick asked the hefty special FBI agent.

"I met Jackie on that case. Six years later, she married me."

"Never realized that." *At least something good came about from that regrettable period*, he thought. "By the way, I told Mack you were a cop from Bawstin."

"Close enough," Lee said as they exited the golf cart.

Lee was bigger than life and well-known at the country club. They sat at Lee's reserved table overlooking the green. Dick sat between Mack and Lee and across from Meghan. His mind couldn't shed the vision of her in a red bikini.

"Thank you for everything, Lee," Meghan said. "You've saved Saint Paddy's Day!"

"God luv ya!" Mack said.

Dick knew Meghan and her dad noticed Lee carrying different phones in separate pockets. When Lee stepped away from the table to take a call, she asked Dick, "You and Lee were in the military together—what branch?"

"Army. We did basic training together. I became a medic, and he joined the MPs."

They sipped Irish spirits as they waited for their lunch to arrive. This time, Dick's phone went off. It was a text from Clay Marshall: their conference call was canceled due to COVID-19. *I'll call him later.*

Meghan asked Lee, "How long have you played on this course?"

"We vacationed here nine years with my father-in-law. He passed away, so my wife took ownership. Now we're snowbirds. I can work remotely, and the airport is ten minutes away."

Mack commented, "Your father-in-law was a lawyer in Newton?"

"Until the day he died," Lee said. "He was flying home on business when the cabin's air pressure caused him to have a brain hemorrhage upon descent at Logan. DOA at Mass General."

"My God, what a horrible way to go," Meghan said. Her eyes widened when Dick jumped up from his chair.

"Excuse me! I have to return a call," Dick exclaimed. *I gotta make sure Jo doesn't drink.*

He moved safely out of earshot and called Jo. No answer, so he called Dan, "Where's your mother? She's not answering her phone."

"In the shower. She's upset. COVID canceled the Miami Open, which she and Marie had tickets for. Marie and Ted offered to take us to Pinchers for lunch."

Misery likes company, Dick thought. *And Pinchers has two-for-one drinks all day.*

"Great. Uhm… make sure your mother doesn't have any alcohol."

"Okay, Dad. Don't worry."

Easy for you to say. Marie drinks like a fish, and so will Jo.

He called Ted and left a message: "Ted, thanks for taking Jo to lunch. She's on blood pressure meds, which can't be mixed with alcohol. Please keep an eye on her."

Now, back to business. Dick called Clay, "What's up? Who has COVID?"

"Hi, Dick. Charles Canfield, the managing director, is in ICU. Everyone in his VC firm is quarantined. They got COVID from a biotech conference in Boston."

"Geez, that's awful… I'm sorry, Clay. But for now, I'm hesitant to invest until we see how COVID impacts all VC."

"I understand, Dick," Clay said with disappointment.

Dick returned to the table, apologized, and explained how COVID canceled his meeting with a Boston VC firm.

"No wonder you turned pale as a ghost," Meghan said. "My former colleagues at the Lahey Clinic are worried about COVID, too."

Dick nodded, "Yeah, I need another drink."

"We all do," Lee said, waving at his attendant. "ESPN said Tom Brady left the Patriots. He signed with Tampa Bay."

"Traitor!" Mack shouted. "How can the Irish GOAT leave us? And on Saint Paddy's Day. Make mine a double." His face turned beet red. Meghan touched Mack's arm to calm him.

Lee put their tasty lunch on his country club tab. Then, Meghan had their server take group photos. Dan assumed she posted them on Facebook on the ride home.

Still buzzing from their lunch, Mack insisted he join them for a drink in their condo. Dick didn't want to disappoint his mourning Irish friend on Saint Paddy's Day or his shapely daughter, so he agreed. Upon arrival, she excused herself to freshen up as Dick followed Mack and his dog to the couch on their lanai. Dick stroked Bruschi's shiny black fur.

When Meghan joined them, her sleeveless, low-cut top drew his attention, especially when she leaned over and placed a bottle of Jameson and three shot glasses on the coffee table.

She then reached up and pulled the chain on the ceiling fan as Dick's eyes moved from her perfect rack to her lovely face. Meghan then adeptly squeezed in between him and her father. Mack poured the Jameson into their glasses and called for a toast. With their glasses raised, Mack said with a tear in his eye, "To Peg, up above in Irish heaven."

Dick felt the sting in the back of his throat as the smooth Irish whiskey warmed everything it coated on the way down. *Nice.* He also felt Meghan's right leg brushed against his left calf. *Whoa.* The screened-in lanai felt much warmer. Dick shifted in his seat. Meghan then put her shot glass next to his and brushed his forearm with another subtle move.

"Forget about namin' the next dog, Brady," Mack bellowed. "He's a traitor."

Meghan nodded and leaned closer to Dick when she rubbed Bruschi's head.

"Look on the bright side," Dick offered, "Now we get to watch Brady play in Florida."

"You still going to root for him?" She asked, moving her right hand from Bruschi to his left leg above his knee.

"Um, sure. I want him to win every game to add to his legacy," Dick said. "Except when he plays the Patriots."

Everyone laughed, and Bruschi barked. Meghan then patted Dick's thigh and squeezed it.

"To da Patriots," Mack slurred and overfilled their glasses again.

"And to the Red Sox," Meghan raised her glass and smiled at Dick, "For bringing us together." She threw her shot back in one gulp.

Dick swallowed half, then downed the rest. He wondered if her subtle overtures were the booze or his imagination. *Both*, he concluded. Beads of sweat clung to his polo shirt as he looked up at the ceiling fan, willing it to go faster. *I need to hydrate and compose myself.*

"Could I trouble you for some water?" he asked.

"No trouble at all," she said, placing her right hand on his shoulder to boost herself from the couch. Her long blond hair fluttered in the fan's breeze, casting an image like a swimsuit model in a photo shoot. *Mercy.*

"Dad, do you want anything?" Meghan asked.

"Cold Bud… thanks, Meg."

Bruschi followed her inside.

"To the Celtics," Mack poured booze in his glass, then Meghan's. Dick covered his glass with his palm. *No more.*

"Thank you," Dick said when she returned and placed two tall glasses of ice water on the table. While Mack opened his beer, she squeezed back into position between them. Dick gulped his water.

"To da Bruins!" Mack drunkenly shouted as he reached for Dick's shot glass. He put his hand over it again.

"Sorry," Dick said. "I'm Irish only one day of the year. Can't keep up with ya."

"I can't either, Dad," said Meghan. Then she expertly rubbed her dad's back with her left hand while she stroked Dick's bare knee with her right hand. *Yikes, she's a handful.*

Saved by the bell. Dick pulled his phone from his shorts and looked at Dan's family chat post, a caption intended for Sam.

Happy St. Patrick's Day from Fort Myers

He eyed the picture of Dan standing behind Jo, who was sitting next to Marie and Ted. They were all wearing their green at Pinchers restaurant with a view of the river behind them. He felt Meghan's eyes on him when he enlarged the picture. There were two beer mugs near Ted and two margarita glasses in front of each woman. *Two-for-ones. Dammit!* Dick stood up.

"It's been great," he said. "Thank you for your hospitality." He shook Mack's hand.

"Thank *you*, buddy," Mack staggered. "You're a good man."

Meghan followed him through the condo. When they reached the elevator foyer, she said, "We had a great time today. Thanks, it meant a lot to us."

"My pleasure," Dick said, then pushed the elevator call button.

Meghan swiftly grabbed his left wrist with one hand, put her other hand on his right hip, and said sweetly, "You *are* a good man."

"Thanks," said Dick. He hugged her gently, but she held him tight. "You're a great daughter."

Meghan buried her head in his chest and hugged him even tighter. His hands moved methodically from her shoulder blades down her spine. He then felt Meghan press her breast against his chest as his fingertips gently traced their way down the curve in her lower back. Meghan's soft hands caressed his back in circles as her breathing got heavier. Then, the elevator finally stopped on their floor. Dick lurched from her grasp and into the open elevator.

"Take care of Mack," he said. Before the door closed, he looked at her, expecting a warm smile on her pretty face, but saw only sadness.

When he got to his car, he considered calling Ted and giving him hell. Instead, he took a deep breath and texted his son.

Told you and Ted to make sure your mother didn't drink. WTF?

We tried, Dad. We got overruled by his wife and Mom.

Chapter 45

Dan had celebrated St. Patrick's Day with his mom, Marie, and Ted Bates, taking in the views from Pincher's riverside dining deck. He told Ted, who devoured his salad that he was an environmental engineer focusing on oceanology, and they hit it off. They agreed Florida's precious water and coastline were under siege by self-inflicted toxic runoffs and climate change. After two sixteen-ounce drafts, he asked their waitress to take their photo. He posted it on the family chat for his sister. Sam posted her typical edgy reaction.

> Some of us have to work on St. Paddy's Day. We're green with envy. Take it slow.

Soon after, his dad's angry text about his mother frightened him. *Dad won't be helping me with PT later.* He'd let him down. After reading his mom's printouts, he knew how dangerous her situation was. He felt guilty; she came home, buzzed from Pinchers, and was stretched out on the lanai couch with an ice pack on her head.

Dan sat in the great room and turned on the TV. ESPN talked about COVID affecting athletes. He changed the channel to cable news, focusing on California's devastating wildfires. Then the front door slammed, and his father rushed in. "Where's your mother?"

Dan motioned to the lanai.

"If she comes inside, change the station," his dad pointed at the fires on TV. "I don't want her worrying about Sam and Khori staying in their cabin."

Dad sat next to Mom on the lanai. He then came back inside with the ice pack.

"I'm making decaf tea for Mom, coffee for me. Do you want anything?"

"I'm good, Dad."

Dan checked the free movies—most were old or boring. After their coffee and tea, Dad came back in.

"I need a shower. Give me ten minutes. Then I'll help you with your

PT."

You got it, Dad.

Dan changed the channel back to ESPN when Mom came in to sit beside her blood pressure monitor. Dad then appeared in his gym clothes and had a rolled-up yoga mat. Dan followed him to the study. He brought the curtain rod and pillows; Dad played the phase one PT video on his phone. They'd gone through a few reps when Mom rushed toward the study and shouted, "Oh no!" Dan and his father froze. *Her blood pressure?*

They relaxed when she explained her friend Michelle, who had Chemo, was dangerously vulnerable to COVID and couldn't attend the fashion show.

"Ask Marie to go," he suggested to Mom, who'd bought the tickets months earlier.

"Her and Ted will be at a rally for their trans daughter," Mom added. "She's running for reelection to the Virginia House of Delegates."

"I knew I liked them," Dan said. *Supportive parents, vegans, and activists!*

Dad said, "Jo, why don't you ask Meghan? She needs to get out, too."

"Good idea," Mom said. "And we can have dinner downtown before the fashion show starts. Now, what did I do with my phone?"

Mom's been forgetting things lately. Dan sighed. He and Dad exchanged smiles, knowing they'd both escaped from being drafted to go to the fashion show.

* * *

Meghan's dad was sleeping on the lanai couch. She thought he had a fun day. *An Irish blessing*, she thought, and wondered how many more she'd have with him. She took the glass of water off the table and emptied it into a stainless-steel bowl on the floor. Bruschi slurped it up.

"That's a good boy," she said, patting his head.

She then checked her email and read through two from the DNA firm 23andMe. She reviewed her genetic health profile and her mother's in a separate profile; there were no cancer flags between them. Meghan expected to see more Scottish and Irish ancestors instead of German and Polish ones, but she couldn't be sure since her father refused to submit his DNA.

Meghan had a 50 percent DNA match with her mother. The others were 25 percent, most likely cousins, as she didn't recognize the names. She'd used initials for family tree placeholders: MM for her and PM for her mother, Peg McCormack. Meghan had received an email from Karen Marcotte asking if her mother, PM, was Phyllis Marcotte. She ignored it and changed their privacy settings, shutting off contact info to her family tree.

Meghan then checked Facebook. Her golfing posts received numerous comments and St. Paddy's Day wishes. She passed out hearts and hugs to her Boston friends. The ultimate compliment came from Allan, her former lover and boss, who taught her how to play golf.

Great form, Meghan! Paige and Hailey have nothing on you.

The gorgeous blonds Paige Spiranac and Hailey Ostrom—both twenty-something pro golfers—were glam TV stars on the golf channel and had huge Instagram followers.

She saw Joanna had checked into Pinchers restaurant with a picture of her, an older couple, and her son. The handsome guy in green looked like his father. *Oh, Danny Boy,* she still had the Jameson buzz.

She chuckled at how easily she got the virile young man into his bedroom for PT and how quickly the package in his gym shorts rose to the occasion. *Fun with a sweet guy and an unexpected boner until it turned sour.* Meghan remembered the desperate look on Dan's face when she shattered his hopes for oxy refills and told him to deal with it.

She then thought about how rugged and handsome Dan's father looked swinging his golf clubs. As a nutritionist, she could tell he ate right and worked out by the healthy veins in his forearms and large, firm biceps. *He'd have stamina for fun in the sack.* Meghan felt flush recalling their lengthy embrace by the elevator. She pulled him in tight and tingled when Dick's caring hands gently stroked her back on the way down to her butt. He broke away when the elevator door opened, and it broke the spell, leaving her feeling sad and vulnerable. Like Dan, lonely and desperate for attention and oxy, she was lonely and desperate for the attention and affection of an older man.

Meghan blamed the alcohol and Irish celebrating for her emotional hugs and lapse in judgment. She gave away her hand to Dick. Like his vulnerable son or Allan, her playful boss, he wasn't an easy mark. Dick's a good friend to Dad, a kind and caring gentleman. *And he now knows what I need.* She hoped her secret was safe with him.

She recalled her mother's words when she told her about sleeping with Allan, *"Tread carefully. You'll always want the one you can't have."*

Her phone startled her. It was a text from Jo.

Meghan, I have an extra ticket for the fashion show at the Berne Davis Center; the link is attached. Shows at 8. Plan to eat downtown first. Please let me know if you are interested. I'll make dinner reservations. Luv Jo.

She replied: I would love to go! TYSM. Luv MM

Fantastic, she thought. Whatever tests Jo had, she was well enough to go out. Her father was still sound asleep. She patted Bruschi's head, "Ready for your walk?"

He barked and followed her to the elevator. "Such a good boy."

* * *

After work, Rachel's St. Paddy's Day celebration consisted of barbecued chicken and Sam Adams beers with Aunt Kelly and Roger by the pool. She felt homesick. She went to her room and called Becca.

"No celebration for me and my big belly. Brandon's working, Brianna's sleeping, and I'm sipping tea."

"I've been cravin' corned beef an' cabbage," Rachel sighed. "Sean and I would eat it at the Glenview Pub, followed by shots and karaoke Irish songs."

"You don't miss that jerk, do you?"

"Miss the good times. Not the pain, heartache, an' lookin' over my shouldah."

Becca said, "I texted Ma, 'Happy Saint Paddy's.' She called me a few hours ago."

"Not me," she sighed. "Nevah returned my call when I left her a voice message."

"Sorry, Robin. I know she loves you."

"Balls in her court," she added. "My birthday's coming up; see if she calls me then."

* * *

Sean texted Greg when he landed. He dragged his luggage to the curb and adjusted his green Celtics cap. Greg pulled up in his white Chevy Silverado pickup and jumped out.

"Hey, Sean. Welcome to Florida!"

They gripped their right hands and leaned into each other for a manly hug. The strapping dude with a five-o'clock shadow wore his black HTS polo shirt.

"Thanks, Greg. I owe ya, man!"

"You'll meet Lacy at my place, and then we'll go to a poolside party at the mobile park's community center to celebrate Paddy's Day."

"Sounds good. How long ya been dating her?"

"'Bout a year. She's divorced, no kids. Lacy cuts hair in the park; I fixed her microwave. Bought my place eight months ago; she moved in when her lease ran out."

The slender, attractive woman with a sleeve tattoo said, "Nice to meet you, Sean."

"Pleashah is mine. Greg say's ya half Irish?"

"My mom's maiden name is Dunn. Happy Paddy's Day." The cougar with stylish blond hair tinted green, snug cutoff jeans, and an emerald green

T-shirt looked ready to party.

Sean dropped his bags in the back room. He peeked into an adjacent bedroom, which had been set up as a hair salon for Lacy B's LLC, then joined them for the celebration.

The mobile park's owner, Brian Haggerty, organized the community pool party. The gray-bearded Irishman with a limp and a beer gut greeted them warmly. After hearing Sean Cassidy's name and Boston accent, he shook his hand and tugged on his green Celtic cap.

"Much bettah wheathah here than Bawhstin," Sean said.

"Good ole Irish lad," Haggerty said, shoving a cold beer in Sean's hand.

Greg said, "Sean's starting with me at HTS on Monday."

"Well, if you want to work this week. I need my lawns mowed. Can't rely on my stepson. He only shows up when he's broke." Haggerty then lowered his voice, "Pay ya under the table."

"Got a lab test tomawrah mornin'. Be glad to cut grass after that."

Sean figured one beer with food wouldn't hurt. He filled a paper plate with pulled pork, baked beans, and corn on the cob, then sat with Lacy and Greg.

"Lacy, can you drive Sean to his lab test tomorrow?" asked Greg.

Lacy said, "No problem. He'll be back here mowing lawns before my first appointment."

"Thanks, Lacy! 'Preciate it!" replied Sean. "You evah work at Cape Cod Cuttahs?"

"Ha-ha. You mean Cape Cuts in Cape Coral. No, but my girlfriend Roxy does. Why?"

"My ex, a redhead from Bawhstin, might be workin' there."

"What's her name?" asked Lacy.

"Robin. Her aunt, the owner, doesn't care for me. I'd want to surprise her," said Sean.

"Okay. I'll gossip with Roxy about who works there now and not mention you."

The drinks and Irish toasts flowed throughout the night. Haggerty sang the Irish lullaby, "Too-Ra-Loo-Ra-Loo-Ral," as Sean and Lacy closed ranks on the old man and joined the chorus.

Chapter 46

Dick's wife and son were sleeping when he headed for the gym. Ted Bates had finished his workout, his tank top revealing big biceps and bulging veins. He was disappointed Ted couldn't stop Jo from drinking yesterday, but he felt guilty about partying with Mack and his gorgeous, irresistibly dangerous daughter. Dick fist-bumped his buffed, shorter friend, "Hey, Ted. Thanks for taking Jo and Dan to Pinchers."

"My pleasure. Dan's a bright young man. Cares deeply about the water and rising seas."

"Thanks. We're proud of him," he said and waved goodbye to Ted.

"Hi, Dickie. How're you?" Laura Britt, the cheery personal trainer, greeted him.

"Good, thanks." He smiled at the lovely certified trainer with the certifiably flawless body as she counted reps for his much older neighbor, George.

"Looking good, George," Dick said.

The thin, bald gentleman sat up on the mat and said, "Welcome back, Dick. How was the Green Conference in Boston?"

"It went well. Glad I'm back as COVID is breaking out there."

"Scary stuff," George said, wiping the sweat off his brow with his T-shirt.

"They postponed the Boston Marathon," Laura said with concern.

George added, "Laura runs marathons all over the world." *It shows. She's superbly fit.*

George once told Dick, "I think of Laura like paying premiums on a health insurance policy. She adds years to my life."

He wished Jo could get Laura's insurance benefits, but the doctor said no strenuous activity. Dick cut his workout short and headed upstairs to check on Jo. After that, he helped Dan with his PT, then left to get paint to touch up his rental condo.

* * *

Dick entered Lowe's; their employees wore facemasks. He put on his face-mask, placed the old Sherwin-Williams cans in a shopping cart, and wheeled it down to the paint department. He waited in line behind a heavy-set man wearing a shabby tank exposing his hairy back and flabby tattooed biceps. The grungy guy leaned on his cart full of caulking supplies and silicon tubes and leered at the young red-haired woman behind the counter.

Dick noticed the name tags on the employee's red vests. Phil, a gray-haired guy, mixed paint for a customer while Rachel, the redhead, motioned for the hefty guy to move up. The man grabbed another silicon tube off the counter and told Rachel, "Painting all the rooms for the little woman. Do you think I have enough *caulk* for the bedrooms?"

"Woah," Dick blurted.

Phil glared at the jerk and turned toward his redheaded coworker.

She replied, "Bettah, get more. You look like you'll always come up short."

Dick snickered. The shamed fat guy asked, "What are you laughing at?"

Dick leaned over his cart and pointed at the guy's red face, "She pegged you perfectly."

The jerk threw the silicon tube on the counter. It hit the young woman's forearm. She scolded, "Sir… please pay for your items at the registahs up front."

The belligerent caulk-spewing creep swung his cart around and banged into Dick's.

"Use the self-service," Dick said to him. "I'd say offhand, you're good at that."

The paint employees and customers laughed. Dick adjusted his face-mask and moved up.

"You handled that buffoon well," Dick said to Rachel. Her ocean-blue eyes widened when he got close to her.

"Thanks, he's a wicked jerk. How can I help ya?"

Heavy Bawstin accent, Dick thought. "Need to match these paint formulas," he said.

The young woman, in shapely blue jeans, mixed the paint and eyed him several times.

"All set, sir," she handed him the paint. A shamrock tattoo on her wrist stood out.

"Thank you," Dick said, then he asked, "You from Bawstin?"

"Use ta be. Cape Coral now. How 'bout you?" she inquired.

"Fort Myers, now," he said on his way out. "Go, Red Sox."

Dick loaded the paint and supplies in his Audi. Something about the redhead was nagging at him. Then it dawned on him: the tattoo. He called Dan, no answer. He called his wife, "Jo, how ya feeling?"

"Okay. Where are you?"

"Leaving Lowe's and heading to the rental to get started."

"Started—on what?"

My God, I told her this morning. "Touching up the walls."

"Oh. Okay."

"Where's Dan? He didn't answer his phone."

"Gone to the pool deck. He's in the hot tub."

"Good for him. I'll see you at dinner."

"Don't forget, we're grilling beef tips by the pool," she said.

"I won't." *But you never told me.* He sighed.

* * *

Rachel ate lunch in the Lowe's breakroom. Her friendly coworker, Viviana Longoria, said, "I heard how you put the caulking creep in his place."

"Ha-ha, thanks. I wish that cute guy who works for Ryan Painting made passes at me," said Rachel. "He has a small boy. I think he's divorced."

Viviana said, "Kyle Ryan was divorced. He's now married to my cousin, Catalina." She showed her picture of Kyle with his son and a little girl in the arms of a beautiful Latina woman.

Rachel said, "The good ones are always taken. I need to get out more."

"Want to join me and my friends Friday for a drink?"

"I'd love to," Rachel replied without hesitation.

Rachel thought about the Boston guy she mixed paint for. The way he spoke and his mannerisms reminded her of Dan. He wore a facemask, but her intuition made her curious. She used the thirty minutes left on her lunch break to get some answers. She created a new Facebook account as Rachel Gibbs, Aunt Kelly's last name. She used a photo of her face cropped out for her profile picture with her niece Brianna sitting on her lap. She then searched for Dan's mother's account. *Bingo.*

> Joanna DeCosta checked into Pinchers Restaurant, Fort Myers, Florida, Celebrating St. Patrick's Day with Dan DeCosta and Marie Bates.

Oh... my... God. "He's here!" She enlarged the picture of Dan. He looked different; younger, he'd shaved his beard. She wondered why his arm was in a sling. *But he looked wicked handsome in his Paddy's Day green.*

His mom also checked into Izzy's last Saturday night. Joanna DeCosta posed between Dan and his father, who had bought the paint earlier. A comment posted by Meghan McCormack stuck out.

> Lovely Joanna, the luckiest lady with the two best-looking men in town.

Curious, she clicked on Meghan McCormack's profile: Physical Therapist, Lahey Clinic, Burlington, MA, now lives in Fort Myers. She scanned Meghan's celebration of life posts. The pretty blonde in a blue dress stood proudly between Dan and his father. She scrolled further and admired the Marco Island beach pic of the gorgeous blond in a revealing red bikini. *She's hot!* Probably a friend of Dan's family. *Either way, too many friggin blondes in Florida.* Rachel angrily yanked out a handful of her red strands.

* * *

Sean finished cutting the grass around Haggerty's pool. He then parked the rider mower by the storage shed. *Damn, it's hot.* He removed his drenched and beat-up baseball cap and wiped the sweat off his face with his faded U2 T-shirt. Sean entered the tool shed and drank water from a jug. He found the garden trimmers next to a sharp hunting knife with a jacket. Lacy had told him a redhead named Rachel was the new part-time receptionist at Cape Cuts. She worked her other shift at Lowe's in the next plaza. Sean slid the knife into the pocket of his camo cargo shorts.

"What're you doin' in there?" a voice behind him asked.

Sean looked at a thin, long-haired dude in sunglasses. His slim arms, covered with sleeve tats, stuck out from his Rage Against the Machine T-shirt.

"Mowing lawns for Mistah Haggerty," Sean said as he stepped outside the shed and pulled a pack of Marlboros from his shorts.

"He's my stepdaddy. I usually help him out," the thin man explained as he stuck out his hand, "Rand Carter."

"Sean Cassidy," he said, shaking the nervous man's thin hand. "I'm helping this week 'til I start my full-time job Monday. Stayin' with Greg Gaudette."

"Ah, and Lacy. Good folks." The man took a drag on his vape, blew it out, leaving a strong scent of pot, then said, "I live at the corner home, four down from the office. You ever wanta party, need anythin'—smoke, blow, Molly, Apache. Drop by. I'll hook ya up."

"Thanks. Uhm, good." *It's the last thing I need,* Sean thought, *but good to know.*

* * *

Meghan sat across from her father as she sipped her coffee. "Dad, I'm sorting out Mom's stuff. Do you want any keepsakes?"

His frown told her he wanted no part of it.

"I trust you, Meg. Save what you like in the storage cage and toss the rest."

She sorted out most of her mother's possessions and ate lunch. Meghan then put on her new ice-blue bikini, went to the pool, and spotted Silvia.

"Stunning bathing suit. Is it new?"

"Arrived yesterday, Amazon Prime. Never know how they'll fit."

"Perfect, but you'd make a burlap sack shine with your figure."

"Thanks. You're too kind. Take my picture." *I want to taunt my Boston friends.* Then she posted it on Facebook.

"I've had enough sun. Enjoy your day," Silvia said, leaving the pool area.

Meghan opened her Nora Roberts novel. She kept an eye on the two young boys, errantly tossing a rubber ball in and out of the pool. *So annoying. Where the hell are their parents?*

A petite brunette with thick, curly hair pulled off her T-shirt and settled into the lounger vacated by Silvia. The young woman smiled at Meghan, adjusted her sunglasses, and sat back.

"Watch out!" she heard the young woman shout.

Meghan ducked behind her book, and the young woman reached over and snagged the bouncing ball.

"Nice save! Thanks," Meghan said as the thin, agile woman tossed the ball back to the boys. She was drawn to her black thong bikini that split her sculptured tush.

"No problem," the wavy-haired cutie said. Then she turned to her, "I'm Rikki. I moved in last week."

"Meghan," she said, extending her hand to the dark-skinned woman.

"Ah. Megan Monahan. Thought so. The weekend anchor at Wink News."

"Sorry to disappoint you. Doctor Meghan McCormack. Physical therapist at Fort Myers Rehab Center."

"Not disappointed. Rikki Rossetti," she smiled. "And nice to meet you."

"Nice to meet you, Rikki, or is it Erica?" *Italian sweetie with sexy hair.*

"Just Rikki. My parents are big Steely Dan fans. They loved that song."

"Me too. And I love the Steely Dan song 'Peg.' My Dad calls my Mom Peg, short for Margaret. She uh… recently passed away."

"I'm so sorry," she said as she reached over and touched Meghan's arm.

"Thank you. So, Rikki…" *Don't lose that number.* "Where do you work?"

"I'm a meteorologist at NBC2 News. I recently joined their morning weathercast team."

"Nice!" Meghan said as she watched Rikki reply to a text.

"Oh, I'm meeting a friend. She's at the lobby now," she said, pulling a Tampa Bay Rays jersey over her slender body. "Bye, Meghan."

"Bye, Rikki." She watched her rush off before she googled Rikki Rossetti. She'd previously worked at Tampa Bay's NBC-8 station. Based on her Florida State University graduate date, she figured Rikki was in her mid-twenties.

Meghan checked her Facebook feeds. She received lots of compliments from her Boston friends about her blue bikini. Lydia, her former intimate roommate, commented:

Gorgeous—miss you!

Joanna's recent post of Dan lying on a float in their condo's pool intrigued her. She expanded the picture, focusing on his shoulder scar. *He's not well enough to swim. Hope he doesn't hurt himself; he'll never get off the oxy.*

He looked hot in his Speedo swim trunks. Meghan chuckled as she recalled the bulge in his shorts. *If I keep staring at this eye candy, I'll have to find batteries for my vibrator.*

Nice Pecs, Steely Dan.

She then replaced her comment with,

Looking good, Dan.

* * *

Dick touched up the rental's master bedroom and bath. He noticed the faucet in the double vanity leaked and took a picture to find a match online. He then set himself up in the other master suite. Dick opened the drapes for more light, looked down at the pool, and scanned the sun worshippers on their lounge chairs. He focused on a buxom blond with a shiny blue bathing suit. *Meghan!* He started sweating. *Not again; I need a break.*

He drank water and started painting again. He thought about Jo's forgetfulness—and Dr. Royce's concerns about mild cognitive impairment—early onset of dementia. He'd read the risks of coils versus clipping surgery. He didn't like either of them, but they agreed she'd get the noninvasive endovascular procedure if her symptoms worsened. Dick now wondered if she even remembered their discussion.

After he finished painting, he looked back out at the pool. Meghan was lying on her stomach, reading a book, showcasing her perfect rear. Her bikini was not as skimpy as the red one but still intoxicating. It was time to go swimming, he thought.

Chapter 47

Dick swam two laps in the pool. He climbed the ladder, cleared the water from his eyes, and then she handed him his towel. Dick wiped his face, leaned over, and kissed her on the cheek. They walked to the umbrella-covered table where she had set places for their family dinner.

"Dan's tending to the beef skewers," Jo said, motioning towards the grill. The sizzling aroma made Dick realize he was starving.

"How do you feel?" Dick asked Dan, his bathing suit and hair still damp.

"Good. I started in the hot tub, then used the float in the pool."

"Guys, turn around," they heard Jo say. She photographed them by the grill.

* * *

Dan felt good about his progress. He washed the steak tips down with a cold beer. Dad brushed the grill grates off while Dan sat in the chair next to Mom. *Man, another beautiful evening.* He thought about job searching in the area. Or maybe he'd enroll in FGCU's graduate program, which had research projects in his field. *But how will I sell my house in a pandemic?*

His mother said, "Look at these Facebook pics Meghan commented on."

He leaned over and looked at her phone. There was a picture of him lounging on a float and Meghan's comment: Looking good.

The following photo showed him and Dad by the open grill.

Meghan wrote: Looks delish, Jo! So do your two handsome grill masters. 🫶 🫶

He took his mother's phone and jumped to Meghan's posts. There were Marco Island beach pictures of her in a fiery red bikini. *Hello!* Then Meghan in a blue bikini at her pool today. He shook his head. *So, much, woman!* His phone chimed. He read Sam's family chat comment to Mom's earlier post of him in the pool today.

Hey. Good to see you without your sling. Enjoy.

He was happy to hear from Sam and concerned about her. Dad told him not to worry Mom about his sister. Rather than comment on the family chat, he chose to text her.

How r things with u n Khori? Worried about u and wildfires. Dad doesn't want Mom to know, cuz of the blood pressure on her brain aneurysm.

Sam replied: Dan! WTF r u talking about?
Shit, sorry. Call u soon to explain.

Dan told Mom he had to pee and take his meds. He looked down at the pool deck, kept an eye on his parents, and explained to Sam what he read in his mom's printouts.

"She's also forgetful. I think she's scheduling surgery soon. You should get out here."

"Geezus... Okay. I got stuff to move from my flat to Khori's house. Don't let Mom know. I'll text Dad when I have a flight booked. Take care and keep me posted."

His phone dinged again: a surprise text from Meghan.

Good to see you're making progress. Don't try any breaststrokes. 😊

Ha, breaststrokes. Did she mean swimming or the ones she rubbed across his sling when she had him on the mat? Either way, he didn't know what he did to deserve the sudden attention, but he'd promised her. *Time to follow through.* He grabbed the oxy vial and set one aside. He used his phone to videotape him, flushing the rest of the pills down the toilet. He replied to Meghan's text and attached the video.

Thanks! As promised. I'm good now.

Moments later, her reply warmed his heart.

Yes! You are! 👎

When his parents returned from the pool, Dan turned on the TV. Dad loaded the dishwasher while Mom opened her medical bills.

"My gosh, Dick. Most of this isn't covered!"

"Don't worry about it," his dad said, touching her shoulders.

"But the procedure will be fifty times that."

"Jo, we have plenty of money," his dad said in a hushed voice.

"I better wait 'til you sell the rental unit."

"Don't let it interfere with your thinking," he heard Dad emphasize.

Dan and his parents tuned into the evening news. It was March 19, and California's governor had announced the first statewide mandatory shelter-in-place order.

"Oh God," his mother reacted. "I gotta call Sam."

"Mom, she's been staying at home," Dan said, hoping she'd calm down and not call Sam.

"Don't worry, Jo. She and Khori work from home," his dad said, putting an arm around her. "She's probably writing programs; it's only three thirty out there."

The local news continued, "The Sydney & Berne Davis Art Center canceled tomorrow night's annual fashion show. Ticket holders can get refunds or a credit for future events."

"Oh dear," his mom sighed. "I gotta tell Meghan. Guess I'll cancel our dinner reservation."

"Keep the reservation," his dad said. "Mack is going to the casino. Meghan is all alone; go to dinner with her."

"Okay. Good idea," Mom said, then looked at Dan, "Maybe you and Dad can join us?"

His dad frowned, "I don't think—"

"I need to get out, too," Dan interrupted. "And we all need to eat. Haha."

"What restaurant?" Dad asked bluntly.

"Cabos. Meghan said she hadn't been there and heard the margaritas were good."

"Okay. But promise you'll only have one drink?" Dad waited until they both nodded.

* * *

Meghan carried a box of her mom's mementos to the storage cage. She moved her mom's dusty ten-speed beside her bike. She pried open a storage tote and flipped through photo albums of fond memories with her brother, family vacations, and holidays. She missed Mitch and pined for her mother. *Both are gone; not fair.*

Beneath the photo albums were manila folders with Mom's medical records and a metal box at the bottom, secured with duct tape. She opened it and found more photos of Mom at Marco Island and others at an Emerson Hospital holiday party.

Meghan then opened a mailer-sized envelope and pulled out yellowed newspaper clippings of *Boston Globe* articles. She glanced at an investigative series about cesarean surgeries and articles on sexual assault allegations by several women against an obstetrician. She read an old obituary for Dr. Benjamin Samuel Friedman of Lincoln, Massachusetts; he left a wife and three young children. The deceased OB-GYN's picture matched a doctor who often appeared in her mom's Marco Island photos. *Mom, why'd you save all this?*

She locked the cage, carried the envelope to the condo, and planned to research the articles on her dad's computer. He was in the den, glued to his crazy conspiracy-filled cable station, which claimed the flu kills more people yearly than COVID-19 would.

I'll do this when he's not around. Meghan hid the envelope in her bedroom. She then lowered the TV to get his attention.

"Dad. I put Mom's stuff in the storage room. Lots of baby pictures. Mitch and I were both born at Emerson Hospital. Were you in the delivery room?"

"I was for Mitch. With you, she needed a C-section. I sat outside the operating room."

"Ah. Do you remember the doctor's name?"

"Hell, that happened decades ago. I can't remember what I had for lunch."

She thought about her mother's old health files from storage. *I'll get them later.*

"Dad, you still going to the casino?"

"Yeah, Friday."

"I'm having dinner downtown with Joanna DeCosta, then going to a fashion show."

"Great! Park behind the library, on Second Street. No meters there."

Chapter 48

Rachel sat in Lowe's break room, checked Facebook, and scanned Dan's mother's posts. She zoomed in on a picture of Dan lying on a float. *He's looking better without his sling.* She loved Dan's photo with his father beside a grill—they both looked buff in their bathing suits. The comments between Dan's mother and Meghan, the flirty blond, were helpful.

Thanks, Meghan. My two grill masters will be joining us for dinner tomorrow night. See you at Cabos at 7:00 sharp. *Sweet lady,* Rachel thought.

She googled Cabos. *Hmm...* tacos, tequila bar, downtown Fort Myers.

"Hey... what's up for tonight?" she asked Viviana, who entered the breakroom.

"Camilla and I usually grab a bite downtown, then hit the clubs."

"Sounds good. I'll text you my aunt's address."

At 6:30 p.m., Rachel jumped in the back of Viviana's Honda Civic in her white tri-rocker tank top, high-waisted denim shorts, and open-toe sandals. Camilla and Viviana's hourglass figures in the front seats filled out gray halter tops and tight black jeans with pumps. She thought. *I'm hanging with two smoking hot Latina babes. Fun Friday night, for sure.*

Viviana circled downtown in search of parking.

"Use the library's lot," Rachel suggested.

They pulled in next to a BMW. Its blond driver stepped out of her car, flashing long legs with beige ankle-strapped high-heeled sandals. She carried a matching beige handbag and filled out a sexy sage green one-shoulder minidress in all the right places. Rachel and her friends walked behind the hip-swaying, shapely blond.

"Pretty woman," Viviana said.

"A lotta woman," Camilla said.

Rachel eyed the woman's grandiose glutes as she strutted confidently toward First Street.

* * *

Dan and his parents walked casually along First Street. They would meet up with Meghan at the restaurant downtown. His parents always dressed well and looked amazing for their age.

Dan asked, "Mom, how old is Meghan?"

"Uhm, thirty-three?" Mom looked at his dad.

His dad said, "Mack told me she'd be forty in October."

"She doesn't look it," Dan said. *Ten years older than me, oh well.*

They approached the entrance to Cabos, where Meghan, in a light green minidress and stilettos, stood out on the crowded sidewalk. *She looks twenty-nine and mighty fine,* Dan thought.

"You look fabulous. I love your dress and sandals," said his mom as she embraced Meghan.

"Thank you, Jo. So do you. I got this outfit for the fashion show. Hi guys."

"Hi," Dan said with a wide smile.

His father grinned and raised his eyebrows.

Cabos' cute hostess led his mom and Meghan inside as Dan and his father trailed behind. It was obvious that all eyes were on Meghan as they made their way through the restaurant. They exited a rear door to a roped-off area of tables in the plaza. Dan pulled a chair out for Meghan and peeked at her deadly derriere before she settled in.

Meghan said, "Thank you, Dan."

My pleasure.

Her intoxicating perfume lingered. He took a seat to her left. His mom sat beside Meghan opposite him, and his dad sat across from Meghan.

The waitress asked, "What can I start you off with?"

Dad said, "Watah with chips and salsa."

Then, they ordered margaritas.

* * *

Rachel, Viviana, and Camilla sat at an outside table at Patio de Leon while they nibbled on their giant pizza slices. Rachel had a view of the 10 Twenty Five restaurant's patio but kept an eye on Cabos' outside tequila bar. A hostess led a lovely older woman in a shapely black dress and the vivacious blond in the green dress they'd seen earlier to a table in the roped-off area.

Rachel thought her head would explode when she saw Dan pull out a seat for the blond. *It's Meghan, the Facebook nemesis.* His handsome father pulled out a chair for his attractive mother. Smartly dressed in a colorful shirt and beige shorts, she thought Dan was underdressed relative to the classy bombshell. *She's way out of his league.*

"Rachel," Viviana instructed. "Let's hit the Skybar before it gets too crowded."

"Where's that?"

"Top floor of Firestone's. It has great views."

They walked by Cabos' tables. Rachel looked over at Dan and thought about waving at him. But Viviana pulled her through the crowded patio. *Go, Red Sox,* she wanted to shout but said nothing. *Life goes on; try to have fun tonight.*

* * *

Friday night, Greg and Lacy took Sean downtown for a bite. Lacy snagged an upstairs spot at 10 Twenty Five. They ordered burgers and drinks—Sean had a nonalcoholic O'Doul's. He scoured the crowd below for any signs of Robin. But was overwhelmed by the many scantily dressed women out on this warm tropical night. In the distance, two big-breasted Latina girls sat with a redhead eating pizza. *Robin? Or just my Floridah sun-bleached brain?*

He bit into his burger. The three shapely women left their table and crossed the plaza. The redhead's stride, mannerisms, and turned-up nose all unmistakably matched Robin's. *I gotta get to her, and soon.*

Sean was determined to execute the plan he'd been working on ever since Lacy told him Robin's typical work schedule. Her restraining order said he had to remain more than a hundred yards from where she lived and worked. Sean would use his iPhone to map her walking path from her aunt's salon to Lowe's. But he needed transportation. Haggerty's truck would only be available at night, and he had other plans for the old man's pickup if she didn't cooperate.

"Greg, you're not working tomawrah, right?"

"Saturday, I get overtime pay. I got two repair appointments.

Can't use Greg's truck.

"And I do a lot of haircuts on Saturdays. Don't sleep in," Lacy said.

"Can I use your cah? I'll pick up steaks and beeah at the market. I owe you guys."

"I'll drink to that," Greg said.

Everyone clinked their beer bottles.

* * *

Meghan clinked her glass with the DeCostas and sipped the gold margarita. She enjoyed the moment, the meal, and the delightful conversation with Jo. It made it easier to avoid eye contact with her husband, who patiently let Jo talk about last year's fashion show and their upcoming fall trip to Portugal and Spain.

"It's six months away, Jo," Dick finally said. "You already agreed to cancel the flights because of COVID."

A sad, confused look came over Jo's face. She shook her head slowly.

"You did, Mom," Dan added.

"Another round?" the waitress asked as she cleared their dishes.

Meghan nodded.

"Yes, please," Dan said.

"Why not," Jo said.

Her husband shook his head no at her.

Woah, what's his problem? Meghan wondered.

Dick mumbled rest room and excused himself from the table. *Geez, who brought the pin to the balloon party?* She thought Dick was acting like a prick.

Meghan turned to Dan, "How's the PT coming? Did you swim again today?"

"Little bit, but no breaststrokes," he smiled on cue. "There would be too much strain on my ribs." He patted his chest and pretended his heart was beating fast for her.

She chuckled. *Aww, you're so sweet. You're going to give me diabetes.*

"When do you start at the rehab center?" Jo interjected and broke the spell.

"Monday," she said. "Looking forward to it."

Dick returned, leaned over, and whispered something into Jo's ear. The waitress arrived with two jumbo margaritas and placed them before Meghan and Dan.

"Did you take the trolley?" Dick finally spoke directly to Meghan.

"I drove and parked at the library."

"Great," he looked at his son. "I promised Jo we'd get her favorite ice cream and head home," Dick said, helping Joanna up. "The tabs covered. Enjoy."

That was abrupt and way too controlling, Meghan fumed.

"Thanks, Dad," Dan said.

"Thank you both for a lovely evening," Meghan hugged Jo. She then leaned into a brief, awkward hug with Dick. *Why'd you ruin it?*

Meghan sipped her drink as she watched Dick and Jo walk off.

"Your dad likes casinos. Does he play blackjack?" Dan asked, breaking the silence.

"I don't know. I don't do casinos," she snapped, then asked. "Did your father say that?"

"He told us Mack invited him to the casino, and you'd be all alone. He suggested my mom ask you to attend the fashion show and dinner."

He's trying to control me too. "Why didn't he let your mother have another drink?"

"She's not supposed to have any alcohol. She has a brain aneurysm and will—"

"Oh God! I'm *so* sorry," she reached out and patted his hand.

"Thanks. She's forgetful lately. Probably having surgery soon."

Shame on me. Dick was protecting Jo and being considerate to me.

"I feel terrible. Your mother never said—"

Dan held up his hand and leaned close. "They don't talk about it with me, so please don't mention it to them."

They both took a big gulp from their jumbo margaritas.

"Your secret is safe with me," she said softly, touching his forearm.

He smiled, "Well… I guess they trust us alone."

She leaned closer, "That could be dangerous."

They chuckled and took another sip. By the time they licked the salt off their lips, their knees were touching under the table.

Chapter 49

Rachel tried to forget about Dan and the blonde. She sipped her cocktail and took in the amazing river and city views from the Skybar's hip rooftop club. The original Firestone Tire's four-story brick warehouse was converted into a fine restaurant on the first two floors, with nightclubs on levels three and four. The bar was packed two rows deep, mostly Gen Xers and millennials jockeying for drinks. They seemed impervious to COVID.

The dance floor filled when the DJ cranked up Bruno Mars's "24K Magic." But when Pitbull's "Timber" started playing, Viviana and Camilla dragged Rachel to the packed dance floor. Rachel tried her best to emulate freestyle salsa moves. As soon as the song ended, Viviana shouted to Rachel, "Ladies' room! Follow me!"

Good idea, she thought as her hair stuck to her sweaty neck. Viviana led her down the back steps to the third level. On the way, they passed by the Blues Brothers, life-size statues of Dan Aykroyd and John Belushi, posing on a landing. She followed Viviana through another crowd in the glittering disco ballroom on level three. After they freshened up in the ladies' room, Camilla caught up to them and said the party was moving.

They circled back to Patio de Leon. Music was blasting from Space 39's outside speakers. Inside the hopping art and martini bar, a live band was playing a cover of The Weeknd's big hit "I Can't Feel My Face." The jam-packed joint had a crowd at the entrance. *No COVID concerns here either,* she thought.

"This band, The Night Owls, is great," Viviana said as they squeezed inside.

This place is wicked cool. Rachel eyed the interesting paintings and artful sketches hanging on the walls. The raucous crowd was a mix of millennials and boomers, all bopping to David Bowie's "Let's Dance." The three women worked their way to order martinis.

The lead singer then belted Bruno Mars's "Uptown Funk." People swayed and danced in any available space. Rachel froze when she saw Dan trying to squeeze his way inside. She kept her eyes on him, hoping he'd see her. *What will I say to him?*

A tall Black dude dancing and grinding with a sexy older blonde woman momentarily blocked her view. When she looked again, Dan was gone. Rachel approached the doorway and saw Dan walking away, arm and arm, with the deadly blond in the green dress. *Damn, Facebook bitch is more than a family friend.* Her heart sunk to the tiled dance floor and got trampled by the crowd.

* * *

Meghan and Dan, both lit from their jumbo margaritas, were drawn to the sound of the live band playing "Uptown Funk" at Space 39. Dan tried to pull Meghan through the jammed entrance, but she held her ground and discouraged him.

"Too rough, Dan," she insisted. "They'll bang into your ribs and shoulder."

"Thanks!" he said. "You're always watching out for your patients."

Especially the vulnerable ones. She hooked her left arm around his waist and he put his right arm around her shoulder. Thoroughly buzzed, they giggled and wobbled along the sidewalk toward the library.

"Thanks for escorting me to my chariot," she said in the brightly lit parking lot.

"The pleasure was all mine," he said, releasing her at her SUV.

"I'll ask the rehab center if you can come in for PT," she said softly, touching his chest.

"Great. But I'll need muscle relaxers working next to you," he said smoothly, slipping his arms around her waist. Then he pulled her close and gently kissed her on the lips.

"I will, too," she kissed him back. Then she slipped her tongue between his lips.

His tongue circled hers back. He moved his body closer; her butt now rested against her BMW's tailgate. She pulled Dan in tighter; they separated when they heard someone approaching.

"Good night," he said and stepped away.

"I'll give you a lift to your parents' condo."

Meghan considered driving him to her father's condo but couldn't risk her dad walking in on them. She envisioned them in her bedroom and Bruschi barking outside her door. *Tequila makes me wild. I'd hurt him. He'd be back on the pain meds.*

She stopped at a traffic light and said, "If you're free tomorrow, I can show you safe routines with a Styrofoam noodle in our pool."

"Sounds like a challenge—I'd be up for."

They both giggled.

Meghan entered his condo complex and chose a visitor's parking space beneath a palm tree. She then turned to him.

"So, where were we?" she flirted.

Dan leaned over and kissed her. As she stroked the hair on his head, their reciprocating tongues took it to another level.

* * *

Rachel sat at Space 39's bar, watched Viviana dance with Camilla, and finished her martini. A tall, smooth-dancing Black man left an attractive, mature blond on the floor and squeezed in beside Rachel. He told the barmaid, "Bourbon on the rocks and another martini for her."

"Thanks," Rachel said to the handsome, sharply dressed man. Then asked, "Why me?"

"Cuz you're a natural redhead and the most stunning girl here."

"And you want to have sex with me."

"Damn. You're the smartest one, too. Ha-ha. But with another drink, you might act like a redhead. You ain't smilin' nor dancin'."

"I danced at the Skybar. It's too crowded here," she forced a thin grin.

"Shame," he said. He leaned close to her, "Ginger beauty like you got a rep to live up to like us bruthahs have about size and endurance—you're every dude's wildest dream."

Bad pickup line and a bragah. "Your rep's safe with me." *Just keep your hands and dreams to yourself.*

She gulped her drink and said, "So, what do you do?"

He handed her his used-car business card, "Trey Jackson. Call anytime for a test drive."

"Cool. I'll give it to Large Marge. She does test runs for our fair-haired group."

"Is Marge a big redhead?" Trey raised his eyes and stirred his drink.

"Nah, she's blond with a *big* mouth and *loves* tall guys." She drained her drink.

"So, how tall is she?' He sipped his bourbon and waited.

"Five-eight with heels. Five-six without. Three-foot-two if she likes you *a lot.*"

He spit out his drink and roared.

"Sweet dreams," she said, leaving him at the bar and pulling Viviana outside.

* * *

Dick got a text from Sam. She was arriving Saturday night. He told her to call her mother. Jo was thrilled. They agreed it would be better for Sam to stay in the rental as she'd have more space and privacy to work. "Lots to do tomorrow," Jo said and kissed him goodnight.

Dick went to his study to search online at Lowe's for a replacement faucet. An ambulance siren drew him to his window. His attention then went to an SUV in the visitor's lot; its brake lights were lit. The security guard approached the SUV and spoke with the driver. He then spotted his son exit the passenger's side.

Moments later, Dan sauntered down the hall and then stopped in his study. His hair was disheveled, smeared lip gloss lined his mouth, and per-spiration marks were on his shirt. *Meghan drove him home ... and probably drove him crazy.*

"Dad—didn't think you'd be up."

"Searching for plumbing parts," he added. "Sam's coming tomorrow night. I gotta get the rental ready for her."

"Fantastic!" He then asked, "Can you give me a ride there tomorrow? Meghan invited me to the pool to do water PT."

"Ha, sure. I'll get you there after I get some things at Lowe's."

"Thanks, Dad. Good night."

"Good night." *Wet dreams for him tonight.*

Chapter 50

Saturday morning, Joanna discussed with Dick their preparations for Sam. Dick would go to Lowe's for plumbing items. She'd go to the market for items Sam would need, then bring new linens, bath, and beach towels there. "I'll take Dan there," she told Dick.

"Great." He kissed her goodbye. She felt they had a good team plan, and she'd finally have her family together. *Monday, I'll schedule my surgery, but which one?*

* * *

Rachel slept poorly and woke up feeling like crap; a hangover and heartbreak made her want to stay in bed all day. *I have commitments*—a shift at Lowe's, then the afternoon at Kelly's.

"Rachel, you went out on the town last night, and it looks like you lost your best friend," Auntie K said, driving on their way to work.

"Can you color my hair this afternoon to blond?"

"What are you crazy?" she braked hard for a yellow light. "You're young; you don't color your hair until—"

Rachel twirled her hair and told her aunt about the Black man who bought her a drink at the bar and his pickup line, then added, "I don't want to be guys' wildest wet dreams. Too many losers out there watching porn on their phones."

"Well, you put that one in his place." Auntie K said as she stopped at Lowe's.

"Yep, thanks. So, will you color my hair?"

"No! Sweetie, your hair is beautiful, and lots of women would kill to have it."

* * *

Dick put on his mask, searched the Lowes's plumbing department, and found the parts he needed. He then hurried in line to get his military discount. The redhead was scanning items for another customer. He spotted the tattoo on her wrist, opened his phone, and found the text from Dan. He enlarged the sexy photo of the girl with the wine glass; on her wrist, a green shamrock tattoo with a red heart in the center. *Coincidence? We'll soon find out.*

He put the plumbing items on the counter.

"Hi," they both said in unison.

Dick then handed her his military ID, which she examined closely.

He said, "Lowell girls must be too colorful to work in the paint department. Ha-ha."

She smiled and returned his ID. "How do ya know I'm from Lowell?"

"Wild guess. I was born there." *And I've seen your provocative photo.*

"I saw you and your family at Cabos last night," she said, scanning his items.

"Really? Were you at Cabos?" *Rachel, or is it Robin?*

"No, House of Pizza."

Dick snapped her picture.

"Please don't." She frowned and handed him his receipt and the bag with his items.

"Have to. Dan won't believe me when I tell him you saw us last night."

"Won't mattah. He was all ovah that blond."

"She's a friend of the family helping him with PT. He had shoulder surgery."

"Well, tell 'em. I'm truly sorry about his setbacks."

"He'll appreciate that." Dick handed her his business card and said, "Hit me up, and I'll pass your contact info to Dan."

"Thanks. Have a good day," she said, slipping his card into the back pocket of her jeans.

"You too," Dick said. Then he began whistling the Beatles song, "Good Day Sunshine." He didn't know if she wanted to hear from Dan, but having his card left the next move up to her.

No pressure, Robin. Or is it Rachel?

* * *

Saturday morning, Meghan checked her father's room. He never returned from the casino. She was angry at him and herself for letting alcohol interfere with another DeCosta man last night. When Dan explained his mother's medical issues, she felt terrible. But the golden margaritas changed her mood and fired up her libido. She hadn't had intimacy in months, and the charming guy easily amped her up.

They kissed when she parked her car and were primed for paradise by the dashboard light. Their tongues tangled, and their hands roamed freely. She had to be careful with Dan's injured ribs, then remembered her teen parking dates. *This won't take long.* She grabbed Dan's bulge, then tugged on his zipper. Unexpectedly, the security guard appeared, and they both froze.

Meghan ate her morning fruit and thought—*you're better than that.* She filled Bruschi's water and food bowls and called her father, who finally answered.

"Mornin,' Meg." He coughed and cleared his throat.

"Dad, why didn't you call?"

"I just got up. The casino comped me a room, meals, and drinks all night."

"When are you coming home?"

"I'm hanging with friends I met. Be home by five, six at the latest. I promise."

"Call when you leave. And don't forget to take your meds." *God, I sound like Mom.*

Meghan considered retrieving her mother's medical records and researching the articles but had already committed to water PT with Dan. She took Bruschi for his walk, and they ran into Emily, the neighborhood dog sitter, who agreed to watch him.

She put on her red bikini and pulled on an oversized pink T-shirt she got for participating in a Boston 5K run for breast cancer. Meghan then loaded her mother's red canvas pull cart with Styrofoam dumbbells, noodles, and a float. She went to the pool and waited for Dan. *Keep it professional today,* she smiled to herself.

* * *

Dan woke up excited about the pool time planned with Meghan. She drove him crazy last night. He couldn't take his eyes off her when he saw her in that seductive minidress. And they couldn't take their hands off each other while making out in her car. Fortunately, the security guy didn't shine his flashlight on her head, hovering over his crotch.

His mother drove him to their high-rise rental. "Did you get your lump sum payoff from GreenEx?" she asked on the way.

"Not yet. But my first short-term disability check got deposited."

He helped her carry bags up the elevator to the apartment where Sam would stay for the next two weeks. "Did you sign up for unemployment?" His mom asked.

"Not yet. I'm seriously considering looking for work in Florida."

"Get unemployment in Mass, first. Then, apply for jobs there and here. It's required."

"Okay, Mom."

Meghan walked into the pool with him, wearing a pink baseball cap and a T-shirt over her bathing suit. She stood beside him and helped him lie on an air mattress. His dark sunglasses helped him focus on her instructions instead of her wet T-shirt clinging to her rounded red bikini bottom. They used noodles and foam dumbbells to do PT routines.

"Good job, Dan," she said, holding the float for him. "Now, turn over on your stomach."

The pool was getting busy, and two little girls playing Marco Polo moved closer to them. Simultaneously, somebody swam by and splashed water in his face. During the commotion, Dan slipped off the float, and his sunglasses drifted to the bottom of the pool.

"Hey! Be careful, Rikki!" Meghan shouted on his behalf before retrieving his sunglasses.

"Thanks," he said, wiping the water from his face. Her soaked T-shirt highlighted the bullets projecting from her voluptuous breasts. "Permission to take a break?" he pleaded.

"Yes. It's too crowded now."

Meghan gathered the floats, and Dan followed her to their lounge chairs. They drank water and were toweling off when the woman who'd splashed him earlier approached them in a dripping wet black thong bikini.

"Sorry, Meghan. I tried to avoid the little girl playing Marco Polo," the slender young woman explained. She then turned to Dan. "Are you okay? Sir?"

"No problem," he smiled at the pretty girl and looked at Meghan for help.

"Dan, this is Rikki Rossetti… NBC's morning weather forecaster."

"Pleased to meet you," he extended his hand, "Dan DeCosta."

"Likewise," she shook his hand, "I just moved here from Tampa."

She toweled off and took the lounge chair between his and Meghan's.

"Must be a boring job, with all this sunshine to report," he teased Rikki.

"Ha-ha. You won't need an umbrella or jacket this week," she replied. "But it does get dangerous with lightening in the summer rainy season and hectic in the hurricane months."

"I bet. And all the toxic runoff from the heavy rains damages the seas and water supply."

Rikki nodded at him, and he continued, "I'm an environmental engineer from Massachusetts; been here a few weeks. Considering oceanology jobs in this area."

"Glad to hear it. We need all the help we can get in the Sunshine State," Rikki said, peering
at Meghan as she pulled off her wet T-shirt, exposing her red string bikini.

* * *

Dan's mother walked across the pool deck toward the group. She stood and greeted Meghan, "Hi. I saw you helping Dan from our rental unit."

"We were making progress until Rikki arrived." Meghan teased.

"Rikki did me a favor," Dan said in her defense, "I needed a break."

"Have we met?" Jo smiled at Rikki.

"Rikki Rossetti," she replied.

Dan added, "NBC's meteorologist."

"How nice! I'm Joanna. Can I get your picture with me and my son?"

Rikki nodded. Jo handed her phone to Meghan, posed behind Dan and Rikki's chairs, and then between Rikki and Meghan.

Meghan pulled Jo aside and lowered her voice, "How are you feeling? Dan said you had tests done."

"Tired, frustrated. My blood pressure's up. I can't play tennis or drink. But I'm excited, my daughter's coming tonight. After she leaves, I'll have surgery to improve my situation."

"Oh, good! You let me know If I can help with anything," Meghan replied with sincerity.

"Thanks," Joanna said warmly. Then, she turned to her son and said, "Dan, I'm leaving now. If you want a ride?"

Dan replied, "I'm in no hurry to leave."

"Ah, we've both had enough for today," Meghan advised him. "You can work on those pool routines at your parents' condo," Meghan noted the disappointment on Dan's face and Rikki's contrasting smile. *Perhaps my instincts are right about her.*

As Dan and his mom left, Meghan laid back in her chair. Rikki then turned toward her, "Dan seems nice. Is he a PT patient?"

"Friend of the family. His father and my dad worked at the same computer company. We're all from the Boston area. You and Dan hit it off well."

"We're both into ecology and biodiversity—but he's not my type." Rikki smiled.

"I see. So, not your Steely Dan?" Meghan grinned and looked at her.

"Nah. Mine's in my underwear drawer. Hehe."

"Mine too … and I need batteries. Bahaha."

"Don't ya hate when that happens." They both laughed louder.

Meghan's phone dinged. "Excuse me," she said."

It was a text from her old boss, Dr. Allan Hansen.

> GL. In your area today. D If you're free?

GL stood for green light—Allan's family wasn't with him. And D meant dinner if she could make it. Meghan knew he had friends who lived in a Naples golf community. *Oh, why not? A girl's gotta eat, and Allan's always a treat.* She replied to his text.

Maybe. Call me later with specifics.

"Gotta run," she told Rikki abruptly, loading her canvas wagon.

"Well, I hope I see you tomorrow. Should be a perfect pool day again."

"Yes! Good to know. Bye now."

Meghan then headed to the storage room to gather her mother's health records. Her inner voice sang Steely Dan's upbeat song, "Peg." The documents might shed light on what happened in her mom's past.

* * *

Sean opened the trunk of Lacy's red Toyota Corolla. He put the Corona twelve-pack, a bag of ice, and the rib eye steaks in the cooler. He then grabbed the case of water bottles from the shopping cart and placed it in the trunk next to the heavy-duty trash bags and zip ties he hoped he wouldn't have to use. Sean then grabbed two water bottles, shut the trunk, jumped into the front seat, and drove to the end of the supermarket's parking lot.

He parked near the trees facing the walk along the road connecting the two major plazas. He pulled out a Marlboro, lit it, opened a water bottle, and checked the time on his phone. Sean wasn't sure when she'd appear, but he planned to sit there and wait for her to walk by.

Robin loves steak and beeah. Sean couldn't wait to tell her about his new job and introduce her to Greg and Lacy. She'd be proud of him for how far he'd come. *Or maybe not.*

Sean reached into the pocket of his cargo shorts and found Haggerty's knife and the zip ties. He could snap Robin's neck as he did Miggy's before he dumped his body in the woods, beat on it, and made it look like a gay hate crime. He could keep her body in Haggerty's tool shed until dark. Then, borrow the Haggerty's truck to get gas for the lawn mower.

Earlier, he'd driven by North Fort Myers's enormous, capped landfill on Route 41 and checked out the access roads. It gave him options. Sean knew the putrid methane gas would mask the decaying corpse smell in the trash bag. Preferably, he'd douse it with gasoline, flick a Marlboro at it, and torch the body and surrounding trash.

Chapter 51

It was eighty-nine degrees, sunny, with no breeze, and humid when Rachel left Lowe's for Kelly's salon. She had received a text from Becca to call her ASAP. She was too tired and depressed to hear more drama about her mother or the Subaru needing brakes. And she stressed over the photo Dan's father had taken. Rachel knew she looked as bad as she felt and would never measure up to that knockout blond with Dan last night. She reached into her back pocket and pulled out the card.

Dick DeCosta Renewable Energy Consultant

It had a number with a Massachusetts area code. She stopped under a shaded tree to create a new contact. Before she opened her phone, Becca called.

"Hey. Where are you?" her sister asked anxiously.

"Walking from Lowe's, a few minutes from Auntie K's salon."

"Well, you need to know. Sean's in Florida!"

"What? Where? I thought you said he got arrested."

"He got off no charges. I got a call from Ashley, the *Lowell Sun* reporter. She's dating a Lowell contractor who knows Sean. She heard he got a job in Fort Myers."

Rachel took a deep breath. She was trembling.

"You still there?" Becca asked.

"Does this reportah know where I live?" replied Rachel.

"She thinks you're in Orlando. I said you were waitressing there. So, be careful."

"Thanks. I gotta go."

Rachel slid her phone into her back pocket and sat near the tree's base. She then closed her eyes and rubbed her temples. The noisy vehicles driving by did not drown out her scream, "Ahhhhh! Fuck noooo!" She covered her face with her hands and wept uncontrollably.

"You, okay?" She heard a man ask behind her, "Can I help you up?"

Rachel jumped when she felt his hand on her shoulder. Looking up through her teary eyes at the caring gray-haired man, she said, "I'm fine. Jus havin' a bad day."

"You sure? It's hot out." He glanced at the parking lot, where a woman with a water bottle stood by an open car door. "Want some water?"

She shook her head, pulled herself up, and leaned against the tree. Her stomach tightened when she spotted a younger man with closed-cropped hair running hard toward them.

"Outa da way!" the red-faced guy shouted before he shoved the older man aside. "Robin… drink watah!" Sean handed her a plastic bottle.

"No!" Rachel screamed as she swatted it from his hand.

Sean then grabbed her wrist.

"Get *away* from me, Sean!" she screamed.

"Leave her alone!" the man intervened, grabbing Sean's other arm.

"Stay outah this, Mista!" Sean tossed the older man to the ground, pulled his knife out, and pointed it. "Take off, ole man, it don't concern you."

Rachel clawed at Sean's wrist but couldn't break free. "Let go! I got a restraining ordah!"

"You're comin' to a suppah with my friends and me."

"Oww!" she screamed when he twisted her wrist and tried to bend her arm behind her back. Rachel bit down hard on his other hand, forcing him to drop the knife. But then Sean grabbed her hair and jerked her head toward him. Rachel spit in his face, grabbed the tree with her free hand for balance, and kicked him as hard as she could in his balls.

Sean let go of her hair and wailed, "Farhk." He bent over in pain, covered his crotch with both hands, and yelled, "You *vicious* cun—!"

She kicked him in the head. As soon as Sean fell backward onto the ground, Rachel took off. But when she looked back, she stopped. A silver-haired woman—she guessed was the gray-haired man's wife—handed a gun to the old guy, who then pointed it at Sean.

"Use your damn knife," dared the old man. "This is a stand-your-ground state. I'll blow your friggin head off!"

Rachel resumed her flee and bolted down the sidewalk, cut across the parking lot, and zig-zagged through the cars. She ducked behind an SUV to catch her breath and to see what she left behind. Her heart raced while the old man aimed his gun at Sean, who was now sitting on the ground with his hands raised. The man's wife was now talking into her phone.

Cars pulled over, and other people gathered near the older man and his wife. With sirens off in the distance, Rachel walked briskly and diagonally across the parking lot to the other plaza, where her aunt's salon was. She hustled along the storefronts until she reached the entrance to Cape Cuts.

* * *

Dick finished the paint touch-ups and installed the new faucet and the toilet's flush valve. He had one more task left when he got a text from Jo; she'd brought Dan home with her. Dick removed the AC's old air filter, wrote today's date, 3/21/2020, on the new one, and installed it. He washed up, grabbed the paint can, and took the elevator to the storage area, where he locked the paint supplies in his steel storage cage.

Dick was headed down the main corridor when he spotted Meghan up ahead with her phone to her ear. Her other hand pulled a red cart with pool gear and Manila folders; a pink T-shirt barely covered her red bikini bottom. She looked over her shoulder at him, closing their distance, and stopped.

"Got it, Allan. I'll meet you at The Indigo Room," he heard her say as she ended her call.

"Dick… Fancy meeting you here." Meghan gave him a devilish grin.

"Storing paint. Getting our rental ready for my daughter arriving tonight."

"Aha. I thought maybe you were stalking me. Tee-hee."

"No. Just lucky," he said, winking at her. "How's Mack doing?"

"He's coming home from the casino," she said by the exit. "Just in time to watch Bruschi, as I'm going to dinner with a friend from Boston."

"Good for *you*. What restaurant?" he asked, holding the exit door for her.

"The Veranda. Is it a nice place?"

"Ah, The V. Elegant place, great menu." Dick gave her a thumbs-up. "And they have a cool piano player in their bar—also known as Courtroom V because lawyers stop in from the courthouse."

"Ooh. You got me excited, now."

Your friend from Bawstin must be, too. "Have fun. You deserve it," he said as they parted ways in the garage.

"Thanks, that's the plan," she said over her shoulder.

He watched her pull her red cart behind her perfect red caboose.

* * *

When Dick got home, Jo was in a good mood; Sam was arriving tonight. The TV's music channel had Tina Turner belting out "The Best." She'd dedicated Turner's song to him three years ago when they'd celebrated their thirty-fifth wedding anniversary in Aruba. He hugged her, kissed her, and asked, "Where's Dan?"

"In his room."

He walked down the hall and found Dan resting on his bed.

"How'd the PT pool session go with Meghan?"

"Good. Learned a few water moves. And Mom and I met Rikki Rosetti, an NBC News meteorologist. She's sweet, into biodiversity, and knowledgeable about climate change."

"She better be. She's a meteorologist," Dick said, then added, "The rental's ready. Sam will have a great view, privacy, and room to work."

"Yep," Dan said, "I'm going to start looking for work here. Might enroll in FGCU's master's program. Think I can sell my home in North Chelmsford?"

"Maybe. But the pandemic will make real estate and the job market shaky now."

"I know. But it can't hurt to try."

Dick nodded and headed for the bathroom to shower.

* * *

Meghan finished showering and dried her hair. She was looking forward to having fun with Allan but was apprehensive. She'd quit working for the needy orthopedic surgeon three months ago and wondered about the surprise he said he'd tell her about over dinner. The Veranda was a short walk from Allan's hotel. *Perfect, no driving,* she thought, knowing he'd prime her with drinks to have his way with her later.

She set aside a mauve satin midi dress with spaghetti straps and put on her hottest Victoria's Secret undergarments. Meghan vividly recalled when Allan invited her to play golf at a Myrtle Beach resort. They had played eighteen holes, then had lunch and cocktails in the clubhouse. It was late September and too cool for the beach. They went to their ocean-view suite, undressed, donned white terry cloth robes, and sipped white wine. After her lusty romp on top, she rested beside him. He had gently stroked her breasts and tummy, then found her inner thigh.

"I doubt all surgeons have your soft hands and magical touch," she said coyly.

Meghan giggled when he said, "I also studied to be a gynecologist."

She moaned when he slipped two fingers inside, found her G spot, and pressed down on her stomach with his other hand. "Ooh, aah," she said. "My checkups will never be the same."

He chuckled and said, "I also interned as a proctologist."

"Really?" She rolled over. "Prove it."

Meghan's phone startled her reverie. "Meg, I'm leaving the casino lot now."

"Good, Dad. I have a dinner date downtown. I'll make you something when you get here." Her father had diabetes, and as a certified nutritionist, she worried about his cholesterol and not getting enough protein.

"Don't bother. I've ate all day," he coughed. "They comp my meals."

"Oh, right," Meghan said, putting her bathrobe over her undergarments.

She had an hour before Dad got home. Meghan spent the time going through her mom's medical records. The most recent were her cancer and chemo files. Older records in a tattered ob-gyn folder: Dr. Benjamin Friedman had performed a cesarean section and tubal ligation surgery on Meghan's birth date. *Mom's tubes tied made me the last one.*

She opened the envelope with the obituary that confirmed Friedman died fourteen years after Meghan's birth. She read through the investigative articles and one describing an FBI raid at Friedman's office—a few months before he'd committed suicide. The same *Boston Globe* journalist, Jackie Adams, had written the series on both the C-section investigations and the sexual allegations. *Hmm, why does that name sound familiar?*

Chapter 52

Sam's nonstop flight from San Franciso would arrive in Fort Myers at 6:05 p.m. She was glad passengers wore facemasks. The last two days were exhausting, filled with packing, moving, worrying about her mother's health, Khori on edge about anti-Asian harassment, COVID-19, the nearby wildfires, and the thought of being gone for two weeks. All of the tension was unbearable.

Sam made solo trips in Khori's SUV to move her things from her apartment to Khori's hillside cabin. She'd regretted selling her Honda and buying her expensive mountain bike. She ordered an Uber back to her apartment so she could stay there the night before her flight.

"I know you don't want to go near my place. That's why I didn't renew my lease," Sam told Khori as she waited for her Uber. "But don't say I'm not sympathetic because I need a ride back there. You'd never have to leave your car."

"You wouldn't know. You're a White-privileged blond who can go wherever you want and get whatever you need."

"That's not fair, Khori," Sam said, too pissed to say goodbye.

After boarding the plane, she swallowed her pride and texted Khori.

I'll be back before you know it. Love ya. 😘

Safe travels 🖤

A token response, Sam thought and closed her eyes to try to sleep on the flight.

When she landed in Fort Meyers, Sam texted her dad and Khori. She adjusted her mask and waited in the baggage area for her luggage, annoyed that most people did not wear facemasks. While she waited, Sam got caught up on the family chat posts. Her parents had dinner with a beautiful blond woman. In the next photo, her mom stood between Dan and an intriguing petite brunette in a bikini, captioned:

Rikki Rosetti, NBC-2 weathercaster.

Sam enlarged a photo of the stunning blond in a red bikini. Dan smiled proudly with his arm around the gorgeous, curvy woman's waist. *What's going on here, big brother?*

She pulled her suitcase off the carousel. Then she hoisted her computer bag with her company's laptop and iPad on her shoulder and dragged her luggage and carry-on bag to the curb. The warm eighty-four degrees and balmy breeze reminded her she was still in her flying clothes. Before she could take off her biking jacket, an Audi SUV e-tron pulled up.

"Hey, Sam!" It was her brother. He hugged her, grabbed her suitcase, and pulled it toward the car's rear.

He doesn't look like he had surgery three weeks ago. Good for him.

Her mother then met her with open arms. *No one is wearing face masks!*

"Samantha, mmm," she hugged her. "So glad you're here."

"Me too, Mom," she said, then joined her brother in the back seat. Her dad reached between the bucket seats, patted her extended hand, and drove off. With trepidation, Sam removed her mask.

"I'm hungry, but I need to freshen up and get out of these clothes," she announced.

Her mom said, "You can change at our condo. See that first. Then we'll walk to Joe's Crab Shack."

"Not crazy about seafood or inside dining," Sam said.

"Kings Kitchen," Dan suggested. "Cuban food with an outdoor patio."

"The governor just closed all bars in Florida for thirty days," Dad said. "Not restaurants."

"Great. Maybe they'll take COVID more seriously," Sam said. *This fuck'n state is crazy.*

"Let's hope so," her parents said in unison.

Her parents' impressive and spacious condo had incredible views. Her brother was right—the photos he posted didn't do it justice—you had to see this yourself.

Sam changed into shorts and a T-shirt, then said to her waiting family, "Let's get this party started."

* * *

Lacy Birch removed the extra place setting. *We won't be partying with that stalker.* She brought two beers outside to Greg, who was grilling steaks. Hours earlier, Sean called Greg and said the police detained him for a misunderstanding with a gun-toting man in a plaza where he shopped for their dinner. Greg had driven Lacy to Cape Coral, where they arrived just in time to halt the police from towing her car.

But the story changed. The cop said Sean was arrested for assaulting a senior citizen who tried to break up a fight between him and an unidentified red-haired woman who fled the scene.

Lacey said, "Let's go, Greg. We got my car and the cooler. This doesn't concern us."

After they finished their dinner, Greg called the police station for an update on Sean. He learned Cassidy had a restraining order against him filed by a woman in Massachusetts; they did not reveal her name. His first-degree assault charges had been reduced to simple battery; he would be released soon with his personal belongings.

"The bastard used us," Lacy fumed.

Greg said, "I texted him and said he won't have a job with HTS. And I won't pick him up at the station."

"And he ain't sleeping here," Lacy said. "Tell'm his bags will be at Haggerty's office."

* * *

Meghan looked at the full-length mirror and pivoted on her pumps. The clingy satin mauve dress showcased her tan and figure. She found her dad on the lanai, "Don't wait up. I'm having dinner with Allan, my old boss. He's flying back to Boston tomorrow."

"Have fun, Meg," he said, coughed, and lit a cigarette.

She drove downtown, knowing the married doctor was as risky and addictive as her father's gambling. But she'd let this one ride until a safer bet came along. She pulled up to The Indigo's valet, took her stub, and entered the hotel.

Allan sat in the Indigo's empty lounge, his back to her, talking on his phone. His blond, thinning hair exposed the bald spot on the back of his head. He turned, ended his call, and rushed to greet her, "Wow, Meghan. You look amazing."

"Thanks! You look good, too," she said. His sunburned face and arms blended with his papaya-colored Tommy Bahama shirt. He pecked her cheek, then hugged her to his chest.

"The concierge said the governor closed the bars today," reported Allan. "The restaurant's got a piano bar, which should be open with fifty percent seating," he said as he took her hand and led her to the street.

"About time. Covidiots here… and we have so many vulnerable elders," she said as they strolled over colored pavers toward The Veranda restaurant.

"Florida looks good on you," he said, his eyes focused on her cleavage. "You have a great tan."

I bet you can't wait to see my tan lines. "Thanks, you got some color. Been playing golf with your friends in Naples?"

"Fort Myers. At The Legends," he said to her surprise.

"I played there on Saint Paddy's Day."

"I saw you on Facebook. That's why I checked it out."

Interesting, she thought as they entered the elegant Veranda's refurbished 118-year-old historic home—forty-two years in business, it was the longest-running restaurant in Fort Myers.

"Twenty minutes," the hostess wearing a facemask said, motioning toward the piano bar. "We'll find you."

A boomer couple sat on the front side of the polished dark wood-paneled bar. They grabbed two end stools to social distance. The bartender mixed a Cosmopolitan for Meghan and a dirty martini for Allan.

She toasted, "Welcome to Fort Myers."

Several parties were enjoying cocktails at the lounge's socially-distanced tables. The talented piano player Rick delivered a smooth Satchmo rendition of "What a Wonderful World."

"The Legends is a private club. How'd you get in?" she asked Allan.

"I bought a condo with a golf membership. Barring COVID, I'll return to close or wire the funds and use electronic signatures." He then toasted, "To my Legends surprise."

"I'll drink to that," she said. They drank, and he explained.

"From Boston, I contacted Patti Long, the club's on-site realtor, whose husband, Pete Long, is the resident golf pro. Patti set me up with property viewings and a round of golf with Pete. She also told me to book The Indigo and The Veranda for dinner before I arrived."

"Excellent realtor," Meghan smiled.

He guzzled his drink and asked for another. "She set me up to play twenty-one holes," he grinned and caressed her thigh.

"The Legends is only an eighteen-hole course."

"Yes," he leaned closer as he stroked her upper thigh. "I'm including *you.*"

"Easy, doctor," she patted his hand. *Booze makes a pig brash and overconfident,* she thought, then pivoted. "Deal-closing realtor and a golf pro. A dynamic duo."

"Yeah. They're a popular couple who know everything about everyone at The Legends. At the Sunset Grill, they introduced me to the club's president. Then to Lee Grisham, a huge guy, and his tall, attractive wife, Jackie."

"Ah, Yes! I was impressed by Lee… big generous guy with a big swing."

"And a big job. Heads up the FBI in Boston!"

Hmm, I thought he was a Boston Police detective.

"Lee said his wife inherited their place from her father, a wealthy attorney." She sipped her drink and added, "Or maybe that's a smokescreen, can't trust the FBI. Ha-ha."

Allan shrugged, "Lee's wife, Jackie, worked for the *Boston Globe*."

FBI, Globe reporter? Meghan racked her brain, trying to recall Lee's father-in-law's name. *Dad or Dick DeCosta would know.*

The piano player tapped the keys to the distinctive beginning of Leon Russell's "A Song For You." The hostess arrived, "Your table's ready." Allan settled the bar tab and dropped a tip in Rick's jar.

They sat at a private table by a window, viewing the outside garden diners. They started with spinach salads. Their server refilled their glasses with Pinot Gris; it complemented her Chilean sea bass and his Atlantic salmon.

Meghan noticed the bags under Allan's eyes. "Spinach and salmon, healthy choices."

He smiled, "Says the nutritionist who routinely bugs me about getting more protein."

She opened her phone and read a quote, "'If you don't eat adequate protein at each meal, you can end up anxious, depressed, hungry, and tired.' Says Doctor Mark Hyman."

Allan pretended to read from his phone, "Same symptoms are suffered by older men who don't get adequate sex, says Doctor Ruth Westheimer." They both had a good laugh.

When their key lime pie arrived, Meghan asked, "You talked about buying in Naples. Why The Legends?" She wanted to discuss this, and she had mixed emotions about it.

"Less expensive, near the airport and Jet Blue Park. My family's not into golf, but they love the Red Sox. They'll be down next spring if COVID is behind us. And I knew—"

"You knew I wouldn't be going back to Boston."

He nodded, "I knew you found work here, loved golf… and I hoped you missed me."

"Well—two out of three ain't bad," she chuckled, thinking about Meatloaf's hit song.

He pursed his lips, drank wine, and then pecked at the key lime pie.

Meghan patted his other hand and said, "I'm kidding."

He looked at her with his steely blue bloodshot eyes, "Prove it."

"You'll have to sleep on the plane," Meghan replied, then drained her wine glass. She smiled as the watchful waiter adjusted his facemask and rushed over.

Allan said, "Check, please."

Chapter 53

Sam enjoyed dinner and a fun time with her loving family. She'd missed them. No Facetime or WhatsApp chat would ever replace the close-knit family feeling of holidays and vacations with them. She sat on the couch with her mother out on the lanai while her father and Dan were inside watching TV.

"You did a fantastic job decorating and remodeling your amazing retirement home. And it's in a great spot. I see why you and Dad love it here."

"Thanks, we do. I'm so happy you're here." Her mom hugged her again. "And how are things going with Khori?"

Sam put her head on her mother's lap and her feet on the couch. Mom stroked her short hair and comforted her while she explained Khori's recent experience with anti-Asian harassment.

"Invite Khori to visit; you can get away to Key West for a few days."

"I did. She knows Key West is LGBTQ-friendly. But she's afraid to go anywhere with COVID and won't commit to anything."

"It's understandable if she feels abandoned. But you've done all you can to support her. If it doesn't work out, it wasn't meant to be."

"That's how I feel. I told her I was worried about you, Mom. So… what are you dealing with, and what can I do to help?" Sam sat up and held her mother's hand.

"I have an aneurysm. You helped by being here. I've decided I'll call Monday to schedule surgery. After a few days in the hospital, I'll be playing tennis in a few weeks."

"Oh, Mom." Sam hugged her. "I hope so."

Her mother was tired and retreating to bed.

"Good night, Mom. Ask Dan to come out and talk to me."

* * *

Dan and his dad were watching a flick they'd seen before. John Travolta and Uma Thurman were doing the Twist in the Tarantino classic *Pulp Fiction*.

"I know you don't want me to meddle," his father said, "but I have to let you know—"

"Here we go…You think I'm getting too close to Meghan, right?"

"Not where I'm going. But yeah, I do, and that's understandable."

"How so?"

"You're attracted to one another, both vulnerable, in a new town with no social life yet."

"She's gorgeous, not vulnerable."

"She's *lonely*. She lost her brother last year and now her mother. She's worried about her father. Personally… I think she's been frustrated and un-happy for quite a while."

"She's smoking hot. She can't be too lonely or lacking attention."

"She's got beauty, brains, and doctor's creds, plus she's highly com-petitive. That intimidates most guys who don't want to get upstaged."

"Guess I can see that," replied Dan. *She is assertive.*

"And she's pushing forty now," Dad added. "Successful, accomplished men who wouldn't be intimidated are usually married. Others want to bed her, not compete with her."

"I see what you mean," said Dan. *I don't have a shot.*

"Forget her, look," his dad said, showing him a picture of a red-haired woman wearing a facemask working at Lowe's. Dan took his dad's phone and said, "This isn't who you think it is. Her name tag says Rachel, not Robin."

"Expand it, look at her wrist. I met her last week in the paint department at Lowe's. She's got a wicked Bawstin accent," said Dick. "And this morn-ing, she was a cashier and examined my military ID."

Dan found the shamrock tattoo. "She looks upset," he said.

"We chatted. She said she saw us at Cabos last night."

"Oh wow!" Dan felt queasy.

"I took the photo and told her I needed proof for you."

"What'd she say?"

"Thought you were dating Meghan," said Dick. "I said she was a friend of the family giving you PT because you had surgery. She said to tell you she was truly sorry."

"She should be," Dan sighed.

"I gave her my card and told her to send me her contact info, and I'd pass it on to you."

"But she never followed up?"

"Not yet. I didn't want to meddle, but I thought you needed—"

"You, uh…you did the right thing, Dad. Forward her picture to me."

* * *

Sam looked out at the glittering cityscape, the marina, and the cars crossing the bridges. Dan joined her on the lanai with two cold beers. They clinked bottles and he asked her, "How's things out West?"

"Work's cool, but COVID and wildfires make everything pretty intense."

"I bet. How's things with Khori?"

"A bit rocky. Asians are getting harassed now. She got assaulted by a guy who also keyed her car at my apartment," said Sam. "She won't go near my place now, so I had to relinquish my lease. I'm now stuck in her cabin."

"Shit. She all right?"

"Physically… but bitter and struggling with everything else."

"Geez. I'm sorry," Dan said with genuine concern.

"Hey, remember the DNA test kit I sent you?" asked Sam. "Khori and I got our reports back. Mine are strange; let me know when you get yours."

"I sent my kit over a month ago," said Dan. "But I haven't heard back anything since."

"How are you doing? Considering how bad you looked three weeks ago in the hospital, you look pretty good."

"Thanks. I was hurting then, but Meghan and Dad helped with PT," said Dan. "Plus, Florida sunshine helps, too. I'm going to look for work here."

"Ha, I bet. You and that atomic blond look pretty friendly." *She's scary gorgeous.*

"Dad worked with Meghan's father years ago. Her mother recently died, and opioids killed her brother last year." Dan took a sip of his beer. "Meghan's my physical therapist. She's beautiful and a beautiful person."

"That's all?" Sam looked sideways at her brother. *Fess up.*

"That's all, Sam," Dan grinned. "She's ten years older than me and a doctor."

"Wow. She don't look it. … Is she friends with that cute weather woman, Rosie?"

"Rikki Rosetti. She just moved into the condo complex," said Dan. "She's *really* nice! Younger than me. She's heavy on ecology and knows a ton about climate change."

"Duh, she's a weathercaster," said Sam. "And you asked her how old she was?"

"Give me some credit—I googled her. She graduated from college the same year as you." *Interesting. I'll check her out.*

"Cool. So, how's your lust life going?" she drank some beer.

"Ha. I wish I knew."

"Did you hear from Robin?"

"Not yet. But she ran away and changed her name to Rachel," said Dan. "Dad bumped into her at Lowe's—here! She was supposed to send her contact info to him… but didn't."

Dan showed Sam the picture on his phone.

"Nice hair, but she looks sad."

He showed her another photo, "This is her on the last night we spent together."

Sam stared at the long-legged beauty sitting by the fireplace. Her thighs were barely covered by a football jersey with nothing else under it except her pale, curvy body. "Wow… she's hotter than the fireplace." *Never been with a ginger; keep her away from me.*

"She was that night," said Dan. "I thought we had something going 'til she took off."

"Did she seem happy or moody and distant before she left?" Sam asked.

"She was always upbeat and never complained," said Dan. "And she never said her ex was stalking her. I don't get it."

"Maybe she was trying to protect you," replied Sam. "But you know where she works; go after her. If she's honest, she'll open up to you."

"Maybe. I miss her. But the ball's in her court."

"Why do guys always think relationships are about gamesmanship?"

"We don't… I don't," said Dan. "I just don't want to get crushed again."

"I hear ya. But at this point, what do you have to lose?"

Her brother nodded and then downed his beer.

"I'm beat," said Sam. "Can you give me a ride to the rental now?"

"Love to, but I'm not supposed to drive yet," explained Dan. "Dad will take you there."

"Okay. Can you come to the pool tomorrow and introduce me to your friends?"

Dan smiled at her and said, "Big brothers—that's what we do."

Sam chuckled, *especially since your pool friends are sizzling hot babes.*

* * *

They entered his hotel room. Allan put his wallet and change on the nightstand, used the phone, and ordered an early morning cab to the airport for his Boston flight back.

Meghan said, "I'll be gone long before that," then kissed him.

Allan replied, "You have tropical sun exposure! You'll need a full skin exam."

"I'm due for one," she said, letting the doctor undress her and examine her tan lines.

"What's your findings, doctor?" she asked, unbuttoning his shirt.

"Anatomically perfect… chronically hot."

Chronically horny, she felt. "What's the cure?" she said, reaching into his shorts.

"Incurable… but treatable."

"I'll take my medicine now," she said. Then, she yanked his shorts down.

Allan grabbed a quarter from the nightstand and asked, "Heads or tails?"

It won't matter who wins the toss, she thought. *We've played this game before*

Meghan awakened with the urge to empty her bladder. She gently removed Allan's hand from her thigh, eased out of bed, and sipped the water she'd left on the nightstand. She rubbed her eyes, yawned, and felt the lockjaw pain. The illuminated alarm clock displayed 1:27 a.m. and cast a dim light on the carpet littered with condoms, lube, and the towels she stepped over on her way to the bathroom.

She was tender, and it burned when she peed. She hadn't felt this raw since their week in Myrtle Beach. She wasn't surprised after they played Feel of Fortune, a wild spinoff from "Wheel of Fortune." Their uninhibited game has simple rules: the coin toss winner picks a vowel for the first letter of the act, and the loser performs it. His yellow weekend pills, her salacious skills, and their pent-up yearnings to satisfy each other kept them flipping for vowels and performing until they finally dozed off around midnight.

Meghan cleaned up, dressed, and left him a mock message on the notepad by the phone.

> *Pat,*
> *Safe travels, and good luck with The Legends deal.*
> *Looking forward to the next round.*
> *Vanna.*

Meghan left without waking him. The Indigo's night clerk took another fifteen minutes to find another staffer to take her car out of valet parking. It was 2:12 when she tiptoed into her father's condo carrying her pumps. She then undressed, slipped under the covers, and wondered when she'd get a chance to play golf with Allan at The Legends. But before she fell asleep, she thought about Lee Grisham and his wife, the reporter, and why the FBI had raided her mother's ob-gyn's office.

Chapter 54

Sunday morning, Joanna felt better. She'd slept well knowing her family was safe, and she could now schedule surgery. She took her tea outside to the lanai and joined Dick and her son, who asked, "Mom, can I take your car to the rental today? Sam wants me to join her at the pool and introduce her to the neighbors."

She looked to her husband for help. He asked Dan, "How do your ribs feel?"

"Not bad. And my shoulder's stronger. I can handle Mom's automatic."

Dick asked, "You still want to sell your house and move to Florida?"

"Yeah. If I do, I can work or return to college for my master's."

"I'll check with Christina; she said her assistant is house hunting."

"Think she'd buy my house?"

"You never know—"

"Unless you ask," Joanna finished her husband's sentence. "Dan, my keys are on the counter. Bring Sam back with you. Tell her to dress up. We have dinner reservations at Cristof's on McGregor Boulevard."

* * *

Sam slept late Sunday. Her body was still on California time. Khori called and explained how the winds had shifted; the wildfires were now headed toward her cabin.

"Oh, Christ. You better make plans to evacuate!" Sam said, pecking at her bowl of fruit.

"I am, but I'm not sure where I'll stay," Khori said, and then they ended the call.

To take her mind off Khori, Sam headed to the fitness center. She put on her facemask and entered the quiet gym. A thin, bald man was running hard on a treadmill. *No mask.* Sam slid onto a recumbent bike and started pedaling. She scanned her phone for Twitter updates on the California fires and checked her crypto wallet. The gym door opened, and a fit woman in black spandex pants and a matching jacket entered. The attractive blond with no mask smiled at Sam when she approached the adjacent elliptical. The woman put her water bottle in the cup holder, adjusted her pink base-ball cap, and pedaled.

"Do you prefer the elliptical over the bike?" Sam asked the stunning woman.

"I'd rather ride my trail bike or the recumbent, but this one's fine."

"Me too," Sam said, "I usually ride my mountain bike in the California hills, but this will have to do for the next two weeks."

"I brought mine with me from Massachusetts."

"Where in Mass? My family's from there."

"Bedford. I'm Meghan." *Ah, my brother's hot PT, babe.*

"Sam… Samantha DeCosta, from Chelmsford. I took a job in San Francisco."

"I know your parents. I've been working with your brother, Dan. I'm a physical therapist." *And a physical specimen,* Sam thought, admiring Meghan's incredible body.

"Dan's made great progress. You must be good."

"Thank you! You're kind, like your lovely mother. How's she doing?"

"She looks okay but has a brain aneurysm. She's scheduling surgery—that's why I'm here."

"Oh, wow. That's so scary. You tell her I was asking for her."

"I will. Maybe I'll see you around the pool later," said Sam tentatively.

"Probably. And if you're up for a bike ride, I have my mother's in storage."

"That'd be great," Sam said.

The bald man got off the treadmill and said, "How ya doing, Meghan?"

"Good, Fred. And you?" she replied.

"Great!" the man then asked, "Is this your sister?"

"Ha. No." she smiled at Sam.

Sam got off the bike. "Great meeting you!" she said.

"You as well, Sam."

* * *

Dan adjusted the seat and mirror of his mom's Audi convertible. He hadn't driven in weeks; it felt strange. He was disappointed that Robin had yet to follow up. *Oh well, I can't wait to see Meghan and Rikki today.*

He wore his Speedo bathing suit and carried a change of clothes into the rental unit. Sam drank from her fruit smoothie, then asked, "How's Mom doin' today?"

"Good. She made reservations at a nice restaurant. She wants you to dress up and come back with me later."

They grabbed water, towels, and noodles and headed for the pool.

Sam said, "I met Meghan at the gym this morning. She's nice."

Hot and sunny in the high eighties, they laid their towels on lounge chairs. Sam beat Dan into the circular pool, pushed off with her long legs, and swam to the other end. He used the noodle floats while Sam swam back and stood next to him.

His sister's gaze followed Meghan, who was strolling across the pool deck with the confidence of a Miss Universe contestant and the body of a Hooters pinup. Meghan stretched out on the lounge chair next to theirs. Before he knew it, Sam left the pool and flanked Meghan. While they chatted, Dan dangled his shoulder from the float and made circular arm motions.

Several seniors occupied chairs on the pool deck. Dan realized there were far more retired people here than anyone his age. His spirits rose when Rikki tossed her towel on a chair and entered the pool. She swam by him, then circled back.

"How ya doin'?" He asked Rikki.

She smiled, "Great. Nice to have a beautiful day off." Rikki then looked past him toward Meghan and his sister. "So, Dan, the Jennifer Lawrence look-alike—is that Meghan's sister?"

"Nope. That's my little sister. She got in last night from San Francisco."

"She's a cutie. And resembles Meghan."

As are you, he wanted to say. "A little bit. But they're night and day and years apart."

"Seriously?"

"Yeah, I'll be thirty next month. My sister Sam turns twenty-six in May. And Meghan … amazing Meghan, will be forty in October."

"Wowzah. She doesn't look it. I'll be twenty-seven in May, like, Sam?"

"Samantha, we call her Sam."

"What's Sam's occupation?"

"She's a software engineer for Coinbase, a crypto company."

"Hmm. I've always been interested in Bitcoin, but clueless."

"I've shied away from it. Want to meet Sam?" Dan said, leaving the pool.

"Yes, please," Rikki said and scooted alongside him.

* * *

Meghan fascinated Sam. The woman was beautiful, intelligent, confident, and comfortable in her evenly tanned skin.

"Love your bathing suit," Sam said, admiring the flawless fit.

"Thanks! Victoria's Secret, Burlington Mall."

She should be an Instagram brand ambassador. "Thought so," Sam said, "You couldn't wear that too often in Boston."

"Exactly," Meghan said, "I don't miss the snow up north… nor my old boss. He cared more about my anatomy than my PT skills.”

“Oh. I hear ya. I had my hands full with jerks in power roles,” said Sam.

“Just get what you need to level the playing field,” replied Meghan. “Have fun, but make sure to maintain your dignity.”

“Maybe,” Sam said, “But it’s risky. I think women are more trustworthy.”

“Speaking of girls,” Meghan said with a grin, “Dan’s walking over with Rikki, our lovable local weather forecaster. I think she’s been checking you out.”

“Ooh! Thanks for the heads up.”

Sam’s brother approached, followed by a cute-as-a-button brunette with thick wavy hair and a wet string bikini.

Her brother said, “Sam, this is Rikki Rosetti.”

“Hi. Nice to meet you,” Rikki extended her hand to Sam.

“Hi!” Sam said, reaching Rikki’s thin hand, “I heard you forecasted this gorgeous day.”

“It should be perfect bikini weather… for the next two weeks.”

“Hope so, that’s how long—” Sam looked at her snickering brother.

“Smooth, Rikki,” Meghan said. Everyone laughed, knowing Dan tipped Rikki off.

Rikki turned to Meghan and said, “I thought you and Sam were sisters.”

“I’ll take that as a compliment,” Sam said, exchanging smiles with Meghan.

“You should,” Dan added and then looked at Meghan, “You both should!”

Meghan said, “Compliments will not get you any PT today. It’s Sunday, my day off.”

“Ha-ha. How’s your dad doing?” Dan asked. “Did he get back from the casino?”

She nodded.

To Sam’s delight, Dan took a chair on the other side of Meghan so Rikki could sit beside her. Sam was now hemmed between the women she’d asked Dan to introduce her to. She felt awkward. Then Sam read a scripted tattoo on Rikki’s upper thigh: *“Embrace the unknown.”*

“I love that,” Sam pointed at the tat high up near Rikki’s bikini line.

“Thank you! Something tells me you get it.”

Oh yeah. “Yup. I need the unknown,” Sam said. “But my parents would freak over a tattoo.” She sensed Meghan was listening in.

“My mom didn’t care—she’s a high school art and music teacher,” explained Rikki. “My dad, a college professor, teaches philosophy and tells his class to embrace change. He liked the quote and was glad it wasn’t a flashy sleeve tat that my TV viewers would see.” *Viewers won’t, but I know it's there.*

"Your parents seem pretty cool," Sam said. "And they blessed you with beautiful hair."

Rikki's pretty smile grew as her chestnut brown eyes and almond skin glittered.

"Thank you! Yeah, my mom's African American, and my dad's Italian. They live in Saint Petersburgh."

"I bet they're proud of you," said Sam. *She's adorable like Zoë Kravitz—with a finer body than Khori's,* she thought with a twinge of guilt.

"Aww…" she touched Sam's wrist, "I love *your* haircut. Perfect for swimming and hot humid weather."

"Thanks," Sam said, pushing her short hair behind one ear. *Don't you dare cut yours. It's as beautiful as Zendaya's,* Sam thought.

Rikki then asked Sam about Bitcoin and what blockchains were. She commended her for being at the forefront of technology and apologized for being woefully uninformed.

"Don't apologize," Sam said. "Most people wrongly believe it's a pyramid scheme. So, what got you interested in meteorology?"

"I grew up in Florida, where lightning killed my eight-year-old childhood friend. Later, I witnessed the destruction of hurricanes. I wanted to learn about the forces of Mother Nature."

"Wow, you turned your loss and curiosity into an excellent career," replied Sam in awe.

"Thank you," Rikki said. Sam felt the charge when Rikki touched her wrist again.

She admired the weathercaster's lifesaving information on hurricanes and was envious of Rikki's passion for her job. She thought Rikki's trusting voice and disarming personality were perfect for television. *Unreal. No one is this authentic and attractive—be careful.*

* * *

Meghan was worn out and sore. *Too much fun with Allan, not enough sleep.* She liked that she and Sam hit it off in the gym and took to each other at the pool. Meghan thought Sam was energetic and straightforward about her preference for women. She overheard the candid chatter between saucy Sam and adorable Rikki. She wasn't surprised by how quickly the sparks flew between them, though a bit jealous. *I saw the cute mulatto meteorologist first.*

Her thoughts shifted to Dan. She'd grown to appreciate him for dealing with his pain meds and his surprising progress in rehabbing his injuries. Meghan also appreciated how he inquired about her father. She wanted to ask him about his father and if he knew anyone in the FBI but decided this could wait with Sam and Rikki nearby.

Silvia approached them, said hi, and asked, "Who is this pretty young lady?"

"This is Samantha DeCosta," Meghan said, touching Sam's arm.

"Call me Sam," she said. "I'm staying in my parent's rental unit."

"The next two weeks," Rikki added, and everyone chuckled.

Silvia smiled and did a double take. "You know you have the same color hair and deep blue eyes as Meg?"

"Would you take our picture?" Meghan handed her phone to Silvia.

Silvia took a picture of Meghan and Sam, then stepped back and captured them all. She then returned the phone to Meghan, "All beautiful kids."

"I'll text these to you and Dan," Meghan told Sam. "What's your number?"

Sam rattled off her number. Meghan entered it for a group text with Dan. She heard both phones ding. "And if you want to ride bikes, now you have my number."

"What about me?" Rikki pleaded. "I'd like the pics."

"Oh, Rikki, you'd lose that number," Meghan teased.

Everyone laughed. Rikki said, "I fell into that one."

"Put your number in mine," Sam said, handing Rikki her phone, then added. "I expect up-to-the-minute warnings about clouds ruining my next two weeks."

"You got it. My fair-weather fan." They giggled.

Meghan watched Sam, Rikki, and Dan slip into the pool. She sighed. *I'm too tired to play with the millennials. I'll rest and then research Mom's past.*

* * *

Late Sunday morning, Rachel emerged from her room and forced herself to eat a bagel with coffee. Her scalp hurt where Sean had pulled her hair. She'd spent the evening hiding in her bedroom and complaining to Auntie K about a headache and cramps from her period; she never mentioned Sean. Rachel went to the laundry room, removed the clothes from the dryer she'd washed last evening, and then picked off the lint and shredded paper.

"Uh oh," she said. She'd left Mr. DeCosta's business card in her jeans. It was unreadable.

"Can't text him my contact info now." *Probably an omen since sicko Sean's in Florida. Maybe I need to move to Reno with Mom.*

She joined her aunt and uncle, reading the Sunday papers on the pool deck.

"How ya feelin' today?" her uncle asked. "Hope you didn't get that Corona bug."

"Little bettah. Don't think it's COVID."

"What happened to your wrist?" Aunt Kelly pointed at the bruises.

"I jammed it between paint cans as I pulled them off the shelf." She rubbed her wrist, "It's fine, and I'm off 'til Tuesday."

"Good, you need a few days off," Kelly said.

Then the doorbell rang. Roger went to the door and returned a moment later.

"Deputy Cruz, you know the one I tiled his kitchen?"

Her aunt nodded.

"He needs to speak with Rachel."

Rachel's heart sped as her head pounded. She sat on the couch beside her aunt to answer the middle-aged cop's questions. A younger police officer stood by the door.

"Miss O'Rourke. Where did you go last night, and when did you come home?"

"I never went out. Been here since my aunt drove us back from her hair salon."

Her aunt and uncle both confirmed.

"So… the last time you saw Sean Cassidy was yesterday afternoon when he assaulted you in the plaza parking lot? Why didn't you tell the police?"

Rachel's eyes welled up as she touched her badly bruised wrist. "Yes. I ran away. I didn't want him to know where I worked and make trouble for my aunt. He's dangerous!"

"Well—he won't be causing any more trouble—they found his body at a North Fort Myers mobile park. Drug overdose."

Rachel collapsed in her aunt's arms and began to bawl.

"Sorry to disturb you. We had to follow up and close the loop on this as we knew Miss O'Rourke had a restraining order against Cassidy," said Deputy Cruz as he left.

Chapter 55

Monday morning, March 23, Dick watched Jo write in her calendar—noninvasive surgery, Tuesday morning, March 31.

He hugged her. "Jo, you made the right choice. And I'll be there with you."

"I know, Dick. Just wish I'd decided and done it sooner."

"Good news," he said. "Christina's assistant, Chantel Jenkins, and her husband are interested in Dan's house. I'm overnighting Christina the keys."

"Oh, good! I hope it works out for Dan," Jo said.

He knew Dan's traumatic experience with the Chelmsford cops, plus Robin's disappearance had left him disenchanted with a home he never wanted. Since Dan had gone off on him in the hospital, Dick felt guilty about pushing him into buying it. He was happy to give him this news.

"Wow, Dad. It would be amazing if we sold it without listing it."

"Especially in this COVID market." Dick added, "The Massachusetts governor issued a lockdown. Only essential workers can go to work."

"Things are shutting down everywhere. Jobs are hard to find," his son said. "So not having to worry about a mortgage is key. I hope it sells."

Dick still hadn't heard from Robin. He felt bad for Dan but needed to work on his second book, which was falling way behind schedule. He decided to help Dan with his PT first.

"Want to hit the gym?" Dick asked.

"Sure," Dan said, grabbing his beer gut, "I'm getting a spare tire."

* * *

Dan spotted Ted Bates pumping iron in the gym. He did stretches while Dad set up the cable pulleys for him. An attractive personal trainer with a blonde ponytail who was working with an older woman smiled at his father and said, "Hi Dickie. Is this your son? He looks just like you."

His father grinned, "Dan, this is Laura Brit. She keeps everyone hopping in here."

"Hi," Dan said, smiling at the lovely woman with the slim, sculptured body that drew the eyes of all the guys in the gym.

Dan did everything his father suggested with the pulleys and then on a padded mat. Ted watched Dan do his last reps, complimented him on his progress, then asked his Dad, "Dick, want to hit the driving range with me tomorrow?"

"Sure," his father replied.

"Can I go too?" Dan asked.

Dad looked at Ted, and they both shook their heads. "You're not ready to swing a golf club. You could hurt your rib cage, set you back another month."

Dan and his father returned to the condo, where his mother was glued to the TV. The local NBC station had breaking news at a North Fort Myers mobile home park where a man's body had been found. They listened to the reporter, Jenn Walker, on the scene.

"The coroner's office confirmed Sean Cassidy of Lowell, Massachusetts, died of street fentanyl poisoning—the fourth area overdose in the past two weeks. Ironically, the sheriff's department had Cassidy in custody Saturday for assaulting a man in a parking lot. The police dropped him off at the mobile home's office. The next morning, Brian Haggerty, the park's owner, found Cassidy in his storage shed. Sadly, opioids kill more than a hundred people every day nationwide. Reporting live from North Fort Myers, Jenn Walker, NBC2 News."

"Oh wow! That's Robin's ex," Dan said.

"Poor Robin," his dad said. "Maybe that's why she hasn't followed up."

Mom looked at Dad, "What's going on? What have I missed?"

"Saturday, I ran into Robin at Lowe's and took her picture," said Dad. "I left her my card so she could send me her contact info, which I'd pass on to Dan." He pulled up the photo and showed it to her.

"Oh wow! I met her. That's my hairdresser's niece. She calls her Rachel."

"You sure?" Dan asked.

"Yes. She's a receptionist at the salon. And walks to Lowe's to work her other job. Wicked Bawstin accent."

His father nodded. Mom added, "She's nice. You should drop in on her. The salon is closed on Mondays, but she'll be there on Tuesday."

"I don't know, Mom. It's not that simple," Dan said, rolling his tender right shoulder.

* * *

Sam texted Khori pictures of her river view. She then posted photos of her, Rikki, Meghan, and Dan on the family chat. She felt guilty about not sharing them with Khori, knowing she'd ask about the two attractive women in bi-kinis she sat between at the pool.

At last night's excellent dinner at Cristof's, Sam promised to meet her mother downtown for shopping and lunch. Dad suggested Sam take the free trolley that stops at the high-rise buildings. Before leaving, she caught Rikki's weather forecasts. She looked different in a conservative black dress, silver hoops, and a chain with a Catholic cross around her neck. Her phone rang; she muted the TV.

"Hey, got your text," Khori said. "The fires are heading our way. They're telling us to be ready to evacuate if we don't get rain soon or the winds pick up."

"Shit, Khori. Don't wait. Go to a hotel in town… Come to Florida."

"I got email matches on Ancestry.com. I connected with a second cousin and her husband, who live in Chinatown. They know about the fires and said I can stay with them."

"That's great. I sent my DNA saliva kits weeks ago. I haven't heard anything from either site." Sam lied; she couldn't admit she had surprises in her reports.

"I got mine last week. Check your spam filters," Khori said.

"I will. You get your car packed to be ready to evacuate. Keep me posted. Love ya."

After Khori's mammogram revealed a tiny benign lump, she submitted her DNA to 23andme. The health report showed no cancer in her family's history. Khori then ordered test kits for her and Sam from Ancestry.com. She teased Sam about having blond hair and blue eyes, unlike her father and brother, who have dark hair and brown eyes.

Sam explained. "My Mom's family is mostly French Canadian. She has green eyes and dirty blond hair; I favor her."

Khori guilted Sam into submitting her saliva kit to Ancestry.com. She also gifted Dan a kit but never told Khori. When Sam learned of her mom's health issues, she also submitted to 23andme to understand her family's genetic history, especially since her aunt had breast cancer.

Sam used her iPad and logged on to her Ancestry account. There were no email updates or indications that her brother's results were in, so she looked again at the composition profile.

"What the hell. This can't be right!" she shouted at the screen. It did not show all the world regions she expected, and her DNA composition breakout startled her.

Sam shut her iPad off. *Shit, I can't ask my parents about this—especially Mom, with her delicate condition.*

She had several DNA matches from names she didn't recognize. Based on the DNA percentages in the low twenties, they were projected to be cousins, half-siblings, aunts, uncles, or grandparents. Parents and full siblings are typically 50 percent. She'd get another email match notice when Dan's Ancestry.com reports came in. She wondered when her 23andme reports would arrive.

Sam unmuted the TV when Rikki appeared and said, "Droughts in California, tornadoes, torrential rains, and floods in the southern states, but another perfect weather day in Southwest Florida. I'll return in fifteen minutes to give you the seven-day forecast."

Sam shut the TV off and texted her mother. She'd catch the trolley downtown.

* * *

Meghan enjoyed her first day at the Fort Myers Rehab Center. All the employees now required to wear facemasks supplied at the door warmly welcomed her. *Maybe all the patients should wear masks.* Many of their clients were elderly and far more vulnerable to COVID-19. The director was older, and the administrative staff were closer to her age. The physical therapists were much younger and typically assigned to younger patients recovering from sports injuries or auto accidents.

"We'll get you oriented here first," the director said. "Before sending you out to long-term care facilities."

Many older clients, especially those recovering from strokes, require physical and occupational therapy, managed care, and nutrition guidance. They were counting on Meghan to deal with an aging clientele, including nursing homes and assisted living facilities. Older, more mobile men also required physical therapy. *Maybe I'll find a wealthy sugar daddy who needs special care after rehab.*

Meghan then texted Dan. Walk-ins with insurance were allowed, but he'd probably get assigned to a younger therapist.

After work, she picked up pizza and salads on the way home. Over dinner, she told her dad she liked her new job and told him about Sam.

"Wednesday, my day off, I invited Sam DeCosta to ride. She'll use Mom's old bike."

Her dad said, "Dick DeCosta invited me to the driving range tomorrow morning."

"Oh, good," she said. "By the way. Do you remember Lee Grisham said his father-in-law had a brain hemorrhage on a flight to Boston? What was his name?"

"Adams. Bob Adams… like the beeah from Boston."

"Figures you'd make that connection." They both laughed, and Bruschi barked.

"Why do you want to know about Adams?"

"I'm worried about Joanna. Dan said she's got a brain aneurysm. I remembered Lee's frightful story and how pale Dick got at the table."

Her father coughed, "Yeah, Dick and Jo keep things to themselves. Always have."

She recalled how upset her mother was about the DeCostas and her warning, *"Stay away from them—they're trouble."*

After dinner, she read Jackie Adams's investigative newspaper articles. She then googled Adams and found her *Boston Globe* mini bio. Jackie Adams won an investigative journalism award for her series on BRCA1 tests for women with breast cancer genes. As a result, many young women were getting mastectomies even though they did not have cancer. She also won an award for a series on unusually high volumes of cesarean births—it led to women coming forward about Dr. Friedman with sexual harassment allegations. Jackie Adams is married to Leland J Grisham and resides in Newton, MA. *And winters in Fort Myers,* Meghan thought.

She went to the storage room and cleaned her mother's old bike to prepare it for Sam. She hoped to get information about Dick DeCosta on Wednesday.

* * *

Rachel was torn with mixed emotions for Sean, her first true love, who had put her through hell for the past two years. She felt empty but relieved, knowing he'd never harm her again. She needed to find Dan. Rachel was disgusted with herself for destroying his dad's business card in the laundry. *They must think I'm a psycho bitch.*

Eventually, Rachel grew tired of crying and lying in bed. She called Becca, who said she read Sean's body would be cremated in Florida and his remains sent to Lowell for a future memorial service.

"I'd still like to say goodbye to him," said Rachel in between tears.

Becca said, "Don't go through the stress and expense of attending. Pay your respects online and send a card to his mother."

"You're right. And I need the money for college," Rachel added.

She found the *Lowell Sun's* online obituary for Sean Cassidy and posted:

> My sincerest condolences to Sean's loving mother, his uncle Bill Cassidy, and their families. We'll miss Sean's big smile and even bigger heart. Please know that his struggles are over, and he's in a much better place. RIP Sean.

Her aunt Kelly entered her room and said, "You've been moping all weekend. Clean up. We're having Gary and Jill Gagnon over for dinner."

She'd met Jill Gagnon at her aunt's salon. Gary owned a plumbing company and worked for the same builders Roger installed tile for. They barbecued steaks in their outside kitchen and drank beers by the pool.

The conversation turned to builders and contractors. Rachel listened closely as Gary explained, "We've been busy over at Babcock Ranch. The planned community is powered by a massive seventy-five-megawatt solar voltaic array for all the homes in several subdivisions, including the stores, restaurants, and municipal buildings."

"It's the largest solar farm in the state," Roger added. "And it has the biggest battery storage in the country."

Rachel thought that a city powered by solar energy made sense in the Sunshine State, then remembered that Mr. DeCosta's card was for his solar business. After their guest left, she used her phone, "Hey Siri… Find Dick DeCosta Solar."

It found Sold on Solar in his LinkedIn profile. She added the Massachusetts phone number to her contact list, named it Mr. D, and then texted him.

> Hi. This is Rachel from Lowe's. Thank you for reaching out to me! Please tell Dan I am truly sorry about everything. And that Robin from Lowell hopes he'll give her a chance to explain what happened.

Swish, her text was now in transit. Rachel then made the sign of the cross, hoping she had the correct number and that Dan would find it in his heart to forgive her.

* * *

Tuesday morning, Dick received a text from Rachel. He replied.
> Got it, Rachel. Will do. Thanks!

Dick copied her number and message, then texted it to Dan, who was still sleeping.
> Red alert. Her number and message follow. Be kind

Dick then forwarded a COVID email directive from the condo's management to Jo and Dan. Essentially, the CDC now recommends face masks, social distancing, and shelter in place for people over sixty or with preexisting conditions. Florida's bars are closed, and restaurants could operate at 50 percent, but there were no restrictions on golf courses. Dick left a box of facemasks on the kitchen counter for them before he headed out.

Ted rode with him to Golf World's driving range in North Fort Myers. He told Dick, "Sometimes the driving range is better than a round of golf. It's a good workout and a way to release my anxiety and frustrations."

Ted was an activist and an outspoken progressive. His transgender daughter, a Democrat state representative in Virginia, had been treated harshly by the opposing party. Ted expressed his anxiety about how many Floridians, especially around Fort Myers, were not taking the pandemic seriously. Dick shared similar concerns, in addition to Floridia's lawmakers and developers disregard for the environment.

They pulled into Golf World and parked next to Mack's top-down Mustang. Mack was smoking a cigarette. Dick introduced Mack to Ted, who cautiously elbow-bumped him rather than shake Mack's hand. Dick and Ted put on their facemasks before they all entered the Pro Shop, paid for their buckets of balls, and walked to the driving tees. After they each hit long drives, Mack asked Dick, "Want to go to the Seminole Casino with me on Thursday?"

"Love Blackjack, but I don't trust indoor crowds with rising COVID numbers. I'll pass."

"The numbers ain't rising in Florida," countered Mack. " And the president said the virus will be gone by Easter."

Ted raised an eyebrow to Dick, shook his head, and took a big swing. The ball soared further than usual. Ted said, "We need to eliminate the Electoral College. And we need term limits in Congress.

Dick nodded and watched Mack drive a few balls, cough hysterically, and then clear his throat. They all soon emptied their buckets.

"Thanks again, guys," Mack said as he slid into his silver Mustang.

The Mustang backed up, then stopped, when Dick put up his hands to tell Mack, "Your right rear brake light and the blinker aren't working."

"Thanks, Dick," Mack said. He cleared his throat and added, "I must be emotionally constipated. Cuz, I haven't given a shit in weeks. Ha-ha." Then he sped off.

Dick shrugged and looked at Ted, who said, "Not surprised. Florida doesn't have auto safety or emissions inspections."

"You're shitting me! Since when?" Dick was curious, as he'd only lived in Florida for six months.

"Since the damn climate deniers running this state did away with them. Another reason why the third most populated state has so many fatal accidents and sky-high insurance rates."

"Damn. So much for the elderly drivers and the fuckin' environment," Dick fumed.

* * *

Tuesday morning, Dan called the rehab center where Meghan worked and made appointments for Wednesday and Friday. He then used his father's computer again. Yesterday, he updated his résumé and LinkedIn profile and applied for jobs. No one was hiring—the pandemic saw to that.

Dan hoped that if his house sold, he'd enroll in graduate studies at

FGCU's unique college, The Water School. The program focused on climate change, natural resources, ecosystem health and well-being, restoration, and remediation.

Dan received Robin's forwarded message in a text from his dad. *Hallelujah.* He read her message twice. *Yes, Robin. I want to hear your explanation.* Dan wanted to know why she didn't wake him when her car wouldn't start. Why didn't she trust him with the truth? Why didn't she call him when she left for Florida? She had to have known about the hospital and his trouble with the law—it was all over social media. Did she follow up only because his father guilted her into it? He had too many questions to text or call her. It would be too apparent that he didn't trust her.

But he also couldn't wait to see her, hold her in his arms, and hear her out. Dan knew Robin worked mornings at her aunt's hair salon and afternoons at Lowe's. He called the store; the girl at the service desk gave him Rachel's schedule for the next few days. Dan then worked on a plan.

Chapter 56

Wednesday morning, Meghan put her Guru mountain bike on the BMW's rear rack and her mother's bike in the back of her SUV, for Sam. They drove off.

Sam said, "I love your Guru."

Meghan paid over four grand for it and wondered if Sam knew her mother's Culver cost less than six hundred bucks. "Thanks. What do you ride in California?"

"I have a Trek Remedy. It's great for the hillside trails."

"Nice!" Meghan exclaimed, knowing a Remedy cost between six and ten grand and a custom titanium Trek as much as twenty thousand. When they were stopped at a traffic light, Sam took out her phone and showed Meghan a picture of herself on the shiny black mountain bike. Meghan also noticed an Asian woman and a dog standing beside Sam in the photo.

"Beautiful bike. Who's the pretty woman with the French bulldog?" Meghan said as she accelerated through the green light.

"Oh, that's Khori, my partner," Sam said. "And her dog Bulova."

Bit surprising, Meghan thought. She'd guessed Sam might be bisexual but didn't expect the young woman to have an exclusive partner. "Ah, they're beautiful, too."

"Thanks. I'm worried about them; the wildfires are getting close to her cabin, and California is in COVID lockdown."

"That's really tough," Meghan replied.

Meghan pulled into the Trailhead Neighborhood Park, passed the playground, and parked near the paved trail. The two women put on their helmets, mounted their bikes, and began at a leisurely pace. It was sunny, with temperatures in the low eighties, but the humidity made it feel like ninety. Meghan knew the area well. She changed her gears and sped off. Even though her expensive bike was much better equipped, Sam quickly caught her.

"Trying to lose me?" Sam asked.

Meghan smiled, "Not a chance."

She rode alongside Sam and thought about how well she'd gotten to know the DeCosta family—and how perversely attracted she was to all of them. Jo made an instant impression on her at the Red Sox game and made her feel welcomed. The lovely older woman had a hunky husband and a beautiful family—a life she envied. But Meghan worried about what would happen to the family if Jo's aneurysm ruptured.

She'd also gotten comfortable with Dan through PT and had to curb her desire to sleep with him. Last night, Sam told her about the cops putting Dan in the hospital and a runaway ex. Meghan did her own digging and read the stories online about the arrest, the social media mess, and the follow-up stories that cleared Dan's name. She now understood why he'd been so susceptible to pain meds and felt guilty about toying with the sweet, vulnerable guy. *Your secret's safe with me, Depot Dan.* Meghan also wondered if tall, lean, steely Dan preferred heads or tails. Or both, like Allan.

Meghan decided to steer the conversation, "Our dads were at the driving range. I appreciate how your father always checks in on mine, especially since my mom passed."

"My dad said they're both engineers and go way back," replied Sam

They sure do. Meghan wondered what Dick and Lee Grisham might know about her mom's ob-gyn. She said, "My dad said your father was well connected with VC, politicians, military police, and even the FBI. Is that just hype?"

"Well, he's a Desert Storm vet and into everything from AI to real estate and renewable energy," explained Sam. "He knows TV talk show hosts from his book tours. He gets harassed on Twitter for his stance on climate change. My mom said the FBI knows about threats to him and our family."

"Wow. You must be proud of him."

Sam shrugged, "Meh."

They chuckled and veered off the paved trail to a narrow path thick with trees. Meghan led them to a shaded area, where they removed their helmets and took a water break.

"It's not as challenging as the mountain trails," Meghan explained. "But the weather, tropical vegetation, and wildlife in these preserves work for me."

Sam looked around, "I could get used to it. Plus, the beaches. I bought a new bikini yesterday shopping with my mom."

"Can't wait to see you in it," Meghan winked. "We'll have time for the pool later."

"I'll be at the pool, but I'm saving my new suit for Marco Island," said Sam. "Mom booked a family getaway before her surgery. We're going late afternoon."

"Good for her. You'll love Marco. My dad and I were there recently. My mother's wish was to have her ashes spread there."

"Aww… I'm so sorry for your loss," Sam said, leaning in to hug her. "I don't know what I'd do if I lost my mom."

Meghan wasn't sure what to make of Sam's lingering hug, but she enjoyed it. Nearly two inches taller than the Jennifer Lawrence look-alike, she smelled Sam's shampoo in her short, styled hair and felt the heat emanating from their perspiring bodies.

"You're as sweet as your mother," Meghan said as she cupped the pretty face that looked up at her with ocean-blue eyes and perfect lips that she fought off the urge to kiss.

* * *

"Thanks," Sam said. She pulled away from Meghan and felt the sweat on her upper lip and the tingling in her shorts. *That was awkward.* She drank more water. Sam was in awe of the beautiful, confident woman who always seemed in control. She felt like Meghan had taken her under her wing like a big sister. But there were also sensual nuances between them, which confused her.

Meghan put her helmet back on and said, "It's my only day off, so I'm going to make sure my dad eats a healthy lunch before I relax poolside."

They rode back in silence, exchanging smiles along the way. Sam wondered if she should feel guilty or flattered that Meghan shared her day off with her.

Sam returned to the condo and made a smoothie. She worried about Khori and texted her. She also logged into Ancestary.com. There were no other matches or notices about her brother.

Khori texted back. She had no new positions to fill at work as companies were putting hires on hold because of the pandemic. The winds had also picked up, and the fires were getting closer. Despite the bad news, Sam didn't want Khori to ruin her vacation and time with her family; she chose not to tell her about her Marco Island plans. She called her back, briefly updated her about her bike ride with Meghan, and told her that she missed her and Bulova. When she hung up, Sam felt guilty—she wasn't entirely truthful with Khori—she didn't really miss her.

Sam lounged by the pool and checked her crypto balances on her digital wallet. They continued to drop as the number of COVID cases rose.

"Hey," she heard Rikki ask, "Saving this chair for your brother … or Meghan?"

"All yours. So, what hours do you work? You're always here," Sam teased.

"I usually work the early shift and sometimes weekends to cover for others."

"I share a hillside home with a friend near the fires. Is California going to get any rain?"

"Gosh. No storms or even moderate rain along the Pacific. Sorry," replied Rikki.

"It's okay," said Sam, then changed the subject. "I'm going to Marco Island tonight. You said sunny the next few days?"

"I see." Rikki sighed and looked dejected.

"What's wrong with Marco?"

"Nothing. You're only here two weeks. I thought we might get together for dinner."

"Aww… That's so sweet." *And tempting.*

"Guess I'll ask your big sister," Rikki said. "She'd have chaperoned anyway," she laughed.

"Not funny," Sam said, "I'll be back on Friday night."

"That might work," Rikki said. "But I don't know any restaurants in Fort Myers that accept Bitcoin for payment."

"Meaning we go Dutch?" Sam grinned.

"Dutch? No, I thought you made a killing in crypto and had money to burn."

"You thought wrong, Sunshine Girl," said Sam.

"Will you at least pay for the Uber?"

Sam snorted. *Most women are after my body, but this one wants my crypto or maybe both.* She then leaned over and touched Rikki's forearm. "Let's take the free trolley downtown."

The two women were chatting up a storm when Meghan placed her towel on the lounge chair beside Sam. Meghan slipped off her wrap gracefully, unveiling her bikini and overwhelming hourglass figure.

Wow. Pull it together. "Um, how's your dad doing?" Sam asked.

"He's doing okay. I just wish he'd stop smoking and gambling. He's going to the casino tomorrow. I'll have Emily walk and feed my dog, Bruschi. I work the next three days."

"If he's well-behaved, I can watch him from time to time," replied Sam.

"Thanks, Sam. I'll keep that in mind. Any updates on the wildfires?"

"The wind's getting stronger. Khori might evacuate if it gets closer," Sam said.

Sam felt Rikki's hand on her arm, who interjected, "No rain in the Pacific region either."

"Feels kind of steamy out here," Meghan said, grinning at them.

"The humidity makes it feel like ninety-four," Rikki answered quickly.

"The water will be refreshing," Sam said as she headed to the pool with

Rikki in tow. She had forty minutes before packing and getting ready for her Marco trip.

"Text me when you get back. We'll sort out our plans Friday night," said Rikki.

Sam nodded. *Looks like I have plans this weekend.*

Chapter 57

Dick and his son were having coffee on the lanai when Christina called. She received the keys to Dan's house and would show it to her assistant, Chantel, and her husband. His son was happy, then said, "I read Robin's text…better late than never." Dick was relieved.

Jo joined them on the lanai. She'd booked a family Marco getaway at Marriott's Crystal Shores. They were all leaving late afternoon. His wife said, "Dan, pack an overnight bag. Use my car for PT and come to Marco tonight. Then return to Fort Myers Friday with Sam and take your other PT session."

"Ok, Thanks, Mom."

Great idea, thought Dick. He and Jo would then have the place to themselves. He helped Jo pack, then rubbed her neck and shoulder. "I'm looking forward to our time alone," he said before he kissed Jo's forehead.

"So am I," said Jo with a flirtatious grin.

Dick went to his study. He focused on completing his second book about the looming dangers of climate change and what he believed governments, private sectors, and individuals could do to address it. The past month, he was consumed with one family crisis after another. He viewed climate change as a pressing global crisis and was determined to raise awareness in any way he could.

* * *

Rachel left Lowe's feeling down. Mr. DeCosta acknowledged her text yesterday morning, but she hadn't heard from Dan. *He doesn't want anything to do with me.*

She sauntered to her aunt's salon. Still paranoid about Sean's attack, she avoided walking along the road and went through the plaza parking lot instead. A convertible with its top down rolled by her. The driver stopped beside an elderly couple and asked them for directions. Based on their headshakes, Rachel figured they couldn't help the guy with sunglasses and a tennis cap.

The man in the convertible then looked at her. She put her head down and kept walking. He shouted, "Excuse me! Do you know where the Wash 'n Wag is?"

"Yeah," she said, pointing, "Othah side of the pahkin lot. Next to Cape Cuts Hair Salon."

"Thank you," he said.

She nodded, looked down, and resumed walking. He slowly rolled alongside her and explained, "I'm picking up a Boston Terrier. Hope she don't bite."

Bawstin Terryyah, she mumbled under her breath, *Bite me!* She ran behind the car, aimed her phone, took a photo, and shouted, "Keep going, Bustah! I got your fancy cah plate!"

The guy shouted, "And I got your cell number!"

He removed his hat, pushed the passenger's door open, and demanded, "Robin, get in! It's time to talk!"

Oh my God! It's Dan. She hesitated, then slid into the passenger's bucket seat. He looked unhappy but said calmly, "Sorry, I didn't intend to scare you."

"Not how I imagined seein' you again," she said, shutting the door.

He said, "Put on your seat belt." She did, and he drove off.

"Nice cah," she said to break the ice.

"Thanks, it's my mom's. Your aunt does her hair."

"Small world. How long have you known that?" she sassed.

"Just recently. But it's my turn to ask questions."

He parked under a tree for shade and shut the car off, "Why didn't—"

"Look, Dan, I'm sorry. I didn't mean to deceive you. I planned to stay with Becca. But Sean got out of rehab and was stalking me. My sistah has a four-year-old and is eight months pregnant. Sean knew where Becca lived, and—"

"Yeah, but you could've—"

She held up a hand, "I couldn't get you involved. He's … he was too dangerous."

Dan shook his head and drank from a water bottle in the console's cupholder.

"My aunt's expecting me. Will you wait 'til I let her know what's up?"

He nodded.

She jumped out, "I'll be right back. I promise." *I knew this wouldn't be easy. But I owe him. I hope we'll at least be friends.*

* * *

Dan watched Robin walk by the dog grooming place and enter the hair salon. He'd scoped out the area earlier and waited for her in the Lowe's parking lot. His surprise pickup hadn't gone well, but he needed answers and preferred to get them face-to-face. The sun and late afternoon heat were stifling. He put the Audi's top up and it's A/C kicked in. Robin climbed back in.

"My aunt's with a customer. She'll be another hour. Would you mind giving me a ride home? It's only five minutes from here."

She gave him directions as they left the parking lot.

Dan began again, "The last night at my house… we partied. You never said a word about leaving for Florida, or in your note—"

"You didn't deserve to be caught in the middle, Dan. I didn't want to ruin what might have been our last night. It was wonderful. I'll never forget it."

Yes. But Saturday sucked—it was the worst day of my life. "You could have told me the next morning. I'd have taken you to the bus terminal."

"Becca was supposed to get the Outback at the bus station. I didn't want to wake you, try to explain everything, and miss the bus to Bawstin and my train to Orlando. So, I called an Ubah drivah, a friend of mine."

"You could have texted me and let me know."

"I texted my sistah about the cah in your driveway, and then my phone died."

"Her husband snuck into my house!" Dan shouted over the road noise. "I called nine-one-one before your sister did. Cops pounded on me and hauled me to jail. Luckily, my dad's lawyer got an ambulance to take me to the hospital."

"I know. I know. I'm sorry!" she touched his hand resting on the shifter.

"Before that, I learned my Home Depot card had crazy things charged on it. But you weren't answering my texts so I had a huge argument at the store and got crucified by social media." His heart raced with the fast-moving traffic. "I then woke up in the hospital with cracked ribs, shoulder surgery, and I lose my friggin' job. *And you… you* never called me."

"I planned to call you when I got on the bus or the train. But I left my chargah behind and couldn't find anyone with one that fit my old phone." She pointed, "Next light, take a right."

Dan turned onto a side street with rows of lovely landscaped homes.

"There's the house. Pahk on the right. My aunt and uncle will be home, latah."

He pulled into the driveway of a three-car garage, parked, and kept the car running. "Why didn't you call me when you got to Florida?"

"I lost my phone on the train. It took me four days to get a new one. Then I lost all my contacts."

"You could've called the hospital and left your new number. I—"

"Dan, I have to pee," Robin got out of the car. "Come inside, please."

He wanted to leave, but he knew he needed to calm down. Dan followed her inside and looked around the enormous, great room. "I need a bathroom, too."

Robin pointed at a powder room and continued toward a back bedroom. After he composed himself, he found her in the kitchen.

"Do you want a beeah or watah?"

"Water, please."

She filled two glasses from the stainless-steel fridge. They both took a drink, put their glasses on the shiny quartz counter, and faced one another.

"Why didn't you trust me with your escape plan?" Dan asked. The smile on her freckled, sun-tanned face faded to a frown.

"Why'd you follow me in the pahkin' lot? You scared the shit outa me. Coulda called or texted me with ya—"

"I know," he said, moving closer to her. Robin backed up against the counter as he took another step closer. "But I needed to hear… I needed to see you."

He then placed both of his hands on her hips and kissed her gently. Robin wrapped her arms around him, and they hugged. Neither one wanted to let go. He felt her rapid heartbeat against his throbbing chest; he didn't mind the twinge in his cracked ribs. Dan pushed her hair aside and kissed her neck, then her cheek. Their lips found each other's.

Robin pulled away and smiled, "Want to see the house?"

She led him through the great room, down a hallway, and into her bedroom.

"Nice," he said, looking around at the queen-size bed and furnishings.

"I love it. Beats sleeping on Amy's couch or my Outback," she replied.

"Sure does. And you deserve this. I'm happy for you."

"Aww, thanks," she said, then turned and kissed him.

Dan fought the urge to push her down on her bed. His phone bailed him out. He pulled away to read a text from his sister.

Where r u? Mom has reservations for 7:30.

"I better go."

"Stay for suppah," she pleaded. "You can meet my aunt and uncle."

"No. I can't," he started walking down the hall. "I'm meeting my family for dinner."

"Dan," she grabbed his arm. "You still upset with me?"

"No. I have to go. I'm already late."

"Can we get togethah tomawrah night?"

"Can't. I'm going to Marco Island with my family."

"Dan…." She moved closer, her blue eyes tearing up, "Are we good?"

"Yeah… Uhm. I think so." *I want us to be.*

"You sure?" A tear rolled down her cheek.

"Yes," he sighed. *Please don't cry.* He explained, "My mom's having brain surgery next week. She booked a family getaway at Marco for a few days."

"Oh wow, I'm so sorry." Robin hugged him and patted his back.

"Thanks. I'll be back Friday for my last PT session." Dan said as he headed for the door. "Can we get together that night?"

"I work till four. It's also my birthday, and my aunt's taking me to din-nah," she said by the door. "I missed you."

"I missed us," he said before he kissed her. "Let's work something out for Friday night."

She nodded.

"I'll text you later."

Dan was relieved he'd cleared the air with Robin. But he was running late and worried about upsetting his mom and raising her blood pressure. Dan got in the car and sent an update to the family chat with his ETA.

Chapter 58

Thursday's warm breeze felt great to Sam. She spread her legs on the lounge chair and used her feet to frame a photo of the white sun-bleached sand and the Gulf's turquoise water. Earlier, she'd taken pictures of Marco's Crescent Beach, with its swimmers, boats, and high-rise resorts. She had asked an older woman to take a picture of Sam with her family. She was proud of her parents with their tanned, fit bodies and watched them head off hand in hand for a walk along the water's edge. Sam then texted the pics to Khori.

She liked the resort's pools and hot tubs filled with vacationers but loved frolicking in the warm Gulf's waves best. Due to COVID, her family preferred the safer, wide-open beach. She shared an umbrella with Dan, who was texting with Robin. He was pumped that he'd finally hooked up with "the redhead from heaven or hell," as he called her last night over dinner. Everyone felt happy for Dan when Dad announced, "The Jenkins loved the house."

Sam posted her photos on Instagram and Facebook and tagged her mother. She received several comments from her West Coast friends and one from her mom's sister, Aunt Paula.

> Great family photo. So glad you made the trip to be with your mother. Love ya.

Paula's my favorite aunt. She always checks up on Mom.
She loved Meghan's comment on the family pic, too.

> Marco, it is a beautiful setting for a beautiful family.

She felt bad for Meghan, knowing she'd recently spread her mother's ashes at Marco. Her parents returned from their walk, settled under their umbrella, and read the books they had brought.

Sam recalled how, six years earlier, her father had shrugged off criticism and numerous threats for authoring a controversial book at the time. It highlighted the effects of greenhouse gases and how global warming deniers and politicians gaslighted the facts to keep themselves in power and to subsidize fossil fuels. Thankfully, today, most millennials and educated older generations with a conscience accept that climate change is an existential threat to the Earth and its inhabitants.

Sam was glad she was on vacation. She turned on her iPhone's playlist, adjusted her earbuds, hummed along with Brandi Carlile, and tapped her hands on the lounge chair.

* * *

Joanna finished putting on her makeup at their Marriott villa and noticed her right eye drooping. *Too much sun glare at the beach,* she thought. She then checked her new sundress in the full-length mirror; it fit her well. Dick, preparing a sales contract for Dan's home, closed his laptop and kissed her cheek.

"Jo, you look great."

"Thanks. Let's take pictures with Sam and Dan on the balcony."

She lined her family up with the setting sun glistening upon the water in the background.

"Now, just Sam," she directed her. "Smile, you look great in your new sundress."

"Crypto Cutie," her husband said. Sam's smile broadened.

"Thanks, Dad," Sam said. "We'll both make a ton of money."

"Climate change culprits!" Dan howled. "Energy-hogging distributed computers!"

Joanna frowned. Dick stepped in. "You're both right. As I do with most new technologies, I'm investing in blockchain. Eventually, their computing centers will be geothermally cooled underground and solar powered above."

Dan and Sam nodded.

"Time to go," Joanna said. "Reservations are at seven."

They wore facemasks and appreciated that Marriott had posted COVID-19 safety rules. They dined outside and were relieved that Marco's restaurants and clientele were vigilant and cautious about COVID-19.

Her children talked about their Friday night plans. Jo was proud of how her college-educated kids turned out and pleased that they loved Marco. She wanted them to see that their parent's hard work and sacrifices had paid off and they were enjoying a comfortable retirement. But she worried if that would always be the case. Jo did not want her health to pose a burden to her family.

* * *

Thursday after work, Meghan fed Bruschi. Her dad was at the casino. She finished dinner, sipped an iced tea, and admired Jo's Facebook post of Sam and Marco Island's sunset. She recalled her father's words at Marco. *"Your mother came here on a hospital boondoggle and always wanted to return."*

She stacked the old newspapers and photos on her dad's computer desk. Then Meghan launched a private browser and got dozens of hits when she typed into the search engine: Dr. Benjamin Samuel Friedman, cesarean births, FBI, sex allegations.

The Boston Globe's original story, by Jackie Adams, protected every-one's identities. *The Boston Herald* reported someone had anonymously sent *The Globe* and the FBI a list of women who had cesarian deliveries by Friedman. The FBI raided his office after his former receptionist, who also had a cesarean delivery, filed a sexual harassment case.

The Boston Herald ran a separate story headlined,

Farmer Friedman, Perversion for Profit.
Two unidentified women claimed they had unexpected pregnancies. The debonaire, Dr. Benjamin Samuel Friedman, often examined women alone and administered nitrous oxide well over the 50 percent gas-oxygen mixture. Many may have been unwittingly impregnated via insemination syringes, while a few were consensually seeded. His surgical assistants nicknamed him 'Benny Bikini Cut' and 'Sammy C-section.' The ob-gyn had performed more C-sections and tubal ligations than all the other surgeons at Emerson Hospital combined. Undoubtedly, to maximize his earnings and feed his penchant for gambling, Friedman was often spotted at the high-rollers' tables at the Foxwoods Casino.

Meghan read other stories. Friedman's list of cesarean births went back twenty years before his Concord office was raided on April Fool's Day, 1997. They took his records, nitrous oxide tanks, and a mini fridge with a special compartment full of frozen sperm. A month later, Friedman died from carbon monoxide poisoning in the garage of his luxurious Lincoln home while parked in his Mercedes. And just two days before celebrating his seventeenth wedding anniversary with his wife, Victoria, whose three children were also delivered as cesarean births.

Friedman's faded obituary picture matched her mom's Polaroid of the tall, blond, dashing man standing beside her at the Emerson holiday party. The notation on the Polaroid's back was Ben, Christmas 1979. The Florida photo of her mother with her coworkers and Friedman was taken at the Marco Marriott resort on Jan 21, 1980.

Roughly nine months later, Meghan was born on October 20, 1980. Her cesarean birth included tubal ligation surgery. *Coincidence?*

Chapter 59

Friday morning, March 27, Rachel was awakened by her phone's ding. She grabbed it off the nightstand, rubbed her eyes, and read her sister's text.

> Happy Birthday! Hope you have a great one. Luv, Becca, Brandon, and Briana.

> Thanks, Becca! ♥ Luv and miss you all.

Last night, Dan texted a picture from Marco. She replied:

> Beautiful family, you're lucky. Looking forward to tonight.

They'd work out the details when he returned from Marco.

She opened the card from Kelly and Roger, who had already left for work. Inside, a $500 check and a note, "Your college fund." She wiped the tears and hugged her aunt.

Rachel received good news: FSW State College would accept credits from her community college in Massachusetts.

"I'm considering three different majors at FSW," she told Aunt Kelly as they drove to the salon. "I can't afford to pick one I might hate."

"Which programs?" her aunt asked and pulled into the parking lot.

"Dental hygienist pays the best, but I'm not crazy about working in people's mouths, especially with COVID. Radiology tech looks interesting and pays well. And social services, as an addiction counselor—we have an opioid epidemic, and I'd like to help."

Auntie K said, "Go with your heart; don't rush your decision."

Rachel sat behind the salon's reception desk when a delivery guy walked in with a massive bouquet. The card was addressed to Robin. *Sure, Mom. Send flowers to show up, Auntie K.* Everyone in the shop saw her open the envelope.

"Aww! So sweet," she said, fanning her face with her hand.

> *Happy birthday!*
> *Let's celebrate tonight.*
> *Dan*

* * *

Dan sat in the Marriott's hot, bubbling spa. The pulsating water jetting on his right shoulder felt good. Sitting beside him, his father said, "Florida's weather is great, and there are no state income taxes, but the politics are harsh. The emphasis on development and disregard for the environment and climate change sucks. You sure you want to sell your house and move here?"

"I know," he said. "But I'm tired of the snow and want to help protect the water and coastlines. Plus, you and Mom and Robin are here."

Shortly after, Dan and Sam said goodbye to their parents. He had to return to Fort Myers for PT and couldn't wait to celebrate with Robin later. As Dan drove his mother's convertible, Sam said, "I'm looking forward to dinner downtown with Rikki, but I feel guilty about Khori."

"You're on vacation. Have fun," he said.

"I don't want an expensive place, but I don't want pizza. Suggestions?"

"Burgers at Ford's Garage or Mexican. Cabos Cantina has *great* margaritas."

"Sounds good. Where are you taking Robin?"

"Her birthday, her choice." He envisioned taking her to his parents' place after dinner.

"Does she like Mexican?"

"Not sure. But she *loves* margaritas."

"I'd love to meet her. Go to Cabos, and we'll help celebrate her birthday."

"You need cover if Rikki turns out weird? Ha-ha."

"Guilty. I don't want to ruin your time with Robin. Maybe just for drinks there first."

"That should work," he said. " Besides, there are plenty of places to go our way later."

Sam checked her phone and asked him, "Did you check your email before we left Marco? You should have one from Ancestry.com."

"No. But I limited the notices—they were annoying," he said, pulling up to the high-rise entrance to drop Sam off.

"When you get home. Check your DNA matches and family tree. Send me the report."

Hmmm...Something's bugging her. Now, he was curious.

Dan entered the rehab center with a facemask. He then sat in the waiting room and read Robin's text. She said she'd be ready by 6:15 and didn't care where they ate. He made reservations and texted Sam.

See u at Cabos. Reservations for 7:00.

* * *

Sam texted Meghan that she'd walk Bruschi and watch him until she returned from work. She then texted Rikki that she'd meet her to catch the 6:40 p.m. trolley and that they'd be joined by Dan and his date for a birthday drink at Cabos. Rikki replied.

Perfect. I'm looking forward to it.

And so am I, thought Sam. She was nervous but glad that Dan would be there. She had an out if she had second thoughts about betraying Khori. She also wanted to meet the redhead and hoped she wouldn't crush her brother again.

* * *

Friday, at 1:35 p.m., Khori's bulldog, Bulova, started barking when police and forest fire crews blasted through their loudspeakers to evacuate. She'd lost power earlier, and cell phone coverage was weak, to say the least. Since yesterday, she'd been loading her Range Rover with luggage, clothing, non-perishables, and financial records. She placed the cooler with food and drinks on the front floor mat and put Bulova's doggie cushion on the passenger's seat.

Khori's nose and throat burned from breathing the thick smoke obstructing the sun's rays. She adjusted her facemask and returned to the house to lock up and get Bulova. Yesterday, she took photos for insurance records of the furnishings, Sam's mountain bike, and items she'd have to leave behind. She'd forgotten to take pictures of their new deck furniture. She opened the sliding door and stepped outside. High winds fueled the fires burning off to the north. Her phone dinged; she had cell reception on the deck. It was a text from Sam with pictures she'd look at later. Khori then sent a group text to Sam and Alyssa Stroud, her assistant.

Police said to evacuate. Leaving now. Will let u know when I reach my cousin's house in Chinatown.

Her group text was marked as sent. She put her phone in the pocket of the denim shirt she wore over a t-shirt and jeans. Khori then stepped inside and called for Bulova. She checked the bathroom where he'd been hiding from the sirens. There was now a pee puddle. She checked under the bed. No Bulova. Then she smelled smoke.

"Oh no!" She'd left the slider ajar. "Bulova!" she shouted from the deck.

He barked and ran down the sloping backyard. Khori pulled her mask down and screamed again, "Bulova! Come back!"

He sprinted down the narrow path into the woods, where she walked him daily. Khori ran down the steps and tripped on the landing. She got up, ran to the front of the house, jumped in her car, and started driving. She knew Bulova had taken a path that would end at the creek. A red pickup truck with flashing lights stopped in the oncoming lane. A firefighter jumped out on the road. She zipped down the window; gusting wind and smoke hit her face.

"It's not safe to go that way," warned the man in the yellow suit with black soot on his face. "The roads at the bottom of the ridge are overtaken by fire and are impassable."

"I'm chasing my dog. He'll be down by the creek, half a mile off to the right."

"Okay, but double back and take the road down the other side of the ridge."

"Will do. Keep an eye out for a black French bulldog. His name is Bulova. He might return to my house, second driveway on the left." She motioned over her shoulder.

"Got it. But we don't have much time. High winds are pushing the fire this way!"

"Thanks!" She closed her window. Her phone was not in her shirt pocket. It must have slid out when she fell near her deck. *I'll find it after I get Bulova and double back.*

* * *

After completing his last PT session, Dan drove to his parents' condo, showered, shaved, and dressed. He had an hour before he'd pick up Robin. He used his mother's computer and attempted to submit a reimbursement insurance claim for his PT but failed. He left Mom the paperwork and a note; she'd get it done right.

He logged onto Ancestry.com for Sam. He downloaded the PDF reports, sent them to himself, and spooled them onto his mother's printer. The PDF file showed he had a DNA mix of French and English and a much higher percentage of Portuguese ancestors. It listed regions in Canada, Portugal, Spain, and France. He had 50 percent DNA matches with his parents, but his sister was only 26 percent. His aunt Paula, his cousins Eric, and his sisters were on his family tree at 12 percent. *Weird.*

Dan never met his Portuguese cousins, scattered in Rhode Island and California. He was fascinated but would hold off sending the reports to Sam until he understood them better and could ask Dad about his side of the family tree. This would have to wait. Dan realized the most important thing to do in the next five minutes was to pick up Robin.

* * *

Silvia thanked Sam for relieving her. Sam slipped a leash around Brusch's powerful neck and took him for a walk around the high-rise towers. Bruschi found a bush to water. Her phone chimed. It was a group text from Khori to her and her assistant, Allyssa. *Khori evacuated!*

She imagined Khori, terrified and fleeing the burning mountainside. She'd seen the TV coverage of the homes burned to the ground. Sam hoped Khori's cabin would somehow be spared. She thought about posting it on the family chat but didn't want to upset her mother. Sam walked along the pavers circling the towers, then entered the lobby. Bruschi pulled her around the corner where Meghan stood by her mailbox.

"Hi," Meghan said, patting Bruschi's head, his tail wagging. "Was he a good boy?"

"Very good. He's the king of the condos."

"How was Marco? And how's your mother doing?"

"Marco's beautiful. Mom's relaxing and happy."

"So, what're you doing tonight? Want to go downtown, grab a bite and a drink?"

"Uhm. I'm taking the trolley with Rikki downtown. Meeting Dan and his date, it's her birthday. We're starting at Cabos for margaritas at seven."

"Oh… And who is the lucky girl?"

"Robin. A girl from Lowell he hooked back up with. You should join us."

"I don't want to be a fifth wheel," she said, walking up the hallway.

"You won't. Besides, I don't know if I can handle Rikki. I'm worried sick about Khori. She evacuated. Wildfires are headed toward her neighborhood!"

Meghan stopped, put her arm around her shoulder, "So sorry. I hope she's all right."

Sam looked up at Meghan's caring eyes. "As for downtown. I'll think about it. You take care," Meghan said, turning the corner toward her elevator with Bruschi at her heels.

Chapter 60

Rachel floated on air all day after getting Dan's flowers. She carried the vase with the bouquet into her aunt's house. Kelly grabbed the mail and handed her an envelope with a return address for Reno, Nevada. Rachel went to her bedroom and read her mother's thoughtful birthday card. Inside: a handwritten note and a check. The tears poured down her cheeks.

> *Dear Robin,*
> *I pray this card finds you well. I'm sorry about everything you endured this past year and about Sean's passing. Although it pains me, moving in with your godmother was a wise and under-standable choice. I'm proud of you and always will be. I know you are working hard and saving to finish college. We hit the slots last month! I hope this helps with your tuition. Happy Birthday.*
> *Love you to the moon and back.*
> *Mom*

Rachel held the thousand-dollar check and cried her heart out. She called her mother and left a voicemail. In a heartfelt message, she thanked her and explained how happy she was to have a date tonight with a wonderful guy whose parents were from Lowell.

She used the bathroom and was relieved her period had ended. *The birth control pills keep my cycle regulated.* She squeezed into her new destroyed denim shorts and adjusted the spaghetti straps on the black satin Cami V-neck top. She hoped Dan would think she looked hot.

Uncle Roger greeted her in the kitchen, "You look nice, Rachel. Happy birthday." Then he kissed her cheek.

"Thanks, Rawjah," she hugged him. "And thank you for the generous birthday gift."

"You're welcome. We'd planned to take you to dinner, but Kelly says you got a hot date."

"Yes! Dan's on his way here. Wicked nice guy from Chelmsford."

"You could join us. We booked an outside table, eight o'clock at

Izzy's."

"She needs to be alone with her guy," her aunt said, her heels clacking on the tile floor. *Thanks, Auntie K.* Rachel smiled at her.

"What's this Chelmsford guy doing in Florida?" Roger asked.

"He's got a house there. He had surgery and came to Fort Myers to recuperate with his parents. They're retired," she said, pulling out her phone. "This is him with his family at Marco."

Roger said, "His parents look too young to be retired. Must be loaded."

Her aunt frowned and shook her head at Roger. The doorbell rang. Rachel raced to open it.

Dan looked smartly dressed, sun-tanned, handsome, and happy. "Robin, you look great," he said, pecking her lips.

"Thanks, so do you," she steered him inside.

"Dan, this is my Aunt Kelly. And my uncle Rawjah."

"Nice to meet you both," he said. "You have a beautiful home."

"Thank you. Come sit in the kitchen," Kelly said.

Rachel said, "Rawjah's a contractor. He did the tile work in the house and the patio."

"It shows," Dan said, shaking Roger's hand. "You did a great job."

"Thank you," her uncle nodded proudly. "Want a beer?"

"Thanks, but I better not. We're celebrating later."

"I cut your mother's hair, Dan. How's she doing?" Kelly asked.

"She mentioned that. She's doing okay. Having surgery next week."

"Well, you tell her I wish her a speedy recovery," said Kelly.

"I will. Thank you."

"Heard your folks are retired," Roger inquired. "Where do they live?"

"In a high-rise condo that overlooks the river and marina. Short walk downtown."

"We installed a lot of tiles there," Roger said. "Thirty-three floors, tallest in Southwest Florida. What floor are they on?"

"Twenty-seventh. Magnificent views."

"I know. The upper floors go for big bucks."

"I wouldn't know, sir. They never said what they paid for it."

"What do you do for work?" Roger asked. Dan caught Robin's eyes.

"I'm a LEED-certified environmental engineer. And I focus on oceanography."

"Good, we need energy-efficient buildings and clean water. Who do you work for?"

"I'm uh… between jobs. Might sell my house up north. Go for my master's at FGCU."

"Rachel's going to FSW college this summer," Kelly said, smiling.

"Yup. But we gotta go," Rachel said, ushering Dan toward the door. "We're meeting his sistah at Cabos."

Dan opened the door for her, and she slid into the bucket seat. "Thank you. And thanks for being so polite to my aunt and uncle."

"Felt like a prom date," he grinned and drove off.

"I know, huh? They're my surrogate parents—they nevah had kids."

"You going to FSW State College?"

"Yes! They'll take my credits from Middlesex. I've been saving my wages. And my mother and my aunt gave me birthday checks for my tuition."

"That's great! Happy birthday," he said as he touched her wrist.

"Thanks! You serious about selling your house ?" She thought he'd return to Chelmsford after his mother's surgery.

"Yeah. My parents' friends are interested in it. I'd love to get my master's and land an oceanology job."

"That would be wicked awesome," she said.

They crossed the bridge on US-41, heading to downtown Fort Myers. Robin pointed at the majestic high-rise buildings and asked, "Is that where your parents live?"

"Yeah. Want to see it? We can park there and walk downtown."

She followed Dan through the fancy lobby and onto the elevator. He punched in a code and pushed button twenty-seven. She grinned, and he asked, "What?"

"It's March twenty-seven. I'm now twenty-seven, going up to floor twenty-seven."

"And you're my redhead from heaven." Dan kissed her gently and hugged her until the elevator door slid open to a beautiful entrance. They passed through double doors, her sandals clicking on tiled floors as she eyed the expensive furnishings. "Oh… my… Gawd," Robin said, approaching a high wall of glass and a fantastic river view beyond.

"This is wicked gorgeous," she said, following him to the lanai. She looked down at the marina filled with yachts. The setting sun, bursting through the clouds, cast a golden path across the water. Stunning," she said and took a photo.

"I'll show you the rest of the place."

Rawjah was right: big bucks. Tasteful decor with a large open-concept great room and dining room. A roomy kitchen with quartz counters, white cabinets, and top-end appliances, similar to her aunt Kelly's. Robin followed him into his father's study, which had beautiful city views, and then to a back bedroom with a private bathroom. "My sleeping quarters," he said.

A king-size bed, a yoga mat, and a curtain rod leaned in a corner. "What is this for?" she asked, picking up the rod.

"PT exercise for my shoulder." Dan grabbed it, laid on his bed, and showed her how he raised his injured arm with it. She playfully grabbed the bar, and he pulled her down on top of him. Robin kissed him as Dan's hands slowly slid down her back to her denim shorts. Then she thrust her breast on him.

"Ouch," he said. The rod had dug into his chest.

She pushed herself up. "I'm sorry. Are your ribs still sore?"

He frowned and rubbed his rib cage. "Cracked ribs take longer to heal than my shoulder."

His phone dinged. "It's my sister. She's waiting for us."

"Can I use your bathroom first?"

He nodded toward his adjacent bathroom.

Robin closed the door, looked in the mirror, wiped her smeared lipstick from the corner of her mouth, and fluffed her hair. An Advil bottle and two vials on the vanity piqued her curiosity. They were the familiar pain meds and muscle relaxers she'd seen Sean load up on after his car accident. Her mind jumped back to when she'd flushed Sean's pills down the toilet. He choked her, threw her against the wall, and pounded on her. *Oh God*, she thought. *Not Dan, too.*

Robin freshened up and walked down the hall where Dan was waiting.

"Beautiful place," she said as the elevator descended.

Dan held her hand as they walked through the parking garage, over the pavers, and down the sidewalk toward downtown.

"Why so quiet," he asked when they walked past Joe's Crab Shack.

"I feel bad. I didn't mean to hurt your ribs," Robin said, gently squeezing his hand.

"I'm fine."

"Do you have trouble sleeping?"

"Only if I lay on my injured shoulder."

"You take pain meds?"

"Just Advil if I have any pain from swimming or PT."

Sean denied it, too. She sighed.

Chapter 61

Sam texted Khori and left another message. She then texted Khori's assistant, Alyssa, whom she'd gotten to know well.

Please call if u hear from Khori or have fire updates.

She felt nauseous and thought about canceling her plans. *I promised Rikki and Dan, and I want to meet Robin.* She spotted the back of Rikki's black wavy hair near the trolley stop—a backless belted romper fit perfectly on the petite woman.

Rikki exclaimed, "Hi! Thought you'd chickened out."

"Nah, never pass up a free trolley ride with a TV celebrity."

"Ha. You look fantastic. Your colorful dress will light up the whole trolley."

"Thanks. I *love* your romper," Sam said as she touched the soft black belt around Rikki's tiny waist.

The wooden electric-powered trolley arrived, and they boarded with their facemasks. Thankfully, nearly everyone onboard was wearing one. Sam grabbed a two-person wooden bench and sat by the window. Rikki slid next to her like they were already a couple enjoying a warm, balmy evening in downtown Fort Myers. After they departed the trolley, they walked another block. Sam used the time to text Dan.

Waiting outside Cabos. Where R U?

Walking there from the condo. Reservations on the back patio. Safer for Covid.

The hostess said, "Yes, I'll check when a table is ready."

Sam scanned the street toward her parents' place for Dan and a redhead.

"Oh, wow! Look who's headed this way," Rikki said.

Sam turned and saw the striking, glam-like star approaching. Her high-heeled sandals supported long legs and a breathtaking body that filled out a floral mini dress with a V-neck top featuring Meghan McCormack's magnificent cleavage.

Sam was glad to see her but was jealous when Megan greeted Rikki.

"Cute jumpsuit, weather girl," Meghan said, exchanging air kisses with Rikki.

"Thanks. You look fabulous," Rikki said, then asked, "You missed the trolley and walked downtown in those heels?"

"I drove. No trouble parking. COVID is keeping people home."

Meghan air-kissed Sam's cheek and whispered, "You look adorable. And your secret's safe with me."

Sam couldn't help but blush.

Meghan asked, "What are you guys up to?"

"Waiting for Dan and his date to arrive," Rikki said.

"We're celebrating her birthday," Sam added, "Want to join us for a drink?"

"Thanks anyway. I'm going to Space 39... the Martini bar."

Rikki exclaimed, "But the governor closed all the bars because of COVID!"

"Forgot... And you two could probably use a chaperone."

"Yes, they could. Ha-ha," Sam heard Dan say behind her.

She turned and extended her hand to the ginger-haired beauty with him, "Hi. I'm Sam."

"Rachel, nice to—"

Dan raised his arm, "Hi everyone, this is Robin."

"Hi," said the well-endowed woman in a sexy black Cami top. Sam studied the blue-eyed woman's face—a turned-up nose and a warm freckled smile surrounded by red wavy hair—and thought, *Lowell Babe—pretty as Amy Adams.*

Sam's date extended her hand, "Hi there. I'm Rikki."

"Yes. Dan told me all about you," Robin said, sidestepping Sam to take Rikki's hand.

Sam read a scripted tattoo on Robin's shoulder blade: "Still I Rise." She wondered what the story behind that tattoo was.

"Hey, Dan," Meghan said, embracing her brother and eyeing the red-head.

She saw Dan's hand slip down Meghan's back to her waist, turning her toward Robin.

"This is Doctor Meghan McCormack... my physical therapist and health adviser."

"Nice to meet ya, Dawktah." Dan's date forced a smile.

"Please. Call me Meghan. Robin... or do you prefer Rachel?" She held the redhead's wrist.

The redhead replied, "Call me anything; just don't call me late for din-nah. Ha-ha."

* * *

Robin thought Dan's sister was nice and could pass for a fashion model. She thought Rikki Rossetti was as petite and pretty as Zoë Kravitz. *But why is Meghan here and dressed to kill?* She tried to be respectful to the wannabe movie star who tried to intimidate her, but she harbored resentment, imagining that the bombshell PT's hands had free rein to Dan's body.

"Come on, Birthday Girl," Dan said, grabbing her hand. They followed the others to Cabo's outside patio. Sam and Meghan wore pretty sundresses, Rikki in a dynamite romper. *I'm underdressed in my denim shorts.*

Dan then pulled out a chair for her. He sat between her and Rikki at the large round table, and his sister sat between Rikki and Meghan. With the same blue eyes on the two blonds sitting across from her, Robin thought they could pass for sisters.

They ordered various margaritas, and when they arrived, Dan toasted, "To Robin—Happy birthday."

Everyone repeated the sentiment. Her eyes met Dan's as the glasses clinked. The smooth tequila and Grand Marnier tasted great.

"I like your tattoo," Meghan said, pointing at Robin's wrist. "I've seen many shamrocks, but none with a heart in the center."

"Thanks," Robin said, surprised by the compliment.

"It is nice," Sam said. "Does it mean love the Irish or lucky in love?"

"Both," Robin said. She smiled at Dan, and he touched her hand.

"Robin, where do you work?" Meghan asked.

She touched the other tattoo on her bruised wrist: a long stem rose with the words *"Be Kind"* above it. "Part-time at my aunt's hair salon and part-time at Lowe's."

"And she's going to FSW this summer," Dan said proudly.

"Good for you," Sam said. "What are you majoring in?"

"Either radiology or social services—addiction counseling. We have an opioid crisis, and I'd like to help." She patted Dan's knee, hoping he'd pick up on it.

"Noble vocation," Meghan said. "I lost my brother to opioids last year."

"Sorry for your loss," Robin paused. "I lost my ex last week to fentanyl."

The table went silent. The waitress appeared and asked about appetizers and meals.

"Large nachos with chicken," Rikki said. Sam shrugged.

"Haven't decided yet," Dan said.

Robin wanted to move on and be alone with him. But then Dan's phone dinged.

"It's my dad," Dan said. "I got an offer on my house. Will you excuse me?"

Robin nodded. Everyone watched him walk away.

The server delivered the nachos. Rikki, Sam, and Meghan took some. Robin passed and looked over at Dan, who was still on his phone. Then Sam's phone rang.

"Alyssa. Any news?" Sam ran her free hand through her short hair. "Oh God! No!"

She hung up, "No one has heard from Khori. Fire has destroyed every home in the area." She leaned into Meghan's open arms and sobbed. Rikki tried to comfort her as well.

"I'm sorry, Sam," Meghan said. "Take a deep breath."

Sam wiped her teary eyes, looked at the nachos, and said, "I'm going to be sick." She cupped her hand over her mouth and ran for the rear door. Rikki rose to follow her.

Meghan shouted to Rikki, "She's going to the lady's room to compose herself. She lost everything in a fire and is worried sick about Khori."

Rikki sat down and shook her head. "That's rough. Is Corey the guy she works with?"

"No," Meghan shook her head at Rikki. "Khori... is her female partner."

"Oh!" Rikki's mouth was wide open. She lowered her head, sighed, and said, "I uh... feel like I'm just spit in a hurricane here." She gulped her drink and pushed her share of nachos away.

Robin felt bad for Rikki and terrible for Sam, whom she just learned was a lesbian. *Not a problem, Dan, but you could've tipped me off.* Robin eyed him in the plaza.

The dejected weather girl said softly, "I guess I'm not going to be much help to her now."

"Probably not," Meghan said curtly.

Rikki slipped cash under her glass, "You have your car? Please get Sam home safely." Megan nodded, and Rikki added, "Tell her I'm sorry. I'll catch the next trolley back."

She turned to Robin, "Nice meeting you. Good luck with school and Dan."

"Thanks. Take care," Robin said. She felt terrible for everyone except Meghan.

Dan returned and explained, "I've got to do an electronic signing on my phone—my dad's working me through it. I'll be back."

"Okay," Robin said. Her phone displayed 7:48 p.m. She guessed her aunt and uncle were having drinks before dinner at Izzy's.

Meghan began, "Always drama in this wealthy, close-knit family. They protect one another and their secrets."

"I wouldn't know," Robin said. She wondered why Dan never mentioned Sam was in a relationship or let on how well-off his family was.

"Not everyone gets in the DeCosta circle. Have you met his parents and been invited to their swanky condo?"

"Not formally," she replied. *But, so what?*

"They raised their soccer kids with braces in the burbs. His mother's having brain surgery and doesn't know Dan is dating a girl from Lowell, with tats and drug issues."

What a judgmental bitch. "My ex had a drug problem, not me."

"And you'll have your hands full with Dan."

"Meaning what, Dawktah?"

They both looked over at Dan.

"I've seen his package. I gave him muscle relaxers so we could finish PT. Then he begged me to write him a script for oxy."

"Did you fill it?" *And fuck him anyway?*

"Hell no! I grabbed my gear, left his bedroom, and told him to fix his problem."

Sam approached the table, looking distraught. Robin jumped up to greet her, "You, okay?"

Sam sniffled in return.

She then touched Sam's arm. "So sorry. My turn to powdah my nose," she said and left Dan's sister with Meghan.

Chapter 62

Dan was excited about the offer on his house until his father asked again, "You sure you've thought this through? You've only seen the perfect spring weather. Summers are hot, humid, and rainy. Then comes hurricane season. Christ, there are no auto inspections here. It's nice for retirees—but no place to start a family."

Dan looked at Robin and said, "Dad, I'm not getting married or having kids. And I told you—I want to protect the water—start over in Florida."

"All right. They didn't offer the full price. I have the e-forms ready to go."

"You've been through this dozens of times. Tell me what I have to do," he said. He saw Rikki wave goodbye and leave the restaurant. *What'd I miss?*

Dad said, "You sign electronically, reject their offer, and meet them halfway with your counteroffer. Later, we'll offer them all the furniture— you don't want to pay to move any of it. Sell the rest online. You can stay in the rental 'til you finish school."

After Dan e-signed, he said, "Thanks, Dad. Let me know if they take the deal."

"You'll get a message when all parties have signed—we need both Jenkins signatures.

"Great! I'm going back to the restaurant before Robin shoots me."

Sam and Meghan were alone at the table now. He saw the cash under Rikki's empty margarita glass. Dan sipped his drink. Sam was engrossed with her phone. She announced, "Over six hundred acres destroyed—Mendocino, Glen, Riverside, and Yuba counties evacuated. No cell towers. No one's heard from Khori since she said she evacuated."

"Horrible," Dan said, hugging Sam. He then looked at Meghan, "Where's Robin?"

"Ladies' room," Meghan said, gently rubbing Sam's back.

He asked, "Are you guys having anything else?"

They shook their heads. Meghan tossed cash on the table, "We're heading home."

"Tell Robin, happy birthday," Sam said. She walked away, leaning heavily on Meghan.

Dan swallowed hard. Sam had lost her possessions and expensive bike and he hoped Khori survived. *God damn, climate change!* He finished his drink and pocketed the cash.

The waitress appeared. He asked for the check and gave her his credit card. He drummed his fingers on the table and stared at his phone while waiting for the e-signature confirmations. He couldn't wait to move on and celebrate with Robin. *What's taking her so long?*

Then his phone dinged. He read his dad's text.

> Congratulations. They both signed. How's the party going?
> Thanks! Dad. Khori's house is torched, and she's missing! Sam's a wreck. She left with Meghan. You should call her.

Dan checked his email—all parties had signed. The waitress returned. He added a generous tip and headed to the restrooms. Two giggling blonds and a curvy Latina were waiting to use one of the restrooms. He guessed Robin was inside one. He sent her a text.

> I cashed out. I'm in the men's room. Please wait for me in the hallway.

After finishing his bathroom business, he checked the hallway and half-empty bar inside the restaurant. There was no Robin. His waitress walked by, and he asked her if she'd seen the redhead.

"No, sir… Thanks again. Have a good night."

* * *

Robin's margarita buzz was replaced with raging resentment toward Meghan. The heartless woman had highlighted how delicate the DeCosta family was. The longer Dan stayed on the phone with his father, the more disappointed she felt. She never made it into the ladies' room. *Not how I want to celebrate my birthday.*

Robin exited the restaurant onto First Street, found her bearings, and passed the sidewalk diners until she reached Izzy's. Her aunt and uncle were outside drinking cocktails. She slid into a chair and told their waiter, "I'll have fish 'n chips. And watah for now."

"What happened? Where's Dan?" Kelly asked.

"I got tired of all the dramah, and I need a restroom." Robin went inside. When she returned to the table, her aunt asked, "So, what drama?"

"His sistah from California lost everything in a wildfire and hasn't heard from her partner. The poor girl used the restroom to toss up nachos." Robin drank water and continued, "Dan's snooty physical therapist thinks

I'm a tattooed druggie loosah from Lowell and will nevah be accepted by his family."

Roger blurted, "What the hell?"

Kelly asked, "Why does she think you do drugs, and what did Dan say?"

She explained that Meghan's brother died from opioids and learned Sean did too, then jumped to her conclusions.

"Ridiculous," Kelly said. "His parents live comfortably. But Jo's kind and down to earth. She wouldn't treat you that way. Something else is going on."

She didn't want to mention Dan's meds or that he probably slept with his physical temptress. Their dinner arrived, and Robin dug into her fried cod and fries.

"Where's Danny Big Bucks now?" Roger asked.

"Probably still talking with his fahtha, signing electronic stuff."

"That ain't right, Rachel," Kelly chided. "He sent you flowers and acts like a gentleman. He seems focused, with a bright future. Don't you think?"

"I guess … but I don't really know him yet."

Robin's phone chirped.

"Is Dan texting you?" Kelly asked.

She nodded, swallowed more food, and said, "His family's close-knit. Maybe I don't belong."

"Nonsense," Kelly said. "Forget about what others say."

Robin got another text and read it out loud.

> "Robin, I'm out front of Cabos. Where are you?"

She pressed the microphone symbol and dictated her response.

> "Drank too much. In an Ubah headed home. Gotta work tomawrah."

Her aunt shook her head slowly while her uncle smiled and nodded his approval. Robin put her phone on silent mode and didn't mention Dan's follow-up texts or her responses.

> Seriously?
> Sorry, just following ur doctor's orders.
> WTF does that mean?

Means I'm wicked pissed and a fuckin' mess. Robin wanted to scream. Her birthday had started great but turned to shit. Maybe her expectations were too high? Perhaps she had PTSD from Sean? Fear, insecurities, and the potential of another train wreck relationship made her paranoid, confused, and disgusted.

Robin considered replying to Dan. *Hope Khori's safe, you sell your house, your mom's surgery goes well, and you and your douchebag doctor fix your oxy problem.* Instead, she shut her phone off for the night.

* * *

Khori drove her Range Rover down the narrow wooded path, searching for Bulova until the trail ended at the creek's edge.

He always comes here. Her small dog often barked at the turtles and wildlife but never ventured into the running water. She jumped out of her car, placed dog food along the bank, and shouted into the smokey air, "Bulova! Here, boy!"

She coughed and looked around the pristine spot. She recalled years past, smoking weed and skinny dipping with Barry, her ex, who'd owned the cabin before they'd wed.

Barry Brantley was the founder and CEO of a cybersecurity company, and she was his top talent recruiter. He loved entertaining vendors and clients with private dinner parties at their six-bedroom home in San Francisco. Sometimes—for select out-of-town guests—he made Khori part of the drug-laced booze and entertainment via partner swapping and three-ways. The next day, he'd act like nothing happened, focus on his company, and treat her with kindness, respect, and affection. Khori was confused and trapped until Barry brought home Olivia (Livvy) Loubier, an attractive chief information officer at an international bank.

He kept the wine flowing that night. Then Barry sent Khori and Livvy off to a guest bedroom where he'd joined them after they warmed one another up. They locked the door, and Livvy deftly showed Khori how a woman should be handled tenderly. Barry could only listen to their giggling and intimate action all night. Livvy helped Khori realize that no company loyalty nor marriage was worth more than her dignity. Livvy said, "Strong women are more caring and trustworthy than powerful men."

After that night with Livvy, Khori found the courage to end it all. She signed an NDA in exchange for a comfortable divorce settlement, which included the hillside cabin.

"I'll always love you," Barry told Khori when they signed the documents. His eyes moistened when he rubbed Bulova's head and said, "Be a good boy for her."

In retrospect, Khori wished she had taken the city home, but it had too many bad memories of Barry's sordid parties. She beeped the horn and shouted, "Bulova, time to go!"

The strong whistling winds blew hot ashes across the tree line. No flying insects, birds, or other animals were around. *They must have fled from the fires. And Bulova ran back, too. Time to circle back.* She jumped back into her Rover and started the engine.

All at once, a burst of flames roared over the treetops. Khori drove into the creek, which would give her a wet buffer. She then headed downstream, hoping to get around the bend in the creek and away from the fire. The four-wheel-drive Rover quickly climbed over the bumpy rocks beneath the shallow running water. As she rolled by the creek's bend, the front end of the Rover sank into the deeper waters. Khori had to slow down. The Rover was losing traction, and water began to seep through the car door's seal. Then Khori's foot slipped off the accelerator, and the engine stalled.

Chapter 63

Dick appreciated that the Marriot had set up the Friday night entertainer on the pool deck. It allowed Jo and the resort's guests to enjoy the music from their balconies safely. He sent the final e-docs on Dan's house sale to all parties and then read his Twitter feed. #CaliforniaWildfires: Hundreds of homes evacuated across four counties; many people are unaccounted for. He retweeted his daughter's plea to search for Khori.

#prayersforCalifornia, #prayersforKhori, #Wildfiresearchpartys #findKhoriChen, @SamanthaD, @sold-onsolar @CCallahan.

Dick had to tell Jo. He sat beside her in a cushy lounge chair and held her hand while the entertainer finished the final song: John Lennon's "In My Life."

Dick kissed Jo's cheek, "Deal's done. Dan's happy."

"Oh, good. We'll see him more now," she said with a smile.

"Yes. Might see Sam more, too," Dick said as he patted his wife's hand. "Khori had to evacuate. The wildfires destroyed most of the homes in her county. Khori's one of many still unaccounted for."

"Oh God, no!"

They went inside, sat close together, and FaceTimed Sam, who was in the rental. They saw their daughter's bloodshot, misty eyes peering back at them. Meghan was sitting beside Sam, consoling her.

Sam explained, "It's been six hours since Khori's last text. She was headed to her cousin's house in Chinatown."

"We're praying for her," Jo said.

Dick added, "It's good you tweeted about searching for Khori. It will cast a broader net for her in the Bay area."

"Dad, thanks for retweeting that at Curt Callahan—the head of Google's artificial intelligence division. He has a bazillion followers. Didn't he publish his first AI paper with you… like thirty years ago?"

"Yeah, I moved into management. Curt became a sought-after consultant and published dozens more AI papers."

Sam said, "Curt's wife, Cyndi, commented on my post about Khori. She's friends with Mom on Facebook."

Jo said, "We were in Curt and Cyndi's wedding party. I got her the receptionist job at my gynecologist's office. She worked there until Doctor Friedman delivered her first child, Kerry. Cesarean like you were seven months earlier."

Dick said, "Then they moved to Silicon Valley, and Curt ended up at Apple. Curt's followers on the Google campus will organize search parties."

"Hope so. Thanks, Dad."

Then, silence on both ends.

Jo said, "Meghan, thank you for being there for Sam. We love you both."

After the call ended, Jo wiped away a tear and leaned on Dick's shoulder. "Thank God Sam came to visit us."

Yes. But I wish she'd kept her lease like I suggested.

Their alone time didn't unfold as he had hoped. Dick held his trembling wife in bed and kissed her gently goodnight. He said prayers for Jo, Khori, and Sam. He turned over and thought, *at least Dan was happy—he had his house under contract and was celebrating with Robin.*

* * *

Dan left Cabos pissed. He called, but Robin didn't answer. He had a headache. *A burger at Ford's will help.* He hustled across the street and dodged a pickup with a loud muffler, bald tires, and a broken taillight. His dad's reminder, "They don't have auto inspections here," echoed. *That dangerous piece of shit wouldn't be allowed on Boston roads.*

He entered Ford's Garage. The inside tables spread out for social distancing were all occupied. He then scanned the bar, and two bulky middle-aged guys were drinking as heavily as their waistlines. A server brought them plates with full racks of ribs and fries.

Dan grabbed a seat on the other side of the bar. He ordered a Sam Adams draft and a cheeseburger. He tried to understand why Robin had split early and what she meant by *"Following your doctor's orders."* Was she drunk, pissed at him for leaving her alone, mocking Meghan, or all the above?

He gulped the top off his beer, took a bite of his juicy burger, and thought about what to do with Robin. His redhead from heaven drove him crazy—he wanted to tell her to go to hell. But he didn't want to give up on her. Dan needed to know why she ran away again and if they'd have a chance together in Florida.

* * *

Meghan appreciated the DeCostas' FaceTime call and Jo's acknowledgment of her consoling Sam. Meghan wished she could adopt the loving family as her own. But Jo's comments about Dr. Friedman and his receptionist Cyndi gave her pause.

When the call ended, she said, "Your parents are so supportive."

"Thanks," Sam said and blew her nose on a tissue.

"So, your petite mom needed a cesarean delivery for you?"

"Yeah, and Dan, too. Then she had her tubes tied."

"My mom delivered me through cesarean and also had a tubal ligation." *By the same Dr. Friedman. We have more in common than you know.*

Sam asked, "What should I say to Rikki now that she knows about Khori?"

"Explain why you gave up your apartment and moved in with Khori. And text me with any news on Khori." They hugged goodbye.

Meghan left feeling bad for Sam but had a hunch. She googled "Cyndi Callahan, Friedman receptionist, harassment" and got several hits. One story covered an altercation between a reporter and Curt Callahan outside their Maynard, MA, home. The reporter claimed Callahan's wife filed the harassment case and leaked the women's names to *The Boston Globe* and the FBI. *Maybe that's why they moved to the West Coast.*

Meghan read Friedman's obituary and got the names of his children: Gina, David, and Benjamin. She then searched Facebook and found Gina (Friedman) Goldberg. She married Joseph Goldberg, lived in Wellesley, MA, and was born in Lincoln, MA. *Definitely, Dr. Friedman's daughter.* She scanned Gina's posts, most of which were of her two young children. Meghan's antennae went up when she saw Karen Marcotte tagged Gina, her brothers, and the 23andme Facebook page, but the author had hidden the content.

In turn, Gina Goldberg tagged Karen Marcotte and 23andme with a post.

Please leave me and my brothers alone! We are all full siblings.

Meghan clicked on Karen Marcotte's profile; she lived in Acton, MA, and was single. Many of Karen's recent posts were captioned "Welcome to the family," tagging new half-siblings. Each post had comments from their related siblings, all with different surnames, raised in Massachusetts towns, and born via C-sections at Emerson Hospital. *Wow, these patterns are unreal,* Meghan thought.

Meghan then launched her 23andme app. Meghan had a 50 percent DNA match with her Irish mother and 12 percent with cousins on her mother's tree. She then found Karen Marcotte had linked her to her family tree. Meghan had a 25 percent DNA match with Karen and potentially twenty-one other half-siblings, including Dr. Friedman's three children.

She understood why Gina Friedman posted she and her brothers were full siblings—they all shared Gina's mother's and Dr. Friedman's German genes. However, Karen's half-siblings group has Friedman's paternal DNA and their birth mother's DNA.

My DNA report shows I'm half Irish and half German. Meghan hovered over Karen's Facebook profile and blocked her. The nosy do-gooder couldn't tag her with a "Welcome to the family" post. All this sleuthing brought Meghan to the conclusion that her mother had gotten pregnant in Macro with Dr. Friedman years before all the other cesarean births occurred. Sadly, her mother had duped her stepfather, Mack, who had provided for Meghan and her brother. She thought about her promise to her dying mother—she'd never mention this to Mack. *The only father figure I have known and loved. He's all I have left, and it might kill him.*

* * *

Dan finished his meal at Ford's and returned to his parents' empty condo. He tossed and turned all night, trying to figure out what to do about Robin. Then he remembered what his dad said: "It's okay to lose sleep to work out important matters you must get under control. No one ever remembers the nights they got plenty of sleep."

His iPhone said 3:07 a.m. He created a note on his phone with a list of things to do and calls to make. Dan took a muscle relaxer, returned to bed, and quickly fell asleep.

Chapter 64

Saturday morning, Meghan fed Bruschi and sent Sam the elevator code. Her dad had not responded to her voice messages. She then called the Seminole Casino's hotel. The manager said her father had not checked out yet, but he'd check on him and get back to her.

Meghan had a full slate of appointments scheduled at the rehab center. The office was buzzing about the fourth death in Lee County; COVID had taken the life of a well-known local DJ.

"He was only thirty-nine," Latisha, the admin, said. "I saw him playing at the Celsius downtown. I heard he played for the spring break crowd at the Lani Kai at Fort Myers Beach last week. They're worried about how many people could have been exposed."

* * *

Dan ate breakfast and made a few calls. He checked his online accounts; he received his final GreenEx check and a month's severance pay. He wasn't worried about making mortgage and car payments or using his credit card for emergency fun. He exchanged texts with Sam, but she still hadn't received any updates from California. He sent her the Ancestry report to help keep her mind off Khori.

He then caught Rikki's forecast for a beautiful weekend. She added, "The average temperatures in Florida were four degrees above normal every month this winter."

Thanks for reminding us about climate change.

While his parents drove back from Marco, his father put him on the car's speaker. Dan updated them on Sam and his plans for the weekend after his debacle with Robin. Mom said he could use her car, and she'd submit his insurance forms when they got home. His father said Eric needed to replace his truck and might buy Dan's Toyota pickup.

After the call, Dan exchanged a few texts with Eric and negotiated an offer to pay off his Prius loan. Now, all he'd have to worry about was clearing his furniture and driving his Prius down to Florida after the closing. *Life is good for now*, he thought.

* * *

Sam had a miserable night. Then her phone pinged. *Not Khori*. Meghan texted her the private elevator code. Bruschi wagged his tail as she put the leash on him. She was surprised at how many residents walked for exercise, many with their dogs. The older people with facemasks seemed happy to see her wearing one.

While Bruschi sniffed a bush near the gym, Sam spotted a padlock and sign on the door:

CLOSED UNTIL FURTHER NOTICE

She texted her dad, who then forwarded her an email notice. The condo's board voted to lock down the gym in accordance with the CDC's guidelines on social distancing and recommended that everyone wear facemasks in the elevators and common areas.

Sam returned to the tower and entered the lobby. Jessica, the facemasked receptionist, was dealing with an angry, tall, thin man with a gray ponytail and a goatee who never wore a mask. The man stood close to Jessica's desk, ignoring the tape on the floor and the signs that said *Please social distance.*

He shouted, "Who locked the gym?"

Jessica answered, "The board sent the notice this morning."

The man pointed his finger at Jessica, "Better not shut the swimming pool down!"

Sam shortened Bruschi's leash and said, "Don't take it out on her. The board's trying to keep everyone safe."

He took a big step toward Sam, "Mind your own business, *kiddo*."

Bruschi growled, and Sam shouted, "Back off!"

The beady-eyed guy folded his arms and stood his ground.

Then Sam heard a calm voice from behind. "Sir, please keep your distance."

It was Rikki, standing by the lobby door in her facemask and sunglasses.

The man spun around and said, "No big government or commie condo board is gonna take my freedom away."

"COVID is deadly, and we're all in this together," Rikki said.

Then he stormed off.

"Thanks," the receptionist said to Sam.

"No problem, Jessica. People have a right to be stupid, but he abused that privilege."

Sam led Bruschi toward the elevators. She heard Rikki behind her. "Sam, hold up, please." Rikki caught up to her and asked, "Any word on

Khori?"

"Nothing yet." Sam looked down as they kept walking. "And, hey. I'm sorry I didn't tell you I was in a relationship. I didn't mean to mislead you."

"I know you didn't."

"Long story short, Khori's a recruiter. She got me several jobs, and we were both vulnerable after the problems we had with bad guys. The pandemic made me give up my apartment and move in with her. And I had to visit my mother. Again, I'm sorry."

"It's okay," she said, touching Sam's wrist. "You don't have to apologize. You've got much more to worry about. If it's any help. I'm here as a friend."

"It is a help. Thank you." Sam leaned into Rikki, and they gently embraced.

"Gotta social distance," Sam reminded softly and pulled away.

"Stay safe," Rikki said as they took separate elevators.

Sam gave Bruschi water inside her kitchen, opened her iPad, and read Dan's email with the Ancestry.com reports. They left her more puzzled and frustrated. Dan's DNA should have been a 50 percent match with hers, but it was only 26 percent.

I have to talk to Mom about the Ancestry report and not mention it to Dad. Given her mother's delicate state, it would have to wait. Sam also sent a DNA kit for 23andMe when her mother began having medical tests. Those reports were due soon. They might provide clues about her family origins and the unrecognized matches she had that did not appear on Dan's family tree.

Then, Alyssa, Khori's admin, texted Sam a link to an Instagram reel—Bulova had been found. The viral video showed Bulova drinking water from the firefighter's helmet who had rescued the French bulldog. Sam's stomach churned, and her hands were shaking when she called Alyssa.

"Thank God Bulova's safe. Did you hear from Khori?"

"Not yet. Her ex, Barry Brantley, tweeted he'd rewarded the fireman, and Bulova was with him. As you know, he bought the dog for Khori's birthday and has the papers."

"I didn't know that. But screw him, he cares more about Bulova than Khori."

"I worked for Barry. It's not like that," Alyssa said defensively. "Khori divorced him."

"Whatever... Why is Khori still missing?"

"Sorry. All we know is the fire raged through those towns. And rescuers are searching along the roads that weren't passable yesterday."

Sam ended the call. She was scared, angry, and felt helpless. She pounded on the couch to compose herself. She then created a Facebook post with a picture of Khori sitting on her deck, holding Bulova in her lap. She captioned it.

> Prayers for Khori. Wildfires destroyed her house. They found Bulova, but Khori is missing. Please join the search for Khori and others in the community.

She added the link of the firefighter with Bulova, then tweeted the post with hashtags and tags:

> #bulovarescued, #findKhoriChen, #prayersforKhori, #Wildfire-searchpartys, @sold-onsolar, @coinbasestaff, @Alyssastroud, @CCallahan, @BarryBrantley.

Within minutes, retweets came back at her, which went viral. Her father, Curt Callahan, and Barry Brantley all retweeted it. Sam then read the Facebook comments on her posts for prayers and help searching for wildfire victims.

Her mother gave it a virtual hug. Poor Bulova.

Her aunt Paula commented:

> Thinking of you, 🙏🙏.

Meghan posted:

> 😢🙏🙏.

* * *

Robin regretted ditching Dan last night. She felt miserable during her Saturday morning shift at Lowe's. Thankfully, it ended at noon, and she was off until Tuesday. She entered Kelly's salon. The reception area had three clients waiting. A woman sat in Kelly's styling chair with dye applied to her hair. Meanwhile, Kelly cut a man's hair in her private chair at the rear. Robin answered the phone, "Cape Cuts, how may I help you?"

Another client wanted to book an appointment with Kelly.

"Not available and closed Monday. We have Tuesday afternoon," Robin offered.

She heard Kelly say to her male client, "All set. You can pay Rachel. She'll book your next appointment. Good luck today."

Robin penciled the woman in for 2:00 on Tuesday with Kelly. She then looked up. Dan stood before her with freshly cut hair and a shit-eating grin. *Oh shit.*

He handed her his credit card and said, "I need another appointment."

Robin looked back at her smiling aunt, who said, "Men's special. And he is *special*."

"Twenty," she said and ran Dan's credit card. He added a tip. She flipped through her appointment book, "When would you like to make your next—"

"Immediately."

"Huh, what?" *He's crazy.*

"Grab your stuff, let's go. I'm taking you to the beach for the weekend."

She shook her head, "Oh, Dan! I can't… It's too busy today."

"I already cleared it with your aunt."

Kelly nodded and said, "Go. Get out of here."

Robin crossed her arms. Everyone in the salon was watching for her response. Her aunt waved at her to go as the other stylists shouted in unison, "Go, girl!"

"I guess I'm not wanted here," she said, grabbing her handbag. "You gotta take me home so I can get my bathing suit and pack my stuff."

"That's the plan," he said.

As they left, everyone cheered. Dan then led her across the parking lot.

"Why did you pahk your cah so far away?" Robin asked, exasperated.

"I didn't want you to see it and run away again."

Fair enough, she thought. "You're very calculating," she said as she entered the car.

"My dad said, 'You have to be two steps ahead.'" He started the car. "He also taught me to focus on the most important thing to do in the next five minutes… to get the benefits later." He leaned over and kissed her quickly.

"Took you six minutes," she said.

They chuckled, and he drove off.

"Last night's most important focus was selling my house, which I don't regret. But I'm sorry. I apologize for leaving you alone at Cabos on your birthday."

"Apology accepted. And I'm sorry I left without telling you. Now, where are you dragging me to?" She eyed his overnight bag, a cooler, and beach towels in the back seat.

"Fort Myers Beach," he said as they turned onto her aunt's street. "I booked a room at the Outriggers Hotel. They have a pool and beach on the Gulf, a tiki bar, and restaurants."

"Calculating and confident," she said, then chuckled.

"Thanks, I'll put that on my resume," he said.

And you know how to keep a hostage occupied. Robin felt excited.

Chapter 65

Dick made lunch while Jo unpacked from their trip. He heard her phone ring and the start of the conversation.

"Hi Sam, I saw the Bulova posts. Any news on Khori?"

Jo looked at Dick and shook her head no.

He returned to writing his new book, *Climate Change is Chilling*. He was behind schedule but determined to finish the last chapters for his editor. Dick didn't care about deadlines, promos, or TV appearances. This time, he'd used a pen name and pacified the publisher by writing a forward with his real name.

Now Dick's phone dinged. It was a text from Meghan.

> Sorry to bother you. Are you guys back from Marco?
>
> Just unpacked. Why, what's up?

Meghan immediately called. Her measured, sultry voice was replaced with an anxious, businesslike cadence.

"My dad's at the casino's hotel. Housekeeping opened the door and found the place reeking of alcohol and vomit. He's sick in bed. They want someone to pick him up." She sighed, "I have clients all afternoon. I uh… didn't know who else to call."

"I see… Tell the hotel I'll be there in an hour."

"Thank you so much, Dick. I owe you."

"Don't worry about it. I'll call you later with an update."

He explained to Jo.

"Oh, dear. Wear a mask and bring Sani wipes." Jo said.

Good suggestion. Dick kissed Jo on the cheek. He didn't like leaving Jo alone. His mind then went to his son. He wondered if Dan's plans with Robin fizzled. He sent him a text.

> Hey, you at the beach? I'm off to the casino's hotel to get Mack.
> He's sick. Mom's alone
>
> At Robin's. She's getting her overnight bag.
>
> K. Have fun! Tell her I said hi.

* * *

Rachel put her bag in the back seat. Dan put his phone down and drove off, "My dad said hi. He's going to get Meghan's dad at the casino. He's ill."

I don't care about Meghan. "Without your beard, you look like your dad. I wouldn't be here if it weren't for him."

"He's always pulling for people from Lowell. He appreciates that you're working two jobs and saving for college."

"Aww." *He's such a nice man.* She recalled the paint department incident. "I'll be lucky if I become a radiation technician or drug councilah."

"I think you'd do better as a radiation tech."

"Me too. But Meghan said you begged her in your bedroom for oxy."

"I was hurting so much physically and mentally that I needed meds," explained Dan. "The first time I did PT with her, I was so sore I couldn't hug a pillow."

Robin pushed further, "She said she left you frustrated and told you to fix your drug problem."

"I did fix it." They stopped at a long light. Dan scrolled through his phone messages and handed it to her. "This is why she gave me a second chance and helped me with PT."

Robin read the text exchanges between Dan and Meghan and then played the video of him flushing his oxy down the toilet.

That lying bitch! "Well, she sure thinks she's your family's therapist."

"She lost her brother and then her mother recently. She's close to all of us like we're her adopted family from Boston," Dan reasoned.

Hope so, but I'll never trust that woman.

When they entered the Outrigger Hotel at 1:25 p.m., it was eighty-four degrees with scattered clouds. The desk clerk said check-in was at four, but they could use the pool and beach.

* * *

Sam called to check on her mother.

"How're ya feeling? Worn out from Marco?" *She looked tired yesterday.*

"A bit. I'll have lunch and then relax on the lanai."

"Good. What'd you have for dinner last night?" *Probably seafood.*

"I had scallops; Dad had Grouper."

"Like Dan, you guys always eat fish... must be a Portuguese thing." *And maybe I'm not Portuguese.*

"You hated fish when you were little. I thought you'd acquire a taste for it by now."

"Nope. Guess it's not in my genes." *So, what is?*

"You always ate your fruit and veggies, though. And you look great, Sam."

"Thanks, Mom. I gotta take Meghan's dog for a walk."

"Okay... Prayers for Khori. Love ya."

* * *

Dan carried the cooler across the soft white sand as Robin put her beach bag under the hotel umbrella. "Ah, life is so much bettah in flip-flops," he heard Robin say. *It beats boots and snow rakes,* he thought.

They each applied sunscreen, and then she did his back.

"Now do me, please." *Love to!*

He rubbed the lotion on her back and was looking forward to their love-making later. *I trust she's still on the pill.*

"Gorgeous day," she said as they walked to the water's edge.

They took a selfie with the Gulf behind them. He took one of her in a sexy pose. *Gotta love Big Red,* he thought.

After getting their fill of sun, sand, and swimming, they entered their waterfront room, where he couldn't wait to do the boom-boom. They dropped their bags and beach gear by the king-size bed, kicked off their flops, and stepped onto the balcony.

"Great view of the pool and beach," Robin said, snapping photos.

"Love it," he said, following her inside the chilly air-conditioned room.

Dan pulled his sweaty T-shirt off as Robin removed her top, revealing a pair of white globes and pointy bullets. *AC chill or anticipation?* He hoped the latter. She stepped out of the bikini bottom and hung her swimsuit on the bathroom door hook.

"You thinking about a shower, then dinner?" he asked.

"I'm thinking about the most important thing to do in the next five minutes."

She then spread her beach towel on the sleeper couch, laid down, and motioned him over. *Heaven must have programmed Robin.* Dan promptly removed his Speedo swim trunks.

"You're very calculating," he said.

"And confident, too," she said, pulling him toward her.

* * *

Dick entered the Seminole Casino's hotel. Rojas, a young Cuban attendant, let him into Mack's room. The stench of stale food, booze, cigarettes, and vomit penetrated his facemask. Despite it all, Mack was snoring in bed. His clothes were piled on a side chair, his sneakers on the carpet. A service tray, empty whiskey nips, and beer bottles were all over the table. Cigarette butts floated in a plastic cup; the filtered ones had lipstick on them. On the nightstand were casino chips, quarters, condoms, and vials with diabetes meds, statins, and Viagra. *Mack wasn't just plugging slot machines.*

Dick gently nudged him. "Mack. Hey, Jimmy Mack. Wake up, Buddy."

The poor guy was gasping for air and sweating profusely. Dick retrieved a wet face cloth and hand towel from the bathroom. He bent over the bed and rolled Mack toward him to wipe his sweaty forehead and red, bulbous nose.

Mack coughed and rolled his eyes. He coughed again and phlegm sprayed everywhere. Mack's lips were parched, the gray whiskers on his three-day-old beard caked with dried vomit.

Dick then grabbed two casino chips off the nightstand and tossed them to Rojas, standing by the door. "He's in shock and burning up. Get medical help from the casino. Bring ice and orange juice."

The clerk pulled out his phone.

"Go!" Dick shouted.

He heard Rojas run down the hall.

Dick then tapped three digits on his phone.

"Nine-one-one," a female operator answered, then asked, "What is your emergency?"

"I'm with a very sick, elderly, diabetic man. He's in shock, running a fever, coughing, gasping for air. Might have pneumonia."

The operator asked, "What is your location?"

"Seminole Casino's hotel in Immokalee… Room 210."

"Okay, sir. Have you notified the hotel staff?"

"Yes, they went to get medical help."

"Good, sir. First responders are on the way. Please stay on the line."

Dick gave the dispatcher more info while hotel staff arrived. Two without masks stood at the door, the other with ice and a first aid kit moved to the bed.

"Peg…ca-cold," they heard Mack say when they put the ice on his head and chest.

Dick used the bathroom to wash Mack's phlegm off him. He then found Mack's carry-on bag in the closet and tossed Mack's clothes into a plastic laundry bag. Dick then used the sani wipes he brought on Mack's phone and wallet and dumped them into the carry-on bag, along with the quarters, casino chips, meds, and condoms. Dick signed off with the 911 dispatcher when the EMTs arrived; one wore a white hazmat suit and pushed a gurney into the room.

"You called nine-one-one?"

"Yes, sir."

"Go out in the hall and give all the information to the others."

Dick took Mack's overnight bag and stood in the hall, where two unmasked policemen and a face-masked fireman met him.

A silver-haired EMT told Dick, "Diabetic shock, possibly COVID. They'll test him at the hospital."

"What hospital is that?" Dick asked as they rolled Mack out on the gurney.

"The closest is NCH, North Naples."

Dick checked the directions on his phone. Forty minutes eta. About the same for Meghan in Fort Myers. He headed for his car and called her.

"Your dad's in the ambulance. They're taking him to North Naples Community Hospital."

"Oh, God, I was afraid of this. I begged him not to go there," Meghan's voice cracked.

"I advised him as well."

She sighed, "I'm leaving soon."

"The ambulance is heading out now. See you at the ER."

Dick tossed Mack's bag into his SUV and followed the two cruisers, a fire truck, and two ambulances with flashing lights. He called Jo, but she didn't answer; he left a message.

The traffic worsened when they got into Naples. Forty-one minutes later, they pulled up to the hospital. Dick put on his facemask and watched them push Mack's gurney into the ER. He then spotted Meghan in her work scrubs.

"They just brought him inside," he said.

Meghan threw her arms around him and smothered her face in his chest. "Oh, Dick, thank you."

He held the back of her head. Her perfume-infused collar and shampooed-scented hair permeated his facemask. Dick then gently pushed away from her to make eye contact. An intense stare with moist, determined eyes and a stressed, wrinkled forehead didn't detract from Meghan's beautiful face.

"We should check in at the ER desk," he said.

She nodded and pulled an N95 facemask from her smock's hip pocket. Then they entered through the ER's automatic sliding doors.

Chapter 66

They were sticky and gritty from sunscreen but ripe for the action. She'd lured him to the couch to avoid messing up the bed. A beach towel on the narrow cushions hindered Dan's ability to find a position where he could drive with authority and maintain a rhythm. Then, a jolt of pain in his healing shoulder disrupted his thrusts, and he lost all control and collapsed on top of Robin. Their long-awaited reunion was a bust.

"Sorry," he mumbled when she slid out from under him and bolted to the bathroom, leaving him wilting and wondering how badly he'd blown it. Dan eyed his flops and swimsuit on the floor. *Way to go, Speedo boy*. He rubbed his aching shoulder and thought about the past month of setbacks, pain, and despair he'd endured.

Dan heard the toilet flush and hoped Robin would want another go at it. But then he heard the shower running and entered the bathroom. He put his hands on Robin's shoulders and kissed the tattoo on her back that said, *"Still I rise."*

"Damn, I missed you."

"Missed you more," she said, stepping into the shower.

He followed her in.

She giggled. "Trying to save on watah?"

"I'm a trained conservationist," he said, "Got a standard to live up to."

"And you're up," she teased, reaching for his stiffy.

They lathered each other with soapy washcloths. Then she stood under the water with her back to him. Dan cupped her breasts as she braced herself with her hands on the wall. Dan then held her hips, eased into her, and slid in deeper.

"You… you drive me insane," Dan whispered in her ear.

"I'm sorry," she said seductively.He started thrusting.

"Ooh…ooh. Not that sorry," she purred.

Dan felt the urge and need to perform his best Peter Gabriel "Sledge-hammer" maneuvers. He increased to rapid thrusts as wet slapping sounds masked her moans.

"Ga-ha-ho, Dan!" she wailed.

He knew she was nearing her desired pinnacle, so he slowed and reached up with both arms to hold her hands. As Robin arched her back, Dan repeated his thrusts until she bellowed, "Aw, ho, God!"

They climaxed in unison. Dan's knees weakened and buckled as he clung to Robin's backside and wrapped his arms around her waist. He did not want to let go.

After they toweled off, Robin slapped his butt, like athletes do to acknowledge a great play. *I might get the Comeback Player of the Year Award.*

Dan pulled on his beige shorts and buttoned up his tropical shirt while Robin stepped into red bikini panties and a denim skirt. She filled out a white halter top with sun-kissed cleavage, and her hoop earrings disappeared under her thick, red, wavy hair. Robin's sunburnt freckled face and natural beauty captivated him.

Robin caught him staring. "What?"

"You… You clean up nice." Dan moved closer, "You're … so unbelievably beautiful."

"Aww! You're unbelievably sweet… and even more handsome with a tan."

"Last month, I was in a hospital bed, wondering what hit me and what happened to you."

"I'm sorry." Robin put her head on his chest. "I didn't think you'd evah fahgive me. But now we're here, in paradise like we dreamed about."

"Yep, it's all behind us now." Dan patted her soft round tush. "You hungry?"

"Wicked hungry."

* * *

Joanna worried about Dick helping Mack, who went on benders. Her sister Paula called; they talked about Marco and her health. She felt nauseous from the tuna sandwich Dick made for lunch. Paula reassured Jo she'd made the right decision to have the noninvasive surgery.

Joanna changed the subject. "So, how's Eric doing?"

"Great. Still dating Ashley, the *Lowell Sun* reporter. She keeps him grounded. He needs a new truck and is thrilled Dan's selling him his."

"I'm glad something good came out of that roof fiasco with Dan."

"Speaking of Dan," Paula added, "I got a notice about him on my Ancestry family tree. Did you have your kids check their health histories?"

"No, I didn't get a notice. I use twenty-three-and-me." *I Hope Sam's not on Ancestry.*

"I'm on both sites. Anyway, good luck on Tuesday. Love ya, sis."

"Love you too."

She'd promised Dan she'd submit his PT invoices to the insurance company and found his paperwork near her computer. Joanna completed the task, printed the confirmation, grabbed it off the tray, and found a report Dan had printed earlier. It was his family tree and DNA report from Ancestry, like the one she received from 23andme. As expected, Dan had 50 percent DNA from her and Dick but only 26 percent from Sam.

"Oh, hell no." Her head was pounding. She massaged her temples, wondered why he was on the DNA site, and hoped he didn't share his findings with Sam. Joanna called her son.

"Hi, Dan. Are you at the beach?"

"Yeah. It was fun. We're now going to dinner at the tiki bar."

"Oh, good. I submitted your insurance refund and found DNA reports on the printer. Did the Lowell General suggest you research your family's medical history?"

"No. Sam sent me a kit last month. I emailed my report to Sam this morning to take her mind off Khori," replied Dan. After a pause, "Mom… you still there?"

"Sorry... I was thinking about Khori. She's still missing."

"It's awful," said Dan. "Well, Robin's waiting. I better go."

"Stay safe. Love ya." She ended the call.

"Oh God, nooooo!" Joanna screamed. "I hate technology."

Joanna held her pounding head in her hands. *Sam must hate me and Dick. But I can't explain this to her now. She's worried sick about Khori. I should have done it years ago.*

Heartburn left the taste of tuna in the back of her throat. The pain in her head was now unbearable. Joanna's eyes blurred as the room spun, and her stomach erupted. Her lunch was coming up! *I'll never reach the bathroom.* Joanna held a hand over her mouth and rushed toward the guest bathroom, spewing on the hall floor. She then lunged to the toilet and vomited.

Joanna fell to her knees and puked until she had nothing left inside. She held her pounding head with both hands and felt faint when she tried to stand. As Joanna fell forward, her chin smacked against the bowl, and she bit through her tongue. Then everything went black.

Chapter 67

Meghan straightened her nameplate on her white smock, adjusted her N95 mask, and told the ER nurse she was Dr. Meghan McCormack. She then relayed her dad's information and asked, "Which exam room is he in?"

The nurse said, "He's in isolation. Please take a seat, and we'll let you know when we have a full diagnosis."

Meghan and Dick settled into seats socially distanced from the other visitors. She was terrified, knowing her father's comorbidities lessened his chances of survival. Meghan also felt foolish for leaning on Dick during a pandemic. She needed an icebreaker.

"Do you know where my father's Mustang is?"

"There's a valet stub in his wallet. It's in my car."

A nurse in navy blue scrubs with an N95 mask approached them. "Doctor McCormack?" the RN asked.

"Yes."

The tall nurse with short dark hair led them down the corridor to a private seating area with cushioned chairs. They took a seat.

"What's my father's diagnosis?" Meghan asked.

"He has pneumonia. His oxygen level is dangerously low. It will take a while before we get the lab results back," she explained. "The respiratory specialist and I looked over his chest X-rays; we believe he has COVID."

"But he's a smoker, so his lungs are always congested," replied Meghan.

"Yes. But the pervasive cloudiness in his lungs is consistent with images COVID patients shared with us from California and New York. He's on a respirator but laboring. We may have to intubate him."

"Oh God," Meghan said, squeezing Dick's hand.

"He was brought here from the casino?" asked the PA.

"He's always there. My mother passed recently, and he's been on a three-day bender."

"Sorry for your loss… So, you weren't with him at the casino?"

"No, I haven't seen him since Wednesday morning," Meghan said, then motioned to Dick. "He found him in the hotel room and called nine-one-one."

"He may have contracted COVID a week ago based on how bad his lungs are," said the PA.

Dick explained, "I wore a mask. And I washed up after I tried to bring him around."

"Sir, that's good. But the EMTs said you've been exposed to COVID. You need to quarantine for two weeks. If you start feeling sick, go to a hospital immediately and get tested."

"Am I already contagious?" Dick asked with worry.

"The CDC says it takes a few days to incubate before you become contagious. Stay away from elderly and immunocompromised people in the meantime."

He stood up, "Well, I better go."

Meghan said, "Dick. I'm sorry!"

He nodded, "Take care."

Meghan watched Dick leave and felt horrible.

"Is that your partner?" the PA asked.

"I wish. No, a close friend of my father."

"You should get tested soon."

"I will. I work at the nearby rehab center… As a doctor, can I borrow a surgical gown and face shield to see my father?" Meghan asked.

"I can't authorize that," the PA said. "I'll check with the department head. Meanwhile, let's get you tested. You should quarantine a few days and get retested before returning to work."

* * *

Dick raced out of the ER. He had several things to do in the next five minutes. He called Jo, left another message, and then got the number of the Indigo Hotel, which was minutes from his condo.

"Yes, Mister DeCosta. We have a suite with a fridge and microwave available. How long will you be staying?"

"Five to fourteen days." Dick figured it would be three or more days before he'd feel symptoms.

He made another call.

"Ted… Are you home?" Dick hoped.

"Yes. What's up?"

"I just left Mack at the Naples ER. They think he has COVID."

"Why am I not surprised? Those—"

"I need a favor. I have to quarantine. Jo might be asleep on the lanai. Go to my place and have her pack for me. After she's done, bring my bag, laptop, and phone charger to the Indigo."

"Damn. You got it! Talk later."

* * *

Sam was worried sick about Khori and frustrated with her DNA results. She scrolled through social media. Cyndi Callahan commented on her Facebook post about the search for Khori.

Google teams up with Cal Firefighters with drone searches.

Sam tweeted the drone search, called her mom, left a message, then called her dad.

He answered. She heard road noise in the background. "Dad, is Mom with you?"

"No. I'm—"

"She didn't answer her phone. I left a message. Firefighters and Google are using drones to search… But no one has seen Khori yet."

"I'm sorry, Sam," said her father. "Meghan asked me to get her dad at the casino. He's ill. The ambulance took him to the hospital. They think he has COVID."

"Oh, no! Poor Meghan."

"I just left her. Mack's cah is at the casino. Perhaps you could help Meghan retrieve it."

"Sorry, I have other things on my mind. Ask Dan."

"He's at the beach with Robin for the weekend."

"You know the roads better than me—go tomorrow."

"I have to quarantine. I need Mom to pack for me. Ted will drop stuff off at the hotel."

"Shit!" *Fuck-sake.* "You gonna be okay?" She felt terrible for being short with him. He was trying to keep her mind off Khori and help Meghan.

"I wore a mask and used hand sanitizer. So, it's just a precaution."

"Hope so."

They ended the call.

Geezus, what the fuck else could go wrong?

* * *

Ted explained Dick's needs to his wife. Marie had Jo's elevator code. They stepped off the elevator, rang the bell, and waited. No sign of Joanna.

Ted said, "She might be on the lanai."

They entered, and Marie shouted, "Hello! Jo! It's just us!"

Marie checked the lanai. "Not there. I'll see if she's sleeping in her bedroom."

Ted said, "I'll get Dick's laptop in his office."

He walked down the hall and gagged when he saw the vomit on the floor by the guest bathroom. The nasty odor worsened inside where Jo was lying on the floor by the toilet.

"Marie!" he shouted, "She's in here!" He checked her carotid artery.

Marie came running.

"Call nine-one-one!" Ted yelled to his wife.

"Oh God. Get her up," Marie said before she made the call.

Ted sat Joanna up and gently leaned her against the bathroom wall.

"Jo, wake up."

No response. There was blood on her chin and drool hanging from her mouth. Her pulse was weak. Ted called security, then her husband.

"Dick, where are you now?" He tried to remain calm.

"In traffic… horrible accident. Pickup demolished a motorcycle."

"Jo had an accident. She's unconscious in the powder room. Marie's on her phone with the nine-one-one dispatcher. EMTs are on their way," Ted reported. "Dick, you there?"

"Yeah, uhm … You'll need Jo's ID and insurance card…Wallet's in her purse on the kitchen counter," Dick stammered.

"We'll get it. Security is here now, and the ambulance is pulling in. Talk later."

"Thanks, Ted!"

* * *

Dick's heart raced as he pulled into the plaza to find the card for Dr. Royce, Jo's neurosurgeon, in his wallet. He left a message with Royce's answering service—Jo was on her way to Lee Memorial Hospital with a possible ruptured brain aneurysm. By the time Dick got to the hospital, they'd know if her aneurysm had ruptured and would require emergency surgery. He'd wait until it was confirmed before notifying his children. Dick was ten minutes from Lee Memorial when the Audi's screen indicated an unrecognized incoming number. He answered.

"Mister DeCosta? … This is Doctor Royce. I'm on my way to the hospital. They did a CT scan—her aneurysm ruptured. They're prepping her for surgery; I'll be assisting."

"What does that entail?"

"This requires invasive clipping and a craniotomy. We'll cut her skull open, insert a metal clip to the neck of the aneurysm to stop the blood flow to her brain, and then put the skull piece back. It will be a lengthy but necessary operation. We can't hold off."

"I understand. How long will it take, and what is the recovery period?"

"Surgery will be four or more hours. The amount of blood and fluid that seeps into her brain will impact her recovery. She'll be in the ICU for at least a week, hospital for another week… much longer if there is neurological damage."

"I see," Dick swallowed hard. "How soon will we know if there is brain damage?"

"We won't know all the complications for a few days. I'll call you after her surgery."

"Thank you, doctor." *Godspeed.*

Dick called Ted to relay the latest. He then drove home and considered quarantining there. Dan could stay with Sam in the rental, but if he became contagious, it would be safer for everyone if he quarantined at the hotel. He grabbed a cart by the lobby door and brought it up in the elevator.

Even with his facemask on, he smelled the putrid stench as soon as he entered his home. Dick cleaned up Jo's mess in the bathroom and sanitized everything. He then threw his clothes in the washer, showered, and scrubbed repeatedly, hoping he'd washed away his COVID exposure. He considered calling Dan, but he'd been through a rough month and needed the time alone with Robin.

Dick added Tylenol to his shaving bag and packed a suitcase and gym bag. He filled the cart with bags of food he'd need for breakfast, snacks, a case of water, wine, and vodka. He moved to his study and grabbed his laptop. Dick noticed Jo's phone and paperwork were on her workspace. He examined a report on Dan's Ancestry findings.

Ding—it was a text from Meghan.

> My dad's PCR test came back positive. They had to intubate him. God help us.

Yes. God help us, Dick thought.

> So sorry! 🙏 🙏 🙏

He prayed for Jo, Mack, and Khori. Then Jo's phone rang, and he froze.

Chapter 68

Sam held Bruschi's leash while he led her along the pavers bordering the towers. Every hour that passed made her more fearful that something terrible happened to Khori. She wondered why her mother hadn't returned her calls or commented on her Facebook posts. She sat on a bench by the river and texted Meghan.

> Heard about ur dad. Prayers 🙏 🙏 for u both. Don't worry about Bruschi. Sending hugs.

Meghan called, "Hi, Sam. Sorry, I forgot to check with you. I'm at the hospital."

"No problem. I feel so bad about your dad. Any updates?"

"He's got COVID. He's on a ventilator, and they just had to intubate him."

"What's that?"

Meghan's voice cracked with emotions, "They put a tube down his throat and attach the other end to a ventilator to clear his lungs."

"Oh wow."

"I saw your posts about Khori. I hope she turns up safe. If you need to go out, leave Bruschi with Silvia."

"Okay. Good luck, stay safe, and keep us posted."

She'd never heard Meghan sound so vulnerable. She must be terrified after losing her brother and mother. Sam called her mom and left another message.

She then entered the lobby with Bruschi. Rikki was in the adjacent sitting room, on her phone. She overheard her wrapping up a call, "No worries, Mum. Stay safe... Love ya too."

Sam held Bruschi's leash and sat on a chair across from Rikki, who looked stressed behind her facemask.

"Everything okay?" she asked.

"My parents planned to visit but canceled due to COVID. My dad is a cancer survivor," replied Rikki.

"Understandable," Sam said, fidgeting with her facemask. "My dad had Meghan's father rushed to the hospital. She's there now. He's on a ventilator, struggling with COVID."

"That's awful! Poor Meghan recently lost her mother. She must be scared."

"Yeah, lots of scary things happening," Sam said. "My dad has to quarantine for two weeks. The firefighters found Khori's dog. But no one has heard from Khori yet."

"Aww geez," Rikki said.

Sam's phone rang; she answered, "Dad, are you at the hotel? Mom's not answering."

"Sam, uhm… She's had an accident—"

"What? Where?" She handed Bruschi's leash to Rikki and walked away.

"Ted and Marie found her passed out in the powder room. An ambulance took her to Lee Memorial. I spoke with her surgeon. Her aneurysm ruptured…. They are operating to stop the bleeding—"

"Nooooo!" she screamed, stamping her feet.

Bruschi lifted his ears. Rikki's eyes welled up.

"I can't fuckin' believe this is happening!" Sam paced back and forth.

"I'm sorry, Sam. But she's in good hands. They know what to do in these emergencies."

"Are you there now?" she asked.

"No. I—"

"Right, *you* have to quarantine." *Christ, will this nightmare ever end?*

"I'm home packing. Then going to the Indigo," he replied.

"I'm going to the hospital … If I can get a ride." Sam looked over at Rikki.

"The operation will take over four hours. Dr. Royce will call me when they finish. She'll probably be in recovery another hour or more before they'll let visitors in."

"Don't care. I'll stay all night with her," Sam insisted.

"After the doctor calls me, I'll call you with an update. *Please,* don't call Dan. I'll let him know what's going on later. Okay?"

"Whatever…" *He's your son.*

She hung up, collapsed on the lobby couch, and cried.

Rikki sat next to her. "Is your mother okay?"

Sam wiped away her tears. "She's having emergency brain surgery." Then, she fell into Rikki's open arms and cried on her shoulder.

"I'm so sorry, Sam. How can I help?"

* * *

Dick had been reading Dan's Ancestry report in his office when he saw Sam's incoming call on Jo's phone. He had to make the difficult call to Sam, who was already upset about Khori and Meghan's dad. Now, she was terrified about her mother. Dick knew she was frustrated with him for not being at the hospital with Jo. He felt her resentment and wondered if Sam knew about the DNA reports, which may have put Jo over the edge and caused her rupture.

But none of that mattered now. He couldn't focus on the most important thing to do in the next five minutes. *What happens to Jo in the next five hours is the only thing that matters.* Dick gazed out his office window at Lee Memorial Hospital in the distance. He prayed for his wife to survive the surgery in one piece. Then he headed for the Indigo Hotel.

Chapter 69

Robin held Dan's hand as they approached the tiki bar. A woman serenaded Patsy Cline's "Crazy" for the raucous happy hour crowd; none were social distancing. Robin and Dan grabbed a table far from the bar, overlooking the sun glistening on the Gulf. They sipped tropical drinks and shared appetizers. Robin asked their waitress to take their picture.

"Came out wicked perfect. Huh?"

"Yes. Perfect… like you," Dan kissed her. "But don't post it anywhere."

"No worries. I love that you don't stare at your phone like everyone else."

"It's off to save the battery and avoid crappy news. I just want to be with you."

"You're a special guy," Robin kissed him.

"Hey… do you wanna get some ice cream?" he asked.

I wanna lick you all up. "Sure."

They dropped the top on his mother's convertible and cruised to the center of Fort Myers Beach. They licked their melting ice cream cones, listened to the live band playing near the huge clock in Times Square, and watched the crowd dance.

"Let's go for a nightcap," Dan suggested.

They sipped Robin's favorite—margaritas—at the Pier Side Grille's Blow Fish Bar, crowded with mostly boisterous boomers. Two guys playing guitars covered Chris Stapleton's "Tennessee Whiskey."

A slow-dancing, silver-haired couple's T-shirts made her chuckle. His read, DRINK 'TIL YOU WANT ME. Hers read, I CAN'T DRINK THAT MUCH.

Robin touched Dan's arm and said, "I drank enough… Let's go."

* * *

Meghan had her nose swabbed for the PRC test and then sat in the hospital's waiting room. At 8.31 p.m., she finished her lukewarm coffee. The PA approached her and said, "No change. He's still laboring."

"Can I suit up and see him now?"

The PA frowned, "We have shortages of protective gear. Sorry, only authorized staff in the COVID isolation rooms. I know you don't want to hear this, but you should go home and quarantine."

At 9:40 p.m. Meghan got Bruschi at Silvia's place. She was drained. She sipped a cup of tea, thought about her mother's affair with Dr. Friedman, and wondered if her stepfather, Mack, who treated her like a princess, knew she wasn't his child. *I'd give anything to hug him now.*

She'd considered posting on Facebook that he was in the ER on a respirator. But didn't want to panic anyone, especially coworkers, now that she was quarantining. She'd wait until she knew her test results. Meghan scanned her Facebook feeds to pass the time.

Sam's post about praying for her mother having emergency surgery jolted her. She started a text to Sam and then deleted it. She wanted to contact Dick, then realized he didn't need to be reminded of why he couldn't be at the hospital—he'd risked his life for Mack and her.

Bruschi rubbed up against her leg. "Tell me, Boy… why is everything so fucked up now?" He barked, then sat on the floor.

She commented on Sam's Facebook post.

OMG 😣 So sorry, Sam! 🙏 🙏 🙏

* * *

Sam sat in Lee Memorial's small waiting room down the hall from surgery. She defied her father, texted Dan, and left him a voice message. She got no response. Rikki sat patiently in the adjacent cushioned chair. Earlier, she'd talked Sam into going downtown to Capones for pizza and a drink to calm her nerves and kill time before they drove to the hospital. Sam forced herself to eat a slice and drank a Corona Light.

She felt a chill in the waiting room. She turned to Rikki and said, "It's getting late. You should leave. I can get an Uber home."

"I have tomorrow off. I'll stay 'til you know what happened with your mother's surgery."

"Thank you," Sam sighed, realizing she had no one else in her family to cling to on this gut-wrenching night.

She used Facebook's check-in feature.

> Feeling worried!! At Lee Memorial Hospital, Fort Myers, FL. Praying for my mother to survive emergency brain surgery! 🙏 🙏 🙏

Sam received a bunch of emotional reactions. Her aunt Paula from Lowell commented.

Oh no! I spoke with her a few hours ago.

Paula sent Sam a DM:
Sam, please call me ASAP. 978-452-3778

Sam called her aunt and explained her mother's accident and how her dad was exposed to COVID and had to quarantine. She said she left a message on Dan's phone but hadn't heard from him yet.

"So sorry, Sam. Please keep me updated."

Sam's mind was whirling. She was overwhelmed with anxiety about Khori and her mother and depressed about not knowing her biological father. She thought about the man she had called Dad all her life and why her parents kept it a secret. She then contemplated how Meghan might be feeling knowing she'd lost her mother and was now praying for her father to survive.

She silenced her phone at 10:20 p.m. It would be another hour before her mother's surgery ended. Sam wiped a tear away, clasped her hands, closed her eyes, and silently prayed.

* * *

Dick carried his laptop bag into his hotel suite. The bellhop wheeled the luggage cart in, unloaded it, and Dick tipped him. He removed his face-mask, filled his mini kitchen with the items he brought, and then unpacked his bags. Dick discovered the bellhop had also brought Mack's overnight bag from his Audi.

He opened his laptop and researched his wife's condition and the procedures. Dick reviewed the disheartening risks and the percentage of survivors and deaths in the first year. To lessen his anxiety, he opened the Word doc of his new book. Dick focused on writing his closing chapters and figured he'd finish the book by the time his quarantine concluded.

At 10:31 p.m., his phone interrupted him. It was Jo's sister, Paula. He had always gotten along with her until tonight.

"Sam's all alone at the hospital, worried about Jo and Khori. She left messages for Dan. Have you spoken with him yet?"

No! Dick held the phone away from him.

"And how the heck did you get exposed to COVID?" she asked.

"I'm fine, Paula. Thanks for asking," he said facetiously, then explained the situation with Mack.

"You should never have left Jo alone!" Paula exclaimed.

Don't fuckin' remind me. "Her surgeon will call me any minute... I'll keep you updated."

He ended the call, poured vodka on the rocks, and took a big swallow. Dick felt miserable. He was worrying about Mack's odds of surviving and his wife's chances of making it through surgery with no brain damage. He hoped Dr. Royce would call him before speaking with his defiant daughter.

Then Dick's phone dinged; a family post from Sam.

God help me. She didn't make it. She's gone!

"Nooooo, Jo!" he screamed. He called Sam. *Come on, pick up!* She answered after the third ring, his heart pounding as he paced the room.

"Dad…" He heard Sam sobbing and another voice, perhaps a nurse.

"Sam, you there? Is the doctor with you?"

"Yes, uhm, no," said Sam. "The drones found her burned car in a creek with her remains inside." She began hyperventilating before she could get the rest of the words out. "Khori's ex verified the car. She may have drowned first," she sobbed. "And I… I never got to say goodbye."

"I'm so, so sorry, Sam." He swallowed hard. "Is someone with you?"

"Rikki… She brought me here."

"Maybe you should go—" Dick's phone beeped. "Hang on, the doctor is on the other line."

"Mister DeCosta," Royce began, "She did well."

"Thank God!" he bellowed as he paced the room.

Royce explained, "The titanium clip stopped the hemorrhaging. However, she developed hydrocephalus, and excess spinal fluid built up within the brain. We had to implant a shunt to drain the fluids and relieve the pressure. She'll be in recovery a few hours, then moved to ICU."

"Our daughter's there now. When can she have visitors?" asked Dick.

"Not until she comes around," replied Royce. "I doubt she'll be responsive until sometime tomorrow. And she may not recognize people at first."

"How soon can you do a neurological follow-up?"

"Once she's responding, we'll begin in phases. It may take a few days."

"Okay. Thank you."

Dick switched over to Sam. "Doctor said she did well. The clip stopped the bleeding, and they put a shunt in to drain the fluids."

"Thank God she made it," she sobbed. "When can I see her?"

"She'll be moved to ICU in a few hours. But she probably won't come around until late tomorrow morning. You should leave with Rikki—"

"No! I'm staying here. I'll sleep in her room and wait for her to wake up," Sam cried out.

"Go home and try to get some rest," Dick said calmly. "Then call tomorrow morning and ask if she's responsive."

"I'll think about it." Sam ended the call before Dick could say good night.

* * *

Sam ended Dad's call, texted her aunt, Paula, then collapsed in Rikki's arms. She was wracked with mixed emotions—devastated about losing Khori, relieved that her mother survived the surgery, but anxious to see the precious woman who brought her into this cruel and unfair world.

Rikki handed her another tissue. Sam dried her eyes and blew her nose as Rikki's eyes welled up in empathy.

The ICU nurse told Sam her mother could not have visitors until they checked her progress tomorrow morning. She leaned on Rikki when they walked to her car.

* * *

Dick knew Dan routinely turned off his phone at night and responded to messages the following day. Dick texted about his mother resting after surgery and left a longer voice message with details about Khori, Mack, and his quarantining. He then texted Paula about Jo—it was easier than calling. Paula replied.

Sam updated me. And her partner died too! The poor girl's a mess.

Of course, Dick mumbled. *I'm just a dickhead and a lousy brother-in-law.* He then realized his anger was misplaced. *I should have been there for Jo.*

Dick's heart ached for Jo. He felt utterly useless, miserable, and scared. She might never again be that perfect woman—*to have and to hold from this day forward... In sickness and health, until death do us part.*

He said prayers for Jo and Mack. He thought about how horribly Khori's life was taken. He opened his laptop, launched his new book's Word file, and changed its title from *Climate Change is Chilling* to *Climate Change KILLS!*

He then shut his laptop down and topped his tumbler with more vodka.

* * *

Robin locked and chained the hotel door and turned around to find Dan's lips had found hers. They wasted no time disrobing and hitting the bed. He kissed her neck, her breasts, and then her scripted tattoo, *"Be Kind,"* on her wrist. *He's off to a wicked good start.*

Dan then kissed her tummy before he slid down and kissed her inner thighs. Robin tingled and dug her fingers into the sheets when his lips and tongue performed circles of miracles, sending multiple waves of pleasure throughout her. She quivered and moaned with delight while she climaxed. *Gawd, that was wonderful.*

Robin then gently rolled him on his back. *Your turn.* Her quick kisses traveled from his pecks to his abs, then below until he was rock-hard. She straddled him, easily slid on, and took control. He cupped her breasts as she rode him up and down. He then gripped her hips as she ground him back and forth. Robin rocked and bucked and watched his expressions. He was on the brink, like her.

"Oh ho, yes, baby, yes!" she shouted when she felt him explode. She subsequently collapsed on top of him—her face resting on his good shoulder and her heart racing.

The fan overhead cooled their sweaty bodies as they both caught their breaths. She then felt his fingers gently caress her lower back and bottom. Robin cherished this tender moment.

"You feel so … *perfect* to me," he said. "So perfect *for me*."

No one has ever said anything like that. Robin looked into his dreamy eyes and said, "You make me feel perfect, and I…" *Love you for it.* She then kissed him and said, "I need a breethah."

When Robin returned from freshening up, she found Dan had filled much-needed glasses of water, the lamp was off, and the TV set to the music channel softly playing a Taylor Swift song. He used the bathroom, and she stretched out on the bed and looked up at the fan. *Paradise with a fantastic lovah and sweet, caring man. Don't screw this up.*

When Dan returned, Dua Lipa's rhythmic "Levitating" was wafting through the speakers, and Robin was gyrating to the beat. He stood by the bed, his eyes examining her pointed nipples and her spread-eagle position. Robin threw her arms out to him, and he slid over to her. He kissed her breasts as she ran her fingernails through his freshly cut hair. Then Robin pulled him up to face her.

"You're so good to me! I loved how you planned this getaway. You got a haircut from Kelly you didn't need. Thank you for not giving up on me."

"You have to stop running away. And you have to trust me," said Dan.

"I do trust you, Dan. With all my heart. I love you!" *There, I said it.*

"And I love loving you," Dan said. "I feel like we were destined to be together. Deserve each other."

They kissed tenderly, knowing that they loved one another. There were no more obstacles or fears of another failed relationship; they could get on with their lives and chase their dreams together. Dan nuzzled behind Robin; they melded together, a perfect pair of spooning partners in paradise.

"Love you," she whispered as he pulled the sheet over them.

"Wait…was that my echo or the voice in my head?" he asked.

"Silly…" she hugged his hand tighter to her chest and said, "Nighty night."

"Love you too. Sleep tight."

Slumberland and the soothing sounds of waves slapping the shoreline flushed away their thoughts of the troubled world around them.

Chapter 70

Sam frowned at her reflection. Her puffy, bloodshot eyes had cried all night. At 6:18 a.m., she called and spoke with the ICU nurse. "She's stable but unresponsive. Check with the day shift about visitors." *After eight,* Sam figured.

She ruled out asking Meghan or Rikki for a ride—it was Sunday, after all. She booked an Uber instead and planned to sleep at the hospital. Sam then went on Facebook to read the responses to her post about Khori's wildfire demise. She mustered the courage and posted a response.

> Thank you all for your kind sentiments and prayers. Khori is watching from above.

She'd wait until she got to the hospital before providing updates on her mom's health.

* * *

Dan slipped out of bed without disturbing Robin and emptied his bladder. He jumped in the shower and mused about renting or buying at the beach. *It can't hurt to look.*

As he toweled off, Robin entered and said, "My turn."

Outside the shower door, he asked, "You want to grab breakfast at the Deckside Café?"

"Yes, please. Been craving waffles. Give me a few minutes to catch up to you."

Dan turned his phone back on. It was now Sunday at 8:57 a.m. He noticed he had several missed calls and messages. *Glad it was off. It would've ruined a great night with her.* He then listened in disbelief to waves of horrible news about Khori, his mom, and Meghan's father. *Poor Sam had to endure it all alone, and Dad was quarantined.* Dan felt nauseous and lost his appetite for waffles and for another day at the beach. He hoped Robin would understand. His family needed him.

He sent a group text to Sam and his father.

Sam, so sorry about Khori! 😢 B strong ... I'll C U at the hospital

Robin watched him pack his overnight bag and asked, "What time is checkout?"

"Eleven. But something's come up. I'll explain after we devour those waffles."

* * *

Dick called the hospital again. The ER's lead nurse said, "Your daughter is with her, but she is still unresponsive."

"Has Doctor Royce examined her yet?"

"Doctor Silas did and apprised Doctor Royce, who will examine her Monday. They're more concerned about her blood pressure rising than her not responding yet."

I'm worried about both. "Thank you," he ended the call.

* * *

Meghan spoke with the harried head nurse, who said, "The pulmonologist ordered more X-rays to see if the respirator and antibiotics affected his lungs. They should know more later today."

"Do you know if my COVID test results are—"

"No, the lab will follow up. And uhm, I hope your father has his affairs in order?"

Meghan was his healthcare proxy and had power of attorney. Through teary eyes, she read her father's will. Since her brother and mother were deceased, she was the sole beneficiary of the family trust and would assume the role of trustee upon her father's passing.

The trust included her parents' savings, retirement accounts, the paid-for condo, and Mack's life insurance policy. Meghan also inherited a tax-free estate and would receive the required minimum distributions annually, based on her age. If she were unemployed—due to COVID—she'd have no worries for several years. She'd be debt-free with a hefty bank account. But with no one else in her life, she was scared, sad, and lonely.

Dick had Mack's phone, wallet, and car keys. Before her dad ended up in the ER, she'd planned to ask Dick about his relationship with Lee and Jackie Grisham. Jo's ties to Friedman and his receptionist—who was married to Dick's AI colleague—made her more suspicious about the FBI's raid. If the FBI never investigated, other women may never have come forward—and her biological father might not have committed suicide.

She googled "Leland Grisham FBI" and came up empty, even when she added Dick DeCosta and Jackie Adams Grisham. *Hmm.* She figured the FBI had the means to scrape and remove all internet info on its top cops.

* * *

Dan entered his mom's chilly hospital room and felt a twinge in his chest. His sister was sitting in a chair at their mother's bedside and holding Mom's hand, which now had an IV tube attached to it. He cringed when he saw the bandages around her head—half of her hair was shaved off, and there were black and blue bruises around her right eye and ear in addition to oxygen tubes up her nose and other tubes and wires attached to her arms, chest, and head.

Sam rose to greet him. Dark circles were under her tearful eyes, and her hair was messy. Dan embraced his trembling sister, whose shoulders sagged.

"So sorry about Khori," he said, gently patting her back. Sam wept on his shoulder.

"It's horrible. I never said goodbye to her." She wiped her runny nose and eyes on her long-sleeved shirt, then said, "At least Mom's breathing."

He asked, "Has she been awake?"

Sam shook her head and fell back on the chair, exhausted. Dan moved to the other side of the bed. His mom's hair stuck out from the left side of her head. He took her left hand, leaned over, and kissed a spot on her cheek not obstructed by surgical tape. Dan thought her mouth dropped open. "Did you see that?"

Sam sat up.

"Mom's lips parted. Did she do that earlier?"

Sam shook her head.

Dan gently squeezed her hand. "Mom, I'm here with Sam."

Her eyelids fluttered and popped open.

"You made it! You're a real trooper!" Dan whooped.

She turned her eyes in his direction, weakly squeezed his hand, and said, "Da-da Dick? Oho, Dick… you're home."

"That's Dan... not Dad," his sister said.

Mom's eyes darted from Sam to Dan. "Can't breathe… You're a medic. Help her, Dick—"

"Mom, you can't breathe?" His sister pushed the nurse's call button.

"Dee can't breathe. She's too weak."

"Mom," Sam asked. "Who's Dee?"

"Deidra, poor thing. Dee's too tiny, can't breathe."

They heard the monitor beeping.

"Calm down, Mom," Dan said, patting her hand.

The nurse rushed in, and Sam stepped aside.

"Her blood pressure is rising," the nurse said, adjusting the IV bag. "I'm giving her medication to lower it back down."

"She's awake and talking," Dan said.

"It's too much excitement. You both should leave the room," the nurse replied.

The head nurse dashed in. "Please leave! We'll call you when she's stable."

"Sorry, Mom." Dan put his arm around his sister and ushered her into the corridor.

Sam asked, "Who is Deidra?"

"No idea. She's delirious. The ER nurse said Mom might not recognize everybody."

"She didn't know me ... and she thinks you're Dad," said Sam.

"Maybe… At least she's responsive now. I'll text Dad," replied Dan.

"And I'll call Aunt Paula."

* * *

Sam explained to her aunt, "When Mom woke up, she thought Dan was Dad, and she didn't recognize me. She mumbled about a Deidra and that she couldn't breathe. And that's when her blood pressure shot up. The nurse made us leave. We're in a private waiting room now."

"Oh, dear! Well, Dan looks like your father did when he came home from Bosnia. Put me on speaker so Dan can hear this," said Aunt Paula.

"Hold on… you mean Desert Storm, not Bosnia," Sam replied and looked at Dan.

Paula began, "In nineteen-eighty-nine, your mom was pregnant, and your dad signed up for four more years in the army reserves. He said he'd need extra income to support a family. But your dad never expected to be on active duty, let alone two tours. In ninety-one, your dad was in a Desert Storm MASH unit. After he got home from the short war, your mom got pregnant. Five months later, he was redeployed to Bosnia. The stress—"

"Wrong," Sam interrupted. "I wasn't born until ninety-four."

"Correct," Paula said. "I'm sorry…. They never told you."

"Didn't tell us what?" Dan asked.

Paula explained, "Raising a baby boy, plus being pregnant while your dad was in Bosnia, was too much stress for your mother. So, Dan was at my house when Deidra was born six weeks prematurely through an emergency C-section. Unfortunately, the poor thing's lungs never fully developed, and she died in an incubator."

Sam shouted, "Holy shit! Poor Mom!" *What else is she hiding?*

Dan asked, "Why didn't they tell me?"

"Too painful. Your Dad missed Deidra's birth and her cremation, which the hospital handled. Your mother never forgave him and destroyed Deidra's hospital photos. She still wanted another child. They were on an adoption list when she got pregnant with Sam."

"Awful," Dan said. "So, poor Mom woke up reliving that painful time."

"Exactly," Paula said. "And that's why I told you this. You must be brave and careful not to ask her about it."

"I understand now," said Sam. *Mom blamed Dad. Wanted another child. Probably had a fling with my biological father.*

The head nurse approached them with the news. "We lowered her blood pressure, and the doctor sedated her. She needs undisturbed rest. No visitors for twenty-four to forty-eight hours."

* * *

Dan and Sam were in the hospital parking lot when his dad called.

"So, Mom thought you were me. Hope you didn't tell her Mack has COVID?"

Dan looked at Sam and said, "No, Mom thought you'd just returned from active duty. She kept mumbling about being too tiny to breathe. Then her blood pressure shot up, and they made us leave. They sedated her, and she can't have visitors for a day or two. I'm taking Sam home now."

"Oh… Well, take care of Sam. She needs you now."

He was relieved there was no mention of Deidra. *It might come up someday, but that secret is safe with me for now.* Dan wanted to spend time with Robin but felt guilty. *Dad's right—Sam needs me.*

* * *

Sam rode in the car with her brother and posted a Facebook update.

> Mom woke up in the ICU. Rising blood pressure required meds and sedation. 🙁 No visitors for 24 to 48 hrs 🙏🙏

Comments poured in from Meghan and dozens of friends. Marie Bates and Rikki even offered rides to the hospital.

As soon as they made it to Meghan's rental, she plopped on her couch and read Meghan's text out loud to Dan.

"So sorry about your mother. My dad's condition has worsened. I'm quarantined; all that's confidential. I'm not posting on Facebook. It would panic my coworkers. Stay strong. Sending hugs to you and Dan."

Sam replied:

> 🙁 Understood. 🙏🙏Take care. 😷

She sat back on the couch, closed her eyes, and yawned. Then, she gave her brother permission to leave and meet Robin.

"I can't leave you here alone… You've been through too much," said Dan.

"I'll sleep better if I know you're not hanging around. Tomorrow, we'll check on Mom."

"I'll text later. By then, you might want to join me and Robin for dinner."

"Okay."

Sam closed the door to her bedroom and shut the shades. She flopped on her bed, folded into a fetal position, and sobbed into her pillow.

* * *

Dan drove to Robin's aunt's house and updated her on his mother and Sam. Robin was off work until Tuesday. She packed an overnight bag to stay with him at his parents' condo. They'd planned to eat at Capones; his sister might join them, or he'd bring her a pizza. When Dan stopped for gas, he checked in with Sam over text.

I'm good, thanks. Rikki's bringing me Chinese takeout.

Dan texted his dad from Capones. After dinner, he and Robin carried a salad and a small pizza around the corner to where his father was staying. His dad handed him his mom's iPhone in return.

Chapter 71

Monday morning, Dick felt weak. He struggled to do his core exercises on the rug, then forced himself to eat oatmeal. Harlan and Christina called him on speakerphone.

"The Jenkins are thrilled with Dan's house," said Christina. "They're moving in next month and will be working from home due to COVID."

"Glad it all worked out," Dick said.

Harlan said, "We saw Sam's Facebook posts. How is Jo doing?"

"She's heavily sedated," replied Dick. "Her surgeon should be on his way to check her."

"Jo's a fighter. She'll get through this," Christina said. "Are you with her now?"

"No, uh. I was aiding an old friend who has COVID. I'm quarantined in a hotel—"

"Oh wow, sorry, Dick," Harlan said. "How are you feeling? Any symptoms?"

"A scratchy throat. Unfortunately, vodka doesn't help that."

"Well, Godspeed to you both. Keep us posted, please."

* * *

Sam awoke more rested and in a different state of mind. She was mourning and painfully accepting Khori's tragic passing, worrying about her fragile mother, and sadly accepting that she had a half-brother and a stepfather. All she could do now was hope and pray that her mom would recover with minimal neurological deficiencies.

Yesterday, she welcomed Rikki's Chinese takeout. She no longer felt guilty about spending time with her. Khori, nine years older, had been a dominant force both as Sam's career adviser and her lover. Rikki, her contemporary, was professionally polished, emotionally comfortable about her sexual orientation, and felt like her equal. She was kind, caring, and patient when she held Sam, which she desperately needed. She knew it was too soon to sleep together with everything going on. *That would come later.*

Sam read a tweet from Khori's ex-husband announcing a celebration of life for Khori on Facebook and via Zoom next Friday. Sam was angry that he was running the show but soon realized he was doing her a favor. Sam had too much on her mind to organize anything for Khori, especially from Florida. She retweeted Barry's announcement and posted it on Facebook with a note thanking him and Khori's coworkers for their support.

She then read through her work email. Her boss and colleagues checked in about Khori and her mom's condition. She read an email from 23andme with her DNA results, including her mother and her aunt Paula's family tree. She found numerous cousins and potential siblings from her paternal side. *I might find my biological father.*

Not long after, she noticed Karen Marcotte had tagged her and 23andMe on Facebook.

"Samantha DeCosta, welcome to the family." —Half-siblings group

She jumped to Karen's profile. The older, single woman lived in Acton, MA. All the half-siblings Marcotte had been tagging from 23andMe family trees were born at Emerson Hospital by cesarean and by the same doctor— Dr. Friedman. One woman posted links to newspaper articles about Friedman's sex abuse lawsuits, FBI investigations, and his subsequent suicide. She'd read through them later; Sam was worried sick.

Holy shit, Mom. She wondered if Aunt Paula and Dad knew about this. Dad always told her and Dan, "Focus on the most important thing to do in the next five minutes."

Sam removed her Facebook tag on the welcome post and blocked Karen Marcotte. She then pulled her name from 23andMe's family tree and changed her privacy settings. Later, she emailed Karen via 23andMe and explained that her mother had brain surgery and would not survive this scandalous exposure on social media. Sam appreciated Karen's apologetic reply, who understood the urgent need for privacy and removed her Facebook post. Sam now knew her biological father's name but wished she didn't.

I must speak to the man I've been calling Dad all my life. But when and how?

* * *

Meghan saw Karen's Facebook tag. *My, my, my. Samantha is my half sister!* She considered unblocking Karen so that Sam would know. With her mother in the ICU, social media was not the place for this. *I'll keep this in my back pocket to hold it over Dick's head someday.*

She wondered if Jo had named Sam after Dr. Benjamin Samuel Friedman. She now understood why her mother said the DeCostas were trouble.

Friedman had the motive, means, and penchants to service sexy Joanna during her vaginal exams on prime ovulating days. Dick had the motive, means, and vengeance to destroy her devious biological father.

* * *

Dick explained to Dr. Royce the trauma Jo had relived twenty-eight years ago when she first came around. Royce was concerned about more visitors but agreed with Dick's approach to jog her memory to more enjoyable periods. Royce said that after sleeping in a semi-comatose state for twenty-six hours, Jo's sedatives would wear off. After Royce approved a short, supervised visit that evening, Dick notified Dan and Sam.

He also convinced Royce to FaceTime with him so that the nurses and the doctor could watch Jo's monitors closely during the visit. The goal was to make Joanna aware of her surroundings with her loved ones.

* * *

Sam read the group text from her father about the supervised visit and then FaceTimed him.

"Hey, Dad… Great that you set up a visit with Mom's neurosurgeon."

"I'm hopeful, Sam." He smiled.

"How are you feeling? Any COVID symptoms?" *He looks exhausted.*

"No symptoms."

You wouldn't tell me anyway. She thought he aged ten years.

"So, sorry about Khori. How are you doing today?" her father asked.

"Doin' a bit better." *Still numb.*

"Dan told me Rikki brought you Chinese food… She sounds nice."

"Rikki is wonderful. But I'm concerned about Mom. Can I ask you about her past?"

"Never know unless you ask. Ha-ha." *Dad joke.* He forced a grin.

"Uhm… when did you know Mom conceived me without your help?"

"Geez, Sam." He looked away and scratched his gray three-day-old stubble. "Well… once we knew the due date, I figured it out. I had a hernia operation and was out of commission for a month. The baby couldn't be mine."

Wow, no hesitation. She waited.

"But Sam. I've loved you since the day I held you in the hospital and always will. You don't have my DNA, but you'll always have my heart."

"I know, Dad." She wiped away a tear. "Did you, uhm, tell Mom you knew?"

"Wanted to, but nope. She had a small baby, a home, and a family to care for—no time for a fling. I suspected her ob-gyn took matters into his own hands when he learned about our adoption plans." He coughed and cleared his throat. "He had a reputation for pumping up the nitrous oxide and preying on vulnerable women."

Mom was definitely vulnerable then. "How'd you *deal* with that?"

"Wasn't easy… I channeled my anger and focused on the big picture. Dan would have a sibling to grow up with, and your mother was thrilled. As a result, she needed all of my support to get through a full pregnancy. If I confronted her, she might have miscarried, or you may have been born prematurely—"

"Like Deidra," Sam said.

Her father's eyes widened, and his lip curled.

"Yes… Sorry."

"Aww, Dad. I love you both. But God… how'd you live with that all these years?"

"Honestly—other than re-upping in the army reserves when we started a family—I have no regrets. I always loved your mother and you kids. My job was to provide and ensure a better life for you guys."

"And you did, Dad. You did. Know how I found this out? Facebook and a DNA site."

"Yeah, I was afraid technology would catch up to us one day." He cleared his throat.

"Please don't bring it up to Mom… or Dan. He's not as tough-skinned as you. He might get the wrong impression of his mother, and lately, he's had trust issues with women."

"I won't tell her, but I can't promise about Dan. We've always shared everything—"

"Call coming in. Sorry, gotta go. Good luck with Mom's visit."

The call ended. She rubbed her watery eyes. *Dan and I are lucky to have great parents. Hope we don't lose them anytime soon.*

* * *

Dick took Grisham's call, "Hey Lee, what's going on? COVID keeping you on your toes and off the Bawstin streets?"

"COVID's hell on steroids," Lee replied. "Hey, Jackie saw on Facebook that Joanna had surgery. How's she doing?"

"Surgery repaired a ruptured brain aneurysm. Her blood pressure skyrocketed, and they sedated her. We're hoping for better news later today." Dick coughed and then added, "Mack's in ICU with COVID. I found him at the casino, and now I'm quarantined in a hotel."

"Oh, crap! You all need better news. Do you have any symptoms?"

Dick had a headache and scratchy throat but attributed it to tension and lack of sleep.

"Not yet."

"Here's hoping," said Lee. "So, listen. We got alerts—searches on Google and social media—about Friedman, Jackie, me, and you."

"No problem. It was probably my daughter, Samantha. I just spoke with her."

"The searches were by Mack's daughter—Meghan McCormack."

"Oh—"

"She knows her DNA links her to Friedman."

"Wow, her too." Dick wondered if poor Mack knew

"Meghan was one of Friedman's first C-sections. Your cesarean list only covered six years; we had his entire tenure at Emerson. We interviewed Peg, who was uncooperative and hid behind HIPAA."

Dick replied, "You never said you knew I'd sent the cesarean list on a floppy disk to Jackie and then snail-mailed you the tip on harassment complaints and Friedman's mini fridge."

"*The Globe* thought the C-list came from Peg at Emerson Hospital, as it was mailed from Concord, Mass. Your typed snail mail was postmarked from Lincoln; the bureau thought Friedman's wife tipped me off," explained Lee. "After Jackie ran her *Globe* story, other women and Cindy Callahan came forward with whistleblower details. We figured her husband, Curt, was the source. We then discovered he coauthored an *Artificial Intelligence* paper with you. We compared our C-section list with the shorter one sent to Jackie, which omitted Cindy and Joanna's names. We figured you two AI guys were working together. Cindy violated HIPAA laws but was protected under whistleblower laws."

"Why didn't you say something to me after Friedman killed himself?" Dick asked.

"By then, we had plenty of physical evidence on Friedman and women suing for sexual harassment and unexpected pregnancies. We knew Joanna had three C-sections and a preemie she lost. We figured she was another unwitting victim, so we didn't need to interview her. And we didn't need to implicate you. Whether it was revenge or good intentions to protect other women, no one wanted to hurt a Desert Storm vet."

Both, Dick thought, *and I have no regrets.* "I can't tell you how much I appreciated that, especially for Joanna's health."

"Like I said on the golf cart, you're why I met Jackie and knew I could trust her with my career at the bureau. It all worked out."

"It did indeed."

"Anyway… good luck with Joanna. You think positive and test negative."

"Thanks, Lee. Be well and be safe."

* * *

Meghan got a call from the lab. She tested negative for COVID but had to quarantine until she had another negative result.

She called her rehab center director. He'd keep it confidential. She then read Sam's post about Khori's celebration of life and remembered her mother's.

🙏🙏 Stay strong, Sam. If I can help, don't hesitate to call.

Sam called her and said, "I'm doing better today. Last night, Rikki brought over dinner and kept me calm."

I guess Rikki didn't lose that number, Meghan thought.

Sam then explained the supervised visit with her mom's doctor and a FaceTime call with her dad, which gave Meghan an idea. She called the hospital.

Head nurse Simmonds agreed to press Mack's index finger to access his phone, then FaceTime Meghan, who'd be in a private examining room. But Meghan would first have to get Mack's phone and other items from Dick. She knew Dick had a 5 p.m. call set up with his family. She texted Dick her mission and asked if she could stop by his hotel by 6:15. He replied:

Sounds good. I'm in Room 609

Chapter 72

Dan was depressed about his mom's condition, but grateful Robin had spent the night with him. They talked for hours in his parents' condo about college and living along the water. They checked online sales and rentals in Fort Myers Beach. He booked viewings, then canceled when he got Dad's text about a visit with Mom and her doctor.

"Your mum's recovery is what counts. Those wicked pissah beach homes will be there next weekend," said Robin.

"For sure." Dan hugged her. "I gotta get Sam. Do you want to go home or stay here, and I'll bring back dinner?"

"I have to call my mom when I'm not around Aunt Kelly. I'd love to stay anothah night if you don't mind bringing me to Lowe's in the morning."

"Did I tell you I love you?"

"This morning in bed when you were on top of me. Still counted, ha-ha."

He called his father. "Dad, on my way to get Sam. After we leave the hospital, I'll pick up dinner for Robin. She's still at the condo. I can bring you dinner, too."

"I just ate. Marie and Ted dropped off a healthy rice bowl and a green smoothie."

"Nice of them. How're they doing?" Dan asked.

"They're worried about COVID. They are leaving tonight to stay with their daughter in her Virginia Beach condo. Virginia has stay-at-home orders, so they feel safer there."

"Good for them," Dan said. "Speaking of beaches, Robin and I have been looking at homes on Fort Myers Beach. COVID has dropped the prices, and there are fewer buyers. I can get a cottage for much less than my place up—"

"Don't buy along the coast. Flood insurance is expensive. Too dangerous with the seas rising and hurricanes. Michael's surge wiped out Panama Beach three years ago and is still not rebuilt."

"Don't do this, Dad," Dan barked. "You always tell me what to buy. Let me handle it."

"Most owners ride out storms; protect their possessions. Rent a furnished place. You can leave and not worry about it." His father coughed. "The Gulf's watah gets warmer every year. Just a mattah of time before the big one hits and—"

Geez, he never stops. "I'll think about it," Dan interrupted him. "I'll FaceTime you with Mom's phone. Sam says you need to shave and smile for Mom."

"Guess I do need a shave and a shower."

* * *

Wearing a facemask and white smock, Dr. Royce greeted Dan and Sam as they positioned themselves around their mom's bed. She didn't move as Royce examined her right eye and contorted mouth. Royce nodded to Sam, who pressed Mom's index finger on her iPhone. She FaceTimed their father, and his clean-shaven face appeared.

"Hi, everyone," Dad said over the speaker. "Thanks, Doctor Royce, for arranging this."

Royce said, "Welcome, Mister DeCosta. She's not responsive. Music therapy has helped stimulate memories of amnesia and dementia patients. I trust you picked the right songs."

Dan opened the link with songs from his father. "Should we put an ear pod in, Mom?"

Royce said, "Play the songs on speaker with the volume low. That way, we can raise the volume slowly to see her reactions."

Dan began with "I Love You" by the Climax Blues Band. He'd seen his dad sing it at karaoke to Mom. Everyone listened and watched his mom's reactions.

> *When I was a younger man, I hadn't a care*
> *Foolin' around, hitting the town, growing my hair*
> *You came along and stole my heart when you entered my*
life
> *Ooh, Babe, you got what it takes, so I made you my wife*

There was no reaction. Royce said, "Up the volume a little."

Slowly, a lopsided smile appeared on Mom's face. Dad sang along the last verse; his voice was a little hoarse, but you could feel his emotions.

> *If ever a man had it all, it would have to be me*
> *And ooh ooooooh, I love you.*

Mom's smile broadened, and she parted her lips. But she never opened her eyes. Royce asked Sam, "Did she squeeze your hand?"

"No." Sam shook her head.

Dad said, "But she smiled peacefully. I think it jogged her a bit. Try the next one."

Mom had told the family she wanted this song played at her funeral. Dan hit the link to Lee Ann Womack's "I Hope You Dance," a stirring ballad about a mother hoping her children will learn to embrace life, love, and faith.

> *I hope you never lose your sense of wonder,*
> *You get your fill to eat, but always keep that hunger…*

After the first verse, Mom's mouth opened and shut a few times, and her smile increased.

> *Promise me that you'll give faith a fighting chance,*
> *And when you get the choice to sit it out or dance.*
> *I hope you dance… I hope you dance…*

Mom's cracked, high-pitched voice pushed out a few scrambled syllables. She was hindered by the oxygen tubes up her nose and the contorted right side of her face, but emitted a distorted voice like it was shot up with lidocaine. Mom did her best to form d's when the song reached the chorus, but her words all led with choppy s's, "Sance. I sope soo sance."

Sam sang with her, "I hope you dance."

She blinked and then opened her eyes.

"Oh, Mom!" Sam said. "You squeezed my hand."

Mom looked toward Sam, struggling to mouth the lyrics.

When Dan squeezed his mother's right hand, he could tell she had no feeling. The doctor poked and prodded her right ankle and thigh but got no reaction.

When the song ended, Dad said, "Jo, we're all here."

Mom peered into the iPhone at Dad and said, "Sick, is sis sy sunasal?"

"No funeral, Jo. You just woke up from surgery, and we love you."

"Sove sou, soo."

She smiled, then turned to Sam, "San soo say sothah seek?"

"Aww, Mom. I can stay another fifty weeks."

"Sennis soo seeks."

Dan and Sam forged smiles at each other. Tennis in a few weeks was a pipe dream, but they'd let Mom have it as long as she could breathe. The nurse pointed at the blood pressure monitor, and Dr. Royce motioned that their time was up. They kissed Mom on the cheek.

"Okay, Mister DeCosta. Say good night for now," Royce said. "The nurse can FaceTime you when appropriate. I'll call you later."

* * *

Sam said, "I don't know if Mom will ever play tennis again."

"We'll see. Mom's pretty resilient," said Dan. "But yeah, it will be tough on her and Dad. I hope he doesn't have COVID. He sounded hoarse. You hooking up with Rikki again?"

"Not sure, but I'd like to. Hopefully, we'll see Mom tomorrow," said Sam. "I'll make a playlist with her other favorites. She loves to sing Tina Turner's 'The Best' to Dad."

Dan pulled in front of the lobby to drop Sam off at her rental. She showed him her latest Facebook update and a link to Womack's video for "I Hope You Dance."

> To Mom, she responded to songs ♡
> With love for a speedy recovery 🙏✋

* * *

Dr. Royce called Dick and explained, "Her memory was good today, but she'll have relapses."

"Her face is contorted," Dick said. "Will that improve with PT and speech therapy?"

"Yes, it could take months," said Royce. "She's had a severe stroke—has paralysis on the right side of her face and extremities. She'll need a walker. But the early dementia may diminish her odds of returning to normalcy. Only her determination and time will tell."

Dick ended the call, depressed and sick to his stomach. *Jo's so fragile. She may never play tennis again.* He prayed, then thought about songs to help her recover; he'd be lost without her. He opened his laptop, searched YouTube for the Beach Boys, turned up the volume, and sang with Brian Wilson "God Only Knows." Tears poured down his cheeks. *This ain't helping me.* He closed the laptop, grabbed a tissue, and wiped his eyes and runny nose.

"Oh, Jo. Did I tell you I love you today?" *Or was it just the voice in my head? I must remember to tell you and our kids more often that I love you.*

* * *

Sam sat on the rental's couch. Rikki texted her with a link to Maroon V's "Memories." Sam knew the song emphasized toasting to the people you lost and those you still have. She lost Khori but still had Mom. She read Rikki's message.

> I saw your update on your mother. Good to hear. If and when you

feel up to it, I have cheese, crackers, and a bottle of Merlot 😭 🫶

Sam replied:

♡ Merlot. ♡ Your company. Hurry!!
C U in 30 minutes.

Sam's heart raced when her phone rang, but it wasn't Rikki.

Sam filled Meghan in on the FaceTime call with her Dad and the songs that helped bring her Mom around.

Meghan said, "That's wonderful news and such a heartwarming story."

Sam explained, "Yeah, a one-eighty from the first time my Mom woke up and relived a preemie death that had been kept secret from me and Dan all these years."

"Oh, wow. Your poor mother," Meghan said, then she transitioned to her family secrets and their shared DNA, which floored Sam.

Chapter 73

Dick took Tylenol for his headache and sore throat. It was ten past six; Meghan would arrive soon. He put Mack's bag by the hotel's door. He stuck his facemask in the pocket of his gym shorts and turned on the local news.

"The CDC reports: Monday, March 31, 2020, 875,000 COVID-19 cases worldwide. The US has the most, with 185,200 and over 3,800 deaths. Florida had 5,473 cases and sixty-three deaths. All Seminole and Hard Rock casinos across Florida are closed until further notice."

A little too late for Mack, Dick sighed.

He grabbed a tissue off the coffee table and blew his stuffy nose. *I'll get tested for COVID tomorrow*. He then listened to the meteorologist explain this year's hurricane season would be more active due to increased water temperature in the Gulf of Mexico and record heat nationwide, which had already caused devastating wildfires in California. Dick thought about how badly Sam must be feeling after Khori perished in the wildfire. He sighed.

Dick's phone dinged. He read Sam's gut-wrenching text twice.

Meghan called to ask about Mom. B4 Naples Hospital interrupted our call, she said we're both lucky to have great stepdads. Did u know we're half sisters?

Dick paced for ten minutes before he replied.

Sorry, I honestly never knew you were half sisters.

His phone danced with dots, and then Sam replied:

It's OK, I need a sister. Rikki's here. Talk to u tomorrow.

His head was spinning, and he felt drained. Meghan was twenty minutes late. *Perhaps she changed her mind*. Dick filled a glass with ice and vodka, took a drink, and put it on the coffee table when he heard a knock on his door. He muted the TV and looked through the peephole. Meghan clutching a blue handbag and wearing an N95 mask and white smock. He put on his facemask and opened the door.

"Thank you, Dick," she said and entered.

He closed the door behind her and reached for Mack's bag. But Meghan grabbed his arm, shook her head, and said with emotion in her throat, "Hospital called. He's gone."

She leaned her head against his shoulder and sobbed. Dick embraced her and gently patted her back while she trembled. He couldn't smell her usual seductive perfume. *Shit! Loss of taste and smell are early signs of COVID.*

But Dick couldn't send her away—she'd lost Mack and was all alone. "I'm so sorry, Meghan. Your dad was a good man. Kind and caring… and rightfully proud of you."

"Thank you," she sniffed. "I never got to say goodbye."

He led her to the sofa and handed her a box of tissues from the coffee table. Meghan dried her eyes, removed her face mask, and dabbed at the moisture on her upper lip. Her puffy, bloodshot eyes then looked him up and down. Suddenly, his T-shirt and gym shorts felt too snug. She then stuffed her mask in her smock's pocket and said, "I'm kind of warm."

She took off her smock. *Woah,* Dick thought, *I didn't expect a mini beach dress.* Meghan adjusted the thin, strapped floral dress, and her jutting breasts signaled they were braless. *Yes, it's getting warm.* He adjusted the wall thermostat, grabbed a glass, and added ice. Meghan fanned herself with her hand while he poured vodka into her glass.

Dick then took his drink off the table and sat on the ottoman across from her. When she reached for her drink, her minidress rose, and a flash of lacy blue panties were revealed. Dick maintained his composure, raised his glass in the air, and looked into her watery blue eyes.

"To Mack," Dick toasted. *Poor Jimmy Mack's never coming back.*

"To the jolly Irishman I called Dad."

He wondered what else she knew. Dick then pulled his mask below his chin and sipped half. She downed hers and put the glass on the table.

"Would you like watah or more—"

"Vodka, please," she said, running her fingers over his closed laptop. "Sam said you were writing another book about global warming. What's the title?"

"After Khori died, I retitled it, *Climate Change Kills.*"

"Wow, another bestseller. What're you going to do with all your green energy money?"

"Pay Jo's medical bills. Donate to Greenpeace."

She smiled and said, "Sam told me the songs you played for Joanna. That was clever… and touching. When can she have visitors?"

"Don't know yet. She had a stroke, and MCI will slow her recovery."

"I've cared for patients with MCI and dementia," said Meghan. "Lee

Memorial will refer her to our rehab center. I'll ensure she gets assigned to me and receives the best possible care."

"Thank you!" he said. "Much appreciated."

She lifted her glass, "To Joanna."

"To Jo. She'll need everyone's help." Dick lowered his mask, and they both drank.

"You'll need help, too." Meghan then leaned across the table and patted his bare knee. Her breasts bounced, and her dress inched higher, revealing more blue panties.

Mercy. Beads of sweat dampened his chest. Dick then shifted on the ottoman and reached for a water bottle on the table. He caught her eyes moving to his crotch as she said, "Yours is much bigger than Allan's… He only had a bedroom with a small TV."

"Your friend's hotel room?" he clarified.

She grinned and nodded. "Allan, my former boss, taught me how to play golf. He bought a condo at Legends."

"Nice," Dick said. *She'll have someone else to play with.*

She raised her glass, "To The Legends." Dick drank water instead.

"Allan is neighbors with Lee and Jackie Grisham. They knew about my biological father, Dr. Ben Friedman, who helped Jo bring my half sister, Sam, into the world."

Don't go there! He looked over at Mack's bag by the door.

She continued, "Bars are closed because of COVID. But the golf courses remain open. I told Sam I'd teach her how to play." She paused, and he waited. "Bet you could get Lee Grisham for a foursome. You and Lee—against me and Sam."

Dick shook his head, "I'm just trying to survive the next two weeks then take care of Jo."

Meghan smiled coyly, stood up, and walked to the door near Mack's bag. *Finally got the hint. She'll leave now,* he hoped.

She bent over and rummaged through Mack's bag, the outline of her thong accentuated by her spectacular taunting tush. She giggled, "He's got some surprises in here."

Dick adjusted his package in his gym shorts and regretted that he went commando today. He drank water and looked at the muted TV. Vanna White was now turning over letters on *Wheel of Fortune.*

She brought Mack's bag to the couch. "I found his phone and keys. I wasn't expecting Viagra and safeties. Tee-hee."

"Excuse me while I use the john," said Dick, clearing his throat.

He entered the bathroom, removed his mask, and used both hands to aim his stiffy down at the bowl. The voice in his head sang the guilty lyrics by Squeeze, "Tempted by the fruit of another."

Dick felt guilty, he felt vulnerable. He washed his hands and splashed water on his face. He patted his face dry and pictured Jo lying in bed, her head wrapped in bandages and her contorted face. He put his facemask on and hoped Meghan would have her smock and mask back on by now.

Instead, she stood by the window as the sun's rays filtered through her backless minidress, illuminating her sensational body, lending his mind to believe her panties had vanished. She'd stacked the coffee table with Mack's phone, keys, wallet, casino chips, quarters, pills, and condoms. Dick realized the most important thing to do in the next five minutes was to send her packing!

"Beautiful view, look at this sunset," she beckoned him.

I need to scare her away, he thought and hoped that he'd find the fortitude to deter the seductive temptress in a dignified manner. Dick tossed his facemask on the coffee table. He froze when he spotted her white smock and blue lacy thong on the couch. *She's relentless and reckless,* he thought while he approached the shapely, wanton woman waiting by the window.

* * *

Meghan gazed out the window at the café where she had lunch with her mother. *At least I got to say goodbye to Mom.* She missed that chance with her brother and now her dad, whom she'd never share another sunset with. He left her the debt-free condo and a sizable estate; combined with her 401k, she'd be poised for an early retirement, especially if she snagged a suitable sugar daddy.

She'd work at the rehab center, caring for aging women, and land a wealthy husband who needed companionship. He'd have to satisfy her libido and be proud to show her off in exchange for gifts, travel, and her desired lifestyle. She'd tried online dating in Boston—eHarmony was too committed, and Tinder was good for quickies. She had a condo for privacy now, but with COVID escalating, she wanted no part of online dating or the macho anti-mask fools in Florida.

Allan would bridge the gap when he visited. The discrete family man would never be more than a Salty Daddy—take her golfing and dining for sex. Dick's suite had a better view than Allan's room. She was hopelessly attracted to Dick and couldn't control her desires. She hoped he'd test negative but figured if they got COVID, they'd both get immediate care and be strong and healthy enough to survive.

She felt bad for Sam and worse for Jo. The lovely, fragile woman would become a burden, incapable of meeting the needs of her hunky, highly-esteemed husband. *I'm beginning to resent that big, unflappable prick.* She thought. *He's too aloof for his own good.*

She'd considered threatening him with blackmail—his dealings with

Lee Grisham destroyed her biological father, after all. Ultimately, she'd lose and ruin Dick's life and his beautiful family. She was already part of their extended family—Sam was her half sister, and Dan was like a half-stepbrother. *If only I could be their stepmother.*

Dan had his redhead and Sam now had Rikki. She needed someone; she'd never felt so lonely, empty, and vulnerable. But everyone is vulnerable at some point in their life. *Even the unbreakable Dick DeCosta can have a weak moment,* she figured.

She'd changed from her conservative outfit for the hospital into her minidress. She wasn't used to putting herself out like this, but Dick had rebuffed all of her attempts to seduce him. Most men would have caved long ago. Disciplined Dick: always so respectful and focused on Joanna and his family, and so damned desirable, charming, and challenging. He drove her insane.

Meghan heard the toilet flush. She had one more trick up her dress—she'd set out her props. He'd have one last chance to get lucky with her; she believed they both needed that now. But it was a gamble. If it didn't work, she'd get on with her life, gold-digging in Florida.

"Beautiful view," Meghan said. "Look at this sunset."

Dick came up beside her right hip, put his left hand on her lower back, and said, "Very beautiful." He then peered out the window with her, his handsome face no longer shielded by a mask.

God help us. She made her first move by easing her left strap off her shoulder.

"I'll never see another sunset with Mack." She turned, leaned her head upon his chest, and sobbed. "He left me everything, but I have no one to share it with."

"I'm sorry," he said while his hands caressed her lower back.

Meghan tingled when his fingertips grazed the top of her butt. She pulled him close and rubbed up against his pecs. She then got up on her toes to expose her left breast. And then Meghan put her hands on Dick's face and kissed him passionately. His lips parted, and her tongue slid warmly into his mouth.

Dick backed away slowly. He then placed his hand on her hips and veered her toward the couch before lifting her strap back onto her shoulder. Meghan sheepishly tucked her breast back inside her dress and sobbed.

"Very sorry," he said as he wrapped his arm around her shoulder and walked her to the sofa. She sat down, grabbed a tissue, and dabbed her eyes.

Dick placed Mack's bag by the table. He dropped the condoms and vials of pills back in the bag. She could tell he didn't need Viagra. The bulge in his shorts drove her crazy.

She looked up at the TV and asked, "You like *Wheel of Fortune*?"

"I like Vanna, but I prefer *Jeopardy*. I was watching the news."

"I see. What's your favorite vowel?" she asked, rubbing his knee.

He shrugged. "I like them all."

"Ever played Feel of Fortune?" she stroked his thigh. *I'm not giving up.*

"No, what's that?" he put Mack's phone and keys in the bag.

She stood up, grabbed a quarter off the table, and explained, "You flip a coin. The winner picks a vowel, and the loser performs."

She bent over, lifted her dress, and mooned him, "This is the prize."

Dick's eyes widened while he examined her bare bottom.

"You're a lottery prize for any man," he said, pulling her hem down and covering her rear. "But we can't do this."

"We can," she said, grabbing his wrist. "And should while we can." She then pulled his hand up between her legs, but Dick yanked it away.

"You should leave," he said firmly. His face reddened, and his hands shook as he zipped Mack's bag.

Meghan sat beside him, "I'm sorry. You're right."

He placed her purse on the sofa between them.

"Tell you what," she said, holding up the quarter. "We'll flip a coin... If you win, I'll be on my way... If I win, I stay." *A fifty-fifty chance we play.*

He handed her smock to her; she set it aside. Meghan put one hand on his knee, the other poised to flip the quarter. "Call it," she said.

"Can't," he said. *Can't or won't.*

"Come on, Big Dick," she grabbed his thick package in his gym shorts. "Call it."

He jumped up and shook his head. She waited and waited until he said, "Ladies' choice."

Yes! Win or lose. I choose you for my sugar daddy.

His shorts bulging, she shouted, "Heads!" Then, flipped the quarter straight up.

EPILOGUE

September 27, 2022

Sam looked up at the gray, overcast sky. The air was thick with humidity, and at 9:20 a.m., it was already eighty-nine degrees. It seemed to rain daily throughout the hot, record-setting temperatures in the summer of 2022. Sam held Bruschi's leash as he led her around the high-rise towers. The aging dog had gained weight in the two and a half years she'd been walking him for her half sister, Meghan, who was now the director at Fort Myers Rehab Center.

Meghan's seventy-six-year-old neighbor, Silvia, used to watch Bruschi before she sadly succumbed to COVID along with 90,000 other Floridians and 6.5 million people worldwide. Sam enjoyed walking Bruschi as it took her away from her computer job in the condo she'd purchased from her parents, which has since doubled in market value. Her partner Rikki had moved in with her last year, and Sam was anxious to get back inside and catch her favorite meteorologist's forecast.

Sam and Bruschi walked through the lobby's double doors held open by rubber stoppers. The maintenance staff and volunteers were stacking the pool deck chairs in rooms off the lobby. She could sense the urgency and concern on her neighbors' faces as they prepared for Hurricane Ian, which was expected to make landfall tomorrow afternoon.

Bruschi slurped from his water bowl inside her condo while Sam gulped a fruit smoothie. Sam turned the TV on. Video footage revealed miles of bumper-to-bumper traffic as countless Floridians evacuated north on I-75 and a caravan of electrical repair trucks with lift buckets rolled along the southbound lanes. The coverage shifted to Home Depot, where customers were stocking up on plywood, generators, flashlights, and cases of water.

The station's chief meteorologist announced that Hurricane Ian's Category Four wind speeds of 140 miles per hour with Category Five gusts of 160 would dump as much as twenty inches of rain starting this evening.

Rikki then appeared before another screen and pointed out the projected storm surge heights. They ranged from four to six feet in Sarasota and eight to twelve feet further south in Naples, Fort Myers Beach, and Sanibel Island.

The weather forecast was interrupted by a press conference. State and county law officers flanked the governor in front of a microphone. The regional FEMA head stepped up and said, "We can't emphasize enough how dangerous this storm is. There will be significant power outages. Streets will be impassable due to heavy rains and the storm surge. Everyone living along the coast and low-lying areas, including zones A, B, and C, must evacuate by 2 p.m. today."

Sam trembled. Her brother's cottage on Fort Myers Beach was in Zone A, and Sam's high-rise building and her parents' across town along the river were in Zone B. But she couldn't evacuate, as Rikki was working twelve-hour shifts at the news studio to cover the storm. Sam figured her eighteenth-floor condo would be safe from floods, but she worried about how her windows and sliding doors would hold up to the wind gusts.

Sam's phone startled her. She answered, "Hi, Mom. I'm okay. Where are you now?"

Her mom said, "I'm at Aunt Paula's in Lowell. Next week, we're going to the White Mountains with Harlan and Christina King to see the foliage."

Sam's parents, who were finally healthy enough, were on an extended trip up north, their first since the pandemic subsided. Meghan had helped Sam's mother regain her speech and mobility. Unfortunately, Sam's father contracted COVID and endured a frightful forty-day hospital stay; he still suffered from lingering effects. That was a bleak, terrifying period for Sam and her brother, Dan.

Her mom no longer needed a walker, but Meghan advised her not to play tennis. Sam was pleased that her parents had attended the US Open in New York for her mother's sake. They then flew to Boston, where they took in a Red Sox game at Fenway and then a Celtics game before they dined in the Italian North End.

"Sounds great. You guys are safer there," said Sam. "This hurricane is scary. They shut the airport down this morning."

Her mom said, "I know. Dad flew back last night to button down our condo. He's with Dan now, boarding up windows at his place at the beach."

"Really? No one told *me*."

"Dad surprised them. He wants to ensure Dan and Robin stay at our place."

"Good! I was worried about them," Sam said. She also knew her father was upset when he eventually found out Dan had bought a cottage after he had advised him to rent.

Dan was now teaching oceanology classes at Florida Gulf Coast University, and Robin had just started a radiology job at the Gulf Coast Medical Center in South Fort Myers.

Her mom asked, "Did Meghan evacuate?"

"No. She said the guy she was seeing had a private jet and offered to fly her to Atlanta. But she's got bedridden patients at the rehab center to care for."

"Well, Meghan's in charge of the center now. Thank God she took care of me while your father had COVID," replied her mom. "She deserves a prosperous man. I hope we meet him someday."

Meghan had told Sam she was having a steamy affair with a wealthy guy she'd met at a gala fundraiser in Naples. Meghan hadn't posted pictures of the mystery man, so Sam had yet to learn what he looked like or his name.

***

Dick was exhausted after helping Dan cover the glass sliders on his deck with plywood and sandbags by the thresholds. His ordeal with COVID decreased his lung capacity and endurance. He wiped the sweat from his face on his T-shirt and read the text from the emergency alert system.

Zone A must evacuate by 2:00 p.m.

Dick showed the text to Dan, who said, "Robin is working the second shift. We'll sleep here tonight, pack her things, and go to her aunt's house in Cape Coral or your place tomorrow."

Dick fumed. He was tired of nagging. And he was tired of warning the world about climate change in his books and tweets. This year had been the warmest on record, and the water temperatures in the Gulf were still at ninety degrees. He thought, *everyone along the coast was extremely vulnerable.* The rapidly intensifying hurricane was poised to destroy the coast and everything in its path.

Dick replied, "I can't save you a sheltered parking space in our condo for tomorrow. Come now and have Robin go to her aunt's after her shift."

His son defiantly shook his head no. "I promised Robin."

Dick felt weak and helpless as he drove alone in his Audi SUV back to his condo. All he could do was hope against hope that Hurricane Ian would not be as disastrous as he feared.

AUTHOR'S NOTE

Although this is a work of fiction, many of the incidents and dated headlines depicted in this novel are based on historical events.

—The Centers for Disease Control and Prevention (CDC) reported that in 2020, over 68,600 US deaths occurred from overdoses of opioids. Overdoses increased to more than 80,000 in 2021 and 2023; two-thirds of all drug overdoses were from opioids.

— As of April 2024, the COVID-19 death toll was 1,219,487 in the United States and 7,010,681 worldwide. (Worldometer). And on March 9, 2025, *The News-Press* reported the total COVID-19 death toll in Florida was 99,201. www.newspress.com.

— The Brain Aneurysm Foundation in Hanover, MA, estimated that 6.7 million Americans suffer an unruptured brain aneurysm, with 30,000 rupturing each year.

—The three major San Francisco Bay Area fires, the SCU, LNU, and the CZU Lightning Complex, collectively burned about 846,000 acres and, by mid-September 2020, destroyed 2,723 structures and took six lives. (Wikipedia).

Sadly, devastating wildfires have become a repeated tragedy around the world.

— The National Oceanic and Atmospheric Administration (NOAA) and National Centers for Environmental Information (NCEI) reported that 2022 US damage from weather and climate change disasters totaled $165.0 billion. (Climate.gov). 2024 is now the hottest year on record, and the average yearly temperature was 3.3 warmer. Major category four hurricanes are also occurring more frequently. Living in Paradise is no longer safe.

— On Sept 28, 2022, Hurricane Ian powered through Fort Myers Beach, Sanibel Island, and Pine Island with 150 mph winds and twelve to eighteen-foot storm surges. Across Florida, Hurricane Ian took over 150 lives and caused property damages exceeding $113 billion.

Ninety-seven percent of the property on Fort Myers Beach was damaged. Among the properties depicted in *The Vulnerable*—the Pier, the Pier Side Grille, and the Outrigger Hotel and its tiki bar—were destroyed. Officials estimate it will take five years to rebuild the beach area.

Hurricane Ian's storm surge on the Caloosahatchee River damaged countless homes and high-rise buildings along its shores. Many shops and restaurants in downtown Fort Myers were flooded, and nearly 180 boats were destroyed in the Legacy Harbour Marina. As of this writing, many shops and restaurants have been remodeled, while others have never reopened. But the resilient people of Fort Myers and its beach communities continue to build back strong. It's worth a visit.

ACKNOWLEDGMENTS

Writing and editing novels is a long, arduous, and guilty undertaking. You isolate yourself from your family and friends—while you become the guardian of your story's characters and the world you built for them. I greatly admire the inspirational cities of Lowell, MA, and Fort Myers, FL. My heart goes out to those who have lost loved ones in the pandemic, the wildfires, and hurricanes.

I must thank the many selfless people who contributed in various ways to this project. First, my son-in-law, David Scott Hanlon—read a partial draft, made suggestions, and encouraged me to finish it. I hope he is pleasantly surprised by how it turned out. My enthusiastic beta readers are Bunny Merrill Monteiro from The Spindle City and Donna Jablonski from The City of Palms. My talented editor is Celina De Leon. And my inspirational and long-time mentor is David Daniel, the accomplished author of a dozen superb books.

Thank you to my publisher, the incredible Lisa Orban, for ushering me into the Indies United, her cover design, and so much more! Also, thank you to Jennie Rosenblum, Lisa Towles, and the other talented and supportive IUPH authors.

Last but not least, my unconditional love for those who count the most and set the bar high for achieving any goal. My sensational daughters, Jennifer and Nichole, and my fantastic wife, Janet, I don't know what I'd do without you or when I'd stop to eat. Thank God she pursued her love of tennis, affording me time to write.

ABOUT THE AUTHOR

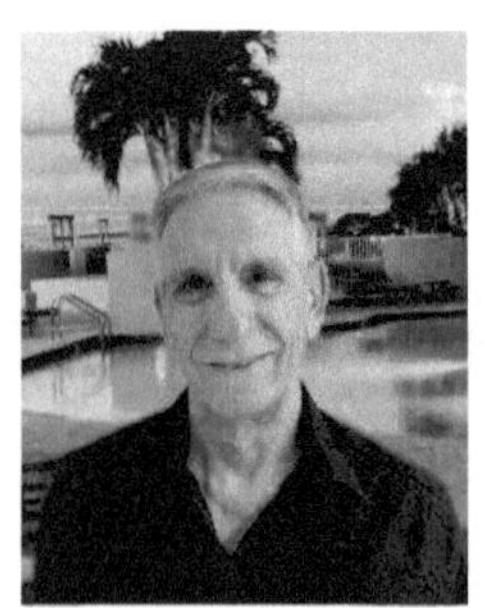 **Ed DeJesus** (pronounced D Geezus) writes contemporary thriller novels. His award-winning short story in *Indies United's 2025 Anthology* offers a glimpse into his forthcoming memoir collection, ***Simpler Times in The Spindle City***.

A technopreneur, he was President of Sightline Solar, CEO of JustZip.com, and VP of Engineering for MSL. Previously, his software work at Digital Equipment Corp was published in the Artificial Intelligence (AI) and Design Automation journals. He served in the US Army Reserves and opened a record store with his wife in the vinyl era.

He was born in Lowell, MA, and raised his family in Chelmsford, MA. He resides in Southwest Florida and is a Gulf Coast Writers Association member. When Ed's not immersed in his writing or at the gym, he finds joy in reading, dancing, singing Karaoke, and traveling the world with his wife and children, who reside in New Hampshire and Australia.

The Vulnerable is his debut novel. If you enjoyed this book, please leave a review. For more information, visit EdDeJesusauthor.com.